CHRISTMAS ANGELS

NADINE DORRIES grew up in a working-class family in Liverpool. She trained as a nurse herself, then followed with a successful career in the health industry in which she established and then sold her own business. She has been the MP for Mid-Bedfordshire since 2005 and has three daughters.

Also by Nadine Dorries

The Lovely Lane Series
The Angels of Lovely Lane
The Children of Lovely Lane
The Mothers of Lovely Lane

The Four Streets Trilogy
The Four Streets
Hide Her Name
The Ballymara Road

Standalone Novels
Ruby Flynn

Short Stories
Run to Him
A Girl Called Eilinora

NADINE
DORRIES

CHRISTMAS
ANGELS

HEAD
ᵒᶠ ZEUS

First published in the UK in 2017 by Head of Zeus, Ltd.

Copyright © Nadine Dorries, 2017

9 7 5 3 1 2 4 6 8

A catalogue record for this book is available from
the British Library.

ISBN (HB): 9781784975166
ISBN (ANZTPB): 9781784975173
ISBN (E): 9781784975159

Typeset by Adrian McLaughlin

Printed and bound in Germany by CPI Books GmbH, Leck

Head of Zeus Ltd
First Floor East
5–8 Hardwick Street
London EC1R 4RG
WWW.HEADOFZEUS.COM

For my agent, Piers Blofeld,
with thanks for believing in me

Chapter 1

It was long gone midnight and Maura Doherty was sitting on the kitchen settle with her second daughter, Angela, lying half on her knee, half against her chest as she hugged the sleeping child close to her. Sleet gusted against the kitchen window, carried on the squalls that flew straight up the dockers' steps from the Mersey and battered the houses least able to withstand it.

Maura's husband, Tommy, set another two pans of water and a kettle on the range to boil, ready to fill the room with yet more steam. 'Here you go, love,' he said, treading carefully as he carried the enamel washing-up bowl filled almost to the brim with scalding water and placed it on the floor next to her. He was in his vest and braces but was still wearing his cap. A damp roll-up, fighting to remain lit, dangled from his bottom lip. 'I've put half a teaspoon of the Vicks on the top, like you said.'

Maura turned her head to the side and could see the greasy film, melted, floating on the surface of the water. Even before she'd looked, she'd smelt the menthol vapour and felt it hit the back of her throat. 'I don't think it's working, you know,' she said, her face etched with worry. 'Her breathing's not getting any better. It's getting worse, if anything.'

Tommy squatted down by the side of her, his head close to Angela's. Like many dockside families, he and Maura dreaded the winter, all too aware of the consequences of living in the rows of terrace houses on the banks of the Mersey.

They both heard the door at the bottom of the stairs open on to the kitchen. In the puddle of amber light thrown down from the bare bulb stood their eldest daughter, Kitty, dressed in her flannelette nightdress and clutching her threadbare teddy with one hand and sucking her thumb with the other.

'Is Angela sick?' she asked as she removed her thumb from her mouth. A long strand of spittle stretched from her face to her hand and remained intact.

Maura nodded her head and looked down at Angela, who was dozing, red-faced, and struggling to breathe.

'Come here, queen,' said Tommy as he strode over and scooped Kitty into his arms. 'Angela's not very well. Your mam, she's going to stay down here with her tonight, but you are going to need to be a help in the morning because I'm on the early shift. The *Cotapaxi* and the *Norry* are both coming down from the bar first thing.' Tommy, along with every other man on the streets, worked down on the docks unloading cargo. 'So, back to bed for you, and I'm coming up meself now too.'

Kitty was still half asleep and her eyelids were heavy, barely able to stay open. She nodded earnestly at Tommy. 'I always help Mammy, Da.'

'I know you do, love. Come on, give Mammy a kiss and let's go back up.'

Kitty wrapped her legs around her father's waist and an arm around his neck and Tommy carried her over to Maura. He bent down so that Maura could just about reach up to kiss her cheek. Kitty's pigtail plaits brushed against Angela's face and Angela opened her eyes and looked straight up at her sister, but she didn't smile. She tried to sit up, but her chest was rattling loudly and within seconds she fell back to sleep.

Tommy walked with Kitty over to the stairs. 'I'll come back on me break in the morning, Maura, and I'll tell Kathleen when I knock on for Jerry on my way down. If there's no change in the morning, we'll take her to the doctor's.'

Maura nodded. She was too exhausted to argue and Tommy was right. It was free now, they didn't have to worry about the money any more. 'Aye, we will,' she whispered as the door closed and she heard the heavy tread of her husband and daughter making their way back up the uncarpeted but well-scrubbed wooden stairs. She sighed and with her lungs full of steam and vapour, shuffled Angela higher up into her arms, lay back against the settle and closed her eyes.

Tommy had brought down some old grey army blankets and pillows from the bed upstairs and tucked them around the two of them, but Maura didn't sleep. She listened to every fresh and ferocious battering of sleet on the window and every breath her daughter took in and out until the night had slipped away and the first light crept in through the windows.

Aileen feared that she would be late for work. She hated to be late for anything, but today of all days would be disastrous. She'd been asked to call in to Matron's office mid morning and she had no idea why. She was dreading it and, as usual, her mother was doing her best to make things worse. Aileen had lost count of the number of times her mother had forced her to take time off, claiming that she was so ill she required

Aileen's personal nursing care at home. Aileen had almost become ill herself with the worry of it all. Even though they now had Gina to help out, it still happened too often, and today looked like it might be one of those days. The wheedling and the complaining, all too familiar.

As Aileen moved over to the bed and laid out her mother's clothes, a sinking feeling settled into the pit of her stomach. She remembered the many occasions she had tried to cajole her mother in the past and how torturous those mornings had been and how weak and futile her own excuses had sounded. 'But, I can't take time off. I'm a staff nurse now and besides, Sister Tapps is a stickler. You have to turn up to the ward half dead and need admitting to St Angelus yourself before she will accept any excuse for absence, Mother.'

When Mrs Paige had first been discharged from hospital following her stroke, she had exploited the guilt she knew Aileen carried for being healthy in the face of her mother's infirmity. She abused her daughter's compassionate nature, her willingness to help, and in the first few months, Aileen had allowed her to do so. That had been her big mistake.

If it hadn't been for Sister Tapps, Aileen was very sure, she would not have remained in nursing. One day not quite twelve months ago, after yet another morning when Aileen had had to make her excuses, Sister Tapps had taken Aileen into the sitting room on her ward and closed the door behind her with barely a sound.

'Take a seat, Staff Nurse Paige,' she had said, in her softest voice.

Her gentle manner had done nothing to ease Aileen's anxiety. This is what you do with parents when a child has died, she'd wanted to say to her. You bring them in here, close the door, ask Branna to fetch tea and sit them in front of the fire, with a clean handkerchief ready on your sideboard.

She was convinced Sister Tapps was about to send her to Matron, to dismiss her. But there was no handkerchief on the polished sideboard. No glass of water to restore the equilibrium when the tears were spent. She looked through the glass panes above the handle of the wood-panelled door. It had been painted buttercream to please the children and keep the atmosphere light and airy, quite different from the dark coffee colour of all the other St Angelus wards. Branna was changing the flower water and cleaning the vases that had been laid out on the highly polished central ward table. It didn't look as though she'd been asked to make tea. The nurses were pulling out the lockers from the sides of the beds into the centre of the ward to clean them.

She decided to be the first to speak. 'I'm sorry, Sister Tapps, it was Mother, she was ill and she was difficult about me leaving the house. I would never want to be late, ever – I love my job, you know that. She's just so difficult and—' When Aileen had sat down, she'd had no idea that she would need one of the handkerchiefs that Sister Tapps kept ready for bad-news days.

'Oh, goodness me, child.' Sister Tapps jumped up and crossed the room.

Tappsy – as she was known to all the nurses – was looking thinner, Aileen thought, though that was hardly surprising. She had to be in her mid to late sixties, she reckoned, and her hair had turned white and fine a while ago. She'd not lost the hint of the soft Irish brogue from her voice though. She'd left Galway some fifty years earlier and had not returned for many years, saying to anyone that asked that the journey was too long and that she didn't like to be so far away from the ward and her charges.

'Look, you have no need to apologize to me. The nurses on ward six have told me how trying things can be for you.' Sister Tapps was doing her best to be discreet. Aileen's mother had a reputation for being one of the most tiresome patients St Angelus had ever known.

She handed a handkerchief to Aileen, who took it without embarrassment and blew her nose. Sister Tapps sat down in the comfortable chair next to her – carefully placed so that she could reach out and take a distressed mother's hand, should the need arise.

'I'm sorry, that was an impertinent thing for me to say. There have been so many telephone calls of late to Matron's office, when your mother has been ill.' Sister Tapps smiled. She was trying her hardest to put Aileen at her ease.

Aileen knew that if it had been any of the other ward sisters at St Angelus, she would have been out on her ear. Reminded of the phone calls, the most recent having been made only that morning, her heart beat madly with the anxiety she felt at letting people down. She hated having to run down the road to the telephone box at the junction with Green Lane and call Matron's office whenever her mother won, which was far too often.

Matron was always sympathetic but firm. 'I am so sorry to hear your mother is poorly, Staff Nurse Paige. Do tell her that we can always arrange for a domiciliary visit from Mr Stephens, her consultant, and that we shall expect you back on duty later today.' In her skilful way, Matron subtly conveyed to Aileen that she didn't believe in Mrs Paige's frequent bouts of illness either.

'Thank you, Matron, thank you.' Tears of frustration would spring to Aileen's eyes, her throat would thicken and her heart would beat so fast and loud beneath her ribcage, she could barely hear her own thoughts as the door of the telephone box clicked shut behind her. As the cold air hit her face, she would take a big gulp and tilt her burning cheeks to the wind. She loathed the smell of the phone box. The lingering aroma was always there waiting for her when she dashed in: stale cigarette smoke, dirty windows, cold metal. It frequently chimed with the way she felt, cheapened by the lies and excuses she was forced to make.

'Look,' said Sister Tapps, 'Matron and I just wanted you to know that we understand what a dreadful time you must be having, looking after your mother full time and trying to be the best staff nurse I have ever had on my ward.' Tappsy smiled.

Aileen sniffed. It was true. She was trying her hardest to be the best staff nurse St Angelus had ever known. In a year or two Sister Carter, the sister on ward three, Aileen's favourite ward, would be retiring and Aileen wanted that job more than she had wanted anything in her entire life. She prayed that Matron might overlook her occasional lateness and consider her for the post.

'We want to help you to get yourself sorted out so that you can do the job you love without any cause for worry. I've noticed how stressed you've seemed just lately and it's obvious you're struggling. So we've come up with a plan.' Tappsy clasped her hands together, stood up and opened the door to call for Branna, the ward domestic.

Here comes the tea and sympathy, thought Aileen, but it was far from that.

'Branna, did you write down the details for your daughter like I asked you to?' said Sister Tapps.

'I did, Sister.' Branna McGinty delved into the pocket of her long overall and took out a piece of paper. She pretended not to see Aileen's tears and kept her eyes on the note as she held it out towards her. 'That's my address, and my daughter's name. Gina. Sister has known her since she was a baby. She's fifteen now and she's looking for domestic work.'

She held out the piece of paper towards Aileen, who instinctively reached out and took it as she looked up at Sister Tapps. Between them, Matron, Tappsy and Branna had come up with a way to help her. A solution she had been too afraid to consider, let alone mention to her mother. But here were her superiors telling her what she had to do, and now that it was mooted as a real possibility, it seemed obvious. They had an answer to her problem and its name was Gina.

It was now almost a year since that conversation in Tappsy's office, and this morning, as her mother continued spitting out her whining venom, Aileen almost blessed herself with relief, as she had many times since. Gina was now a part of the Paige household, paid for by Aileen out of her own pocket to work at the house all the hours Aileen was at St Angelus. Gina had been the answer to her prayers and it was because of her that Aileen had been able to hold it all together. Even though her mother hadn't let up, the guilt of responsibility had faded with the knowledge that Gina was there. Aileen had even managed to join the St Angelus choir last summer, which she loved. She had a Christmas carol rehearsal to go to that evening, in fact. At St Chad's.

Her mother's voice broke through. 'You simply cannot go to work whilst your mother feels like this,' she pleaded. 'What if something happens to me? What if I have another stroke? Do you want me to be here all alone without my daughter at my side?'

Aileen had heard this so many times before, she barely had to even think of her response; it was automatic. 'We have Gina here to look after you, Mother. That is why I took her on and you agreed that would be the best thing. You won't be alone because we have Gina and she is really very good, isn't she?'

'I did not agree, and anyway, what if I did? I had no option. You would have left me here alone. Your sister, Josie, she doesn't approve, you know.'

Aileen had heard this one before too. 'Well then, maybe Josie can call in more often than once a week for a lunch she makes Gina prepare. Maybe she can look after you?' Aileen almost bit her own tongue off. Her mother was doing that thing again, making her say things she would regret for hours afterwards, bringing down her mood.

'I shall tell Josie you said that,' her mother fired back. 'That girl works so hard, with her husband and children to look after. I don't know how you can say the things you do.'

'I'm sorry, Mother, I didn't mean to snap. It's just that I have a busy day ahead on the ward, and a meeting with Matron, and Gina is here, so you won't be alone.'

'Really, Aileen, is that how much you think of me? Leaving me to be looked after by a slip of a girl who doesn't know one end of a thermometer from another. I don't think I will feel very safe if you aren't here. Don't you see that, darling?'

Aileen looked up sharply. Her mother only called her 'darling' when she was up to something.

'Sometimes I feel just like I did before I had my stroke, very light-headed and off my food, and you know how that nearly killed me. You wouldn't want me to be alone with that girl if it happened again, would you now? You know how bad I was last time, and imagine if your father could see you now, what would he think?'

Aileen stared at her mother and the words 'he would be so proud of me' ran through her mind. Her mother saw the look in her eyes and bristled.

Two hours later, Aileen braced herself for the meeting with Matron. She was convinced she was about to be reprimanded or, almost worse, that Matron had made a decision about who was to be the new sister on ward three, now that Sister Carter had finally retired. Please let it not be Sister Antrobus, she prayed. Maybe Sister Antrobus had made a complaint about her – was that what this meeting was about?

Elsie O'Brien, Matron's housekeeper, led her to the door of Matron's office and tried to calm her shaking hands. 'Here now, don't you be getting nervous about seeing Matron, her bark is worse than her bite. That's more than can be said for the dog though. Blackie. Watch out for him, his basket is behind her desk. Look at my leg here.' Elsie lifted up her leg to show Aileen a silvery purple scar that shone out from underneath her stockings. 'The little bugger got me before I got him back with the mop. He's Matron's baby, but don't even try and stroke him, he'll 'ave your fingers off.'

Aileen was frozen to the spot, so Elsie knocked on the door for her.

'Come in!' shouted the voice Aileen had heard so often during her working life but had very rarely spoken back to, other than from the end of a phone.

'It's Staff Nurse Paige, Matron,' said Elsie as she began to close the door.

'Yes, thank you, Elsie, I know who it is, I invited her to the meeting.' Matron smiled, but that did nothing to ease Aileen's nerves.

Blackie lifted his head in his basket and growled, and Aileen's hands became clammy.

'Blackie, stop it, be a good boy.' Matron took something out of the drawer in her desk and threw it to Blackie. He immediately lost interest in Aileen as he began to munch.

'I imagine you are wondering why I have called you here,' said Matron. 'Do sit down, Staff Nurse Paige, and please, do stop shaking. Blackie won't be interested in you while he's chewing that strip of dried beef.'

Aileen attempted to laugh. She would have been grateful for a smile. Nothing came.

'Now, as you know, there is a vacancy for a ward sister on children's ward.'

Aileen nodded as she lowered herself on to the seat Matron had gestured to on the opposite side of her desk. Her auburn hair was tucked under her cap, her ponytail wound into a French knot and her uniform apron immaculate. Matron might be about to give her the worst shock of her life, she might be about to demote her or, heaven forbid, sack her, but if she did, Aileen would walk out of her office with her head held high. She did her utmost, every single day, to be the best staff nurse and, yes, the best daughter too, and she knew it didn't always work out, but, regardless, she always did her best.

Aileen often resented her mother, but no one would ever guess as she was loyal to her too, and if she lost her job would never in a million years blame her. Josie, her married sister, would blame her. She would not shy from making accusations nor waste her words. If Aileen did have to leave St Angelus, it would give her sister ammunition she'd use a thousand times over. Josie had never wanted Aileen to be a nurse. She had never understood. Josie didn't do anything for anyone else if she could avoid it. But Aileen never responded to Josie's complaints. She kept her own counsel and left her own disappointment with both her mother and her sister buried deep within.

At first, when Matron spoke, Aileen had trouble following her words. She saw her lips moving and heard the clock above the fireplace ticking. She was aware of Blackie chewing through his strip of meat. Someone was sobbing outside, and she could even hear the chatter of staff and patients below the window as they walked across the main entrance into the hospital. But she couldn't take in Matron's words and Matron, looking up from her blotter, her elbows on her desk, leaning slightly forward in her chair, hands clasped, silver hair lighting her face as she peered over her glasses, half smiled, as though waiting for Aileen to respond. Aileen didn't, couldn't. Aileen was in shock.

Instead of being reprimanded, demoted or sacked, she had just been given the most coveted job, a job she had not even applied for, believing she stood no chance of getting it. Matron was speaking again. She was waiting for a response. Aileen, calling on all the reserves she had within her, dug deep to deploy something, anything, but she was beyond stopping the tears that rushed to fill her eyes.

Matron looked down at a letter on her desk and, lifting it, shuffled it into the bottom section of her in-tray, pretended she hadn't noticed Aileen's tears and carried on talking.

'Ever since you started as a wartime volunteer at St Angelus, I've been impressed by your total commitment to your training and, of course, by your high exam passes. Sister Tapps is similarly minded. She has been advocating you for this role for the past two years. I am aware of the slight problem you had, but the plan she came up with to resolve it seems to have worked. I do remember your mother, when she was in here as a patient.'

Aileen swallowed hard. Matron spoke again.

'I know that things must sometimes be quite difficult at home.' She was deploying a tone Aileen had never heard her use on the ward. 'But I want you to know that I understand. Not many people know this, but I'm going to let you in on a little secret – after all, you are about to become a ward sister – it was impossible for me to look after my mother at home. I worked long hours in Liverpool, she lived in Lytham St Anne's... Well, I want you to know that I think your devotion and commitment to your responsibilities both here and at home are to be admired and respected. They are values I understand and have empathy with.'

Aileen could barely believe what Matron was saying. All she could do was stammer out her thanks. 'Th... thank you, Matron. I... I will do my very best.'

Matron laid down the pen she had been holding in her hand and looked up at Aileen. 'I know you will. That is why I agreed that it should be you. I didn't take a great deal of persuading. As I said, you have values, Staff Nurse Paige, values I admire and look for in my nursing staff. Many nurses would have given up on either their mother or the job, but you have stuck it out and shown admirable determination. I hope – indeed, I know – that we train all of our nurses at

St Angelus to a very high standard. Sister Haycock sees to that. But what we cannot teach are what one could argue are the most important qualities in a nurse. Respect, empathy, kindness – above all, kindness – and, of course, a love for St Angelus, our patients and everyone who works here. I see all of those things in you.'

Aileen shifted forward on her chair. She could hear the faint rumbling of Blackie growling in his basket behind Matron's desk. He had swallowed the last of his treat and had once again focused his attention on the stranger in his domain. Aileen moved from being tearful to nervous in seconds. Blackie had a reputation and it was one Aileen respected. She was trying to say something more than thank you, which in itself seemed so inadequate, given the enormity of the honour Matron was bestowing upon her, but as she struggled to speak, only two words, words she had no intention of saying, left her mouth before she could stop them.

'But... Mother?'

Matron was more familiar with Aileen's mother than she had led Aileen to believe. There was barely a nurse in the hospital who hadn't heard of Mrs Paige. As soon as she had recovered the power of speech following her stroke, she had taken every opportunity to complain to Matron about every nurse who looked after her. It was hugely embarrassing and concerning for Aileen, who was living at the Lovely Lane nurses' home at the time. She thought she would have barely a friend left at St Angelus by the time her mother was discharged.

'Ah, yes, your mother. Well, far be it from me to interfere in your personal arrangements, but I do think it is about time your sister began to pull her weight, don't you?'

Aileen nodded. She was truly incapable of comment and

if she did start to talk about Josie and her selfish ways, she might never stop.

'Would you like me to write to her – your sister?' asked Matron. 'I did meet her a few times when your mother was here as a patient. I could explain to her the importance of your new responsibilities and how it will take a little more than Branna's daughter to help.'

Aileen shook her head furiously as she finally found the confidence to speak. 'No thank you, Matron. I will deal with this. I shall explain to my sister that Gina needs someone to help with the running of the house and Mother. Gina has been marvellous. She's reliable, and hard-working too. I couldn't have managed without her.'

Matron smiled. 'I forgot to mention your ability to solve a problem too. Anyway, congratulations, Sister Paige. Your new uniform is waiting for you in the housekeeping lodge.' She had left the drawer of her desk open and, slipping her hand inside, she took something out. She leant across the desk and made to give something to Aileen.

Aileen instantly knew what it was and a gasp caught in her throat.

Ward sisters at St Angelus hardly ever left their posts. Most worked until they were well into their seventies, so a ward sister vacancy was a rare event. It crossed Aileen's mind that she was probably the first nurse in quite a while to have risen through the ranks, from the nursing school through to staff nurse and on to ward sister level. There had been Sister Haycock, of course – it had happened for her a few years ago, and everyone had expected it because she was the favourite of the most senior consultant at the hospital, Dr Gaskell. But now here was Matron about to pass on to her, Aileen, a tradition that Aileen had assumed had ended with Emily Haycock's promotion.

Matron moved her hand closer. In it was something firm and flat, wrapped in tissue paper. 'Go on, take it, it's yours,' she said with a smile. 'Think of it as a Christmas present.'

Aileen grinned and as she reached out to take the gift, her eyes met Matron's and she instinctively knew that Matron understood how much this meant to her. She unwrapped it with as much decorum as she could muster. The tissue unfolded like the petals of a flower and there, lying in her own hand, was a St Angelus silver belt buckle. It had been specially designed to reflect the values of the hospital: in the middle was a ship, its mast standing proud, the river weaving around it, and behind was the old workhouse building that had become St Angelus. An angel hovered overhead, its wings sweeping around each side of the buckle and forming the central clasp. Aileen had on countless occasions seen Emily Haycock and other ward sisters grasping the wings on their own buckles as they hooked or unhooked their belts. She was speechless.

Matron always loved this part. This was the sixteenth buckle she had awarded since taking up her post at St Angelus and every one of the recipients had been rendered speechless. The buckles were bespoke, hand-crafted to order by a silversmith in Bold Street. He had designed the buckle himself years ago and she loved it, especially the angel's wings. The silversmith had recently written to her informing her that he was about to retire, so she had ordered ten, to keep in the drawer, ready.

Matron spoke, to allow Aileen to savour the moment. 'This may sound rather unconventional, but I have been told that the best way to clean it is with a damp rag and cigarette ash.

Brings the buckle up a treat, apparently. I use silver polish myself.'

'Matron, it is beautiful. I don't know what to say,' Aileen stammered. 'It is all a huge Christmas present. It's the best Christmas ever – or it will be.'

'Well, off to housekeeping with you, to get measured up for your navy-blue Petersham belt. Give the seamstress the buckle and she will sew it on for you. I know she's running up some new dressing gowns for the children for Christmas, so you had better get in quick.'

Aileen practically floated out of the office, far too distracted to notice that Blackie had stood up in his basket and was eyeing the back of her heels. But she turned back as Matron spoke again.

'Sister Paige...' The words shot across the room and stopped her dead. They were words that only she herself had ever spoken aloud, to the mirror at night as she brushed her hair and dared to fantasize about such a possibility. 'Don't worry about your mother, we will manage. Nothing is ever as bad as it seems, you know. There is always a way around every problem. We sometimes just have to look a little harder than we are used to.'

Aileen nodded, not really knowing how to reply.

As Sister Paige disappeared into the corridor, it was all too much for Blackie, who charged out of his basket, barking at the closed door. Matron sat back down at her desk and picked up her pen. 'Oh do shut up, Blackie, you are all bark. Into your basket now.' She began to fill in the bed vacancy report but found she couldn't concentrate and wrote her last words twice. Laying down the pen, she stood and rang for Elsie, who appeared in a flash.

'That was quick, Elsie,' she said, totally unaware, even after all these years, that Elsie hung around the kitchenette's green baize door whenever she had a visitor. 'I think I need a cup of tea.'

'Yes, Matron. And a nice hot buttered teacake?'

'Why not,' said Matron. 'Yes, please.'

She stroked Blackie and briefly wondered if she'd done the right thing. Both Sister Tapps and Sister Haycock had recommended Aileen for the ward three post, but Matron had had qualms, not least because Sister Antrobus had applied for the post herself. She picked up the phone and rang the school of nursing. Emily Haycock must have been at her desk because she answered almost immediately.

'We have a new ward sister for children's, one Sister Paige.'

'Oh, bravo, Matron,' Emily said. 'She was one of the best student nurses we ever had in the school.'

'I know. And she has one of the most manipulative women I have ever met as a mother,' Matron replied. 'My problem now is how to tell Sister Antrobus she has been unsuccessful. I think she had her heart set on this post and no doubt she'll remind me yet again that Staff Nurse Paige – or rather Sister Paige, as she now is – has missed six days this year due to her mother's supposed ill health.'

Emily was full of sympathy for Aileen. 'That's as may be, but with regard to Staff Nurse, er Sister Paige, you have to ask yourself, what are the qualities required of a nurse on children's ward and does Sister Antrobus possess them.'

An image of the forbidding Sister Antrobus flew into Matron's mind as Emily continued.

'You are always saying that standards are everything and I don't know anyone with higher standards than Sister Paige. Added to that, the patients absolutely love her. I don't know of a better nurse, in every way. I cannot recommend her enough.'

'I'm sure you're right. But her mother is a problem and if that problem persists, we will have to find a solution. Right now, however, I have another problem to deal with and that is what to do with Sister Antrobus.'

'Ah, well, can I make a suggestion, Matron? The maternity department is working flat out. There are four sets of twins due over the next week alone. Perhaps you could put it to Sister Antrobus that you value her experience on maternity more?'

Matron smiled. Emily Haycock was spot on, though she wasn't about to let her know that. 'That could be a solution.' She could easily flatter Sister Antrobus into accepting that. She put the phone down and felt easier having shared her concerns with Sister Haycock.

As Matron swivelled her chair around from the desk to face the window and watched the visitors begin to trickle through the main gate, the St Angelus mafia was in full swing. Elsie had already got on the phone to Madge Jones on switchboard, who had got on to Biddy Kennedy in the school of nursing, who got on to Branna in the kitchen on children's. Before the teacake was toasted, everyone knew that the hospital had a new sister, Sister Paige, and that Sister Antrobus was not about to be granted her wish.

Chapter 2

Kitty held on tight to the handle of the pushchair, with Maura repeatedly reminding her not to let go, as they wandered down the main corridor of St Angelus, scanning the signs for one that said *Children's Chest Clinic*. Maura's hands were warm and clammy and she wasn't sure who was the more scared, her or Tommy.

They had failed to find the clinic so far and were too afraid to ask the way. They felt far too insignificant to bother anyone they had seen pass by so far. Maura opened her mouth as a serious-looking doctor strode past them, his white coat kicking out behind, his stethoscope strung around his neck and flying out in front, but no words escaped. In Maura's world, you waited for someone as important as a doctor to speak to you first. Maura and Tommy both felt awkward. This was not their world of the docks and the streets, where they were both well known and respected. This was a world of education and disease. The first was a stranger to them all, the second a far too frequent visitor, both to their own home and to those of their dockside neighbours.

'Ask your woman here,' Tommy hissed as a lady in a starched navy-blue dress strode past at a very determined pace, her head held high, her frilled and elaborate cap spilling down her back, letting everyone know that she was a very important nurse indeed.

'Why don't you, you eejit! You ask.'

He failed. By the time Tommy had got his tongue around his words, the woman had disappeared.

Maura nudged him as a group of nurses marched by. 'Go on now.'

The nurses were clutching at their black and red capes as flashes of their pink uniforms became briefly visible beneath. Their heads were angled close to one another, starched caps meeting in the middle, and they were whispering as they went.

'What happened there then, Tommy? You're gasping like a fish out of water,' said Maura as they stared at the backs of the departing nurses.

She looked directly at Tommy and, seeing the anxiety etched on her face, he felt helpless. He was, just as she said, a fish out of water and he would have given anything to be anywhere but St Angelus.

Angela began to grizzle in the pushchair. She was uncomfortable and they could both hear the rattling in her chest, but the biggest worry for Maura was that Angela had stopped complaining. Angela had been labelled from birth as a crier and Maura proclaimed almost daily that if she'd been her firstborn, there would have been no more. They'd already tried everything they could think of to ease her cough – a visit to the priest, several doses from the miracle-cure-in-a-bottle that Kathleen had brought back from the west coast of Ireland, and a prayer request to the nuns at Mass the day before. But the morning had brought no improvement.

Tommy had crept down the stairs on his way to his early

shift, careful not to wake their other children, who had slept in the bed with him. As he tiptoed over to his dozing wife, he took one look at the dark circles under her eyes and the red rings around those of his precious daughter and made the decision to call in the doctor. The kitchen was lit only by the waning moon, the struggling flat grey dawn and the dying embers in the fire.

Maura sensed his presence and opened her eyes wide.

'How is she?' he'd whispered as he squatted down at her side, holding on to the arm of the settle to keep his balance.

Maura, ever the vigilant housewife, noted as he spoke that there was a gravy stain on his vest from the night before. 'Still bad. She did sleep for some of it, though,' she whispered back.

As though to let him hear it for himself, Angela's chest rattled with her next inward breath.

'I'll knock on next door and ask Peggy to go and fetch the doctor.'

Maura had nodded. The time had come. Most of the Irish mothers in the streets cured their own, with patience and love and a few herbs sent in the post from Ireland. But they always knew when it was time to hand over to a higher authority. 'Change your vest before you go. I'll wash that one today.' Angela might be sick, but the chores still needed to be done, Kitty and the twins had to be seen to, and Tommy could not miss a day's pay.

The doctor had arrived just after ten. He listened to Angela's chest, complimented Maura on her spotlessly clean kitchen, scribbled a letter addressed to 'children's services' and told Maura that she had to take Angela to the hospital. There was a clinic that started at three o'clock, he said. He would phone ahead and let the consultant know that Maura would be attending with Angela. 'If you have any night things for her, pyjamas and the like, take them with you,' he continued.

'Will she be having to stay in?' asked Maura, unable to bear the thought of being separated from her daughter for several days. At St Angelus, visiting time on the children's ward was on Sunday afternoons only. They knew that from when Kitty had her tonsils out and from other children on the street who were regular visitors to St Angelus, ward four and Sister Tapps. There wasn't a family on the dock streets who did not regard Sister Tapps as the closest they had ever know to the Virgin Mother, but it was the separation from their children that caused the most poverty-hardened women to make themselves sick with distress.

The doctor looked at her with sympathy in his eyes. 'Dr Walker will decide what is best,' he said. 'There are lots of these chests around at this time of year. Best to get her right.'

Maura nodded.

The doctor could have added that his entire morning would be spent with patients trotting in and out of his surgery asking for 'a bottle for the chest, Doctor'. He would oblige, all the while knowing that the cure couldn't be written on his prescription pad. What his patients needed was to move away from the Mersey and into heated housing that was free from mould spores and damp.

Despite having had no sleep, Maura spent the remainder of the morning cleaning her house. Meanwhile, her neighbour, Peggy, spent her time knocking on their neighbours' doors for spare nightclothes, then rushing down to Woolworths in town for two new vests and pairs of knickers for Angela, just in case.

Now that they were actually at St Angelus, Maura

wondered whether the doctor had made a mistake and sent her to the wrong place. Was Dr Walker based in one of the other hospitals? The Southern, maybe? As she looked up at Tommy she felt her energy drain. But Tommy had had a brainwave.

'I know, why don't we go back to that nice lady on the WVS stall?' he said. 'I remember her from when our Kitty had her tonsils out. Maisie, her name is. I bet she's asked all the time where places are. Especially the bleedin' chest clinic, as how is anyone else supposed to find it if we can't and you can read.'

Wearily, Maura agreed, but she was not happy that she hadn't seen the sign and that they were effectively lost and none the wiser. Of the two of them, Maura was the one who really could read. She'd known there was no point in Tommy looking up at the signs. He could read the names of the horses and the times of the races, and he knew how to identify descriptions of form, but that had been the limit to his knowledge until Kitty had taken hold of him. Kitty brought her reading books home from school and every night she taught Tommy a new word. He was not allowed to get away with it, as much as he tried, not one little bit, but even Maura knew it could be some time before he learnt the words 'chest' or 'clinic'.

'All right then. I can't think of a better idea, sure I can't. Come on, Kitty. Let's go back to the doors.' Maura bent down and tucked the blanket around Angela. 'Shhh now.' Pushing down hard on the handle of the pushchair, she turned it all the way round to face the direction they'd come from and they began to retrace their steps back down the corridor.

'Tommy, move,' Maura said as she almost bumped into him

with the pushchair. She was sharp with him and he knew why. Much of what passed between the two of them needed no words of explanation. That left plenty of room for frequent rows and passionate reconciliations, the latter having so far produced two daughters and one set of twin boys.

Maura was full of anxiety and hospital was the last place she wanted to be. One of her closest friends had come into St Angelus by choice to have her baby – not because she needed to, and against the strongly worded advice of Maura and every other woman on the streets. They had all delivered their babies at home, with each other's help, and if there was a problem, the local midwife would be summoned by whoever's husband happened to not be in the pub – usually Tommy – and in most cases it all worked out just fine.

Their friend had walked into St Angelus, waving them all goodbye as she went, but she had never returned. The Irish Catholic community on the four streets of the dockside had not stopped talking about the death of their friend at the hospital. 'Oh and Jesus, didn't she just come out in a box, would you ever have known,' was what they were still saying to one another, and to anyone who didn't yet know the story, on a regular basis. Not one of them had expected a death in childbirth, in a hospital.

They quickly found the WVS stand and Tommy automatically reached for the cigarette tucked behind his ear. It was an instinctive reaction to the smell of tea brewing. Any sense of urgency, whatever the task in hand, evaporated when a cup of tea was in the offing.

He was now on familiar territory. He scanned the area for where he used to sit for hours when Kitty was a patient on Sister Tapps's ward. She had been very little at the time. The rule had been only two visitors to the bedside at any one time, so he would let half the street traipse in and out to see Kitty – her operation being the entertainment of the week and the talk of the neighbourhood – before he took his turn. But today Maura was on to him.

'Don't be thinking you'll be sitting in here drinking the tea and picking out your nags in the *Racing Post* while I take Angela to see the doctor meself. You must be joking,' she warned.

Tommy was affronted. 'You have to, Maura. You have the child in the pushchair, not me. That's not my job. I'm not actually coming in there with you, am I now. That's why we brought our Kitty, isn't it, queen?' He winked at his eldest daughter.

She winked back. Kitty might have been their firstborn and a girl, but she was her da's best friend and they both knew it.

Lifting his head, Tommy could see the steam from the WVS urn rising above the rows of wooden chairs. The air was thick with spiralling columns of blue smoke, chattering voices and the sound of metal spoons clinking against national issue cups and saucers. It was dark and gloomy outdoors and the high windows did nothing to bring cheer or warmth into the wooden-floored room with its walls of dark green tiles. Nor did the single light bulb help much, dulled by its green glass shade, way up high. He squinted through the smoke and patted the outside of his jacket pockets with the flat of his hands, trying to locate his box of Swan Vestas.

'Oh, yes, you are coming in with me, Tommy Doherty,' said Maura, her arms folded as she looked him straight in the eye.

Tommy, his attention back to Maura, responded in a flash. 'No, I am not, Maura. I came and sat here when our Kitty was having her tonsils out and I said on the day we took her home that I was never coming back again. It's the smell, Maura, it makes me ill. Let me go and ask the woman where it is and you and our Kitty can go while I wait here for you both.' He looked confused as the search for his matches moved from the front of his jacket to the back of his trousers.

'What in God's name have you come for then,' Maura demanded, 'if all you wanted to do was sit here and drink the tea?'

Tommy had his answer ready. 'Because you wouldn't give me a minute's peace if I didn't, that's why. I didn't want to be going any further than the gates now and that's the truth. Come to the hospital with me, you said, and I came. You didn't say anything about coming in with you, sure you didn't.'

A smile suddenly spread across Tommy's face and he lifted his cap in the traditional docker's greeting. Maura's head spun around.

'But would you look at that! There's your lovely woman, Maisie, and she's pouring me a cup of tea. See? She just smiled at me, she recognized me. Come on, Maura, Maisie will put us right. Would you look at that!'

To Maura's amazement, Tommy was not telling a lie. The woman he called Maisie, wearing a floral wrap-around apron, was smiling at them. She was standing next to a woman in a hat and an oversized glass hatpin, who looked as though life very rarely threw any surprises her way, and she was not smiling. But this didn't seem to hold back Maisie, who was beaming from ear to ear and holding up a cup and saucer, inviting Tommy to move closer. Before Maura could say another word, Tommy was on a direct path towards the smile and the ashtray being held out to him.

'Hello, Tommy, fancy seeing you back here. Hello, love,' she said to Maura.

Maura felt relief wash through her. During Kitty's stay at St Angelus, she'd been the one to sit at her daughter's side throughout, while Tommy had given up his place for the neighbours, so she'd not been familiar with the staff on the WVS stall.

'You cannot begin to imagine the number of men I tempt across the foyer with nothing more than a cup of tea in my hand and a couple of biscuits from the Huntley and Palmers tea-time range. I get these ones because they are our Stanley's favourites. You look as though you need one too, love. Here you go,' she said to Maura. 'If you don't mind me saying, you look washed out.'

Without him even having to ask, Tommy was handed a large brown Bakelite ashtray by the woman with the hatpin and the sour face. He made to put his hands in his pocket to look for money, but Maisie had already slipped the saucer containing the pennies under the counter so that Tommy and Maura would not be offended.

She waved her hand at Tommy. 'We aren't collecting today, love,' she said. She would slip the saucer back on to the table later, for those who could donate, but not until she was sure Tommy and Maura had left the hospital. As she always said to her helpers on the stall, you couldn't mistake an Irish dockside family because nearly every one of them looked as if they'd just stepped off the boat. 'They have so many children,' she'd say to whoever would listen, 'they don't have a penny to waste, do they? I can't take money from them, even though they always want me to. They are too proud for their own good, those dockers.'

She immediately noted the anxious and suspicious frown that crossed Maura's face as she scanned the table looking for some sign of how much the tea and biscuits would cost. 'Don't worry, really, there's no charge,' she said. 'And don't forget the ashtray for that cigarette I can tell you are searching for.'

The helper with the stern face jumped in. 'We try to keep the ash off the floor, if you don't mind.'

Tommy was left in no doubt that this was a warning, not a request. He grabbed his tea and, thanking Maisie profusely, sat on one of the hard wooden chairs and extracted his cigarette from behind his ear.

'Hello, dear, would you like a glass of squash?' Maisie was now smiling down at Kitty, who looked up to her mam for reassurance and squeezed her hand tighter.

Kitty lived among the Irish, went to church with the Irish and was taught by the Irish. That was her world. Having not moved outside of the four streets, a Liverpool accent was not her familiar dialect. 'Can I, Mam?' she asked. Maura nodded, and Kitty returned Maisie's smile and took the glass of thick orange liquid.

'Say thank you,' said Maura, 'and go and sit with your da now and wait.'

Kitty, who never had to be asked twice, whispered her thank you and almost skipped over to Tommy, careful not to spill the precious squash as she sat down next to him. They never had squash at home. With four children in the house and half the neighbourhood in and out throughout the day, even if they could afford it, it would be drunk almost before it could be unpacked.

'And is it one lump or two for you?' asked Maisie as she poured the tea for Maura.

''Twould be two, er, please,' said Maura. 'And I hope you don't mind me asking, but I wonder, could you tell me, I have to be here...' She pulled the doctor's letter out of her coat pocket, removed a sheet of paper from inside the brown envelope and proffered it to Maisie, who exchanged it for the cup of tea and two arrowroot biscuits.

Maisie looked up and gave Maura a conspiratorial smile. 'Is it for the little one?' She nodded down towards Angela, now fast asleep in her pushchair, exhausted by her most recent bout of coughing.

At least when she's asleep she's free from the coughing, Maura thought as she looked down at her child. Maybe that's a good sign. Maybe she will have turned the corner when she next wakes. Her heart constricted. She was sleep-deprived and emotional but still full of hope. Maisie's kindness was having an effect. She was acting in that Liverpool way, as if she had seen Tommy only yesterday and knew them all well.

'Don't worry, love, she'll be fine. My daughter, she's one of the nurses here. Nurse Tanner. I know them all, I do. The doctors here, they are smashing. I wouldn't worry if our little Stanley had to come and see one of them, not at all. Now, let me see, oh, yes, well, you have to go back outside the building and follow the path around to the left. Children's services is in one of the prefabs. You'll see it, it's attached to the building on the side. There is a sign above the door. Your appointment isn't for another half an hour, though, so sit and enjoy your tea in here first. I think Sister Antrobus is on outpatients, I wouldn't let you be late for her – bit of a battleaxe, if I'm being honest. But you've plenty of time to drink your tea first. There is no WVS around there, although I've told them there should be. They send them to me to look after and that's not a problem, so long as it's not pouring down with rain.' Maisie noticed that Maura's attention was fading. 'You enjoy your tea first. Go and sit with your Tommy, go on.'

Maura blinked, stared at Maisie and stammered a thank you. She wasn't used to such kindness from a stranger and like most of the Irish in Liverpool was often wary of anyone in authority bearing gifts.

'Well, at least I know where to go now,' she said as she sat down next to Tommy and Kitty.

Tommy was mildly agitated, searching for his matches. 'Maura, I haven't me matches. How has that happened? They were in me pocket, I put them there meself.'

Maura flicked open the clip on her battered brown leather handbag. It was her most precious possession, bought at a jumble sale, its seams frayed and the stitching peppered with holes. She had found a sixpence in the small pocket in the bronze silk lining, but she'd never removed it nor felt the inclination to spend it, and she had certainly never told anyone about it. There was a tiny piece of brown paper folded with the sixpence and it read: *Happy Christmas, from your Reggie. Christmas 1914.* She had slipped the note back into the place it had lived for all those years, next to the coin, which had become her lucky sixpence. Even on a Thursday night, the night before payday when she was struggling to make two pounds of potatoes, a couple of carrots and a loaf of bread stretch between them all, the silver sixpence remained in situ.

The aroma from the inside of the handbag wafted up to her. It smelt of a woman who had passed, who had once carried in her handbag make-up and trinkets that Maura would never even encounter let alone own. The stale but reassuring smell of compact, lipstick and Coty L'Aimant perfume calmed her. When Maura opened the bag it was as if, like a genie, the ghostly scent escaped, the invisible signature of another woman's life.

The lady at the jumble sale had given Maura the bag when she'd bought second-hand clothes and shoes for the children. She told Maura it had belonged to a lady who had passed away. 'No one from around here will buy it,' she'd said. 'They all knew her. She was a regular at the church. Her husband died in the war.' Maura's face had fallen. 'Oh, not the last war. He was long gone. The first war. No one around here can remember him. He was only in his twenties – newly married, they were. You take it, along with those clothes you've bought. Have something for yourself. It's good leather, it is. Quality. Has a few years left in it yet.'

Maura had been touched by the woman's thoughtfulness, but then she always found the ladies from the Anglican church who ran the jumble sale to be kindness itself. They never made her feel a lesser person for being a Catholic, nor for being the one buying the clothes rather than donating them.

She extracted a box of Swan Vestas from the handbag and threw the matches on to Tommy's lap.

'What are you doing with those in your handbag?' he asked as he scooped them up. 'Did you take them from my pocket?'

'I did, Tommy. And you are such a dozy bugger, 'twasn't difficult, I can tell you. I thought I might need to bribe you to come to the hospital with me and our Kitty, but then I wasn't accounting for your woman with the tea.' She placed her handbag down on the floor and, taking her cup and saucer from the seat next to her, raised the cup to her lips and began to sip at her tea. She could sense Tommy grinning and, turning to him, she grinned back.

'You are a wicked woman, Maura Doherty, and what's worse, you are teaching our Kitty here your ways.' Tommy struck the match and his face flushed red as he pulled hard on the cigarette.

'I wish you wouldn't do that,' said Maura, tutting.

She always tutted and Tommy always had the same answer. 'I need them for me nerves and they keep me chest loose, Maura. If it wasn't for these...' He held the lit cigarette up to show her, as though it had the secret to a long life written down the side. '... I'd be dead, I would, working in all that dust down on the docks.'

Kitty had finished her squash. She clasped the empty glass in her hand, stared into the bottom and, looking up at Maura, said, 'I've had that squash before. Sister Tapps used to give it to me when I was in here. I remember it. Will we see Sister Tapps today, Mam?'

Maura ran her hand over Kitty's hair and smoothed down an imaginary stray strand. The plaits on Kitty's head were so neat and tight, not a single hair would dare defy her. 'We won't be, Kitty. To be sure, I never want to see her again, because if we do it will be because Angela has to stay in, and that would be just the end of me after all we went through with you. Now, you wouldn't be wanting that, would you?'

Kitty shook her head and her expression was sombre. She wasn't altogether sure whether or not an illness would be a price worth paying to see Sister Tapps again.

''Tis Angela's turn to be in this awful place, and with the grace of God...' Maura blessed herself as she spoke. '... she will be coming right back home with us today. You know, in Ireland no one ever goes to a hospital. Sure, the nearest would be in Galway, but I don't know of a single person who has ever been to it. And the size of this place, you would get lost in it all day long.'

Kitty didn't reply. She wanted to complain. She wanted to visit ward four and say hello to Sister Tapps.

Maura looked into her daughter's eyes and could tell what she was thinking. 'Ah, Kitty, my love, it's been years since you were in here. Sure, you was not much higher than your da's knee at the time. Poor Sister Tapps, she works like a Trojan and she has lots of children to look after, I doubt she would remember who any of us are.'

Kitty looked at the floor. This she absolutely refused to believe.

Tommy shifted forward in his seat. 'Right now, as you know where to go, I'll be making me way back then. You won't be needing me any more. See you later, queen.' He ruffled Kitty's hair as he stood and made his way towards the door at the pace of a trot.

'Tommy Doherty! Don't. You. Dare.'

Maura's words hit Tommy like bullets in his back. He stopped dead in his tracks.

'Sit back down here. Now!'

Tommy shuffled backwards for the first few paces and then, turning, met the eyes of his daughter. Silent, condemning. And then she grinned. His Kitty. He'd swear she held an invisible cord that she'd wrapped around his heart. And now, as though it were winding him in, he walked slowly back to the two women who ran his life.

'Maura,' he pleaded as he sat back down, 'I'll miss the bookie's and there's a winner in the three ten at Kempton. We need a bit of extra cash, don't we, now that you're expecting again.'

'We don't know that yet, do we.' Maura glared at Tommy and then glanced at Kitty, who was staring at the counter, fascinated by the laughing Maisie. Maura put her cup and saucer into Kitty's hands. 'Go and take that back to the nice lady, and say thank you, would you now, Kitty,' she whispered, glad to have a task to keep her daughter busy for a moment. Turning to her husband, she said, 'Tommy, what are ye doing? No one knows I'm pregnant, not even me properly yet. I don't want Kitty to be thinking that, or anyone else.'

'Do you not feel it when you're here, Maura?' Tommy asked. 'Can you not smell the place? What is that? It's enough to make St Michael run for the door.'

He was referring to the pervasive smell of Lysol. It hit everyone as soon as they walked through the hospital doors. Maura looked about her. A group of doctors like the one they had seen earlier with the stethoscope around his neck walked through the main doors and down the corridor, and a gang of nurses almost buried under their oversized capes headed past in the opposite direction. Maura didn't miss the glances and giggles exchanged between them.

They all looked round as they heard a voice shout out, 'Clear the way, please. Patient trolley.'

'Right you are, Dessie,' came the response. 'Toot-toot, please, everyone.'

Maura caught just a glimpse of a woman being transported on a trolley with a drip in her arm. The glass bottle of the drip contained blood. Maura swallowed hard as memories of her pregnant friend flooded her mind. She could see her, remember her, sense her. Her mother-in-law had told Maura on many a day that her friend hadn't left them, that her soul was still in the house with them. It was the Irish way. To hold on to people. To honour and mourn them, and in doing so, to keep the memory so strong that it was as if they were simply in another room. Maura's eyes softened as she thought of her friend. She could hear her whispering to her, warning, *Run! Run! Take the kids, Maura. Run!*

Maura jumped to her feet. 'Tommy, come with me – now!' she said. 'Let's get Kitty.' Her heart was beating a tattoo against the wall of her chest and her top lip was breaking out into beads of sweat. 'Kitty, quickly now!' she called. 'Let's get over to the appointment and then get out of here. I've left the washing out.'

Tommy knew better than to argue. Angela was still in a deep sleep. Maybe she was turning a corner? He might be the biggest eejit to walk the dock streets, but even he knew that two nights without sleep was enough to make Maura hit him over the head with her precious handbag if he made a fuss. He stood up as Kitty, half skipping, half walking and with biscuits in her hand, given to her by Maisie for having returned the empty cups and saucers, made her way towards them.

Maura noticed that Maisie was now chatting to a large lady in a navy-blue dress and a frilled hat. The lady was tall, broad and imposing and stood with her legs apart and her arms folded. Just the sight of her terrified Tommy.

'Feckin' 'ell,' he said, 'she could unload the hull of a ship all by herself, that one. We wouldn't even be needing the crane. Would you look at that. Would you?' His mouth fell open. 'Jesus, feck, sure, come on. Come here, Kitty, we have to be going to see the doctor.'

As the three of them made a hurried and suspicious-looking shuffle towards the main doors and the steps, they heard Maisie shout something to them.

Without turning round, Tommy raised his hand and shouted back, 'Thanking you for the tea and your kindness, Maisie, but we're off to the appointment now.' He held the door open for Maura and Kitty to pass through. 'Come on, faster,' he urged, then continued muttering to himself. 'Jesus, if any of the lads could see this. They won't believe me when I tell them there's a nurse here who's bigger than any of them lot.'

But just as he felt the welcome fresh air on his face, there was a shove in his back and the Amazonian woman pushed past him. 'Mrs Doherty?' she said, addressing Maura.

Maura stopped dead on the red sandstone steps and turned around. 'Yes,' she answered, with a warble in her throat.

'I'm Sister Antrobus and if you don't come with me now, you will be late for your outpatient appointment.' Sister Antrobus was looking and talking to the fob watch she held out from her dress and was peering over her glasses at Maura as though she was daring Maura to challenge her. She looked up sharply towards Tommy before Maura could swallow her breath and reply. 'Mr Doherty.'

Tommy was speechless with fear and simply nodded, fully aware that this was a statement and not a question or a request to verify that fact.

'I have no idea what you are doing here. Or this child.' Again, she peered over the rim of her glasses as though Kitty were not a child at all but rather something which had crawled out of an apple or from under a stone.

But Kitty was neither speechless nor cowed. 'Do you mean me?' she asked, with genuine curiosity.

Tommy paled. Kitty had never met or even seen a person who looked like Sister Antrobus before. Sister Tapps was half her size in both height and width. To Kitty, Sister Antrobus resembled a character from a comic and she wanted her to speak more.

'I do mean you, young lady. Have you never been told, children should be seen and not heard, and that means you. Be quiet.'

Kitty's curiosity faded as quickly as it had arrived and her face clouded with indignation. No one ever told her to be quiet. She was her mother's little helper, and the two of them never stopped talking. 'Excuse me,' she piped up.

Maura wanted the ground to open up and swallow her.

'Jesus, Kitty,' hissed Tommy.

Kitty glared at him. Undeterred, she continued. 'Excuse me, do you know Sister Tapps?'

Sister Antrobus folded her arms. Sister Tapps was her bête noire and far too soft on her patients. In Sister Antrobus's opinion, nurses who were not terribly fond of children made the best paediatric ward sisters. She herself had applied for the job in ward three, but Matron had just told her that an upstart new sister was to fill the post. So now she would set her sights on Sister Tapps's role as the sister in charge of ward four. Tappsy's retirement was way overdue, so it was surely only a matter of time. 'I do know Sister Tapps. Why?' she asked, momentarily taken aback that a mere child had had the temerity to address her without being spoken to first.

'Because I know her too. Will you tell her Kitty was here, please. Kitty Doherty. And that I said hello to her?' Kitty began to feel slightly nervous under the piercing glare of Sister Antrobus. She twiddled one of her plaits and slipped her fingers into her father's outstretched hand. Tilting her head to one side, she let her eyes wander from the top to the bottom of Sister Antrobus.

Sister Antrobus had no response. She squinted and her cheeks flushed, but before she could respond with her customary roar, Kitty's eyes lit up. The little girl squealed, let go of her da's hands and ran down the steps and across the gravel path towards the slight, white-haired figure in a ward sister's uniform who was making her way towards them. In her arms she carried a golden teddy bear and a small doll kitted out in Irish national dress.

'Sister Tapps!' Kitty yelled, and Maura and Tommy were amazed to hear the reply. It was years since Kitty had been a patient at the hospital. Maura immediately thought how Sister Tapps had not altered one little bit, except that she was much thinner than she remembered.

'Well, would you look at you! Kitty Doherty, isn't it?' Sister Tapps looked over to Maura and Tommy, who were rooted to the spot under the gaze of Sister Antrobus, too afraid to move.

Kitty nodded furiously and, overcome with delight, unable to stop herself and with no Maura at her side to reprimand her, she threw her arms around Sister Tapps's waist and hugged her.

Sister Tapps stroked her hair. 'Well now, isn't that lovely, and something I didn't expect to happen today. What a treat. Doesn't it always show you,' she shouted over, 'you never know what lovely surprise the good Lord might have in store for you when you get up out of your bed.' She looked back down at Kitty. 'And what are you doing here? You aren't coming back to my ward, are you?'

Kitty shook her head. 'No, it's Angela. She has to see the doctor.'

Sister Tapps looked over at Maura. 'Well now, if she's been

a poorly girl, that will be the best thing for her. You know that, don't you, Mammy?'

Maura and Tommy, despite their initial fear, couldn't help themselves and began to smile and nod their heads in acknowledgement. Sister Tapps had that effect. She made people smile. Maura remembered that about her and remembered her calm and reassuring manner on the ward. Her fears, her memories of the friend she had lost, which were at the root of all her anxieties about the hospital, faded away in the presence of Sister Tapps.

Sister Antrobus had clearly had enough of Kitty and Tommy. 'Mrs Doherty, come with me, now – you and the patient. Mr Doherty, not you. You and your daughter can wait at the WVS post if you must, but let me tell you, the hospital is no place for children, so unless you are sick, young lady…' She turned again towards Kitty, who, Tommy noted with pride, remained undaunted, but then Tommy hadn't been taught by the nuns. '… and unless you need admitting, let this be the last time I see you here. Unless of course your sister becomes an inpatient and then only at visiting which is between the hours of two and three on a Sunday afternoon.'

The calming, kindly manner of Sister Tapps appeared to have no impact on the curt and officious Sister Antrobus. Kitty backed away from Sister Antrobus and closer to Tommy, instinctively wanting to stick to her father's side and protect her parents and Angela from the unpleasant woman. She reached over to her da and took his hand.

'You come with me,' Sister Antrobus said to Maura, but they all stopped and turned as the thin voice of Sister Tapps filled the air.

'Kitty, it has been a delight to see you again.'

Kitty grinned.

Maura turned the pushchair. 'And you too, Sister,' she said, in the same courteous, reverential tone she used when addressing the nuns. Then, with a very sudden change of key, she said to Tommy, 'Help me down the steps with this pushchair. Kitty, you wait there. Go back inside, it's cold out here.'

Once at the bottom of the steps, and before she turned to follow Sister Antrobus, Maura glared at Tommy. Her eyes sent a number of messages and he understood every single one, as did Kitty, who was now peering through the glass panes of the door, not wanting to let her family out of her sight. The first was: if you want to live, wait for me and be in that WVS post when I get back. The second: look after Kitty, and the third: we have to do this, for Angela.

As Kitty waited for her da, she focused on Sister Tapps. Halfway up the steps, she stopped and grabbed on to the handrail and the expression that crossed her face made Kitty feel funny inside. Something was hurting her and Kitty wondered whether she should run back down the steps to help her, but she found that her feet were glued to the spot in fear. As soon as the grimace of pain had crossed Sister Tapps's face, she looked up towards the door, saw Kitty peering through and beamed a weak smile back up at her. But Kitty wasn't fooled. She could see the tears in her eyes and the blood had all but drained from her face.

Tommy, not aware that anything was wrong, bounced back up the steps and through the door. Passing Sister Tapps, he shouted back down, 'Will I hold the door for you, Sister?'

Sister Tapps shook her head and it was obvious to Kitty that she was waiting to catch her breath before she replied. 'Not at all,' she said. 'I've only gone the wrong way.' And, smiling, she slowly turned as though to make her way back down.

Tommy raised his hand and, letting the door go, said, 'Come on, queen, let's see if I can get you another glass of that squash from Maisie while we wait for your mammy and Angela.' Taking her hand, he propelled her along with him.

Kitty looked over her shoulder and turned back to the door, but she was disappointed as Sister Tapps never returned.

Chapter 3

'Ah, you pair of sods. What kept you? Barbara's been fretting. Cut you the best bit of ham off the bone to go with the chips and when you didn't turn up I thought I was going to get it all for meself. Might of known I'd have no such luck. Bet you smelt it up in Whitechapel, eh?'

The landlord of the Grapes pub lifted up the long wooden hatch and stood aside to let the two tall police officers through to the back of the bar. PCs Freddie Watts and Norman Bartlett both had to duck their heads as they passed through to avoid colliding with the overhead beam and the pewter jugs hanging from it. The jugs were special: each one bore the name of a fallen local hero engraved on the bottom, inscribed there long ago by the men themselves, with a sharp nail and a hammer. They had hung there untouched for a decade now, a fitting memorial to those pub regulars who had paid the ultimate price and would never drink in the Grapes again. More fitting than the stone cross outside St Chad's, where those who had survived assembled after Mass on November the eleventh each year. No one had dared suggest the tankards be taken down. Another ten years would pass before the winds of change would sweep through the community and blow away its superstitions.

'Evening, Dr Mackintosh. Nurse Tanner.' Freddie lifted his tall helmet from his head, both to enable him to pass through the arch and to greet Nurse Pammy Tanner and Dr Anthony Mackintosh, who were sitting at an upturned beer-barrel table in front of the inglenook fireplace. Sawdust covered the floor and the smell of freshly shaved wood was accentuated by the warmth of the log fire that burnt in the wide grate. In the corner of the room stood a tall Christmas tree strung with far too many coloured lights and tinsel. Crepe paper garlands had been looped from one corner of the ceiling to the next and they quivered and crackled with the thermals rising from the fire.

The flames danced up the chimney and there was a sudden scattering of ash as Anthony Mackintosh let go of his Pammy's hand for a moment, lifted a log from the pile stacked up against the blackened brick wall and threw it on to the fire. He clapped his hands together to remove the strands of moss and splinters, then smiled up at the police officers as he sat back on the bench and slid his arm around Pammy's shoulders. She was his girl and he liked to make sure that no one was left in any doubt of that fact, particularly when a fresh male came on to his territory.

Every nurse and doctor who had served their time on casualty knew most of the police officers who worked in central Liverpool by name. Their paths crossed, often.

'Evening, Freddie, Norman. Do you two live in here?' Pammy grinned as she returned the greeting.

'Only when we aren't keeping the streets of Liverpool safe so that you nurses can sleep safe in your beds in Lovely Lane. Isn't that right, Norman?' Freddie gave Pammy a cheeky wink, causing Anthony to hug her a little closer into his shoulder whilst giving the impression that he was simply altering his position.

'Oh yes, that's our top priority, Nurse Tanner,' said Norman, who unfortunately hadn't ducked low enough to miss the beam and was now rubbing his almost bald pate.

At six foot four, Norman was the taller of the two constables but carried with him the visible effects of his leisure-time passion for drinking pints of Guinness. He was considerably older than Freddie and walked with a slight stoop. Freddie had joined the police force when he returned from the war and was much fitter and faster than Norman. He was also single and there wasn't a doctor who worked on casualty who was unaware of this. He loved playing football when he could make the training and he was always being sought to play in the St Domingo's first team on match days. Spending the majority of his waking hours outdoors was yet to play havoc with his olive skin and good looks. His thick dark wavy hair slipped out from beneath his helmet and his dark lashes curled disarmingly, fully revealing his brown eyes flecked with blue. No one was more conscious than Freddie of the effect he had on women, young and matronly alike.

The two policemen were each responsible for a different patch of the neighbourhood, and both territories happened to touch borders at the Grapes, which was where Freddie and Norman convened and took their refs break when they were on night duty. The landlord and landlady ensured that they were well looked after and in return the constables turned a blind eye when necessary – to the numerous goods sold over the bar which had obviously fallen off the back of a ship down at the docks; to the card school down in the basement that played for stakes far too high for most working families;

and to the late-night drinking which sometimes went on until the early hours. The Grapes sat at the heart of the community and Norman and Freddie were well aware that if they made life difficult at the pub, their own jobs would very quickly become much harder. They depended on the goodwill of the community, plus they relished the warmth of the welcome they received every night in the back room.

'How's your da, Nurse Tanner?' asked Norman. Although he had known Pammy since she was a child, he was so respectful of Matron's strict rule about never using Christian names within the confines of St Angelus that he called her Nurse Tanner wherever he saw her, at work or not. 'Is he still drinking down the Irish club on a Saturday?'

'You know me da, Norman – a creature of habit,' said Pammy. She gave the back of Anthony's hand a reassuring pat as she spoke.

'I don't know how your mam puts up with him. A lovely woman like that. And to think she turned me down.' Norman shook his head in mock dismay as though hurt by the memory.

'Well, I've no idea why she did that, Norman, a good-looking fella like you,' said Pammy.

'Ah well, you see, that's what keeps Stan on his toes and treating your mam like a princess. Because I never married, he's had to keep looking over his shoulder all these years. Terrified of me, he is. Go back a long way, me and your mam do, Nurse Tanner. Bet she's never told you about the night me and her went to the Grafton Rooms, has she?'

Pammy laughed. 'Actually, Norman, she has. And about how you weren't allowed in because you were late. You went, but you never actually danced, did you?'

Barbara and the barman began to laugh.

'Are you coming to the rehearsal at St Chad's tonight?' asked Freddie.

'Yes, we both are,' replied Pammy.

She'd been responsible for ensuring that everyone at Lovely Lane signed up to the service-wide concert. Nurses, medics, the Lancashire constabulary and the fire service had joined together and were putting on a carol concert on the steps of St George's Hall on Christmas Eve for all of Liverpool to enjoy. For the nurses, this was in addition to the carol singing on the wards of St Angelus in the days leading up to Christmas.

'Are you coming too, Norman?' asked Pammy. 'It's the reason we're in here so early. Want to make sure our larynxes are warmed nicely before we go.'

'That's a very good idea, Nurse Tanner,' said Norman. 'But someone has to keep the villains away, so I'll be staying here while young Freddie gives you all the pleasure of his warbling tones.'

'Is it all quiet in casualty tonight, Dr Mackintosh?' asked the conscientious Freddie.

Not only did Freddie need to visit St Angelus to accompany the occasional victim, criminal or prisoner, but the hospital was also on his patch and he could often be found enjoying a cup of tea with Dessie Horton, the head porter.

'You are never out of that porter's hut,' Norman would complain.

'I'm intelligence gathering,' Freddie used to reply, and that was the truth. A recent crime involving the mother of one of the porter's lads had caused Freddie and Dessie to strike up a strong friendship and Dessie had discovered it was one that worked both ways.

'Well, it was quiet when I left, Freddie, and they know

where to call for me if they can't cope,' said Anthony as he removed his arm from around Pammy's shoulders and tapped the top of the wooden barrel for good luck.

'Long may it last,' said Freddie. 'At least until I've had me refreshments tonight, anyway. And then, with a bit of luck, all the way through to the other side of Christmas.' He clasped his helmet to his chest and followed Norman to the back room, his mouth salivating at the prospect of ham and chips.

'Where have you two been?' asked Barbara. 'This is the second batch of chips I've cooked. The first lot dried up on the range and the dog had 'em.'

'Sorry, Babs.' Norman unhooked the clasp on his cape, removed the coat and draped it over the back of the wooden chair nearest to the fire.

The room smelt of refried fat and chips. Barbara cooked for the staff, and every night from seven till eight there was pie and chips available for anyone who wanted food and had no one at home to provide it. But she was strict with the dockers. If she thought any one of them was keeping a family hungry by spending his wage in her pub, she would frogmarch him home herself. Weighing eighteen stone and with a tongue as sharp as a razor, she was a force to be reckoned with, and no one, not even in drink, argued with her.

'We wouldn't be late deliberately, Babs, you know that. There was a little lad missing from Vince Street. The Browns' youngest. Frantic, they were. I knew where he would be, which was why I was worried. That kid is fascinated by the water. Always on the dockside, he is. I keep telling his da he needs to do something. Anyway, we found him, didn't we, Freddie? As I thought, stood right on the edge of the dock he was. Tell you what, I didn't half give him a good hiding. His legs didn't touch the ground all the way back to the Browns' house. I told his mam that if that lad is found down on the edge of the Mersey again, I'll put her no-good bloody husband in a cell for the week.'

Barbara put her hand to her mouth. 'It's so dangerous down at the water. What's his mam and da thinking, letting him out on his own? Everyone knows the lad is simple, and the water is so deep. It's straight in deep from the edge and none of those kids on Vince Street can swim. Who can, apart from the bleedin' fishes. Good job you gave him a good hiding, Norman. I bet he won't do it again in a hurry.'

Freddie had taken his own cape off and was pulling the chair out from under the table. He winced as the wooden legs scraped along the ancient slate-tiled floor. He was so hungry, his mouth was watering and he could hear and see nothing but the plate of food before him.

Babs knew that look. Five hours on the beat, walking or cycling through the streets, meant that they were both always ravenous by the time they called in. 'Here you go, lads. Your tongue is hanging out of your mouth, Freddie! Come on, get started on it, love.' She set down two pewter pots of mild next to the plates of food. 'Get that down you before the phone rings and some other kid has done a bunk. Honestly, you're here to stop serious crime, you aren't the welfare.'

Norman popped a hot chip into his mouth and breathed in sharply. 'It feels that way sometimes,' he said.

Barbara placed a bottle of vinegar in front of him. 'There, that's everything, and there are some American ciggies behind the bar that came in off the *Norry*, if you fancy a packet on the way out.'

Norman tapped the side of his nose with his index finger.

'Right you are, Babs. Sounds just the ticket. Where would we be without the *Norry*, eh? Life would be boring, wouldn't it?'

Neither officer needed to be asked twice to get stuck into the food or the mild, and for Norman the gold-foil-tipped cigarettes were a bonus.

Out in the lounge, Pammy and Anthony were deep in conversation. 'What is up with you?' asked Anthony. 'You've been so miserable the past few days. Christmas is less than two weeks away and I don't know about you but I'm really excited. I haven't had a family Christmas since before my mum died.' He'd been invited to spend his Christmas Day with the Tanners, or what would be left of it once they'd both finished work.

Pammy had been twirling the stem of her glass around and around in her fingers and looked up at Anthony in alarm. She immediately felt guilty. 'Oh, Anthony, I'm sorry. I'm missing the others, that's all, what with Dana being in Ireland and Victoria in Bolton. I feel a bit lost without them. I suppose because I'm the only one who's actually from Liverpool it was bound to happen sometime, especially at Christmas, but Lovely Lane isn't the same without them. It's just so quiet.'

Anthony squeezed Pammy's hand and felt his own heart constrict. 'But you are happy I am here, are you? That we are together? That isn't making you sad, is it?'

'Anthony, don't be daft, soft lad. Of course I am happy. Imagine how miserable I would be if you weren't here. We're a team, me and you, aren't we?'

Pammy checked the bar to see that no one was looking. Babs was fussing over Norman and Freddie and they were all busy talking, her and Anthony forgotten. She placed her drink on the table, leant across and kissed Anthony full on the lips.

He blushed, just as he always did when Pammy kissed him in public. And then he grinned, because she was the most impetuous and daring woman he had ever met. 'We are a team,' he said, his eyes shining, his heart wishing they were somewhere private, 'and that's why I worry when I see you feeling sad. When you are sad, I am sad, and my job is to look after you, to make sure you're happy.'

Pammy slipped her hand on to his knee and grasped his fingers. 'I am happy, Anthony. But I'll tell you what, I'm not the only one. Me dad, how much does he love having you round our house! And me mam, I think she thinks more of you than she does me.'

Anthony laughed and, leaning forward, kissed his Pammy back. The light in her eyes had returned. He had lifted her out of her melancholy. The four girls – his Pammy, Dana, Victoria and Beth – had been almost inseparable since they'd begun their training and he wasn't surprised Pammy was lost without them. It was the reason he'd encouraged her to join the services choir, to give them both something to do in the evenings in the run-up to Christmas.

They all turned around as the shrill ring of the telephone on the bar pierced the air.

'Rightyo, I'll fetch him now,' said the landlord into the phone. 'Norman, it's your desk sergeant, he needs to speak to you.'

They heard the clomping of Norman's size-twelve feet on the slate floor as he made his way over and picked up the handset.

'It'll be a cat, sir,' he said into the mouthpiece. 'But if the cat got in, it will get out again.'

Only the landlord heard the raised tone of Norman's superior as he bellowed his response down the line.

'Yes, sir,' said Norman sheepishly. 'On our way, sir.'

As he replaced the handset, Freddie appeared by his side. 'Honestly!' Norman said as he took the cape and helmet Freddie proffered. 'There's an empty house in the station commander's road. He said there were some Germans living there but no one ever spoke to them and yesterday morning they moved out. He thinks they've left a cat in a shed out the back, or so the neighbour who backs on thinks, and he is sending us to go and rescue it.'

Freddie was fastening the chinstrap under his helmet and chewing the last of his mouthful as he did so. 'I'd rather that than a kid in trouble like the Brown boy nearly was,' he said.

'Aye, you're right. At least we have full bellies. Landlord, we are replete.' Norman mock bowed and made a swoop with his helmet. 'We shall return tomorrow. In the meantime, how much are the American ciggies?'

Once the transaction was over, Norman and Freddie made their way out to the bikes they had leant against the outside wall in no particular hurry.

'Night, Norman! Night, Freddie!' shouted Pammy. 'I'm on children's from tomorrow, Freddie, so you will have to find someone else to make your tea on casualty,' she added.

Freddie looked crestfallen and Anthony smiled, relieved. Not that he didn't trust Pammy, or Freddie for that matter – he was a decent young man and a very serious copper who obviously had ambitions in the police force – it was that he just couldn't help himself. If he could wrap his Pammy up in cotton wool and keep her in a gilded house, he would.

'It will taste nothing like yours, little Nurse Tanner,' Norman joked back. 'I shall miss you on casualty, but no doubt you will have a much quieter life on children's and be glad to see the back of me and Freddie here.'

Anthony nodded enthusiastically, then checked himself when Pammy shot him a quizzical look and he realized what he was doing.

Pammy waved to Norman and Freddie. 'Have a quiet night, lads,' she shouted.

Chapter 4

It was their regular weekly meeting in Matron's office and Matron and Emily had just finished discussing which trainee nurse was on what ward and for how long, and who was being moved from days to night duty. Wards and the number of nursing staff, both qualified and trainee, ran down the blackboard on Matron's wall in neat columns. Each square on the board was filled and had been completed to her satisfaction all the way to New Year's Day. It was the most satisfying moment of Matron's week.

Alongside the staff allocation board lay the bed allocation board. Again, there was a column for each ward, with the number of the ward and the name of the sister at the top. In the past, the wards had been named after the ward sister, but the war and the churn of staff coming and going, off to do their duty for King and country, had put paid to that. Below the sister's name, the beds were listed by number and next to the number was the name of the patient, their disease or condition and the length of their stay in hospital to date. This last column had been added following an incident on ward four. Matron had blamed herself and it was something she now guarded against ever happening again. Patients marvelled at Matron's memory. How she knew every one of their names, on every ward. They had no idea how long she spent each day sitting at her desk memorizing them. Sometimes when she arrived back from her rounds she would pick up the chalk and next to a patient's name would write a note, a memory prodder, of something she had been told that day. *Mrs Browne's daughter getting married on Saturday. Mr O'Hara's sister died in a Dublin convent.*

Matron opened the tin box on her desk. It had once contained Scottish shortbread and on the lid was a picture of a Scottie dog crouched on a heathery hillside. He looked just like Blackie, who was right now firmly in his basket, well aware that on meeting days, when Emily Haycock was in the office, he was expected to stay put. Matron placed the chalk and board duster back into the tin, opened her desk drawer and slipped the tin inside, out of sight.

'A very productive hour's work,' she said as the drawer clicked shut and she turned the key. 'Time for our little reward, don't you think?'

She rang the bell for Elsie to wheel in their customary trolley of tea and walnut cake, which they always took on the chairs in front of Matron's fire.

'I won't say no,' said Emily as she finished copying their deliberations into her large book. When she returned to the school of nursing she would copy the lists on to the blackboard in her own office, and that way, whenever she felt like doing a spot-check on one of the probationers or a student nurse, she could glance up from her desk and know exactly who was on days or nights and what ward they had been allocated to. 'It'll give me some extra energy for typing out the off-duty sheets. I'm a dab hand with that new carbon paper now,' she said, looking up and catching Matron's eye. 'It's a lot more efficient once you get the hang of it – typing it up once and sending carbon copies round to each ward. Even Biddy's stopped complaining about my technique. She used to say I banged so hard on the typewriter keys to get it through that they could hear me down in the kitchens.'

Matron laughed. 'Do you know, it seems to me that every day there's something new to adjust to or learn. I have no idea where it's all going to end.'

Emily dabbed her foolscap sheet with the blotting paper before slamming it shut. 'I'm glad we're going to let the ward sisters work out their own off-duty over Christmas. The number of requests are almost too much to deal with. Better that the sisters be the ones to say yes or no, and, really, they can make their own deals with the devil, as long as everywhere is covered.'

'That was a brainwave you had there, Sister Haycock,' said Matron. 'Transferring the recuperating children from ward four on to ward three was an excellent idea. Why have I never thought of that before? Sister Tapps can have a proper break at Christmas for the first time in years, we'll have no pressure on cover for children's ward and everyone will be happy – especially the paediatric surgeon, whoever that will be over the Christmas break. It will be a quieter Christmas for him too.'

Emily had grown to enjoy these weekly sessions. It had taken a long time for Matron to trust her, but she had finally managed to convince her that she was not after her job and that St Angelus was as close to her heart as it was to Matron's.

'Matron, do you think it would be a good idea for you to have a word with Sister Tapps yourself about transferring the children from four to three? Now that we have decided.

I don't think it's my place really. And I don't want her to just receive the pink off-duty sheet and wonder what's happening and where her ward has gone.'

They both sat down in the armchairs, Matron primly tucking her navy-blue dress under her knees, Emily flopping, as was her style. If she had been anywhere other than in Matron's office, she would have kicked her shoes off and stretched her toes out in front of the fire.

Matron folded her hands in her lap. 'Do you know, that's an excellent idea. I think I'll invite her to have supper here with me. I've barely spoken to her about anything other than the patients for years. You know that there was the very sad case of the child...'

Matron didn't have to finish her sentence. Emily nodded. 'I do. To be fair, I think everyone does.'

They both looked into the fire for a moment, both feeling for Sister Tapps, who had fallen into the trap of caring too much for one of her long-term patients.

'I should do that more often, you know,' Matron said. 'Invite people over for supper.'

They both looked up at the familiar squeak of the tea trolley, being pushed by Elsie across the room.

'Do you want two slices of walnut cake today, Sister Haycock?' Elsie enquired as she kicked the brake on the trolley. She lifted the netting cloche with one hand and held a side plate ready, hovering over the cake dish, with the other.

Steam rose from the teapot and Emily realized that she was indeed starving. 'No, thank you, Elsie, just one, please,' she said.

Elsie winked. 'Here you are then, but I'll leave you one cut on the plate, just in case you change your mind. You've been using up a lot of energy just lately.'

Emily looked up sharply at Elsie and was about to ask her what she meant, but the colour spreading across her cheeks was a dead giveaway. Everyone who lived on the dockside streets knew what Emily and the head porter, Dessie Horton, were up to. It was a scandal and there was no hiding from the gossip, the giggles and, in some quarters, the condemnation.

Elsie did what all the domestics had mastered to a fine art – she redeemed herself in the next couple of sentences. 'I always get exhausted myself at Christmas. So much rushing around to be done. Mind you, I haven't missed a single week this year, either in my butcher's club or the greengrocer's. We are going to have a smashing Christmas in our house.'

'Thank you Elsie, we can manage now,' said Matron and Elsie knew she was dismissed.

Emily glanced at Matron and could tell she had no idea what Elsie had been talking about. She let out the deep breath she hadn't realized she'd been holding and sat back in the chair, the hand that held the plate of walnut cake trembling slightly. It was no secret that Emily and Dessie were in love, nor even that wedding bells were in the air, but that was all Matron knew, and Emily wanted to keep it that way.

Emily and Matron had built a new relationship. They had been through enough together to know that they could work as a team, that they shared the same values, almost, and would fight to the death for the St Angelus family. But there were some issues on which their views diverged, and Emily was well aware that Matron would be truly horrified if she discovered that she and Dessie were actually lovers. And it wasn't just the occasional night together – they were effectively living in sin. She was making a big show of returning to her rooms in the hospital each night and ruffling up her sheets, swilling water around the sink, wetting her toothbrush and throwing rubbish into the basket, so that the maids thought she was still sleeping there. The maids were gossiping and laughing along with the rest of them. She was fooling no one, but Sister Haycock was so popular, and had been through so much during the war, that no one wanted to deny either her or the streets' own war hero Dessie the happiness they had finally found in each other's arms.

'Once Dessie and I are married, I'll invite Sister Tapps to join us for the occasional Sunday lunch. It's the least I can do. We go back a long way, after all – right back to when I had my appendix out as a child.' Emily grinned as the memories came flooding back. 'She fed me jelly and ice cream, I remember, even though that was for the children who'd had tonsillectomies. On the ward diet board I was listed as "tonsils" so that the cook didn't deprive me of the ice cream. She was lovely, kindness itself. And do you know, when I came back here as a nurse, the first thing she said to me was, "And how's that scar of yours?" And then she asked me had my bowels been OK! It was fifteen years later.'

Matron chuckled at the thought of Sister Tapps asking Emily about her bowel movements and Emily laughed so much she was scared she'd spill her tea. 'I was amazed that she remembered me. I had changed a lot from the six-year-old she'd looked after.'

'That sounds just like Sister Tapps,' said Matron. 'But she's not been the same since all that to-do with the polio child.'

'That was a long time ago,' said Emily. 'It can't still be affecting her now, surely.' She took another gulp of tea. 'I know what you mean, though. Some of the nurses have become concerned about her recently, but I think it might be that she's lonely. Her life is the ward, the children, and Mass on Sunday. It must have been different when lots of the sisters used to live in, before the war. She'd have had more company then.'

'The war changed everything,' said Matron. 'Would we still have ward sisters living in hospital accommodation if the war hadn't happened? Would I ever have abandoned the "no married nurses" rule?' She checked herself. 'I suppose I'm being a fool. If the war hadn't happened, time wouldn't just have stood still, would it?'

Emily shook her head and bit into the walnut buttercream filling. For a moment she was lost. The novelty of having unlimited access to sugar, flour and butter had taken some getting used to.

Matron was quite used to Emily's loss of concentration when she first bit into her cake. She waited patiently for her to finish and recover her tea. 'All that sadness,' she murmured, half to herself. 'All that loss of life. I hope this country never knows the like again.' She broke off and gazed into the fire.

The sadness that filled the room whenever anyone spoke of the war had arrived and Emily wondered when that would change, when people would be able to talk openly about the days that had destroyed their lives. For her part, she thought that time would never come. She doubted whether she and Dessie would ever have the conversation about how the war had affected them. Look to the future, Emily reminded herself, not back to the past.

'I'm going to invite her tonight,' said Matron with a flourish of determination, 'and at the same time I will tell her the good news – that we are discharging the walking wounded from her ward home for Christmas, that there will be no list admissions in the run-up and that the rest will be transferred to ward three. She will be delighted. Her first Christmas Day off and away from St Angelus in forty years – fancy that!'

There was no response from Emily, whose eyes were fixed on the extra slice of cake Elsie had left for her just in case. Matron smiled at her as she reached out and slid the slice on to her plate. 'Oh, why not?' said Emily as she grinned back.

Later that evening, replete with liver and bacon in onion gravy, and mashed potato, followed by a jam roly-poly suet pudding and very hot custard, Matron loosened the buckle on her belt. 'Do the same, if you feel like I do, Olive,' she said to Sister Tapps. 'Shall we have a cup of tea in front of the fire before you go back to your room?'

Sister Tapps took a moment to respond. She couldn't remember the last time anyone had called her by her Christian name. She had no need to undo the buckle on her belt, even though she had made a good job of eating supper. She often missed supper. It involved a trip to the sisters' dining room, but as she was one of only a few sisters left living in the hospital accommodation, she preferred not to bother. In fact, she would rather go without supper than have to sit at the table with Sister Antrobus. They had their own maid in the sisters' sitting room and Tappsy would often simply ask her to leave a sandwich in her room for when she finished.

Sister Tapps was known in the hospital as one who kept herself to herself and liked it that way. Tonight had been special. The supper had been delicious. Elsie and Cook between them had done Matron proud. Matron didn't like to have alcohol in her dining room, not since the night Sister Antrobus had drunk too much and vomited all over her new red floral Axminster carpet, but Sister Tapps wasn't the type to drink, even if she had gone to the effort of buying it in.

'That would be very nice, thank you,' said Tappsy.

Matron got to her feet. 'I think up here, away from the wards and the nurses, you can call me Margaret, don't you? How long have we known each other? You know, I don't know why we haven't done this before, you and I. You make yourself comfortable and I'll bring the tea tray through to the sitting room. You'll never guess what I have as a treat – a bar of Cadbury's Dairy Milk.'

Sister Tapps smiled. 'We have so much of that chocolate being brought into the ward on Sunday afternoons these days that I have to take it off the parents at visiting time. There's a new chocolate bar arrives every week, it seems. I send two nurses out with a tray to collect it all in during visiting – you wouldn't believe how some of the parents complain. And to think, we never saw a bar of the stuff during the war. As scarce as hen's teeth it was.'

Matron had stopped midway to the kitchen. 'It all seems so long ago, don't you think? And yet it's not even ten years. What do you do with all the sweets and chocolates when you've gathered them in then?'

'I keep them in jars in the cupboard in my office. Every afternoon, after the quiet hour and the sleep, and again after supper, I distribute a small bowlful to each child. That way, everyone has exactly the same and no child is made to feel different or left out because their visitors can't afford such luxuries, or they don't have visitors at all. And the children, they do look forward to them. I've even known some of the nurses to use them as a bribe.'

Sister Tapps laughed and it occurred to Matron that she did

that a lot, whereas she, Matron, rarely laughed. What does she have to laugh about, Matron wondered. Her thoughtfulness, her kindness, and the compassion she showed every child regardless of creed or background never ceased to amaze her. Matron had heard about the weekly sweet collection and twice-daily distribution. Some were grumbling that the nurses had enough to do and what did it matter that some children had sweets in their lockers and others didn't. Sister Antrobus had complained herself to Matron. 'Some of the parents are taking umbrage. They spend good money on those sweets for their own children or charges, only to have them confiscated. Ward four is not a charity. You know me, Matron, I totally disapprove of spoiling children, but, really, I think Sister Tapps has overstepped the mark.'

Matron was herself well used to Sister Antrobus and was also very well aware that she was looking for a new ward to take charge of. She had smelt weakness in the ageing Sister Tapps and was moving in for the kill. Matron had put a flea in Sister Antrobus's ear and sent her on her way.

Sister Tapps rose from the dining room chair with some difficulty. She was the wrong side of sixty, slightly older than Matron, and it was beginning to show. Her now brilliant white hair sat like a cloud beneath her heavy frilled hat and, mid perm, tended to fall in soft loose curls about her ears. She had always been slight and at one time could have been described as swift in her movements. Never tiring, always busy, she had to be persuaded to take her nurses for their morning coffee before they dropped, even though she herself had no need to refuel.

She might have begun slowing down now, but Matron had noticed as they were talking that her eyes had lost none of their youthfulness. They were blue and twinkly, and her smile was still gentle around the edges. But far more notable, and alarming, to Matron was that Sister Tapps's sole topic of conversation was the children on the ward. No matter how many times Matron had tried to divert the subject away to a wider realm – the NHS, the post-war building boom, the new plans for Liverpool and the country – Sister Tapps had engaged only momentarily and had then reverted to discussing a patient, her ward or even her surgeon, who had first arrived on ward four as a houseman thirty years ago.

Now, as she made her way to the armchair, she reprised the topic. 'We had a new admission this afternoon from children's services, and you'll never guess, I only had her sister Kitty in for her tonsils four years ago. The poor mother, there was no stopping her tears. The little sister is in a bad way. She had a turn in the clinic and the doctor thought she was going to go into respiratory arrest. He had Dessie bring her straight up to me, told him, "Take her to Sister Tapps and no one else." Ran with her in his arms, Dessie did.'

'Yes, I saw it on the bed statement that we had a new one in,' said Matron. 'Did they give her aminophylline?'

'They did, or I did. I stayed with her until it was time to come over here. She's breathing much better now. Good job the parents brought her in when they did. The mother couldn't bear to leave the little lass – in bits she was. I had to get two of the nurses to take her away so that she didn't upset the little girl. I think there might be something in this new notion to let parents visit their children daily.'

'Would you agree to that?' asked Matron.

'Oh yes, of course I would. Remember, it's not so long ago parents weren't allowed to visit at all. That was not my notion, you know that. It was already in place when I arrived here.'

Matron nodded. It was she who'd introduced weekly visiting, immediately she'd taken up her post.

'I told the mother, "It's not long until Sunday and I'll look after her just like I did your little Kitty," but there was no consoling her. I had to call down to Maisie Tanner in the WVS post and ask her to send the daddy up. He wasn't much better. But little Kitty, you should have heard her, calming them both down, telling her that their Angela was the lucky one to be in such a nice place. 'Twas funny to hear her, so.' And on she went, not noticing Matron had even left the room to fetch the tea.

As Matron placed the tray on the table between them, it seemed clear to her that Emily Haycock had been right. It was time Sister Tapps had a break and, given what had happened in the past, she was furious with herself that she hadn't been the first to notice. That was her job, her duty of care, and she felt consumed with guilt that she had left this finest of ward sisters to her own devices for far too long. She should have known – hadn't there already been one dire and distressing warning too many?

She settled into her chair and began to pour the tea. Sister Tapps looked comfortable, rested, happy. The image of the polio child, the sound of her screams, flashed though Matron's mind, but, shaking her head slightly, she dismissed them swiftly.

She noticed that Sister Tapps's navy-blue uniform and Petersham belt looked bigger on her frame than was usual. She was losing weight. Working too hard, as always, thought Matron as she handed over the cup and saucer.

'And now for some of this.' Matron tore open the bar of Cadbury's Milk Chocolate and began to slowly peel back the purple foil wrapper. 'I don't know why anyone wants to drink alcohol when you can have this instead,' she said.

'Do you know, Matron... Margaret...' Tappsy flashed that beaming smile of hers, amused at calling Matron by her Christian name, 'I wouldn't know. I have never tasted a drop of alcohol in my life. However, we have a young boy who is eight days post-operative adenoids and his father, well, he smells of it. I may not have tasted it, but I do know what it smells like. I've smelt it on many a parent.'

There she goes again, her point of reference always her charges, thought Matron. And with a start she realized that she was just the same. They were no different. St Angelus was her entire life too and whereas her scope was wider, in as much as she was responsible for a hospital while Sister Tapps was concerned with a ward, they were essentially in the same position. They were the spinsters of St Angelus.

From under her eyelashes, Matron glanced at the belt hanging off Sister Tapps's waist, its buckle almost resting on her thighs, and broke off a huge piece of the chocolate. Placing it on a side plate, she handed it to Sister Tapps. Politeness prevented Matron from passing comment, but she made a mental note to keep an eye on her in future. They had been colleagues for so many years. If she didn't look out for her, who would?

'Now,' she said as she broke off a smaller piece for herself, 'I have some news that is going to delight you. I wanted to tell you myself and that is why I invited you here tonight.'

Tappsy looked up. She was suspicious. Her life had followed a pattern for many years. The variety came from the different children she nursed back to health, from the conditions they were admitted with, and from their parents too – sometimes a challenge, often a delight. She didn't want any surprises. Her life, her routine, was just as she liked it. The effect of Matron's words was to set her nerves jangling. She had been about to pop a square of the chocolate into her mouth but hesitated, long enough for it to begin to melt between her finger and thumb. She popped it in anyway as Matron continued.

'You have worked tirelessly for the children who live around here. You must have nursed a child from almost every family in every street, I would think. Sister Haycock and I—'

Sister Tapps had taken a sip of her tea to wash down the chocolate and she smiled over the rim of her cup. 'Oh, Sister Haycock, she was such a good little girl. She used to love her ice cream. She'd eat it so slowly, you know, savouring every single spoon. And her mother, well, her heart was broken when her little Emily was admitted. So close they were. The stepfather, he was away, fighting. The mother and daughter were inseparable. Even though we fed her ice cream, she couldn't get home and back to her mother quick enough. Some of them, they love the taste of ice cream so much, they guzzle it down on to the raw tonsil beds, they find it soothing, but not Sister Haycock, she was an appendix and such a good girl.' Sister Tapps set her cup on the saucer and looked slightly distracted, as though she was back in time, somewhere else entirely.

Matron felt slightly confused herself. Sister Haycock was over thirty now, many years on from having been a little girl. How did Sister Tapps remember all this detail? Eventually she said, 'Why don't you have some more chocolate?'

Tappsy snapped off a square and looked at it. 'Maybe I should save the rest for the sweetie jar,' she said.

Matron shook her head. 'No, you will not. You will eat it.'

'Pulling rank, Matron?' Sister Tapps smiled. 'I suppose you could be asking me to do something worse – like take Christmas Day as an off-duty. Now that would be bad.' She popped the chocolate into her mouth and gave a little laugh.

'But that's exactly what I am going to do!' Matron spluttered. 'How did you know?'

The clock on the mantelpiece chimed the half hour and Blackie's basket creaked as he shifted his position. He knew the precise time for his walk. It was when the clock chimed the hour. And when that happened, he knew exactly how to persuade Matron to leave her comfy seat.

'Well, not Christmas Day exactly,' Matron continued, 'but we are closing ward four for ten days, to give you a holiday. Because, believe it or not, I know you never take your days off and no one knows when it was you last took a holiday. Actually, I do know. I sent you on it. I had to make you go. You remember too, don't you?'

The air between them crackled. The occasion Matron was referring to had never been spoken about since.

Despite the heat from the fire, the blood had left Sister Tapps's face and she had turned a ghostly shade of pale. 'You can't do that,' she said. 'I don't want a holiday, and what about my children? I've been saving for Christmas all year. I have all number of plans for the ward. The Christmas trees are arriving tomorrow. I have twelve children to look after who couldn't possibly be sent home and even if they could, they will have a much better time on my ward than at home. I have bought them presents and asked Dessie Horton to be Father Christmas.'

The plate of chocolate banged down on to her knee and the final square flew across the floor. Matron shifted forward in her seat to retrieve it, but she was too late. Despite his age, Blackie had left his basket with lightning speed and stood with a defiant glare in his eye and a growl in his throat, daring Matron to take it. Matron had other things to deal with and Blackie, sensing victory, slunk back to his basket.

Matron, playing for time to gather her thoughts, picked up the teapot. 'Pass me your cup,' she said as she held out her hand.

Sister Tapps was silent. There was accusation in her eyes as she extended her hand, and the cup rattled on the saucer, betraying her deeper emotions.

Matron took a breath. This was going to be much harder than she had imagined. 'No, Sister Tapps, you do not have to be there.' She had wanted to sound softer, more comforting. She had thought that Sister Tapps would jump at the chance of a Christmas off. She remembered that she had a sister, down on the south coast. She searched her memory for her name. She'd met the sister once, at Crewe station, and she remembered how caring she had been. Younger than Sister Tapps. Well adjusted, a former teacher – it was coming back to her. Edith was her name and she was married to the headmaster of the local school, which their own children also attended. She was happy. That was what had struck Matron the most. They had sat in the station café for an hour and chatted while they waited for the connecting train. A subdued Sister Tapps had sat between them. Over the years, Matron had enquired about Edith's health and general wellbeing, but her recent enquiries had been met with the vaguest response and she had faded from Matron's memory.

'The children who cannot be sent home are being transferred to ward three so that you can have the break you deserve and need. No one can work every day of the year, day in, day out – it isn't possible.'

'You do.' Sister Tapps's eyes flared as she set her chin at Matron.

'No, I do not. Over the years, I often visited my mother. That simply isn't true.'

'You do now.' Sister Tapps was not backing down.

'Yes, but I'm not always going to. In fact, I am planning a holiday right now. I have always wanted to visit France and next summer I am going to do just that.' She was lying. She knew it, Sister Tapps knew it and Blackie, now sitting quite near, waiting, hoping for a further food catastrophe, also knew something was not quite right.

Matron adopted a gentler tone. She was desperate for a good outcome. Things were not going at all the way she had planned. Her authority had deserted her in the face of a woman who had begun her nursing career even before she had. 'I am doing this for you – you understand that, don't you? I thought you might want to spend Christmas with your sister, Edith, and her family. They must miss you and I'm sure they'd be delighted at the prospect.'

Sister Tapps looked as though Matron had just spoken in a foreign language. 'Edith died six years ago.'

Matron sat back in the chair. It was as though she'd been winded. She'd not been told this, had she? She knew Sister Tapps hadn't left Liverpool since the incident, but she'd simply assumed that Edith came up every so often for a visit. She'd seen her around the hospital, more than once, with her children. Though now it occurred to her that this had been a very long time ago. How long? Years, many years.

Matron recovered her equilibrium and, folding her hands

together, tried to catch Sister Tapps's eye. 'I am so very sorry to hear that,' she said. 'I don't remember you telling me.'

'That's because I didn't tell you,' Sister Tapps shot back. 'If I had, you would have made me leave my ward and attend her funeral.'

Matron drew in a sharp, deep breath. The image of Edith's face flew into her mind. Her benevolent smile. Her concern for the wellbeing of her sister. How she had implored Sister Tapps, in the presence of Matron, over their tea at Crewe station, to leave Liverpool and work in a hospital nearer to her and her family. 'Don't you think that would be for the best, Matron?' Edith had said, and Matron, not wanting to influence Sister Tapps either way, had replied, 'I will always support your sister, whatever she decides to do. She knows that should she ever want to apply for another post, she will have a glowing reference from me. But, of course, she would be missed at St Angelus, very much indeed, not least by the children.' The reference had never been sought. There had been no further incident, no cause for anxiety. Days and weeks had passed without event. The months had rolled into years and the ward that had temporarily become a cause for concern resumed its smooth running and required only minimal input from Matron. And Matron, being caught up with the day-to-day management of St Angelus, had been happy for it to remain that way. The incident on ward four, the broken heart of Sister Tapps, had faded from memory.

'You didn't attend your own sister's funeral?' Matron couldn't supress the incredulity in her voice. 'Why not?' she rasped. She could never have anticipated in a million years that this was how the conversation would unfold. She found herself wishing that she had invited Sister Haycock to join them for supper. Maybe she could have shed some light on this unfathomable turn of events.

Sister Tapps turned her face towards the fire and it was as if the fight had suddenly left her. As though she was struggling to understand herself what she had just said.

The fire was about to go out. Matron stood sharply and, dusting imaginary crumbs off her skirt, moved towards it, lifted the coal scuttle, threw on a small shovelful of coal and watched for a second as the embers glowed red. She was giving them both time. Time to alter the course of the conversation, should they wish to. And then Sister Tapps spoke and Matron realized that these were the last words she ever wanted to hear. It was as if she was listening to herself articulate her own excuses for the many things she had not done over the years. The visits she had failed to make to her mother. The friends she had made excuses to – or had ignored, when the excuses ran thin and repetitive – and who then, weary of being sidelined, had disappeared and moved on with their lives without her. Matron had not always been alone.

'Because Edith's funeral was a list day. I told her husband, I tried to explain, to ask him to make it for the Friday – you know Wednesday has always been our day for the operating theatre – but he wouldn't listen. We had five operations on the list for theatre that morning. I couldn't possibly have left the ward. Two appendixes, one of them an emergency admission from the night before. An inguinal hernia on a three-month-old baby, a pyloric stenosis that shouldn't even have been in my ward, but ward three was full, as it often is in the winter, and to top it all, a tonsillectomy. When is there not one of those needing to be done? There was no way I could leave with all that going on, was there? I am sure you understand. What would you have thought if I had just abandoned all of my responsibilities and left you without a ward sister in the middle of winter at our busiest time? You would never have done that yourself.'

Matron's heart sank. Her heart beat a little faster and tears threatened to fill her eyes. She turned slowly from the fire and flopped back into her chair, feeling wearier than she could remember. This was all her fault. That speech, it had been rehearsed – not out loud, but Sister Tapps had obviously reiterated it to herself over and over. The justification for not attending her own sister's funeral. The sister who had rushed to her in her hour of need. Who had written to Matron to check that Sister Tapps had readjusted back into the ebb and flow of hospital life. The sister who, when she visited Sister Tapps, used to bring a homemade cake for Matron and leave it with Elsie in her kitchen. How Matron would have loved to have had a sister just like that, and how different her life would have been if she had. Her own decision to devote herself to St Angelus had in part been because everyone else had married and she hadn't met anyone who offered more than the life she now had. But Sister Tapps did have relatives and a family.

Matron's voice was small and tired as she spoke. 'How did she die?'

Sister Tapps didn't reply but looked down into her lap at her folded hands.

At least she has the grace to comprehend that what she did was wrong, Matron thought. 'How did she die?' she asked again.

'Cancer. Her womb. It was all over very quickly, before I had time to visit. But it was such a difficult time. As I said, it was winter, the ward was so busy.'

Matron frowned. Her head was almost shaking with the effort of trying to understand. You couldn't even leave the ward for one day to honour the memory of your own flesh and blood, she thought angrily. This was serious. Shockingly serious. Something needed to be done about it at a deeper level, but in the meantime she would enforce the Christmas plans without hesitation.

'Sister Tapps, ward four is being closed from the twenty-first. I will visit the ward tomorrow with Sister Haycock. Any walking wounded who can't be sent home will be transferred across the landing to ward three, under our new Sister Paige. You will be on leave from the twenty-first. Maybe you could visit your niece and nephew and make up for some of the time you've missed with them.' Time you didn't spend with their mother, she had wanted to say. Time you chose to spend with the children of strangers instead. Children you will never see again, unless by some coincidence they happen to end up working at St Angelus or have a sibling admitted.

The clock struck ten. Blackie leapt from his basket and, grabbing his lead from the peg on the back of the door, ran across the room and dropped it at Matron's feet. In a voice loaded with sadness and very different from the one she had used at the beginning of the evening, but nonetheless, one that made it clear that no dissent would be tolerated, she said, 'It's time for Blackie's walk. Come along, we will escort you back to your room.'

Chapter 5

Freddie leant his bike against the lamp-post at the top of the cul-de-sac as Norman, having given up trying to keep up with him, huffed and puffed, pushing his bike as he walked alongside it. 'I thought that hill was going to kill me,' he gasped. 'Hang on, Freddie, I need a fag to help me catch my breath before we find the house.'

'What, one of those gold-tipped things?' Freddie almost laughed out loud.

'No, those are for my lady friend. I'll have one of my Capstans.'

Freddie waited while Norman bent over and flipped open his bicycle clips then dug around in his deep trouser pockets for his cigarettes and matches. 'You still seeing your lady from Skin Street then?' He'd nearly used the word 'young', but then he remembered that she looked considerably older than Norman.

'I am, thank you very much. It is an amicable arrangement that suits us both well. Mrs Poultice has no complaints.' Norman sounded defensive, which is exactly what he was. His Mrs Poultice from Skin Street had done his washing and ironing and made him a supper of cocoa and butties every evening for the past eight years and asked for nothing in return. Norman had met her when her house had been burgled. Skin Street was on his patch and he'd been the officer on duty. What had begun as popping in for a cup of tea during his shift had slowly drifted into the satisfactory arrangement Norman found himself enjoying today. Both appeared to be happy: she liked having someone to look after and he liked having the company at the end of his shift, before he returned to his own police house. A house that Mrs Poultice had never visited and, as a respectable single woman approaching sixty, nor would she.

Norman's face lit up briefly in the flare of the match as flakes of flaming red tobacco flew off the end of his cigarette. Freddie watched the first puffs of smoke rise and noted the pleasure on his colleague's face as he closed his eyes.

'That's better,' Norman said as he exhaled and looked about them. 'I've never been up this way before. They never got the bombs here, too far from the docks, lucky bastards.'

The glow of the orange sulphur street light above them fell across the two lawns at the top of the cul-de-sac and Freddie saw a cat arch its back against the fence as it regarded them both with suspicion. 'Where's the bobby who covers this beat?' he asked.

'I have no idea. My guess is he called into the station for refreshments and refused to come back out again. He probably thought it would take the best part of forty minutes to get here on the bike, and we were the nearest. Do you reckon that's the cat?' Norman inclined his head towards the feline observer as it slunk behind the fence. 'Have we been sent all this bloody way for a cat?'

'I hope not,' said Freddie. 'It's a long way to cycle for a bogus call. Look at these houses – they're all separate. No outhouses or two-up two-downs here. It's the same on all these roads off the avenue.'

'We have indoor lavvies in the police houses too,' said Norman. 'Not everyone has to live like the people on our beat do. I'm just grateful I don't have Clare Cottages on mine.'

Clare Cottages were notorious and they were on Freddie's patch, but he didn't rise to the bait, just looked around at the dimly lit houses. There were trees and hedges up here – something else that was lacking down on the dockside streets – and he craned his neck to see what he could of the white render and pebbledash in the amber glow.

Norman liked to use whatever means he could to assert his authority over Freddie, even though they were both beat constables. It helped that he had the beat with the fewest problems and the cleaner streets. On his patch, steps were scrubbed with a donkey stone every morning and pavements washed. When a dusty cargo was unloaded down at the docks, the women in his neighbourhoods raced out into the street to clean their windows and wash down the sills before the ship had even sailed back out of the dock and reached the bar. Almost all of his residents worked either up at St Angelus or on the docks; Freddie's pretty much all worked down on the docks. Norman's patch took in Lovely Lane, with its nurses' home opposite the park and the undertaker's next door. Freddie's patch included the processing plants, wood yards and smelters that surrounded the docks. There was no competition and Freddie tried hard never to give Norman the opportunity to rub that in.

'Are you done then?' he asked as Norman dropped his cigarette butt and ground it out with the toe of his boot.

'Aye.' Norman surveyed the street. 'Which one looks empty

then?' They were on Vienna Close, off Princess Avenue and the houses stood tall and proud in the middle of their own plots, each with a large lawn to the front and rear. 'Too bloody quiet up here. There aren't even any dogs roaming around. I wouldn't like to work on streets as quiet as this – a bit creepy if you ask me. I bet none of them talk to each other. All keeping themselves to themselves in their big houses.'

'I think you can tell that by the size of the privet hedges around each garden,' said Freddie. 'They can't even see each other's houses, never mind each other. Look, there's not a leaf out of place on any of those privets.'

The two men, away from the comfort of their own familiar patches, stood and stared. Even the grass had taken on a marmalade hue under the sulphur light.

'It does feel creepy. You can't hear a thing. What is the desk sergeant on about sending us out here? I can't hear anything, can you?'

They both stood still and strained to hear whatever the offending noise was meant to be.

'Would you believe it? He's sent us all the way up here and almost killed me in the process, for absolutely nothing,' said Norman. 'I can't hear a peep. Can you?'

Freddie scanned the houses and from the corner of the one window he could just about see came the twinkle of Christmas-tree lights. The night was dark and nearly moonless and they were almost entirely dependent on the street light to see anything at all. 'Come on,' he said as he headed to the gate at the end of the first drive. 'I can't hear anything either, but let's just find the empty house and check it and then we can say we did what we were asked to do. At least the ride home will be a lot easier, eh, Norm – downhill all the way.'

Norman didn't appreciate Freddie taking the lead. He liked to be the one who made the decisions and gave the orders. He had applied for the station sergeant's job on the last two occasions it had become available and both times he had been passed over. The resentment, a slow burn in his belly, manifested itself in the occasional barbed comment fired in Freddie's direction. 'I think, as the senior one out of the two of us, I will make that decision,' he said.

Freddie bit his tongue. They were paid the same money, wore the same cap badge and worked for the same force at the same rank, but Norman appeared to believe that age carried additional authority. Freddie had been a sergeant in the army, whereas Norman had never been more than a foot soldier and had taken his demob at the first opportunity. Freddie had every intention of rising through the ranks of the force. He wanted to work on special investigations. He was just waiting for the one case to come along that would help him prove his worth to his superiors. The petty prostitution, robberies, fights and social problems on his patch had so far not furnished him with sufficient opportunity, but he knew his day would come. He didn't doubt his future and he thought about it every day. The image of his wife and children, the house they would live in and the job he would rise to played out in his dreams. Every morning he woke thinking about his promising future and every night when he closed his eyes a smile crossed his face. His life was going to be wonderful and he would make it happen. He would be a hero and Norman would respect him. 'Oh my, the confidence of youth,' his mother would say when he told her how his life was going to be. But Freddie would not be deterred by the negative comments of those older and supposedly wiser than himself. He would show them all.

'Let's check these houses together,' said Norman. 'We will find the empty one, look around and then, when we set the bloody cat free, we'll knock on every door and let them know what we've done and that they can all sleep safe in their beds. Safe from the marauding tomcat. That way, we'll knock on the commander's door and earn ourselves a few Brownie points. All these God-fearing people who have done well and bought their own houses can appreciate our efforts.'

'I bet most of them have never met a policeman,' said Freddie.

'Oh, don't you believe it. Crime is everywhere – it's just that with the likes of people who live around here, it's not robbing to help pay the bills, it's not a kid being seconds away from death down on the dock, it's secret crime. What they call in the papers "white-collar crime". Embezzling from banks, that kind of thing. The people who live in these houses, they're human too. Just because they live in a big house doesn't mean they aren't capable of straying from the straight and narrow like the women down in Clare Cottages.'

'Wow,' said Freddie as they got to the end of the first drive. 'These people haven't gone away. If they have, they've forgotten to take their brand-new car with them.' He wanted to reach out and stroke the car. In the dim light he couldn't really tell what colour it was – pale blue maybe, or cream – but what he did know was that one day he would own one just like it.

'Right, on to the next one,' said Norman. 'Well, this looks more promising. No lights on. No car. No sign of life. Can you hear anything?'

'I might if you stopped talking and huffing and blowing like a pair of bellows,' said Freddie.

His words were blunt but accurate. Few men who lived as close to the Mersey as Norman did and who smoked forty Capstan Full Strength a day could breathe quietly.

They both stopped talking and Norman, as surreptitiously as was possible, held his breath.

Freddie heard it first, just as Norman let out his breath and began to gasp. He held up his hand. 'Norman, be quiet will you! There. I heard it. Did you?'

Norman was wheezing. 'Hear it? That almost killed me, not breathing.' He loudly and dramatically filled his lungs with the damp night air. 'I'm fighting for me life here, Freddie. I need another ciggie. I can't do that again.' He began to fish around in his pockets as Freddie looked at him impatiently. 'What did you hear? Was it a cat?'

Freddie furrowed his brow. 'Maybe. But it sounded different from that, a bit odd.'

'Jesus, it's effing creepy here. Not a person anywhere on the street. It's not natural. If we were on Arthur or George Street now, we'd have an audience of fifty kids at least.'

Freddie wasn't listening. He was leaning over the gate to try and catch the sound again, but the split seconds of silence were broken by Norman and the lighting of another match. He took in the white-painted five-bar gate and tarmacked entry, also tinged orange in the lamplight, and followed the drive with his eyes. In the distance, just visible over the top of a hedge, he could see a low roof. Despite the wheezing and puffing next to him, the eerie sound came to him again. A wail? A howl? A cry?

'Jesus, I effing heard that.' Norman blessed himself with the spent match. 'Come on, let's go. That wasn't natural. Let's get out of here.'

Freddie shot Norman a look, but Norman was already lumbering towards the lamp-post and the bikes. As if in response to the sound of their voices, the sound came again, this time higher and longer, more desperate. A cold shiver ran down Freddie's spine. He glanced at Norman, who by now had one foot on the pedal of his bike.

'Come on,' Norman hissed. 'Let's go. That's not of this world. Sounds like a ghost to me.'

Freddie hesitated as the realization dawned that this was his moment. His test. This could be all or nothing. He could follow Norman and run away, but if he did, they would never know. What if this was the case that would change his life?

'Will you hurry up!' said Norman, pulling agitatedly on his cigarette.

Freddie could only agree that the noise sounded other-worldly.

'You know Liverpool has more ghosts than any other city, don't you?' Norman said. 'They are everywhere. You can't get away from the buggers, and I'm telling you, that's one of them there, I swear it. Mrs Poultice, she's seen dozens of them and she knows exactly how they sound. She's told me: they don't speak, they wail.'

But Norman was talking to himself. As he threw his cigarette to the ground and looked round at the gate, Freddie was gone. 'Oh, for the sake of Jesus and all the effing saints above,' he said, letting his bike fall to the ground. 'Freddie, come back!' He was still hissing rather than shouting. He didn't want to attract attention to either of them. Right now they were winning and he didn't want the residents to realize they were there and run the risk of being delayed any longer. He plodded over to the gate and rubbed his hand across his forehead. 'Freddie,' he pleaded pathetically. 'Freddie, oh God, come back.'

Freddie could see the house was empty. It wasn't just that there were no lights on; there were no curtains up at the windows either. The house was bleak and dark and as he moved stealthily down the side and further away from the street light, so was the garden. His heart pounded in his chest like a hammer. He was terrified. He had heard some of the ghost stories that thrived among the Irish diaspora and though he'd always taken a neutral stance, neither believing nor disbelieving them, he now realized that perhaps he really did believe them, even if he wished with all his being that he didn't.

He looked back over his shoulder. He'd had to jump the gate because of the chain and padlock holding it to the post. As he'd guessed, Norman hadn't followed him. The grass beneath his feet was wet and obviously hadn't been cut for a while. But at least the night was mild for December, which wasn't so unusual in Liverpool.

He looked at his watch. He could barely make out the time but knew that he would miss the choir rehearsal down at St Chad's. He loved to sing and he was as excited as anyone about the joint carol service at St George's Hall. He'd been sent along by his sergeant as a token contribution. 'Go on, lad,' the sergeant had said. 'There's a dozen or so of you. It'll be nice to put on a good show.' Freddie, always keen to please, hadn't needed to be asked twice, and besides, he thoroughly enjoyed being in the choir. The sound they made at their first rehearsal in St Chad's had sent a shiver through him and he'd become so choked by the emotion of it that he'd had to sit out one of the verses, temporarily too moved to sing.

It was a quite different sort of shiver he was experiencing now. He decided to call out. It seemed to him that the noise had been louder when he and Norman had been talking. 'Hello?' he said. There was no reply. His feet began to feel damp. There was a hole in the sole of his right shoe. A hazard of the job and the hours he spent on his feet every day. He had meant to visit the cobbler's on the way to work tonight, but the cobbler had closed early. Now, standing in the soaking long grass, his sock was absorbing the moisture and his foot was turning cold. Freddie knew he had to look after his feet or in no time at all he'd be like Norman, barely able to move for the bunions and corns and forced to lumber about with an unseemly gait. He'd seen how Norman's face flinched with pain whenever they stopped for a cuppa and he removed his boots and held his feet.

'Hello, is there anyone there?' He was breathing so hard, he could hear his inhalations as well as feel them. 'Hello, is there anyone there?' He tried again and this time his whole body jolted with the shock as an answer came. It was a wail, a terrifying, lost, desperate wail, but it was not a random wail – it was a response to his call.

'Norman!' Freddie now shouted out loud. He would admit to anyone that he was frightened, but he recognized the sound. He had heard it before, in North Africa during the war, following a raid in which they had lost men. It was a cry of pain and helplessness, and he knew beyond doubt that it was human.

He broke into a run. There was no sign of Norman, but he had expected that. Before him loomed a wooden garage.

It was painted white with a black roof and had a row of windows across the top of the double doors, crowned with arched beams painted black in a mock-Tudor style.

Freddie took out his torch and shone it at the double doors. They were not locked. 'Norman!' he shouted again, loudly this time, and from within came a thready wail. He ran towards the doors, lifted the wooden bar that held them closed and pulled one open. He didn't dare stop to think – if he did, he might turn around and run and in doing so discover that he was more like Norman than he thought. He might not be the Freddie he wanted and believed himself to be, in which case, what would be his life? Would his dreams also be a sham?

He flung the second door open and his torch lit up the damp dirt floor. Sweat broke out on his scalp and the back of his neck. He raised the torch and its beam immediately fell on a large coach-built pram. His training kicked in and he flashed the torch around the remainder of the garage. There was nothing. A forgotten grass rake lay across one of the rafters. A spider's web hung from one corner to the other, supporting a large spider, caught mid meal, in the centre. He thought he heard the scurrying of a mouse, but if he had, it had beaten the sweep of his torch. And then he heard the sound again: quieter, defeated. A breath; a moment of life captured in the air, but what? What was it? Just at that moment a tiny hand grasped the side of the pram and made Freddie gasp out loud as he very nearly dropped his torch.

Norman was trying to make the radio work. His battery was low and he was aware that his range might be impeded as they were far from the station. He didn't want to use what battery was left in case they needed to save themselves. From what, he wondered. The ghost? He was nervous that Freddie was out of sight. An uncomfortable feeling had settled in his gut.

'Damnation. You are a little swine, Freddie,' he muttered as he struggled to clamber over the padlocked five-bar gate. Once on the other side, he switched on his torch. 'Freddie!' he shouted. 'Freddie, where are you?'

As he raised his torch, he saw Freddie racing towards him with his arms held out and something white trailing from them. He was running faster than Norman had ever seen him and there were tears in his eyes. 'What the hell is that?' he asked as his beam fixed on the scrap of fabric.

'It's a young child, a baby, Norm, and it's almost dead, God help it.'

Norman paled. 'Right, let's call for an ambulance. We'll find a house with a telephone.'

'No time,' said Freddie. 'It could take an hour to get here. I'm putting it in my jacket for warmth and I'll cycle to St Angelus. You find a house with a telephone and tell them I'm on my way. I'll be half an hour, tops.'

Norman felt rising within him the familiar resentment at being told what to do by Freddie, but it quickly faded. In his arms lay the last thread of a young life and Norman was speechless as Freddie opened the top buttons of his jacket and tucked the tiny scrap inside, resting the child on the belt that fastened around the outside of his uniform. He made one check to the buttons to ensure the baby could breathe and then, draping his cape across his shoulders, he fastened the chinstrap on his helmet and mounted his bike.

'Find a house with a phone,' Freddie instructed. 'Follow the telephone cables – look, that post on the corner has one leading up that drive there.' He pointed to the house with the Christmas tree in the window. 'Pray they are in, and make the call,' he said, his voice full of emotion

Without a word, Norman ran up the path as fast as his bunions and corns would let him.

Maura lay in bed and waited for Tommy to join her. She had cried herself sick all evening. Within moments of arriving home from the hospital, the kitchen had filled with neighbours and children, everyone wanting to know what had happened. Food had appeared and the kettle been set to boil. Maura had sat on the settle and faced the crowd. 'She has pneumonia and she has to stay in, for Christmas.'

A gasp went up around the kitchen. Pneumonia was a killer on the streets. It took both young and old with a regularity that was the price to pay for being poor and living by the river.

'I don't think it's as bad as it was, even last winter,' a voice piped up. 'They have tablets now that can make them better. Mrs Green, she had it last year, remember? And look at her now, she's still turning out two matinee coats a week on her needles. They kept her in though, over a month it was—' The neighbour stopped talking as she was shushed and elbows prodded her sides. She was not helping.

'Did they say how bad it was, love?' asked another neighbour as she sat down next to Maura and put her arm around her shoulders.

Maura gripped her damp handkerchief, twisting it round and round into a knot. From somewhere in the crowd, Kitty's arm appeared, holding out a steaming mug of tea to her mother. Maura never let her make tea, said she was too young and might scald herself, and, unused to the weight of the enamel mug, Kitty's wrist wobbled. An adult hand reached out and whipped it off her.

'Good girl,' Peggy from next door said. 'Did you put sugar in? Your mam's going to need it.'

Kitty nodded. She'd seen the midwife put sugar in her mam's tea when she delivered the twins and she'd thought that this situation was equally serious.

'Come on, love, get this down you. Come on now – you weren't this bad when your Kitty was in, you weren't.'

'No, but that was tonsils. This isn't tonsils, Peggy, this is serious,' said Maura as she took the tea and held it to her lips.

The women looked at each other, eyes loaded with concern. Maura had voiced what they were thinking.

'Right,' said a voice from the sink. It was Kathleen from down the street. 'Come on, everyone, you know what this one is like. She needs to get to bed, but she won't rest until everything is done. Let's get cracking. Now, who's bringing the washing in? I've got a huge pan of scouse on the range, I'm taking Maura's bread bowl to fill it up. Peggy, you get the washing in, it's as damp as when it went out. Put it on the clothes horse in front of the range. Who's filling the coal bucket? Let's get those twins fed and ready for bed.'

And on it went until the kids had been fed and bathed, and the kitchen was spotless, and all Maura's jobs had been completed by the army of women who knew that there but for the grace of God went any one of them and any child on their streets.

*

Tommy was leaning against the bar of the Admiral, sipping his Guinness when his best mate Jerry walked in. No man whose child was in hospital bought his own drinks and there was already another pint lined up next to that one.

Tommy shook his head. 'Don't buy one, mate,' he said. 'This is my third and I can't stop them coming. If I go home reeking of ale, I'm a dead man.'

'I wouldn't worry about going home yet,' said Jerry, 'half the street is in your house. It's panic stations.'

Tommy nodded but said nothing.

'Go on then,' said Jerry. 'What happened?'

Tommy was slow to answer. The experience at the hospital had alarmed him. 'I don't know, Jerry. Sure, Angela was sleeping – you know what she's like, she never stops – and then she just turned blue as the doctor lifted her out of the pram. He started shouting for the nurse and then your man came running in with an oxygen bottle and then he was shouted at by the doctor and told to take her straight to the ward, on the oxygen, and he picked her up and his sidekick picked up the bottle and they ran.'

Jerry lifted the pint, took a long draught of the black velvet and said, 'Your Maura will be demented. She was bad enough when your Kitty was in and that was only for her tonsils.'

'I know,' said Tommy. 'I don't know what to do.'

'You do nothing,' said Jerry. 'Leave it to Kathleen, Peggy and the rest. We only have one job: to keep out of the way. Let's order another pint.'

The smell of stale smoke and Guinness fumes entered the bedroom long before Tommy, who was struggling up the stairs.

Maura lay there, her worst fears realized. It took him a full five minutes to navigate his way across the floor and then he almost toppled over as he fumbled around under the bed for the pot.

'Where were you?' asked Maura.

'Jesus! Fecking hell, Maura, I almost dropped the pot.'

'Don't miss it,' Maura said.

Tommy sighed. There was heat to her voice, but even in his state he could detect too much in the way of despair. He began to relieve himself in the pot and the room filled with the sound and smell of Tommy urinating.

Maura knew to wait until he was in the bed and lying down before talking to him. A minute later, the pot shoved back under the bed, Maura frowning at the sound of the splosh of urine hitting the floorboards, Tommy lay with his arm over her chest. That was all Maura wanted or needed from him. The women in the street provided the rest, but in order to sleep, she needed him there beside her.

'Don't worry, queen, she will be better tomorrow,' he whispered.

'I hope so,' said Maura. 'I went to Mass with Kathleen, but, Tommy, if they had just let me see her. How can she get better if she doesn't know where her mammy is? What if she wakes up now? You know how often Angela wakes in the night. She will be calling for me, wondering where I am, Tommy. I don't think I can sleep again until I know how she is. Will you go back to the pub and ask them can we use the phone to ring the hospital? Someone might be able to tell me how she is.'

But it was no use. Tommy was snoring. Maura, trapped under his arm, looked out through the window to the inky sky and began what for her would be a long night of prayer.

Chapter 6

The weather had turned overnight from warm and damp to sharp and cold and Mrs Duffy felt it deep in her bones. She threw an extra shovel of coal on the fire she was laying in the morning room before the girls arrived down for breakfast. As usual, Beth was the first to show her face.

'Morning, Nurse Harper,' she said as she placed the flat of her hand in the small of her back and, wincing, stood upright. 'Would you move, dog.' She gently pushed Scamp, the nurses' waif-and-stray dog, out of the way with the toe of her slipper.

He shot a resentful glance at her as she shooed him away from the heat of the fire, then crawled under the table on his belly. He always moved there once breakfast was laid, to wait for scraps. Scamp and Mrs Duffy had a love–hate relationship, which amused the nurses. Mrs Duffy gave a good impression of having no time for him, but everyone knew she had grown used to him and would be lost without him now.

Since her first week at Lovely Lane, Beth had made a habit of being the first nurse downstairs in the morning and she and Mrs Duffy had become close. Even so, it would never occur to Mrs Duffy to address her as anything other than Nurse Harper. 'Isn't it exciting, you being on children's today,' she said as the shovel slipped from her fingers and into the coal bucket with a clatter. 'I do love the children's ward.'

'Well, it's fine for Pammy,' said Beth churlishly as she kicked off her shoes and stood on Mrs Duffy's footrest to see herself in the mirror above the fireplace. She pushed kirby grips into the back of her hair to secure her starched cap in place. Beth was the shortest, and without the footrest all she could see in the mirror were her eyebrows. 'I'm with Sister Tapps on ward four – old Tappsy. Nurse Tanner is with the new sister, Sister Paige, on three and then I have to go on to nights. Dana would have been with me, but seeing as she's over in Ireland, I'm all on my own.'

Mrs Duffy rubbed her chapped hands together to loosen her stiff fingers and chose to ignore Beth's plea for pity. She was missing her friend Dana – they all were. She would happily give Beth all the sympathy she required, if it came to it, but she doubted there would be any need. Everyone knew that old Tappsy was the softest and kindest ward sister in St Angelus. Beth was calm and contained and got along with life without fuss. Mrs Duffy was certain she'd enjoy working with the woman everyone loved.

'It's just nerves,' she said. 'And you the most confident one and all. You're always the same on your first day on a new ward. Sister Paige, now… Well, would you believe it? It seems like only five minutes ago she was Probationer Paige. She was one of mine, you know, began her training days here and lived in at Lovely Lane. She was in Nurse Baker's room. Such a lovely young lady. I'm surprised she made it to sister and some young man didn't persuade her to give it all up, after what happened. Have you met her yet? She was staff nurse on ward three for a while, and before that she was with Tappsy herself, so take note. I don't think I'm giving away any secrets here, but all the staff nurses who train under Sister Tapps make the best ward sisters. Everyone knows that. But Sister Paige, now there's a sad story that not many know, and look at the poor life she lives now.'

Beth shook her head as she stepped down from the foot-rest, grabbing the mantelpiece with one hand as she did, and smoothing the front of her apron with the other, to keep it away from the flames that were now leaping up the chimney. Her shins stung with the heat.

'What do you mean? What happened to Sister Paige?'

Usually the most kindly in all situations, Mrs Duffy was most definitely short of comforting words today, turning Sister Paige into a saint in a few short sentences and making Beth even more nervous about being on Tappsy's ward. She hated the way she felt when she started on a new ward and she wasn't best pleased that Mrs Duffy had found her out. Beth was the bossy, organized list-maker. The others depended on her, and yet she knew that Pammy would breeze down to breakfast like it was just any other day, even as Beth felt sick to the stomach.

'What is Tappsy like then? Everyone tells me she is lovely, but she might not like me.' Beth's voice was by now almost a wail.

Mrs Duffy ignored Beth's question and continued with her praise of Sister Paige. 'Oh, Sister Paige, she would take the eyes right out of your head, she would. She's such a beauty. A real looker, and a personality to match. I have never heard anyone say a bad word about her, but then there's always a little more sympathy for those with a broken heart.'

'Really,' said Beth as she retrieved her spectacles from the breakfast table and carefully slipped them through her hair, under her cap and over her ears. It peeved her that not only was she the only one who wore glasses but she also had curly hair that suffered greatly in the damp Mersey mist. 'She could be as ugly as Methuselah and I would still rather be on her ward with Pammy, especially as it's Christmas. And there's safety in numbers.'

'Nurse Harper, that's not like you!'

The reproach missed its mark – Beth's curiosity had been aroused. 'Anyway, what do you mean, "more sympathy for a broken heart"?'

Mrs Duffy blushed. The familiarity that had built between herself and Beth had caused her to drop her guard and she was instantly embarrassed by her faux pas. She turned her back to Beth as she reached for the sideboard and prepared to lift the large bread board over to the table. 'Is Nurse Tanner up and out of her bed yet? She can't be late on the first day.'

Beth knew Mrs Duffy was changing the subject and quickly switched tack. 'Hang on,' she said as she rushed to Mrs Duffy's side and took the bread board from her, 'let me take that. Is it a recent broken heart?' She set the bread board down in the middle of the scrubbed wooden table.

'Oh now, look, I shouldn't have said anything.' Clearly agitated, she began smoothing down the front of her apron.

Beth felt instantly guilty and placed an arm around her shoulders. 'I'm sorry,' she said. 'Don't tell me if you don't want to. I'm a right grump today. I'm always the same on my first day on a new ward – you know what I'm like. But I would never betray a confidence, you know that. I'm not a gossip.'

Mrs Duffy curled her arm around Beth's waist and gave it a light squeeze. 'Oh, don't I just know that,' she said and she pulled out one of the dining chairs and eased herself down. It had not been lost on Beth that Mrs Duffy was beginning to show her age.

The room suddenly filled with the sound of a shrill whistle. For the nurses getting ready upstairs, this was their last morning alert. It followed their own alarms, most of which went off at six thirty. The grandfather clock on the stairs chimed at quarter to and then the dock klaxons went off at seven. If they were not up, dressed and washed by the time the kettle whistle shrilled into every room in the home at seven ten, they risked being late.

Beth knew that the stairs would resound with the clatter of a dozen pairs of feet rushing down for breakfast in approximately three minutes. She hurried down the step from the morning room to the back kitchen to turn down the gas under the kettle. 'Stay there,' she said over her shoulder to Mrs Duffy. 'I will fill the pot. You tell me more.'

'There's nothing to tell really,' replied Mrs Duffy as the whistle died and she heard the slosh of the water being poured into the huge enamel pot. 'It isn't a secret – nothing scandalous at all. It was just very sad, actually. Very, very sad.' She heard the lid being rammed on to the teapot, the oven doors being opened and closed and then the scuttle of Beth's feet as she came back in and pulled out the chair next to her.

'Don't worry,' Beth said as she placed her hand over Mrs Duffy's. 'I lit the grill while I was there – it's not ready yet – and I slid your bacon trays into the oven. Go on, tell me more.'

Mrs Duffy glanced towards the door and the foot of the stairs, then smiled at Beth. They had just two minutes at the most before the first door on the upper landing banged open. 'Well, as I say, it isn't anything really. Staff Nurse Paige – oh dear me, I mean Sister Paige – she and her young man, they were very much in love, and a nicer pair you would never meet.'

Beth grinned to herself. Mrs Duffy said this about Pammy and Anthony, Victoria and Roland, Dana and Teddy...

'It was the war. They got engaged before he left and Matron, she allowed her the time off to see him off at Lime Street station, but he never came back. North Africa.'

Beth being an army daughter, Mrs Duffy knew she didn't need to say any more than simply 'North Africa' for her to understand.

The atmosphere in the room dipped as she took out her rosaries from her apron pocket. 'He died just before Christmas too. Everyone thought that because Sister Paige was so young at the time she would go on to meet someone else, but, over the years, I have heard nurses here say that she just hasn't been interested. When she left Lovely Lane to live back at home and look after her mother, I thought to myself, well then, that's it, isn't it, for the poor girl. I don't like to be speaking ill of anyone, but when I met her mother, I understood right away why Sister Paige had chosen to live in here. I would be leaving home myself if I had a mother like that. And on the day she had to go back home, well, she stood in this room with me, just like me and you are now, and oh, how she cried. As much as she had when she heard the awful news about her David.'

'Gosh, why was that?' asked Beth, calculating that she had maybe another minute to get the rest of the story. But she was wrong. They both heard a van pull up outside and both guessed it belonged to Jake, the under-porter.

'Well now, he's late today,' said Mrs Duffy as she stood up. 'Listen, don't you be telling anyone what I said, or worrying about Sister Tapps and the other nurses. They won't be having a laugh a minute with Sister Paige – she won't stand for any nonsense, mark my words, and Nurse Tanner will find her firm but fair, you wait and see.'

She walked over to the towering wooden front door, turned the brass knob and pulled it swiftly open to reveal Jake, and Bryan, one of the porter's lads, dragging a large Christmas tree up the limestone steps. Her face lit up. 'Oh, would you look! Here comes the tree and it's bigger than ever.'

Beth stood in the cold by her side, her arms folded against the biting wind, and she couldn't help but smile at the joy on Mrs Duffy's face. She and the other Lovely Lane nurses were the closest Mrs Duffy had to a family. They were 'her nurses', as she always called them. She cared for them, fussed over them to the point of distraction, and at times drove them all mad. In return, they were well aware of what was required to make her happy, and that included allowing her to put their washing through – complaining as she did so. When they returned from a split shift or in the evening at the end of a very long day shift, a little pile of ironing would be perched on the end of each bed, immaculate and pressed to perfection. No nurse on nights went to bed without a hot-water bottle and a good breakfast and she was woken at 4 p.m. with a tray of tea and some homemade biscuits or a scone. Letters were posted, jumpers knitted, and cakes baked – the best many of them had ever tasted. Mrs Duffy was a treasure and Beth and the others knew it only too well. She slipped her arm around Mrs Duffy's shoulders and gave her a hug. 'Can we decorate it together?'

'Can you manage, boys?' Mrs Duffy opened the front door wide against the wall. 'We can, Nurse Harper. Sure, why would I want to do it alone? There's no fun in that, is there, and believe me, I know. I decorate my own little tree every year in my parlour. 'Tis a miserable affair, but we have to keep up standards, don't we now.' Their conversation about Sister Paige's sadness had been dispelled; the ghostly legacy of the war banished. 'Look at the tree, isn't it lovely?' she said, using the arrival of a puffing Jake at the top of the steps as a distraction.

'Where do you want it, Mrs Duffy?' Jake asked.

'Same place as usual, please, Jake. In front of the bay window in the nurses' lounge.'

Jake and Bryan shot each other a look of dismay as they both bent down and lifted the ten-foot tree on to their shoulders.

'I saw that!' said Mrs Duffy. 'Did you think I wanted it on the top of the steps outdoors? Now what use would that be? Would you have me carry it meself? Get away with you now. I'm sure a cup of tea and a bacon sandwich will take that frown from your face, Jake. And you, Bryan.'

'This is only the first one, Mrs Duffy,' said Jake apologetically. 'We have twenty-one just like this one to deliver to the wards and outpatients, and one for the main entrance at St Angelus. Matron spares no expense at Christmas.'

Pammy, followed by some of the probationer nurses, clattered down the stairs and arrived in the hallway, which quickly became filled with squeals of delight at the sight of the tree.

'Ooh, can we help decorate it, please, Mrs Duffy?' asked one of the new probationers.

'Nurse Harper has already asked and I have said yes, of course we can. I will make the first batch of mince pies for us to have while we do it, will I? I think we need to make an occasion of it.'

'I love Christmas,' said Pammy. 'I can bang out a few carols on the piano in the lounge as well. We all need to keep rehearsing our singing for the concert on Christmas Eve.'

'I wonder if we will begin our day on children's decorating the wards, if Jake is delivering the trees?' Beth said to Pammy.

'I read in the *Nursing Times* that they're running a competition for the best-decorated wards,' said Celia Forsyth as she led the way into the morning room. She was the only nurse to have been unhappy about the arrival of Scamp, which she felt had resulted in there being less bacon at breakfast. She always made a point of getting to the table first, so as not to miss out. One of the same intake as Pammy and Beth, she was very definitely not part of the inner circle. She lorded it over every new set of probationers, acting as though she were Matron herself and, despite coming a cropper every single time, she had still to learn her lesson.

'Let's hope Sister Paige is feeling competitive,' said Pammy. 'I fancy entering that. But only if we stand a chance of winning. And what better wards to be working on at Christmas than children's.'

'Blimey, who's competitive now?' said Beth. 'But I quite agree. No point in entering something unless you can win.'

Pammy grabbed a piece of toast from a plate on the table and began to speak with her mouth full. 'There was also an article on how not allowing parents to see their children when they're in hospital has a detrimental impact on the children's wellbeing. Honestly, I can think of some kids in our street who would have benefited from being kept away from their parents.'

'Everyone's talking about it,' said Beth matter-of-factly. And she was right: the debate had reached Westminster as well as the homes of families across Britain, and campaign groups were applying pressure on hospital matrons to relax the rules, hospital by hospital. The negative effect of this was that the competency and humanity of hospital matrons was being called into question, and for the first time ever there was a discussion about whether matrons really had the necessary skills to run a modern post-war hospital.

The front door opened again, sending a blast of icy wind down the hall, and framed against the light stood Sister Emily Haycock. 'Morning, Mrs Duffy,' she called out. 'Morning, nurses.'

'Oh, would you get in here and close that door,' said Mrs Duffy. 'It's hard enough to heat these big rooms without the door being left open. It's like Lime Street in here with all the coming and going.'

Emily grinned and did as she was told. She might be the director of nursing, but she was still one of Mrs Duffy's nurses when she walked through the door of the Lovely Lane home.

'Come away to the table, the nurses are just getting down to breakfast.'

Emily untied the headscarf from under her chin, undid the buttons on her coat and hung it on the hall stand, and made her way to the morning room. As she stepped inside, the sight that greeted her warmed her heart. The nurses were bustling around, jostling each other for a moment in front of the mirror to fix their caps, and the room had a pink glow to it from their uniforms. The scrubbed table was heaving with bacon, buttered toast, tea and milk. Scamp was hiding underneath it and his tail thumped the floor hard. He was desperate to slip out and greet Emily, but if he did that, Mrs Duffy would remember he was there and banish him to the yard, where she made him spend meal times. There was bacon, this he could smell. All he had to do was rest his head on a foot and a piece of bacon rind would appear. The chance of a bit of bacon won out over the prospect of an affectionate stroke from Emily and he stayed put.

Pammy was the first to spot Emily standing in the doorway as she fixed her cap in the mirror. 'Sister Haycock,' she exclaimed, 'you haven't been here for ages.'

There was an awkward silence as everyone glanced at Mrs Duffy. Mrs Duffy knew, of course, that Emily Haycock and Dessie Horton were walking out together – indeed, she was looking forward to getting her best hat out for the wedding – but, like Matron, she had no idea that Emily had more or less moved in with Dessie. Everybody else, from the hospital maids to the Lovely Lane nurses knew this, but Emily was determined that Mrs Duffy and Matron should remain in the dark.

Mrs Duffy appeared not to have noticed the momentary silence as she continued to remove trays of bacon and roast tomatoes from the range. As far as she was concerned, Emily lived in the accommodation at the hospital, and Emily's careful visits to ruffle up the bed had kept this impression alive for those who chose to make it their business. Emily knew that women like Mrs Duffy and Matron still lived by the pre-war codes of morality and conduct. For women like herself, however, the war had changed everything. As a woman of the 1950s who had survived the Blitz, she had quite different attitudes to women even twenty years older than her, let alone women of her mother's and grandmother's generation, even if this was sometimes only expressed behind closed doors. A revolution was brewing and women like Emily Haycock were leading the way, secretly pushing back the barriers of expected behaviour, inch by inch.

'Sit down, Sister Haycock, there's enough for you too – but not for that dog! Stop it, all of you! Do you all think I came down with the last shower? I can see the dog munching under there.'

Scamp knew his second name. Dog. It was the only one Mrs Duffy used. His ears dropped and he slunk so low, he was almost as flat as the parquet floor on which he lay. It was his good luck that breakfast was in full flow and Mrs Duffy had no time to throw him out.

'The dog has more bacon than I do at breakfast, Mrs Duffy,' chirped up Celia Forsyth.

The room fell silent and everyone looked at her. She had the good grace to blush and shoved the last of her bacon into her mouth, failing to mention that one of the probationers had slipped her bacon on to Celia's plate.

'Come along, nurses, you're all running late again. I want you out of here in fifteen minutes. I won't have anyone saying I allow my nurses to be late on the wards. Sister Haycock, half of these nurses are to be making their way to your classroom.'

Emily laughed. 'Just five more minutes, Mrs Duffy.'

The room was filled with morning chatter and the clinking of teacups and saucers. Steam rose from the pot and the kettle whistled a low hum, informing Mrs Duffy that it was on standby, ready and waiting for quick refills.

'Actually, I came for a reason other than the delicious breakfast,' said Emily, 'and it's not to talk about assignments either.' She smiled as she buttered the toast Mrs Duffy had sliced and handed to her. She was so busy talking, she forgot to say thank you.

The table quieted as the boys appeared in the doorway, both clasping their caps before them. Like all boys from the dockside streets, they knew their manners. 'All done, Mrs Duffy,' said Jake.

'Ah, good boys, rest your feet a minute. Sit on the sofa in front of the fire in the hallway and I'll bring your bacon sandwiches out. They're keeping warm on the range.'

Jake and Bryan made to protest.

'Away with you now. Did you think I would let you lug that big heavy tree all the way here and you wouldn't leave with full stomachs as a reward?' Mrs Duffy bustled out and the girls watched her leave.

'Look, I have to get to the school of nursing or Biddy will send a search party out for me.' Emily bent her knee and stooped slightly, secretly slipping Scamp a scrap of bacon.

The probationers asked for permission to leave the table.

'Of course. Off you go,' said Emily. 'It's only Nurse Harper and Nurse Tanner I need, unless anyone else is working on children's?'

Celia harrumphed and left the table. 'This way, probationers,' she said as she marched towards the stairs.

Pammy and Beth watched her go. 'Honestly,' said Pammy, 'that girl is the end. She treats those probationers as though they're her handmaidens. Talk about pulling rank. God help us all if she ever becomes a ward sister – she'll be bad enough as a staff nurse.'

Emily knew that there was more chance of hell freezing over than of Celia Forsyth becoming a ward sister. However, the only person who didn't seem to know that was Celia Forsyth herself.

'Right, listen, I need to be hot on the tails of those

probationers. I'll get it in the ear from Biddy if they're making a noise in the classroom and arrive too long before me. Oh, don't tell me, I know very well who's the boss in my school of nursing. I am just a convenience. It's Biddy who has the keys to the kitchen, and isn't that always the most important person anywhere.'

She pushed her chair in and looked from Pammy to Beth. 'Now, we have only weeks until your exams, and Christmas gets in the way, but there is something I want you to do. As you know, Sister Paige is a new ward sister and I thought it would be a wonderful welcome for her if children's entered the *Nursing Times* competition for the best-decorated hospital ward. You have heard about that, I take it?'

Pammy and Beth both nodded, too occupied with the last of their breakfasts to reply.

'I'm asking you, Nurse Tanner, because you have the creative resources of your mam to call upon, and Nurse Harper, you have your organizational skills. Putting those two together, it seems to me that St Angelus can't lose.'

Pammy sat back in the chair. 'Flippin' 'eck – exams, a national competition to win, the St George's concert and Christmas! I was only complaining to Anthony last night how quiet everything was. How fast things change. We'd better get a move on, eh.'

Beth didn't comment; she was enjoying the warm glow brought on by Sister Haycock having mentioned her organizational skills. As an army daughter, she was well used to routine and discipline. They had been moved from camp to camp, and everything in their day-to-day lives had been marched to the beat of a list. There was a list for everything. For all of her life, Beth's daily to-do list had begun with the words *Get out of bed* – included for the sheer pleasure of being able to tick it off. 'I think you can count on us, Sister Haycock,' she said, finding her voice at last.

Pammy nodded enthusiastically. 'Let's have our first day, though, shall we. I've got no idea what happens on children's ward.'

Emily made for the hallway and, lifting her coat from the hook, pushed her arms through the sleeves. Pammy got up to help her. Sister Haycock had known Pammy's family for all of her life. Her and Maisie, Pammy's mam, had been born and raised on the same streets. There was a closeness between them that Pammy would never exploit in the hospital, but in Lovely Lane she felt on safer ground. 'So, what do I tell my mam about you and Dessie Horton then? Does anyone know you have just about moved in?'

'Shhh!' said Emily sharply, looking around. 'No, I don't want anyone to know yet. I'm going to organize a pow-wow at your mam's house about the decorations, so I'll fill her in on all the details then.'

'Does Mrs Duffy know?' asked Pammy.

'Heavens above, no! She'd be the last person I'd tell.' Emily bent down and scratched the top of Scamp's head. 'Right, I'm off.' She picked up her handbag. 'You both need to be too – and it's your first day. And, Nurse Harper, don't worry about Sister Tapps. Be kind to her. Hers is a sad story. I will tell you one day, but all you need to know just now is that like everyone else in the St Angelus family, we look after her. Do you know, she nursed me as a child when I was in the hospital?'

'No!' the cry went up.

'She's that old?' said Pammy, genuinely incredulous.

'Get away, you cheeky articles,' said Emily.

Emily turned back from the front door and looked around the hallway for Mrs Duffy, to say goodbye, but there was no sign of her. 'Did you see where Mrs Duffy went to, boys?' she asked Jake and Bryan, who were sitting on the sofa opposite the hall fire.

Jake looked up from his now almost empty plate. 'I didn't, Sister Haycock.'

Emily glanced back down the hall. 'Oh, well, never mind. I'll catch her soon. If you see her before you leave, tell her I said thank you for breakfast.'

'Right, we need to get a move on too,' said Beth.

They threw their cloaks over their shoulders. Sister Tapps might give Beth a scolding if she was late, and besides, it said on her list to arrive at ward four at 7.30 a.m.

'If the van wasn't full of Christmas trees, I'd offer you a lift, nurses,' said Jake as they all trotted down the steps together.

The Lovely Lane home fell deadly silent as the front door slammed behind them. The sound of the brass pendulum in the dark oak grandfather clock, unheard during the hullabaloo of breakfast, once again filled the hall as it swung to and fro. The whistle from the kettle was now a gentle hum as it stood abandoned on the side of the range. Scamp, sensing he was alone, crept out from under the table and, standing on his back legs, took the scraps of toast crust and bacon bits from Pammy's plate. Having been fed almost two slices of toast and four bacon rashers by the nurses, he padded out of the room, gazed at the shut front door longingly, as if expecting the nurses to return at any second, and with a loud sigh spread himself out before the smouldering fire in the hallway.

He would enjoy the heat on his full belly while he could. The sounds of the coal shifting in the grate, the buses and cars moving along the road, and the children running past the park gates on the way to school all kept his ears pricked with interest, until, unable to keep his eyes open any longer, he fell into a deep sleep.

Mrs Duffy stood in the kitchen, as still as a marble statue and almost as white. Her back was propped against the sink, her handkerchief clasped in her hands, and tears were running unchecked down her cheeks. She had heard every word, even before Emily had delivered the killer blow: 'She'd be the last person I'd tell.'

She hadn't wanted to hear that. She hadn't meant to listen. She'd been returning the boys' empty cups and saucers to the sink and had made her way in through the rear kitchen door and that was when she heard it. Sister Haycock was as good as living with Dessie Horton, and Mrs Duffy was the last person she wanted to tell. The words had cut her like a knife. Did she think she was a gossip? Someone who would judge her? She appeared to have confided in everyone except her. Why? Hadn't she been the one who had comforted Emily when she lived in the nurses' home? Wasn't she the one who kept food aside for when Emily came back from her nights looking after Alf her stepfather? Didn't she worry about them all – all of her nurses, and that included Emily – every single day? Childless herself, she regarded them all as her daughters, pouring all her care and affection into ensuring that they felt a mother's love even though they were far from home. And yet Sister Haycock had said that she, Mrs Duffy, would be the last person to know her important news. Did she think she would disapprove of a lovely man like Dessie Horton, whom she herself had known for years? Was she not a part of their family and they of hers?

'You stupid woman,' she said bitterly as she dried her eyes. 'You think you're their mother, but you aren't. You are nothing to any of them. Just the person who cooks the food and fusses too much.'

She moved over to the table and did something she never did: she sat down and poured herself some tea. She looked over to the jar of mincemeat she'd put on the side only minutes before. She'd been looking forward to the night ahead, to making the pies and decorating the tree. But now she let out a big sigh. Even in the midst of her dejection, her thoughts turned to whether she could fit in making the mince pies on top of everything else. She would need to start soon.

She looked at the tea and felt a pang of guilt. 'Just one minute,' she said to Scamp as he lifted his head and glanced in from the hall. He rose and padded into the kitchen and laid his head on her lap, his big brown eyes staring into her own. She remembered giving Sister Haycock the plate of toast and how her hand had reached out and distractedly taken the plate without any thanks. Fresh tears welled. 'Oh, you stupid woman, what's wrong with you?' But she knew what was wrong, really she did. She felt rejected. Unwanted and untrusted.

Scamp licked the salty tears from the back of her hand. She looked down at him and for a moment studied his eyes. 'I even let them persuade me to keep you,' she said to him. The irony was not lost on her, as he whined in response and gazed back up at her, that the only person who really cared for her was the dog she had initially rejected.

'Oh, pull yourself together, you stupid old woman.' She pushed her handkerchief back up the sleeve of her cardigan.

'This is not how the war was won, eh, dog?' She let her fingers caress the soft spot between Scamp's eyes and, without a second thought, she rose, picked up the remains of Beth's breakfast and placed it on the floor at his feet. 'They think I don't feed you, don't they. I just don't want them doing it, that's all. At least I got that right.'

She retrieved the handkerchief from up her sleeve and blew her nose hard. It was what it was, and no amount of tears or desolate feelings could change that. They had their own lives, every one of them, and when the day came for her to retire, not one of them would give her a second thought.

But despite her disappointment and hurt, Mrs Duffy could not change who she was. She loved her nurses and less than half an hour later she was making a fresh batch of mincemeat for the mince pies and shouting at the maids to get a move on with the rooms. She needed to get the washing dry in time, ready to be ironed and back on to the bottom of the nurses' beds before they returned home.

Chapter 7

Aileen Paige stood in front of the white, panelled door with the laden breakfast tray in her hands. Each morning she said the same thing once she had clumsily gained entry to the room – 'We must find a small table to put outside your bedroom door, Mother' – but she'd never found the time to buy one, and now that she'd just been made a ward sister, there would be even less opportunity.

This morning was no different. She gave a big sigh, raised her right knee, wobbled slightly on the other foot, gripped the tray, balanced it on the knee, quickly let go with her left hand, turned the brass knob, flung open the door and just managed to grab the tray back into both hands before a catastrophe occurred all over the ruby-coloured carpet. Her heart beat a little faster. One day, she thought, I'll drop the lot.

Watery winter sunlight shone through the arch-paned window and illuminated a dash of tea that had shot out of the spout of her mother's favourite Old Country Rose china teapot and stained the white linen tray cloth brown. Her mother would notice. 'Drat,' said Aileen out loud.

'Is that you, Aileen?' came her mother's voice from within.

Aileen took a deep breath. She wanted to shout back, 'Who

else would it be, Mother? Do you have another daughter who would go to the freezing back kitchen to cook your eggs for exactly three minutes and thirty seconds?' But she didn't dare. Aileen never liked to rattle the bars of her mother's cage – the results could be disastrous. 'It is, Mother. I have your eggs for you, just as you like them.'

Her mother had leant forward in her wing-back armchair to watch Aileen as she walked towards her with the tray. She had already taken herself to the toilet and arranged the chair to her liking, but she'd done so when she was sure there were no observers to comment on her agility. She waved her hand in the air as if to dismiss Aileen. 'Oh, take them away. I can't eat them today. I'm just not feeling up to it.'

Aileen froze and stared at her mother, then took another deep breath before continuing towards the chair. 'Don't be silly, Mother. You have to eat. Come along now.'

Mrs Paige grumbled and frowned at Aileen. 'Just because you've been promoted to ward sister, it doesn't mean you can start bossing me around, you know.'

'More's the pity,' said Aileen.

Having laid the tray down on the table between them, Aileen flopped into her own wing-back chair in front of the fire, opposite her mother. She picked up the bone-handled butter knife and began to butter her mother's toast. Mrs Paige didn't like her toast soft. Aileen was instructed to stand it in the toast rack while she carried the tray up from the kitchen to make sure that the steam rose and left the toast crispy on the outside and soft in the middle. She also had to pour the water into the pot as her very last job before she came up the stairs. Her mother drank her tea weak and almost at boiling point and would happily dispatch Aileen back down to the cold kitchen if it wasn't just right. As a High Church Anglican, she would often comment, 'Stewed tea reminds me of the Irish Catholics – thick and bitter.'

Mrs Marion Paige had never been afraid to speak her mind or assert her will and this had not changed after she'd become chair-bound following her stroke. Illness had not diminished her authority or acerbic nature, and Aileen's married sister, Josie, was far from sympathetic. 'You need to get things sorted, Aileen, because I'm not looking after her,' Josie had informed her when their mother had returned home from the hospital. 'My James wouldn't tolerate it, and besides, the children tire Mother out.'

'Mother's food and what she eats is all she has any real control over,' Aileen had retorted. 'She spends a long time in that chair and if she wants to fuss about her food, that's fine by me.'

'She's living in the past, Aileen, as if the war never happened. She's always been like that. Thinks she can still speak to people as though they're slaves, and she has always had you wrapped round her little finger. But I'm afraid I cannot help. I have my own substantial home to run.'

Aileen was not convinced that Josie genuinely wanted her to put their mother in her place. She'd started to sense that there was something else going on. It was the way Josie wouldn't meet Aileen's eye when she spoke to her, the way she shifted from foot to foot and never stayed in her company for more than minutes at a time. Aileen suspected that Josie was not being honest or playing fair, but she didn't know how or why.

There were never any conversations regarding what would happen should Aileen want to marry. There had never been any conversations about David, ever. When he died, their interest in him had died too and it was at that point that Aileen had realized her mother and sister weren't really interested in her, either. She had placed a photograph of David in his uniform on the mantelpiece. A week after he died, her mother asked her to take it down. 'I don't want to look at it all day while you're at work,' she'd snapped, and Aileen had obliged, putting David's picture out of sight on her bedside table.

Day after day she would save her tears until bedtime, and then, once the lights were out, she would sob herself into a well of despair. It was only now, ten years on, that she could think of him without feeling a pain deep beneath her diaphragm, only now that she could even contemplate a life with someone else. But it was too late; she was too old. She had spent her best years grieving for a man who had died of his wounds on the battlefield. Missing in action, along with her heart. She would have given up nursing in a flash for David. But after he died, she put her heart and soul into her job at St Angelus. Even though Matron had now made it possible to be married and continue nursing, Aileen knew that Josie assumed she would never marry, that she would remain a spinster and continue being the one who looked after their mother.

They never discussed this, however. Aileen avoided confrontation whenever possible. Her nature was always to please. She'd had her thirtieth birthday earlier in the year, in the summer, and she could almost hear Josie breathing a sigh of relief. She imagined her saying to her husband, James, 'That's it, Aileen's on the shelf, we're safe. Mother won't ever have to live with us.'

It was a fact that there was no love lost between Josie and Aileen. Mrs Paige knew this and Aileen sometimes wondered if Josie exaggerated the extent of the bad feeling between them, using it as an excuse to spend less time with their mother. Either way, Aileen couldn't bring herself to put it to the test, couldn't face the inevitable upset and drama that would come if she ever had cause to say to Josie, 'It's your turn now.' As a result, Aileen, despite having received many invitations to go out for suppers or drinks with potential suitors, had never allowed things to go any further than a few dates. And anyway, no one could match David.

Most of those dates had been while she was living at the Lovely Lane home, before her mother's stroke. Mrs Duffy used to encourage her, telling her how beautiful she looked when she walked out of the door and leaving a supper in her room for when she got back. Since she'd moved home again, though, she'd been on only a few dates. She never left until her mother was ready for bed and pretended that she was going to a choir meeting at the church. But she always felt so sick with guilt and worry that the date was inevitably a disaster. She couldn't live with herself and the lies she had to tell just to have a night out. It was far easier simply to stay at home, do whatever it took to keep her mother happy and reread David's letters.

Joining the choir, however, had genuinely transformed her life. Although it was an activity her mother didn't exactly approve of – she rarely approved of anything – she had not objected with the forcefulness she was notorious for. Aileen had agreed to take part in the Christmas concert at St George's Hall and even she was slightly amazed by how much she was looking forward to it. When she sang, she forgot her life. Her heart sang with her, and sometimes the words, music and harmonies moved her to tears. They were tears of joy rather than sadness, and why this happened, she couldn't explain. But it was something she wanted to hold on to, and that meant secrecy and managing her mother in such a way as not to endanger the one thing, other than her job, that brought her pleasure.

'Oh, take that away.' Using what Aileen called her good hand, her mother waved away the plate of buttered toast Aileen had made to her precise instructions.

'But you said last night that you wanted me to make you eggs and toast.'

'That was last night. You haven't asked me this morning.'

Aileen sighed and set the plate back down on the tray. As she did so, she glanced up at the framed picture on the mantelpiece of her father and mother, Josie and herself. She could sometimes feel her father's presence, as though he was looking down on her, and right now his eyes were imploring her. Patience, Aileen, she thought she could hear him say.

Aileen had been told for all of her life that she looked just like her father, took after him, and that Josie took after their mother. He had fought with his wife for most of their married life. In the photograph, her mother was sitting on a wicker bench, Aileen and Josie to either side and their father standing behind, his hand on their mother's shoulder, beaming. He'd served as an RAF group captain in the war and had died in 1943, leaving them all devastated. Neither rich nor poor, Mrs Paige and the two girls managed to get by, but as reserves began to dwindle and the cost of living began to rise, Aileen became increasingly determined to rise as high up as she could within the nursing profession and help finance the running of the house.

Always keen to keep everyone else happy, Aileen's secret

was to work as hard as possible. If she was never to marry or become a mother, she would have to succeed at her job. When other women closed their eyes and dreamt of wedding dresses and electric washing machines, Aileen imagined herself wearing a matron's uniform. Her mother's stroke had threatened these plans, but thanks to the intervention of Sister Tapps she now had Gina to help out at home. Gina had proved to be more resilient than Aileen could ever have hoped and was well worth the seven and six a week she paid her out of her nursing wage.

The toast was now back on the tray and Aileen placed a large cup into her mother's good hand.

'I will drink the tea, if it keeps you happy and stops you worrying about me when you're at work,' her mother said with very little sincerity.

'Do you need help?' Aileen asked, her own voice full of genuine care and affection.

'No, thank you, I can manage quite well. Tell me, do you have anything exciting happening today?'

Aileen let the sugar lump drop from the tongs into her tea and began to stir. 'We have a new student nurse from the Lovely Lane home starting on paediatrics this morning. There were meant to be three of them, but I think Matron lost a couple to Christmas leave. Apart from that, I'm expecting nothing out of the ordinary.'

As Aileen ate her breakfast, she thought about the fact that her mother had never once asked her if she wanted to marry and have a family of her own. She never asked if there was anyone Aileen cared for, a sweetheart on the horizon maybe. Even Aileen understood that she was regarded by most as attractive. Enough people had told her so – it was embarrassing how many people commented on her big blue eyes. She was well aware that her long thick fair hair was her best feature and she looked after it carefully, combing it through from her scalp to the ends one hundred times a night as she sat in front of her triptych dressing-table mirror. She often sighed wistfully, knowing that she could take as long as she wished. There was no one waiting for her to finish and only the cold crisp sheets to welcome her into bed.

There were times when she would stare at her own reflection for so long, her vision would blur and then she'd imagine him into the mirror, sitting on the bed behind her. It used to be David, but the man who now appeared on her bed was a stranger, someone she didn't know and hadn't loved. When had David left? When had his face slipped from her memory? The man on the bed was no longer David. It was just her imagination whispering the words she so desperately wanted to hear, if only it could happen, even just the once. The voice of a man who wanted her to join him.

As her mother sipped on her scalding tea, her white hair glowing in the firelight and the drips from the bottom of her cup seeping into the multi-coloured strands of the crocheted blanket that covered her knees, Aileen wondered why they had never had that conversation. Why it was that her mother had never encouraged her to go out and enjoy herself, to find a boyfriend, to marry and have children of her own. It occurred to her that her mother was afraid. Afraid of what would become of her if Aileen ever did want to settle down. Her mother would rather ignore the possibility, believe it would never happen.

The only children in Aileen's life were those she nursed on her ward and then handed back, along with a little bit of her own heart, to their grateful parents. Did her mother not realize that? Could she not sense Aileen's aching loneliness?

Not wanting to dwell on her mother's selfishness, and feeling guilty for entertaining such thoughts, Aileen sprang to her feet and began to clear away the breakfast things. 'Right, I will miss the bus if I don't hurry. Let's move your chair, shall we, Mother?'

Mrs Paige liked to sit in the bay window during the day, once the room had warmed up. She said she needed the light to read by, but she also spent much of her time simply watching the street as it went about its business.

'Leave the tray, Aileen. I might get the girl to pour me more tea. Off you go.'

'Her name is Gina, Mother. She has been here long enough now. Please try and remember her name.'

Mrs Paige snorted her derision. 'Are you going to your choir thing again tonight? You seem to be going rather a lot at the moment. Is it really necessary?'

'I told you, Mother, we're putting on a carol concert on Christmas Eve, so we need lots of rehearsals. We don't have one tonight though.'

'What on earth do you need to practise for? You know all the words and have done since you were a child. What a ridiculous waste of time.'

Aileen's spirits dropped. How could she explain that their choirmaster was doing the most amazing things with the mix of male and female voices. That the harmonies and descants sounded spiritual, as though their words were being lifted heavenwards on the wings of angels. The acoustics sent a thrill down her spine and if she could have called into the Anglican cathedral and sung every night, she would. It was going to be a very special concert, not only because of all the different choirs, but also because everyone, from the sailors in the port to the gentry who lived on Rodney Street, would stand side by side as they sang together.

'Well, I can't let people down. Anyway, I have to go now, Mother. Gina will be up to take you to the toilet as soon as I leave, and she's going to pop down to the shops first thing to catch the post office for you, so give her your list.'

As she stacked her own cup on to her plate, Aileen popped a kiss on the top of her mother's head. 'See you later,' she said, and within seconds she was outside on the landing shouting, 'Gina, can you come and take this tray, please. I have to dash.'

Mrs Paige stared at the closed door, listening. She hated Aileen leaving her alone. She resented the children she looked after and she resented Matron for employing her, but worse than all of that, she loathed Sister Tapps for encouraging and helping her.

The days always felt as though they would last for ever, until Aileen returned home to sit with her. At least today she could ask Gina to buy her the *Reveille*. She would read every one of its gossipy articles, as slowly as she could, to make the paper last.

She used to live in fear of Aileen meeting someone and of her marrying, setting up her own home and returning there each evening after work instead of tending to her. She said a prayer of thanks daily for the fact that this hadn't happened, and now that Aileen had turned thirty, she was confident it wouldn't. Aileen's chances of finding a husband were thankfully well and truly over. Since the war, men had been in short supply in Liverpool. Those who were married stayed married. It was a Catholic city and divorce a shameful, unheard-of option. Even though they never talked about it, Mrs Paige knew that Aileen was sad that she would never marry. But her sadness would pass soon enough.

Leaning back in her chair, she watched as Aileen ran down the road for the bus. There she goes, she thought, as she heard the squeal of brakes and caught a glimpse of her daughter's green Paisley headscarf as she reached the bottom of the road and hopped on. She lifted her good hand and grasped at the gold cross and chain around her neck. 'It won't happen now. No husband for Aileen, please God. Keep her busy. Keep her with me.' She whispered her prayer and, as she did so, felt not a shred of guilt.

Gina tapped on the bedroom door.

'Go away! Come back in twenty minutes when I ring the bell,' Mrs Paige shouted with little grace or gratitude.

Standing up with ease, she pulled the tray table towards her, picked up a slice of toast, bit into it and then speedily began to crack the top of the eggs Aileen had brought her. Her bad hand, which was nowhere near as bad as she made out, held on to the eggs as she cracked them open with the good hand.

'Hard,' she grumbled to herself as she scooped out the yolk and devoured it, but she didn't care. Hard eggs were a small price to pay to ensure that her daughter remained concerned about her and kept her uppermost in her mind throughout the day. Enough to send Aileen hurrying back home as soon as her shift finished.

Chapter 8

Beth and Pammy stood at the top of the stairs. To the right were the large wooden doors to ward three. To the left, ward four.

'Well, good luck then.' Pammy smiled at Beth, who looked as miserable as it was possible to be.

'Thanks a lot,' Beth replied. 'I wonder who I'll bathe and dress first – the children, the special teddy or the dollies that Sister Tapps is apparently so fond of.'

Footsteps came running up the stairs towards them and they both looked down, keen to see who was daring to contravene Matron's strictest rule: 'No running unless in the case of fire, haemorrhage or cardiac arrest.' The mystery was solved as the top of Anthony Mackintosh's head came into view.

Pammy smiled and her tummy flipped.

'Oh, there you are,' he said as he grabbed the banister, propelled himself up the final few steps and stopped short at the sight of the girls. 'I just came to wish you good luck.' A grin spread across his face as he took in their startled expressions. 'Morning, girls, how are you?'

Pretty much any other nurse at St Angelus would have

thought they'd died and gone to heaven if their gorgeous doctor boyfriend had come running down the hospital corridors to wish them good luck, but Pammy was oblivious. 'Thanks, I'm going to need it,' she said.

'Me too,' said Beth. 'Sister Tapps puts the new girls on teddy- and dolly-washing. I've heard that Mr Golliwog can be a very difficult customer and doesn't like having his hair washed, and as for Miss Golden Curls, well, she is very lippy indeed if you don't brush her hair just so.'

They both stifled their giggles and Pammy placed her hand over her mouth to stop herself from laughing out loud. Beth could not have been more grumpy if she'd tried.

'Listen up,' Anthony whispered, 'I've been on ward three all night. There's been a patient in overnight, one of the worst cases of neglect I've ever seen.'

'Oh, gosh,' said Beth, looking around to make sure no one had heard him. 'On ward three? I'm on four, so I won't get to be involved.'

But before she could say another word, the ward doors opened and, to their utter amazement, Matron strode out. The look on her face rooted them all to the spot.

'Good morning, Dr Mackintosh. Have you now abandoned casualty and decided to try your hand at paediatrics after having spent one night here? I had no idea that the rumours about there being no end to your talents were true. Has casualty become too tedious and boring for you now?'

Despite his being an experienced doctor, Anthony Mackintosh's response to Matron was immediate and beyond his control. She had more power over him than either of his late parents. 'Er, no, thank you, Matron, I was just on my way back to casualty to wash up after the night, and then to bed.'

He had the good grace to look guilty. He knew that what he had just said was profoundly stupid.

'Are you indeed? Have you suffered from some form of memory lapse? How often do you run up the stairs to casualty – which is on the ground floor, as well you know.'

Anthony blushed to the roots of his hair. Only Matron could make him do that. She had the ability to make even the most senior consultants feel as though they were back in the nursery and answering to nanny. They discussed this often in the doctors' sitting room, and just that morning on casualty old Mabbutt had been complaining that he couldn't stand up to her, and he was the most abrasive and sweariest of them all. There was nothing quite as funny as hearing Matron tell Mabbutt off when he was using his favourite word, 'bloody'. 'That is quite enough of your bad language, Mr Mabbutt, really,' Matron would say. 'Behave yourself. You are not on the dock streets, you are working in a hospital and I will not tolerate it.' It was the joke of the hospital, how huge, towering Mr Mabbutt blushed and shrank, simpering, 'Yes, Matron. Sorry Matron.'

Matron's eye did not waver as she held Anthony's.

'I'm on my way now, Matron.'

'Well, that's just as well because my nurses are about to be terribly busy, as you are well aware. I would hate to think that you had run all the way up the stairs from casualty, where you are actually needed, to prevent them from going about their duties?'

'No, Matron, of course I didn't. I wouldn't.' And without another word, Anthony was back down the stairs, quicker than he had climbed them, desperate to avoid further interrogation. He was the one who laughed at Mabbutt the most, when he and the other doctors discussed Matron's effect on them all, and yet she had the exact same effect on him.

The trio listened in silence as his footsteps echoed down the corridor towards casualty. Looking satisfied at having reprimanded Dr Mackintosh, and obviously taking some pleasure in his discomfort, Matron continued. Such an obvious endorsement of her authority, despite her progressing years, made her feel surprisingly pleased with herself. But in a flash her small smile of satisfaction disappeared. Her expression became solemn and she turned to face her nurses.

With mouths dry, palms damp and hearts beating faster, both nurses noted the swift sweep of her eyes across their shoes and uniforms. They almost let out an audible sigh of relief when she made no criticism. Beth's hand flew to the fob watch pinned to her apron under her cape and straightened it. As if alerted by the movement, Matron turned to her.

'Nurse Harper, there have been a few changes. You are no longer on ward four today.'

Beth's eyes opened wide in surprise, and relief hovered in the wings as she almost didn't dare let herself believe she might be spending her Christmas on the same ward as Pammy. The Tanners were as close to Beth as any family she had known. She marvelled at their disorder and closeness, and in her heart, Beth, the keeper of lists, loved it.

'We have a very special case on ward three, admitted as an emergency last night. Come with me, both of you.'

The nurses looked at each other and Beth furiously motioned to Pammy to wipe the make-up off her eyelids. She could barely believe that Matron hadn't spotted it. Some ward sisters tolerated a little foundation and blusher, but Matron most certainly did not. Beth had no idea, however, that Matron had been up all night, nor that, without sleep, her eyesight was blurred at best.

The two girls tripped along behind her, Pammy at the back rubbing at her eyelids with her handkerchief. The ward doors opened and they were in for a second shock when they were greeted by a very tired-looking PC Freddie Watts.

The words fell out of Pammy's mouth, as they often did, before she could stop them. Handkerchief held mid air and covered in powder-blue Outdoor Girl eye shadow, she exclaimed, 'Freddie, what on earth are you doing up here in children's? Not following me around, are you?' She laughed and gave him a cheeky wink.

Matron glanced at her. She was well used to Nurse Tanner's impetuous nature. Her eyes narrowed and focused on the hankie, then they moved up to Pammy's face and frowned. They had been through a drama or two together in the time Pammy had been at the hospital, but Matron knew enough from Sister Haycock to make allowances. She had been left in no doubt that Pammy excelled at patient care, and a close second to that was the loyalty she showed towards St Angelus. If a nurse demonstrated an absolute commitment to the St Angelus family, it travelled a long way with Matron.

'Into the office, please, nurses. At once. The night staff are exhausted and will not appreciate your delaying them with chitchat,' said Matron. 'Now, please! Constable, you look exhausted. Is someone on their way to relieve you?'

Freddie looked nervous. Matron's reputation was legendary in Liverpool. 'They will be, Matron. There's a full manhunt about to begin for whoever abandoned the little boy. Norman, er, Constable Bartlett, has been undertaking door-to-door enquiries. It appears that no one in the road had ever seen a baby at the house and the people who lived there spoke to no one. The super will be sending a plainclothes CID officer down this morning, to speak to the doctor. I'm off home for a sleep now, and then I'll be back later, to take over and to help. If that's OK with you?'

'Good man. We'll see you later then. Don't you worry, he's in safe hands with us. Make sure you have your full quota of sleep. We all know what happens when people skimp on that and the last thing you want is to be ill for Christmas.'

She watched Freddie as he went out through the ward doors. Then she turned towards Sister Paige, who was standing in the doorway to the office. Sister Paige was also watching Freddie with more than her usual degree of interest. Matron's heart sank. Only a blind man would fail to notice how pretty Aileen Paige was. She, however, appeared to have no idea of the impact she had on others. Matron had seen heads turn and necks craned as people tried to brighten their day by catching a second glimpse of the passing beauty. She projected warmth as well as professionalism, and that she had a caring heart was abundantly clear. There was something special about her and she was instantly noticed and not easily forgotten. Now that she was a new ward sister, promoted by Matron herself, she appeared to glow with pride in her navy-blue uniform.

Matron recognized the look she'd seen in Sister Paige's eyes as the ward doors swung back and forth and Freddie ran down the stairs. It was unmistakable – she'd seen it in so many nurses' eyes, so often. Including, only seconds before, in Nurse Tanner's – who was also impossible to ignore or forget, though for entirely different reasons – when she'd caught her talking to Dr Mackintosh. Although, Matron would admit, Nurse Tanner had hid it well in her presence – or at least she thought she had. It had been in Dr Mackintosh's eyes too, as he'd looked at Nurse Tanner. Oh, here we go, Matron thought, that's all we need. A flirtation on the children's ward at a time like this, and my best ward sister too, distracted by a police officer.

But as they filed into the office, that was the last thought she gave to it. On the ward, a child was fighting for his life and if it was a battle she was going to win, she needed every one of them on her side. They all had a job to do.

Sister Paige stood to the side of the office door, her back pressed against the wall to let Matron walk in ahead of her.

Matron smiled and stopped in her tracks. 'Not at all, Sister Paige. You may be a new ward sister, but this is your ward now. You are in charge, you are the one who will hand over the report, not me. I am only here to reinforce the conditions of confidentiality we face with the new admission and the added complications of a police investigation.' She could see that Sister Paige was nervous, and so she should be. There would be a great deal of interest in this case and it was a big one to handle in her first week.

As Sister Paige spoke, Beth was struck by the sweet and melodious tone of her voice. She went through the patients, starting with the cubicles but leaving out cubicle number one, the closest cot to the office. 'There is a great deal to say about the baby in cubicle one, so I will leave him until last.' And then, without further ado, she worked her way down the ward, case by case, around the large bay at the bottom with its windows that looked straight on to Lovely Lane and then back up the cubicles on the other side, finishing with a five-year-old boy, post inguinal hernia, due for discharge that morning. She didn't leave out a single detail and Beth found herself imagining what it must feel like to be sitting in the sister's leather chair; to be in charge. She could only imagine how satisfying and rewarding that would be.

'And, finally, nurses…' Sister Paige's voice cut though Beth's thoughts. 'Back to cubicle one. We had a very distressing admission during the night. This will be of interest to the police, the welfare department and the press, and I wouldn't be surprised if it ended up in the news on the new televisions everyone in Liverpool seems to be renting.'

There was a sharp intake of breath from the nurses standing around the room.

'As St Angelus nurses, Matron expects nothing less than your absolute discretion. Not a word of this case must be revealed to anyone outside of this ward, do you understand?'

The nurses were lined up against the wall for day report, each one holding paper and pencil, waiting to write down their duties for the morning. They all nodded in almost stupefied acknowledgement of the instruction.

Only Pammy Tanner spoke, looking up at Matron and Sister Paige as she did so. 'Yes, Matron.'

Matron's eyes scanned the remaining nurses, who, realizing what was expected of them, answered as one. 'Yes, Matron.' Not one of them had ever experienced Matron being present for day report. That in itself was enough to tie their tongues.

Matron, happy that they all understood the gravity of the situation about to be revealed to them, took the report Kardex from Sister Paige's outstretched hands, held it face down at her side and continued. She had been there all night and knew every detail, didn't need to reread her own notes. 'Late last night, a baby was found abandoned in the garage of an empty house. Male, approximately six months old.

He was hypothermic and dehydrated and is malnourished, severely underweight and developmentally impaired. He has pneumonia, with the left lung being much worse than the right. He was lying on his left side when he was found, which would account for this. The houseman and night sister have been with him all night long. The consultant, Dr Walker, was called in from home and was here by 1 a.m. Gone by 1.30.'

The assembled nurses almost gasped at the hint of derision in Matron's voice. It was a badly kept secret that Matron had little time for Dr Walker and his lazy ways.

'He is a very poorly baby and is failing to thrive. There is no doubt that if he hadn't been found when he was, following the drop in temperature during the night and given the fact that his left lung is almost fully congested, he would not be with us this morning.'

Beth swallowed. The air in the room felt heavy and oppressive. The implication that a life had been saved with very little time to spare was something they were all desperately trying to absorb.

'I will let Sister Paige continue, but please be assured that I'll be keeping a close eye on this case, for reasons which will become apparent over time.'

Aileen Paige reached out to take back the long metal Kardex which held the buff cards containing the ward notes. Taking her pen out of her top pocket, she made a note.

Matron's eyes flicked towards her to see what she'd written. *To be special nursed.* A nurse would now be stationed inside the cubicle at all times, leaving them one down out on the ward. She was aware of the wide eyes and bewildered looks on the faces of the nurses around them and decided to fill the silence while Sister Paige read through some of the night nurse's notes.

'Because the child is in a very bad way, nurses, we need you to be prepared before you see him for yourselves. The police are obviously concerned to find who abandoned him and so evidently neglected him for the duration of his short life. They are treating it as attempted murder – as indeed it very nearly was...' She paused for a moment and took a breath. 'And indeed still may be. Whatever the outcome, he is both a patient of St Angelus and the subject of what will be an intensive and sensitive police investigation. This child appears to have never eaten food. He appears to have no real sucking reflex. Dr Walker said that there were some bowel sounds – in his opinion, just enough to try him on a liquid diet. Night Sister attempted to feed him some watered-down milk, but it was impossible as he vomited it straight back up and then, following that exertion, he slipped into unconsciousness. He was found with an empty glass formula bottle in the pram. Its rubber teat appeared to have been chewed and swallowed as it was not found in the pram with him, according to the CID who visited the scene. His skin is chafed from the leather reins that were used to strap him into the pram. He is gaunt and frightened and because of his dehydration on admission his eyes are quite sunken. His clothes were in rags, his skin has broken down in places, particularly along his left side, and he is teetering on the edge. He is alive now, but with the possibility of infection and other complications, he may not be so for very long. Indeed, that is the very definite opinion of Dr Walker.'

Matron paused and shifted in her chair slightly, leaving them all in no doubt regarding her opinion of Dr Walker.

'He requires intensive nursing care. That is why Sister Paige needs an extra pair of hands here on ward three. That will be you, Nurse Harper, until the situation alters.' Matron raised her eyebrows and nodded towards the Kardex, indicating to Sister Paige to continue.

'Right. So, as Matron has explained, this is going to be difficult. I shall pass a nasogastric tube as soon as we finish report. As you all know, that is a tube we pass into the stomach in order to introduce fluids and a liquid diet. I know you would all appreciate the chance to have that procedure ticked off in your assessment books. However, this little boy has been through a great deal. Night Sister attempted to pass a tube during the night and has been unsuccessful…'

'Sister Paige is being modest, nurses,' said Matron. 'She can pass an NG tube in twenty seconds flat, causing minimum discomfort to the patient, and that is what is needed today. Watch her and learn. She is the best I have ever seen. What is your secret, Sister Paige?'

Aileen blushed as she replied. She knew exactly what her secret was: it was confidence in her own ability and the swiftness that resulted. She was unafraid, and she focused on the job in hand to the exclusion of all else during those vital seconds while she pushed the tube up the patient's nostril and then down, following the path of the oesophagus all the way into the stomach until she felt the soft resistance as the rubber tube yielded between her fingertips.

Before she taped the tube into place, she would apply a syringe to the bung at the end of the rubber tube and aspirate. As she did so, she would pray that a sample of green bile would appear in the syringe; when this happened, she would squirt it into the metal kidney dish on the trolley and on to the litmus paper, which would immediately turn pink, confirming that the aspirate was stomach acid and that the tube was in the correct position. Passing the tube into the lung by mistake could be fatal. Had been fatal, in living memory at St Angelus and during Matron's own tenure. Since that time, Matron had insisted that all student nurses had to pass nasogastric tubes under supervision and that it had to be signed off five times in the assessment book before third-year finals.

'I will let the nurses watch me,' she said to Matron. Then she addressed the nurses themselves. 'I'm sorry I can't let you do it yourselves in this instance. The thing to remember is that it is mainly a matter of confidence. You cannot doubt you are going to succeed on first attempt. It is a case of setting up the trolley correctly and making sure you have someone with you to reassure the patient in order that you can give the procedure your one hundred per cent attention. It is impossible to do on your own as you cannot then focus fully on passing the tube swiftly and painlessly. The patient needs to be coaxed all the way through because if they panic and grab at the tube and pull it away, you just have to set up and start all over again.'

Sister Paige paused, looked up and gave the nurses an encouraging smile.

'Don't look so alarmed. Once you are ready to go, it is just a case of taking a deep breath, making sure all the Ts are crossed and, in my case, telling myself and the patient that this will all be over very quickly indeed. Then you need to get right on with it, without any hesitation. If you start dithering or become alarmed by the patient's gagging or attempts to grab at your hands, you'll prolong the distress. It's not cruel to get someone else to hold on to the patient's hands tightly so they can't distract you and by doing so, prolong the entire ordeal for them, it's being kind.'

Matron appeared to be more than satisfied. 'Well, did you hear that, nurses? I would like every nurse in this hospital to be as confident as Sister Paige, because good nursing, the best nursing, should be our only objective. Now, with this case, we must be very careful. As I have already mentioned, it is a CID investigation and that means no talk outside of this ward. Not a single word. Night Sister has given our abandoned baby a name, after her own father – Louis. No one must discuss baby Louis outside of here, not a single word, do you all understand? Not even in the Lovely Lane home.' She glanced straight at Pammy.

More confident now of what was expected from them, the voices came as one. 'Yes, Matron.' They only ever saw Matron on her ward rounds and when they were in trouble. Pammy had needed to visit Matron in her office a number of times.

'Also, be alert as to who comes in and out of the ward. The new cleaning rota kicks in today and you will have Branna cleaning on days up here from this week. You know who the doctors are, but if you see anyone entering the ward and you don't know who they are and you have the slightest suspicion, do not be afraid to ask. There is a thought that if whoever left this baby knows he is here, they may try to remove him. He has a mother, and one assumes there is also a father involved. The police will be looking for them now. However, do not waste your sympathy. Baby Louis was abandoned and almost lost his life. Any longer out there and he would not have been alive this morning. During the war we found our share of babies left on the hospital steps, but we have never had a case of neglect like this. His mother may come looking for him, and, even worse, the press may come sneaking around. There is of course the possibility that his mother is ill, or was forced to abandon her child. The fact is, we just don't know, so be vigilant at all times.'

'There's just one more thing to add to the morning report – something to try and keep things on as normal a footing as possible,' said Sister Paige. 'Although it seems quite trivial now, in light of last night, I will mention it anyway as we do have other patients on the ward, many of whom will not be going home for Christmas and must not be forgotten. The *Nursing Times* is running a national competition for the best Christmas decorations on any hospital ward that will have in-patients over Christmas. I thought we might enter. The Christmas tree is already leaning up against the window in the bay and some of the children are very excited. I would like to keep things as jolly as possible for our post-operative children. Matron and the doctor are discharging as many as they can from ward four and sending them here for Christmas. There will be no new operating lists on four from the day after tomorrow and those children left with us will have their beds wheeled into the bay at the end of the ward. We have a responsibility to all of them to make Christmas as fun as possible. Sister Tapps is having a well-earned holiday...'

'It is such a shame as we have so many children on the ward looking forward to it all. But now, because of baby Louis,' said Matron, 'I'm not sure how you will manage it all, however, I have every faith that you will.'

Pammy put up her hand. Report was a little like school: no one spoke without putting their hand up first.

'Yes, Nurse Tanner,' said Matron, not in the least bit surprised that she was the first to ask a question. Never backwards in coming forwards, Pammy always wanted to know the ins and outs of everything, sometimes giving the impression that she hadn't understood what she had been told when in fact she was simply gathering more information to deepen her knowledge.

'I'm on a split shift today, but I don't mind not going back to Lovely Lane for my split, and I will come in on my day off, to help with the decorations. I know Sister Haycock is keen too – she loves children's – and she and Biddy will be over in a flash. And my mam could come up from the WVS.'

Matron smiled. 'Well, that seems like a jolly good idea. Nurse Tanner, the decorations have just become your sole responsibility. You can inform Sister Haycock. I do love a good competition, so make sure we win, won't you.'

As the nurses bustled out on to the ward, with the staff nurse and a year-three student as their guides and mentors, Sister Paige said goodbye to Matron and then stood in the doorway to the office with a pale and tired-looking Night Sister, who had remained in the cubicle of baby Louis for report, at her side.

'Matron's been here all night, you know,' said Night Sister, who Aileen noted now spoke to her as though she were her equal, following her promotion. 'She came down from her flat to do the ten o'clock medicine round with me. We were just passing through casualty as the call came through that the baby was on his way.'

'I bet she'll just carry on all day too,' said Aileen. 'She's too old to be going without her sleep. She will make herself ill.'

'Ah, well, you know Matron. She would say that of others, but as far as she's concerned, she's invincible. Listen, about Louis – we've done what we could. I washed him as best as

I could manage, but to be honest, his dehydration was the main concern. I can't see him still being here tonight when I come back on duty. I've never seen a baby so neglected. He's a desperate sight. Can't think I will sleep much today for worrying about him.'

'You must sleep,' said Aileen. 'We are looking after him now, just remember that, and I promise you, he will still be here tonight. You go and have a good sleep.' She sounded more confident than she felt as she turned on her heel into the clean utility room.

Pammy and Beth were sent together to collect the clean linen basket from the linen room at the end of the ward.

'I can't believe my luck,' said Beth. 'I thought I'd be spending Christmas with Sister Tappsy on ward four.'

Pammy grabbed the trolley standing outside the linen room and pulled it inside behind them ready to receive the clean sheets and pillow cases. 'My mam loves Tappsy,' she said. 'She says she's the best ward sister in the hospital by a mile.' She climbed the step resting her feet on the bottom shelf of the cupboard, holding on to a slat on the middle shelf with one hand for balance and began to lift down sheets to Beth, who placed them in the trolley.

'Really, does she?' Beth had a lot of time for Maisie Tanner and trusted her opinion. 'Why?'

'Can you see the pillow cases?' asked Pammy as she looked around the shelves. 'Every ward sister has a different way of laying out their linen room. Why can't they just all be the same?' Spotting the pillow cases, she began to shuffle along her perch towards the shorter shelves at the end. 'Mam says that she doesn't just nurse her patients' sickness, she looks after their hearts too. You know what my mam's like, Beth. She's just a big softie.'

Beth took the pile of pillow cases from Pammy. 'She's such a stickler though, you know. They say she even forgets to send the nurses for breaks. I'm the last person to object to hard work, and I am a stickler too—'

'Don't we all know it,' said Pammy, laughing.

'It's just that it is Christmas and, besides, I wanted to be with you.'

'And now you are!' said Pammy as she climbed back down off the step. She turned to Beth. 'All I would say though is this – and I only know this because I'm from around here and grew up on these streets – everyone loves Tappsy. She has a reputation to equal that of a saint. The one question I am asked more than any other by me mam's mates and our neighbours is, "Have you worked with Sister Tapps yet?" I swear to God, she will be canonized one day. Right, just the cot draw sheets to go and we can get this trolley back down the ward.'

Aileen laid up her trolley in the clean utility room and mentally ticked off the items as she went. She had prepared so many nasogastric trolleys, she no longer had need of a piece of paper in her top pocket listing her requirements. She filled and switched on the Little Sister sterilization steamer and then one by one took down what she needed from the scrubbed wooden shelves. Orange rubber nasogastric tubing, neo-natal gauge. Syringe, litmus paper, kidney dishes, Vaseline, aspiration sample pot. She lifted the lid of the Little Sister and popped in the glass syringe.

Once it was at boiling point, she stood and waited for the large black dial on the front to tick away. As she did so, her thoughts wandered unbidden to Freddie: to the concerned and tender smile he had given her when Matron had taken her into Louis's cubicle; to his paternal protectiveness towards Louis and his tenderness as he had helped her lift the tiny boy into a slightly raised position in order to encourage his left lung to drain. And then her thoughts wandered to Freddie's dark brown eyelashes and the way they curled upwards almost to his eyebrows, framing his unusual blue and brown eyes and giving him a startled, wide-eyed expression. Without her even being aware it was happening, a smile hovered on her lips, her face softened and a warm glow spread through her. He was nice, she thought. There was something about the way he had looked at both Louis and herself. His unashamed and obvious attachment to the little boy he had rescued from near death, the way his smile had made her heart somersault. Her smile broke through and it felt so good to have something of her own, something deeply personal that no one else, least of all her mother, could possibly guess.

The black dial buzzed as it hit zero and Aileen was so lost in her thoughts, she almost jumped. She quickly picked up the forceps that were sticking out from under the lid, the end still in the boiling water, being sterilized along with the tubing and the glass syringe. Passing a nasogastric tube was not a sterile procedure, but Aileen still liked to take every precaution.

As she began to lay her trolley, all thoughts of Freddie vanished and the smile slipped from her face. She was Sister Aileen Paige and her only focus was on baby Louis and the task ahead. Despite this, she felt lighter and hopeful. She would keep the memory of Freddie's smile locked away in her heart.

There was nothing she could do about it. Her mother had to be her priority. But it was a gift Freddie had left her and when she was next alone with her thoughts, she would bring it back out and remember the way he had looked and made her feel.

Back in his lodgings, Freddie pulled across the blackout curtains, which had remained in place since the end of the war. 'They come in handy for night workers,' his landlady had said. Freddie had to admit she was right. When they were closed it was as if it was night in the room and he could sleep soundly, though he couldn't imagine that there was a single lodging in all of Liverpool as depressing as his own. He slipped between the sheets and pulled the eiderdown over his shoulders, and as the exhaustion he had fought off began to wash over him, he fell through the folds of his own consciousness into a deep sleep. His last waking thoughts were of Aileen Paige and the tears that had rushed into her eyes as she looked down into the cot and saw baby Louis. He'd been so relieved, instinctively knowing that he had no need to worry about feeling ashamed, she would understand the tears that were filling his own eyes too.

Sister Paige wheeled the trolley into the cubicle and the first nurse she saw was Pammy Tanner, walking down from the bay with a trolley full of half-sized china bedpans. The ward's tiled walls had murals painted on to them depicting well-known nursery rhymes and Pammy was standing directly beneath Humpty Dumpty. Aileen had always thought it sad that the nursery rhymes were painted in dark greens, mustards and murky browns rather than the bright colours the children seemed to prefer.

'Can you see what the others are doing,' she said to Pammy, 'and whether anyone wants to watch or assist? I'm about to pass the nasogastric tube on little Louis.'

Minutes later, Beth and Pammy crowded into the cubicle and stood around the empty cot. There was a hint of tension as they looked towards the staff nurse who was specialling Louis and was sitting on a chair holding him in her arms. Pammy gasped and clamped her hand over her mouth in horror, which prompted a look of disapproval from the staff nurse. Beth held her breath, determined to maintain an inscrutable and professional expression. There would be no dramatic reaction from her.

Sister Paige was more sympathetic towards Pammy than the staff nurse had been. She placed her hand lightly on Pammy's arm. 'I know it will take you a moment to adjust,' she said softly. 'I felt the same myself when I first saw him.'

Beth now gave Sister Paige a sharp look, annoyed that her efforts to remain absolutely professional had gone unnoticed.

The nurses did not – could not – speak. Before them, on the staff nurse's knee, lay a scrap of life with a head that looked abnormally large for his body. His eyes were open but unseeing, the eyeballs rolled back and looking like huge white saucers sunk into his face. His skin was so dry and flaky, it resembled elephant hide. He had no hair on the back or one side of his head and only tufts around the other side and at the front. A wooden splint, twice the size of his arm but still the smallest in the hospital, was bandaged to him and the rubber tube of a now collapsed drip disappeared within. Baby Louis was unconscious.

'The drip has tissued again,' said the staff nurse, looking up towards Aileen. 'His veins kept collapsing on the night staff – it's desperate. If only he could have a cut-down and a leg splint.'

Sister Paige acknowledged this with a grimace. She retrieved Louis's notes from the bottom of the trolley and handed them to the staff nurse. 'You should all know what is going on here. You may want to pass those notes around to the others,' she said, 'so that you fully understand what we're doing and what's at stake. There is a reason there's been no cut-down and that we have been desperately trying to manage with the drip in his arm...' She looked over at Pammy and Beth. 'I expect you're familiar with the venous cut-down procedure? When the cannula is inserted directly into a larger and much deeper vein, sometimes under surgery?'

Beth and Pammy both nodded but didn't say a word. Staff Nurse also made no comment as she read the front page of the notes, but as soon as she handed them to Pammy, she bent her neck and kissed the top of Louis's head. 'Bless him,' she whispered. 'The poor thing.'

Pammy picked up the notes and gasped at the letters scrawled across the front. 'Who wrote that?' she asked.

'The consultant. Dr Walker,' said Aileen. 'Because the police were involved, Dr Mackintosh called him in from home. Dr Walker is away on a course in Manchester this week, so, as you can see, every little thing we're doing to help Louis is being done against his explicit orders and in secret. Matron has really stuck her neck out here. This is his ward. He is responsible for clinical decisions and we work to his orders. Liverpool children's services run this ward, albeit in Matron's hospital. You are all familiar with the Florence Nightingale code. Our duty is to serve the physician and not to question his instructions or challenge him. That was one of the reasons why Matron swore you to absolute confidentiality. To be fair, it was the main reason. It isn't just because of the police and the newspapers, it is because for the first time in her entire career, Matron has lost a battle with a consultant and is expressly defying his orders.'

Pammy handed the notes to Beth. The blood drained from Beth's face and her eyes opened wide. Across the top in a bold hand with a black pen was scrawled three words: *No further treatment.*

'Does that mean...?' Beth's voice trailed off.

Sister Paige finished her sentence for her. 'It means "leave to die". We sometimes receive babies up here who have been delivered downstairs and have serious disabilities, heart or lung problems, or maybe they were delivered too early and the doctors are worried there may be brain damage as a result. You might see that written on notes during your time here, when a cot is wheeled up from maternity. You will only see it on paediatrics, never on an adult ward and always only on the notes of a newborn, always a newborn. However, Louis is not a newborn. I am with Matron on this one: I think Louis has a fighting chance. He is about six months old. That was why Matron was so cross. But we have less than a week to turn him around and save his life – otherwise there could be the most almighty row. Dr Gaskell would be involved and if Dr Walker was being bloody minded, now that we are part of the NHS and under the auspices of children's services, it could go further. In short, Matron is taking a very big risk.'

Pammy, forever outspoken, said exactly what she was thinking. 'I don't get it. The poor child's parents abandon him to the elements, for goodness knows how long, and Freddie brings him in here, all for Dr Walker to just give up on him? Why? It doesn't make sense. Is that why the CID are here?'

Sister Paige looked out through the cubicle window at the plainclothes officers arriving through the ward doors and then down at Louis. 'Yes. Dr Walker assured them last night that this would be a murder case within forty-eight hours. He said that baby Louis couldn't possible survive. Matron begs to differ. Dr Mackintosh, of his own accord and without Matron's intervention, appears to agree with us. He is also defying orders and has prescribed Louis antibiotics – streptomycin. But, despite Dr Mackintosh's best efforts, we are struggling to get it into Louis. The drip keeps letting us down because his veins are collapsing. Hence our own nursing intervention and the nasogastric tube.'

They all turned to look at baby Louis, lying flat in Staff Nurse's arms. A cotton cover adorned with a print of Peter Rabbit was draped across his lower limbs. His breathing was shallow and in the silence that had descended on the cubicle sounded rasping and laboured. His belly was distended, his skin was raw and chafed and still ingrained with dirt, and his eyes, although not showing any signs of awareness of his surroundings, were now half open. Every nurse in the room, even Sister Paige, had tears in their eyes and one thought in their minds: the consultant might well have been right. None of them could imagine how such a poorly baby boy could ever regain full health.

Aileen took a deep breath. 'The night sister specialling him said that he woke for a little while this morning, and he was semi-conscious on arrival, but he appears to have passed out again. He drifts in and out. So, let's get this done, shall we?

The registrar from children's services is on his way, he is covering for Dr Walker and I want to get the tube in before he arrives and stops us. It's the only chance we have. Matron said we have to replace the front cover of the notes before the registrar arrives and put this one in the desk drawer for a week – that is if we have a week.' She handed the notes to Beth.

Staff Nurse stood up from the chair with Louis in her arms. 'Would you like to hold him, Nurse Tanner, whilst I assist Sister?'

Beth was miffed that Pammy had been chosen and not her. Pammy, on the other hand, was terrified at the prospect.

The tension in the cubicle was now palpable. They were defying the explicit instructions of the consultant. Even if it was on Matron's orders, to Pammy that still didn't feel right. But the sight of the pathetic child in Staff Nurse's arms made her heart tighten with pity. Her emotions were running wild and she didn't trust herself to speak – which was highly unusual as she had something to say about almost everything. She sat on the chair Staff Nurse had vacated and Staff Nurse placed Louis on her lap, along the top of her thighs. She cupped his body in her hands.

'Could you come and kneel down here, please, Nurse Harper, and place your hands very gently on each side of his head. Nurse Tanner, just in case, could you hold on to his hands. And don't move, either of you. It is important there are no sudden movements from Louis – he may come to and try to push my hand away. If you could hold his palms on top of his legs, Nurse Tanner, while Nurse Harper keeps his head still.'

Pammy flinched as she placed her hands over Louis's knees. They felt like fragile twigs beneath her fingers and she was afraid that if she applied any pressure, they would snap.

'Right, here goes.' Aileen smeared the end of the rubber tube with Vaseline. 'I doubt he has the ability to absorb anything other than watered-down milk, but it will be something, for now.'

Pammy increased the pressure on her hands imperceptibly as her palms were now hot and perspiring. Her eyes locked on to Beth's. Their heads were close together, Beth kneeling at Pammy's side. They were both aware that Louis was on the edge. It felt as though the air had left the room as Sister Paige nudged the trolley closer to them with her foot.

'Please stay asleep, little one, until this is over,' she said as she reached over towards him. From one raised hand snaked the orange rubber tube, their one hope at keeping death away from the cubicle door, and as she bent, a shadow loomed over them all.

Chapter 9

Aileen's sister, Josie, ran up the steps to her mother's house and rang the bell impatiently. 'You took your time,' she said as Gina flung the door back with one hand, holding a tea towel with the other.

'Sorry,' Gina replied. 'I was washing up in the downstairs back kitchen. It's hard to hear the bell from down there.'

Josie removed her gloves a finger at a time and, pushing them into her handbag, said, 'Yes, well, I'm going up to Mother. Bring the tea and sandwiches up.' She snapped the clasp shut and, receiving no reply from Gina, looked at her sharply.

Gina was standing with her hand still on the door knocker, and she met Josie's gaze.

'Please,' said Josie.

As if by magic, Gina came back to life, closed the door and said, 'Yes, Mrs Harrison, I will be up when the kettle has boiled. The sandwiches are already made.'

Josie didn't knock on her mother's door but let herself in and strode across the room to the chair. Her mother began laboriously making her way back from the window, where she'd been trying to see who was ringing the bell.

'Oh, Mother, really! You don't have to put on such an act

with me. I'm quite aware your walking's not as bad as you make out. It's Aileen and that girl, Gina, you need to keep in the dark.'

Mrs Paige quickened her pace and as she neared her chair began to walk almost normally. 'It is not an easy task, I can tell you, having to keep up this pretence,' she said. 'One day I will forget.'

'No, you won't, Mother. You know it's in your interest, and we don't want any more notions of you coming to live with me, do we? We all know, you can't abide the children. I have a very busy husband, and little Timothy and Susan to look after. If you ask me, Aileen has the easier life. Now, has she discussed Christmas Day with you?'

Mrs Paige looked defensive as she sank into her armchair. Josie was difficult at the best of times, but she could tell by her body language alone that today she was about to be more stubborn and demanding than normal. She tried to inject some maternal authority into her voice. 'I have no idea what she is doing at Christmas; it will be the same as always, won't it? She always works on Christmas Day. That hospital is her life and now she's a ward sister she'll want more than ever to be there on Christmas Day.'

Josie did not look happy with this response. 'That is as maybe, but I am afraid, Mother, this year it has to be different. We have been invited to the home of James's boss for pre-lunch drinks on Christmas morning and it is not an optional invitation. We have to go, and that means we can't be here to spend it with you. So you had better find some way to make sure that Aileen is here and doesn't go to work. There is no way she could protest that her job is more important than my husband's.'

'And how do you propose I manage that?' said Mrs Paige incredulously.

'I really don't know, Mother, but you have worked wonders for a very long time now, keeping Aileen here, pretending you can't walk. Getting her to stay at home on Christmas Day should be no problem at all.'

They both heard the sound of Gina's footsteps on the stairs and Josie swiftly changed the subject.

'Anyway, I saw just the hat I needed in Lee's...' was all Gina heard as she tapped on the door.

Biddy Kennedy sat in Maisie Tanner's parlour beneath a cascade of turquoise-and-cream-striped satin, holding a pair of scissors in one hand and a tape measure in the other. Maisie had been busy working in the parlour all afternoon, and a few hours ago little Stanley had delivered her a message in his usual manner.

'Mam! Mam!' he yelled through the front-door letter box, his eyes pressed into the opening and peering into the small dark hallway.

Being in the middle of pinning a hem and with a mouth full of dressmaker's pins, Maisie was unable to reply straight away.

Impatient at not receiving an immediate response and annoyed that his mother hadn't immediately appeared in the kitchen doorway, little Stanley grabbed the letter-box flap with both hands, shoved it upwards, put his mouth where his eyes had been and yelled once again into the dark void, at the top of his lungs. 'Mam! Mam!'

Maisie's pins flew from her mouth and landed in her lap as she struggled to extricate herself from under the yards of curtain material. 'Stanley, I'm coming! What is it?' she yelled back as she opened the parlour door and brushed the shreds of fabric from her apron.

'Mam!' Little Stanley was very relieved to see her. If she hadn't been at home, he'd have had to run down to the shop and see if she was there instead, and that could have been disastrous. Biddy had called him out of a game of football that he and the other boys were playing on the old bombsite and he was terrified that his mates wouldn't let him back in goal if he was gone for too long. 'Biddy says there's a meeting tonight and shall she tell them to all come to ours?'

Maisie placed her hands on her hips. 'A meeting, a week before Christmas? Is she serious?' She took the five paces to the front door and flung it open, causing little Stanley to almost fall into the hallway. The key dangling on the piece of string inside the door swung like a pendulum, knocking against the wall, then the door and back again. 'Did she say what it was about?' She leant on the door frame and slipped her hands into her apron pocket. 'Oh, come here you,' she said, 'you can hardly see your face for the dirt. It's freezing out here and you've got no scarf on.' She grabbed little Stanley by his jumper and, extracting her handkerchief from her apron pocket with her other hand, attempted to spit on it and wipe his mouth.

'Mam, get off me,' he squealed as he pulled backwards. 'Mam, I'm in goal!' He expected her to fully understand the importance of this comment. 'Give me a jam butty to run back with, quick, Mam.'

'Oh, come on then.' Maisie abandoned trying to remove half of the street from her son's face and turned to walk towards the back kitchen. 'Close that door. You can go back the long way, down the entry, and don't use the front door again for a message.'

Two minutes later, Maisie was washing the jam from her fingers and watching the retreating back of her precious son through the kitchen window. She rapped her wet knuckles on the glass. With his mouth stuffed full of bread and jam and his hand on the back gate, little Stanley turned towards her. 'Don't forget to knock on at Biddy's and tell her that I said yes.'

'Aw, Mam, do I have to?' shouted Stanley, glancing anxiously up the entry and wishing he had made a faster getaway.

'Yes, you do, if you don't want your backside smacking when you get back for your tea. And don't be late, I've a lot to do and I'm back at the hospital in the morning.'

Life had altered in the Tanner household since she'd started working at St Angelus. It had happened by chance, when someone had asked Emily one night if Maisie could cover for one of the WVS ladies who'd fallen ill, and that was it, Maisie was still there and now almost running the place.

The back gate crashed shut and Maisie smiled. Little Stanley was her scallywag, her cheeky, mischief-making son and best friend to his da. She would never let a living soul know, but he was also her favourite.

Biddy had been the first to arrive for the meeting, as usual. She was now sitting in the parlour while Maisie, who was in almost the same position she'd been in when little Stanley had turned up, finished off a hem of the curtains she was making for a customer on Princess Avenue. Dressmaking was the job she was paid for. Everyone in the Tanner house had a job; some had two. Even little Stanley had a paper round and earned his own pocket money.

'Would you look at that fabric,' said Biddy. 'Isn't it just

fabulous. To think, not so long ago you couldn't get a bit of material for love nor money, not unless it came from the Far East and fell off the back of the *Norry*. And then everyone was fed up with the kids walking round dressed like little Chinamen.'

Maisie glanced up at her friend, all sixteen stone of her, as she sat scratching the bright red scalp in between her tightly wound wire curlers. She tried to remember whether she'd ever seen Biddy looking glamorous. The image eluded her. Biddy had looked just the same before the war as she did now.

'Well, the others will be here soon, Biddy, so you go and carry some glasses through to the kitchen from in here.' Maisie nodded her head towards the glass cabinet which had once been her mother's pride and joy. Two of the panes of glass were broken, from the blast of '41. More than a decade had passed since and if Maisie had a pound for every time big Stanley had said to her, 'I'll get that fixed this week, love,' when he walked into the room, she would be a very rich woman and could give up making curtains for half the smart houses in Liverpool. 'And in the kitchen cupboard at the bottom of the press there's a bottle of Golden Shite. I was keeping it for Christmas, but what the hell, let's have it tonight, it's close enough.'

'No, it's not,' said Biddy. 'Still a week to go. You can have a cup of tea and on Christmas Eve you'll thank me for saving it.'

'No, Biddy, we don't have to because there's two bottles in the press. So do as you're told in my house, missus. I'm in charge here. Go and get the sherry out, I need one after the day I've had. I swear to God, I got lost under this fabric this morning and couldn't find a way out. Almost panicked, I did. If our little Stan hadn't come with your message, I could have been lost for ever. Honest to God, I was nearly late for my shift at the hospital.'

Maisie was grinning and it crossed Biddy's mind that she was the only woman she knew who was almost always smiling. 'I heard you had a bit of drama, what with Maura Doherty coming in with her younger daughter. She had a turn, didn't she?'

'Oh, God, it was awful. Do you know them? Sat in the pushchair one minute, the child was, and the next, the mother, Maura, took her off for her appointment and then I got a phone call from Sister Tapps asking me to send the father and their Kitty up to ward four. Did you hear how she was? I said to their Tommy, call in on your way out and let me know how she is, but he was probably too busy, what with everything that was going on. And they've others, haven't they? That poor woman.'

Biddy opened the parlour door and, clasping the handle, chuckled at the sign pinned on to it. It had been put there by little Stanley and was written in a child's hand, in capital letters: *OUT OF BOUNDS. NO ONE ALLOWED IN HERE OR ELSE DEATH BY WALKING THE GANGPLANK.*

Maisie looked up and saw Biddy's face. 'That's our Stanley. What's he like! A case, he is. If I've got curtain material all over the parlour, I'm not having anyone coming anywhere near it. It's good satin, that – this lady hasn't skimped. One finger mark on it and it's ruined. I didn't even ask him to write it, Biddy. The minute I told him how important it was that no one came in here, he ran off to make the sign. He's such a love is our little Stanley.'

Maisie's dressmaker's dummy had been brought down from her bedroom when her sewing business had begun to

Christmas Angels

take off and it stood in the corner of the parlour draped in fabric. The studded brown leather furniture had not been seen for some time as the entire room was now covered in pieces of tissue paper, lace and fabric. She looked around her as Biddy left. When she finished this set of curtains, hopefully in a couple of days' time, she would clear everything away and rediscover her parlour. She would decorate it and put up the tree. As she thought about the lights she had bought weeks ago with her earnings and stored away, a shiver of happiness ran through her.

Biddy found the Golden Knight sherry in the bottom of the press, hidden behind the flour, and seeing that there were indeed two bottles, she took one out and opened it. The pub sold more bottles of Golden Knight, known locally as Golden Shite, over the counter to women to take home than it served in the pub by the glass.

'Right, that's all I can do for tonight anyway,' said Maisie as she followed Biddy into the kitchen. 'My eyes can only manage a couple of hours at a time once I have to put the electric light on. Who else is coming tonight?'

'Elsie is on her way, and a few of the others, I hope.'

The back door flew open and a cold breeze ripped through the kitchen. 'And I'm here,' said Madge.

Maisie bent and threw a shovelful of coal on to the fire. With all the comings and goings and the door being opened every few minutes, the temperature would drop in no time.

'And Noleen is following me. I just caught sight of her at the bottom of the entry. There can't be a meeting around here unless we all come, Maisie – you know that.'

Maisie laughed. 'I should have known. And no one even knows yet that I've opened the sherry.'

153

Just then the back door opened again and Noleen walked in, followed by Branna. 'Look what we've brought with us, ladies.' Noleen held up a bottle. 'Branna and I went halves and we bought a bottle of the Golden—'

'Ooh, lovely, that's two of them then,' said Biddy, interrupting her. 'We're in for a good night. Anyone seen soft girl, Elsie?'

'Who are you calling soft girl?' said Elsie as she appeared in the doorway. 'Not me, I hope, because I bet I'm the only one who's brought any food.'

She was carrying a plate and Branna looked at it sceptically. 'Is that cheese?' she asked, eyes wide.

'Of course it's bleedin' cheese. Jesus, it's not hard to guess why people call you Irish stupid, is it?'

'But it's red. Cheese is not red,' said Biddy.

'Well that's where you're wrong. It is if it's called Red Leicester. It's coming into the shops everywhere round here now and, believe me, it's lovely on one of those Ritz crackers.' Elsie produced a box of Ritz crackers from under a tea towel in her wicker basket. 'Anyway, try for yourself. We are very adventurous in our house, you know. Martha's Jake, he loves his exotic food.'

Elsie laid the plate down in the middle of the table as Biddy set out the glasses and Maisie filled them with the amber liquid.

'Our Gina can't make it tonight,' said Branna. 'She's still up at the Paiges' house, waiting for Sister Paige to get home from the hospital. Can't leave that old harridan of a mother on her own, it seems.'

'Oh, what a shame,' said Maisie. 'She could have given us some ideas for the Christmas decorating competition Biddy tells me we all have to help with. She's good with her hands is Gina.'

Biddy picked up on Maisie's comment. 'Sister Haycock had a word with me today.' Emily Haycock was Biddy's boss and she would only ever refer to her as Sister Haycock, even outside of the hospital. The only person to call her Emily was Maisie, who had known her since she was a child. 'That's why I called the meeting. Matron has asked the girls on children's to organize it, but they are mad busy on kids' ward right now, busier than they have ever been. They're transferring all of the kids from ward four who won't be home in time for Christmas on to ward three now.'

'Is that because of Sister Tapps?' asked Branna. 'That's not happened before.'

'I don't know,' said Biddy. 'I suppose it must be.'

'That poor woman,' said Madge. 'It must be seven years ago since all that upset with the polio child – surely to God she should have moved on by now.'

Maisie began pouring the sherry from the bottle into the remaining unfilled glasses. 'That's what happens to some women when they've no children of their own – they become attached to other people's.'

'I wish I'd known what she was missing in her life,' said Biddy. 'I'd have sent mine to her the minute they were born.'

Laughter ran around the room, but the atmosphere had become more serious as they discussed Sister Tapps. 'What was the girl's name again?' asked Maisie. 'The one she became so attached to.'

'Laura,' said Madge. 'She was eleven years old. Had long blonde hair that Sister Tapps brushed every day. She was a polio case. With Tappsy in ward four for two years, she was.

Came in when she was nine, frail and withdrawn – and they say that the girl's parents never bothered much when she was in there. Her mother was one of the few who never complained about only being allowed to visit once a week. Mainly because she only visited about once a month, if little Laura was lucky.'

'I remember,' said Branna. 'I was cleaning on there. I saw it all happen the day little Laura was discharged, and I heard all the screaming too. Broke my heart, it did, I tell you. There wasn't a person working at St Angelus that day who didn't shed a tear. Everyone knew her – the porters, even old Cook in the kitchen. Sister Tapps used to get Cook to come all the way up to the ward to tempt Laura with things she'd asked her to make specially.'

Branna's eyes clouded over as she took a sip of her sherry. 'She was crying, poor little Laura, sobbing, putting her hands out, and her mother had to drag her along the floor, all the way down the main corridor. They were almost in a tussle and not one person went to help her because, really, everyone wanted Laura to break free and get back to Tappsy. Screaming for Tappsy, Laura was. Matron was there. She put her hands on Sister Tapps's shoulders and held her fast and I swear to God, if she hadn't, Tappsy would have run after that child and wrenched her from her mother's arms.'

They had all heard the story before, and from Branna's lips. But no matter how often they heard it, it always had the same impact; every heart around the table broke a little for the woman who had dedicated her life to making children well. A childless woman who had broken the golden rule and lost her heart.

'They were wailing in the ward kitchen, not because little Laura had got better and was heading home, but because everyone knew that Sister Tapps was a broken woman now. It felt different. We all just knew and no one thought she would ever be the same again. Two years and she never took a day off. She got that child up every morning and put her to bed every night. Carried her in her arms around the ward, she did, until the child got the use back in her legs. Laura Thomas, her name was, and I can tell you this, she was as attached to Sister Tapps as Sister Tapps was to her – loved her like a mother she did, for two whole years. That's what cut everyone up so much. The fact that she had awful cruel parents who couldn't give a fig whether she lived or died. No two parents could have cared less about a poorly child, and her pitiful god-awful screams, all the way down the corridor, and at Christmas too.'

The room fell quiet as they all lifted their sherry glasses in contemplation. Biddy crossed herself in silent prayer.

'Is Sister Haycock coming then?' asked Madge eventually. 'As she's given us all this extra work to do, on top of everything else.'

Emily Haycock had been a stickler about time-keeping throughout her life – until she and Dessie Horton became smitten with each other. Now she struggled to be on time for anything other than work. She seemed to spend her life in the shadows, sneaking between the sisters' accommodation block at St Angelus and Dessie's house, which was rather unfortunately situated next door to one of the nosiest women on the dockside streets, Hattie Lloyd.

'Dessie, I have to go. I'm supposed to be at Maisie's house for a meeting about the Christmas decorations competition.'

Emily made to haul herself out of Dessie's bed, but before she could move, he slipped his arm under her waist and dragged her back into his side.

'Well, I bet you didn't know that I am to be Father Christmas and take the presents to the children on Christmas morning.' His head flopped on to the pillow and he nuzzled his face into her hair as he spoke.

'I did actually,' Emily said. Even though Dessie's eyes were closed, he could tell she was smiling. 'I thought it might be a little arrangement you and Sister Tapps had between you, and I assumed you've been doing it for many years already. Do you think no one knows it's you? Is it you?' She turned to look at him as she laughed. 'What will you do this year, seeing as ward four is being closed?'

Dessie's head shot up off the pillow. 'Closed? How long for?'

'Oh, only for ten days or so, to give Tappsy a holiday – you know, Christmas somewhere other than with the patients she seems to spend every day of her life with.'

'Oh, Tappsy won't like that.' Dessie reached over Emily, took a cigarette from the bedside table next to her and, propping himself up, lit it. 'The kids on ward four, they are her life. Where will she go for Christmas? It will break her heart.'

Emily shifted herself up on to one elbow. 'Dessie, are you serious? Ward four isn't Tappsy's life, it's her job. Anyway, Matron told me she has family of her own. That's who she should be spending her Christmas with.'

Dessie blew his smoke into the air, away from Emily's face. 'But ward four, the kids, they are her family,' he said. 'She has spent every Christmas Day there since before the war. She doesn't know anything else.'

A frown crossed Emily's face. 'Do you always visit the children's ward at Christmas?'

'Me? Yes! I *am* Father Christmas – there is no other. Did you not know that? Sister Tapps, she makes the biggest fuss. Buys all the children presents out of her own money, and do you know what, I swear to God that when visiting time arrives at two o'clock, she finds any excuse she can to delay opening the ward doors. I always make sure I'm up there at two and I always say to her, "Time for me and you to have a glass of sherry now, Sister," and I put my arm around her shoulders and lead her into the office. If I didn't, she would never let the parents in at all. She never has the sherry though. She pours one for me and she has a cuppa and I always buy her a little present and she buys one for me. We open them at visiting time. Last year I bought her a little figurine of a roe deer, for her rooms, and a box of chocolates. She does have family because she has Christmas cards in her office and I peeped at them once.'

'She has personal cards in the office?' Emily frowned again.

'Yes, and why not? If she's working all day, makes sense, doesn't it?'

It made very little sense to Emily.

'She loves those kids and there's always a special atmosphere on Christmas Day. Having no kids of my own either, I've always quite liked being there with her too.'

'Yes, but, Dessie, they aren't her kids and they change every year. It's also not right that she has spent so many of her Christmases working.'

'Oh, she isn't working really – she loves it. It's not like work to Tappsy.' Dessie leant across Emily and stubbed out his cigarette in the ashtray.

Changing the subject, Emily asked him a very different question. 'Did you... do you... ever want children of your own?'

She was nervous about his reply. They were both older and there was no certainty that they'd have children once they were married. Their love for each other was new and fuelled by a high-octane combination of wonderment, passion and excitement. They were yet to discuss the big questions, and as far as Emily was concerned, this was the most important.

Dessie shuffled down the bed so that his eyes were level with hers and before he spoke, he placed a light kiss on her lips. 'I most certainly do,' he replied with a grin. 'How about you?'

Emily didn't trust herself to speak. Instead, she nodded her head, furious with herself that tears were springing to her eyes. Her face flushed as he kissed her again.

'You know the best bit about trying for a baby, don't you?' said Dessie. His voice was thicker, softer, as he stared into Emily's eyes.

'No,' she said, her own voice quizzical in response. The thought of trying for a baby terrified her. What if she failed? What if she was too old? It never crossed her mind that any future difficulties might be down to Dessie. There was so much they had to talk about, together, so many arrangements and plans for the future, but with Christmas coming and the hospital being so busy, there wouldn't be the time to discuss anything in detail this side of the new year.

'It's just that – the trying. That's the bit I'm going to be looking forward to.' He slipped his hand under her backside and pulled her directly into him.

'Dessie!' she protested. 'I have to get up, I'm due at Maisie's house.'

'Not so fast,' he said as he began to kiss her neck and throat.

'Oh, God, don't do that,' she murmured. 'I really have to go.' She placed her hands on to his shoulders to push him away, but all she succeeded in doing was redirecting his mouth down and on to her breast. Dessie, never a man to miss an opportunity, made the most of the moment. Emily smiled. She was lost. 'Oh, honestly, you!' she said as she ran her fingers through his hair.

Dessie lifted his head and grinned up at her. 'Am I winning?' he asked.

She tilted her head to look down at the boyish grin and bright eyes staring back up at her. 'What excuse am I going to make for being late?'

It was properly dark outside by this time and the bedroom fire was lit. Its orange flames seemed to dance across the ceiling, suffusing the room with a warm and comforting glow, enhanced by the spill of the street light just visible through the closed bedroom curtains. In the distance, despite the hour and the gloom, Emily could hear the children shouting as they played on the wasteland. The traffic on the river was quiet; for once there was no wind to set the mooring chains clattering and banging.

'You can tell them that a demon of a man forced you into his bed and had his way with you. They'll be jealous as hell when you tell them it was me.'

Emily threw her head back and laughed. 'I won't be telling them anything, but I'm guessing you would like me to, you show-off.' She slipped the full length of her leg over his hips and in one smooth and seemingly weightless movement he was on top of her. 'You are winning, Mr Horton,' she whispered before his lips came down on to hers. 'I give in. You can have your wicked way.' She wriggled her hips to position herself more comfortably under him. 'But be quick, I'm going to be late. And don't mess my hair.'

Dessie guffawed. 'Too late for that,' he said, and as she arched her hips closer to him, all conversation stopped.

'OK, then,' she gasped, 'take as long as you want.'

'Sister Haycock is supposed to be here by now,' said Biddy. 'It was her that called the meeting. She's got some ideas about the Christmas decorations – something about stars, I think. I hope she gets a move on, I thought I might make the late bingo.'

'Well, I think we can excuse her being late – young love and all that. Her and Dessie Horton can't keep their hands off each other,' said Madge.

They all grinned knowingly except Biddy, who blurted out, 'Don't be so bloody smutty, Madge. Sister Haycock isn't like that. She has a position of responsibility. The second most important person in the hospital until Matron appoints a new assistant.'

'Oh, give over with your precious Sister Haycock, Biddy,' said Madge. 'I'm telling you, mad for one another, they are. I saw them talking in the porter's yard today and I thought he was going to rip her clothes off there and then. When them two walk into the lodge, the paint peels off the woodwork, they are that hot for one another.'

'Well, I'm not sure about the temperature rising, but something does,' Maisie said.

Biddy looked as though she was about to explode. 'Go and wash your mouth out, Madge,' she spluttered. 'And you, Maisie. Full of filth, you are. It's all you talk about.'

'Ladies, ladies,' said Elsie. 'We are all adults and some of us are a bit older and wiser. We don't have to guess at these things. If she turns up tonight, we will know sure enough why she is late. Just like we did with Dessie a few weeks back. It's as clear as day when those two have been at it.'

They all began to laugh but stopped dead as they heard the latch on the back gate being lifted.

'She's here,' whispered Branna.

'Shall we have a little toast to the rundown to Christmas?' asked Madge.

'To Christmas,' said Maisie as she held her glass high.

'To young love,' they all said as they raised their glasses.

'Not so fast! Have you poured one for me?' said Betty Hutch as she slipped in and hung her coat on the back of the door. 'Jesus, Mary and all the saints in heaven, it's freezing out there.'

'Oh, here she comes. Did you smell that sherry down the entry, Betty?' said Biddy.

Ignoring Biddy entirely, Betty turned around and took the glass Maisie held out to her. 'Ooh, the best glasses, eh? Are you warming them up for Christmas?' She looked around. 'I thought Nurse Tanner and Nurse Harper were coming too?'

Maisie flushed with pride. There was not a single thing in the world that she loved more than hearing someone refer to their Pammy as Nurse Tanner. 'They are supposed to be coming, but I haven't heard a peep from either of them. And Sister Haycock isn't here yet either.'

No sooner had Maisie finished speaking than they heard a tapping on the door, letting them know it was Emily, the only person who knocked before she entered. The other women were so used to each other's houses, it seemed an alien thing to do, like knocking on their own front door. In the dockside streets there was nothing anyone had or did that the others didn't know about.

'Hello, everyone.' Emily popped her head around the door. She had at least moved past the stage of waiting for someone to shout 'Come in.' Born and raised on George Street, she and her stepfather had moved away after the bombing that had destroyed their street and killed her mother and brothers; they had gone to live with her aunt, where she had lost some of the ways of the dockside.

She laid her basket down on the table. 'Provisions,' she said with a flourish as she removed the cover to reveal a bottle of Golden Knight and a plate of sandwiches.

A chorus of oohs went up as she turned towards the door to hang up her coat. 'Blimey, is this the third bottle of Golden Sh—'

'Yes, it is,' said Maisie. 'And no swearing in here.'

Emily looked confused, being unfamiliar with the local term for Golden Knight. The group turned to watch her hang up her coat and stared at what resembled a fuzzy beehive on the back of her head.

'Oh, I remember those days,' said Elsie with a grin.

'Me too,' said Madge with a wink. 'A beehive a day keeps the doctor away.'

'What in God's name are you on about?' said Biddy as she followed their gaze.

'Told you so,' mouthed Branna.

'Lucky bitch,' muttered Elsie, and Maisie almost choked on her sherry.

'Who is?' asked Emily as she turned back to the table. 'What's wrong? Why are you all staring like that?'

No one liked to tell her that she still had stubble rash all over her face and that her lips were swollen from their recent bruising. Emily thought she had applied enough face powder to conceal her secrets.

'No one is staring, love,' said Maisie. 'Sit down and get those butties out. You haven't brought them to tease us, have you? Have you heard from our nurses today?'

'Well, I saw them at the Lovely Lane home this morning. Nurse Tanner and Nurse Harper both said they would be here this evening.'

'Not a sign of them,' said Maisie. 'Now, what's all this about a Christmas decorations competition?'

'I'm surprised the girls aren't here yet,' said Emily as she lifted her plate of sandwiches from the basket, laid it on the table and handed the sherry to Maisie.

'Are they still working? Did you see them this evening at all?' asked Maisie of Branna.

'I saw them,' said Branna. 'I can tell you this, they won't be leaving until night staff come on duty. It's been an awful day on children's. They've worked all through their split shift, bless them.'

All heads turned to face her and the room fell quiet.

'Why?' asked Maisie. 'Our Pammy was on a split shift today, she told me so herself when she came for her lunch on Sunday.'

'Oh, I know why. We aren't allowed to say,' said Branna.

Emily looked embarrassed as she accepted a cracker from the packet Elsie was holding out to her. 'I'm afraid Branna is right, Matron has sworn everyone to secrecy.'

'What, and so you came around here with a bottle of the Golden Shite just to keep a secret?' said Biddy.

Branna looked affronted at Biddy's rudeness and shot her an accusing look. But Biddy knew that if there was ever a secret to be told, Branna would break it before the night was over. They all knew that. Even Branna.

'Biddy Kennedy, how dare you cast an aspiration over me, looking at me like that.'

Emily spluttered on her sherry at the mispronunciation, though none of the others had noticed.

'I know what's going on,' said Madge. 'Jesus, haven't I been the one putting the calls from the police through to Matron all day long.'

'The bizzies?' said Biddy with alarm in her voice.

Maisie stopped smiling and looked concerned. 'Look, we have the rules, Sister Haycock. They always apply here. You know we share everything.'

'Yes, share and fix everything, if you ask me,' said Elsie.

'This is very serious, though.' Emily hesitated as she spoke and her brow creased into a deep worry line.

'Look, let me tell them, not you,' said Madge. 'That way, you're off the hook. There's never been a problem we haven't been able to help with and most of them, Matron doesn't even know about.'

'Let's drink to the rules first, though,' said Noleen as she raised her glass.

'The rules,' they all repeated as they drank.

'Now, what is it?' asked Biddy, who had been on a day off, because if she hadn't, she'd already have known. Biddy was the first with any news and was furious with herself for not having been at work.

'They had a shocker of a case admitted on to kids' during the night. An abandoned baby. It's being kept very hush-hush.

The police want to try and lure back whoever it was who abandoned him, so they don't want anything about it in the papers. I heard the chief superintendent telling Matron that this afternoon. Thing is, though, Dr Walker told the police the baby wouldn't last the night and as I speak here in your kitchen, Maisie, it's been twenty-four hours so far.'

An expression somewhere between pride and smugness crossed Maisie's face. 'I'm not surprised, seeing as they've got our Pammy on there now,' she said, raising her glass and draining the last of her sherry.

Emily was looking intently at Madge. 'I think I had better fill in here,' she said. 'Under the rules, of course?'

They all nodded furiously.

'Well, we aren't strictly following doctor's orders, it's more like Matron and Sister Paige's orders. The reason the little boy has lived so long is down to their nursing care.'

Maisie's eyes filled with tears. Madge picked up the thread. 'I know Matron has been ringing around looking for baby clothes and being all secret, like, as to why she needs them. They have a few on the ward but not many that would fit this poor child. She was wanting to speak to Sister Theresa over at the convent, but I couldn't make the connection for her. The poor kid, he's supposed to be six months but looks about three, apparently. I heard Matron say on the phone to the man from the CID that she had never seen a case like it.'

'Baby clothes?' Maisie jumped to her feet. 'I've got loads of them. I never throw anything away, not after the war – you never know when you're going to need things, do you? A little boy, you say? Wait there, Sister Haycock, I'll get some things now, and if the girls don't come tonight, you can take them in tomorrow.'

'Oh, Maisie, that's lovely of you,' said Emily. 'Of course I'll take them in. I'll take them to his cubicle myself. Sister Paige will be delighted.'

Minutes later, Maisie was back with two brown paper bags full of baby clothes. Emily looked inside.

'Don't worry, I've plenty more for if you ever get pregnant.'

Emily blushed. 'I'll just make do with delivering these to the baby on ward three now, if that's all right.'

'You do that, love,' said Maisie as she patted the back of Emily's hand.

As Emily bent down to slip the brown paper packages into her wicker basket, a strange feeling came over her. 'Oh, I think someone has just walked over my grave,' she said to Biddy, but no one picked her up on her comment. In truth, it was something quite different that Emily felt. After all her single, lonely years, people – Maisie Tanner, to be precise – were now talking to her as though having a child of her own was a realistic option. She couldn't help the grin that spread across her face or fail to notice the warm glow inside.

Madge was still talking. 'Anyway, there is a policeman on duty on the ward doors all of the time.'

'No!' went the chorus around the table. 'Why?' they asked as one.

'Because the little boy may have lasted this long, but he has made no improvement all day and they say he won't survive a second night.'

The atmosphere in the room altered. 'Whoever did that, she isn't fit to call herself a mother,' said Biddy with vengeance in her voice. 'She needs putting in a room full of young mothers. She would know how wrong it was then.'

'Calm down, Biddy, there may have been a terrible situation

here that we don't know anything about,' said Emily, though even she realized that sounded feeble.

'Situation? What situation could there possibly be that would force a woman to abandon her child like that? Women in the famine didn't abandon their babies, they fed them first.' Biddy picked up her handbag from the floor, opened the clasp and began rummaging around inside for her cigarettes. Pulling out her lighter, she looked up at Emily. 'There will be no sympathy from me or from many, I imagine, for a woman who does a thing like that, and so close to Christmas too.'

Madge leant across the table and refilled the glasses to create a diversion – always a useful tactic in the face of Biddy's agitation. Each woman whispered a 'Thank you,' and, raising their glasses, they all sipped on their drinks as they tried to imagine the place a mother must have been in to do such a thing.

'Right, ladies,' said Maisie finally. 'Sandwiches, before they curl up. And I'm going to try these Ritz crackers.'

There was a rustle of paper and the clanging of plates as everyone began to help themselves to food. Then Betty spoke again. 'There was another thing that happened today,' she said in her low monotone that cut through any noise more efficiently than if someone had blown on a playground whistle.

Maisie froze midway through unwrapping the muslin cloth from the sandwiches. 'And...?' She hated the way Betty paused for effect when she spoke.

Betty took a sip of her drink. 'The constable who brought the baby in, he had to come back to the ward today to give a statement to the men in plainclothes – all but taken over Sister Paige's office, they have, and they drink tea non-stop.' Betty took another sip of her drink and Maisie popped a sandwich into her already half-open mouth. 'Well, when he was leaving, he asked me did Sister Paige have a boyfriend.'

The room filled with an audible exhalation of relief. 'Ah, that's nice. Did you tell him she doesn't?' asked Emily, who knew Aileen Paige's situation only too well.

Betty gave Emily an offended look. 'I did not. I don't give any information away about anyone, don't you all know that?'

Emily's hopes came crashing down. 'And do you think he asked because he likes her himself, or what?'

Betty furrowed her brow and stared at Emily as though her earthly form had just been replaced by an alien. 'And how do you suppose I would be knowing that?'

Everyone knew that Betty Hutch didn't do idle chatter, and no one ever challenged the quality of her information. With Betty, you listened and if you knew what was good for you, you listened with quiet respect. All eyes turned towards Emily. Her faux pas was a result of her newness to the group. Silence fell upon the kitchen as all glasses were laid on the table.

Biddy made to speak, but it was too late, Emily had dived straight back in. 'Gosh, well, I would have done. Not obviously, but I would have asked him a few questions.'

Biddy opened her mouth, but the next words to be spoken came from Betty. 'Sister Haycock, I mop floors, clean toilets and wash windowsills – I have not the slightest interest in the romantic goings-on at the hospital. I hear nothing, I see nothing, I say nothing.'

The irony contained in Betty's words were lost on Emily. Betty had been asked about Emily and Dessie many times by nosey Hattie Lloyd, but, as always, Betty had put Hattie in her place, responding with the same answer she had just given Emily.

'Well, I will have to see what I can do,' said Emily, undeterred. 'When I take these baby clothes in, perhaps I can do a bit of matchmaking at the same time. It's my day off tomorrow, but I'll have a shot at it the day after, as soon as I can.'

'Oh, that little boy won't be on the ward by then – not a single person expects him to last another day,' said Betty. 'There won't be any need. He'll not even last the night. I told you.'

Noleen, Biddy and Branna immediately blessed themselves. 'Holy Mary, mother of God, be with him tonight, and in his hour of need,' said Noleen, the most religious of the group.

'Amen,' said Branna, and then Biddy asked, 'Has anyone called for Father Brennan? Do we know if the child is a Catholic?'

'I would say he hasn't been called for, no,' said Branna, looking alarmed. 'They are too busy trying to save his life to think of that. Run off their feet, they are. Have you any idea how hard those girls work?'

'I do, but isn't that just the trouble, no one knows anything about him. They're so busy keeping him secret and tending to his body, they've forgotten all about his soul.' Noleen's chair scraped back along the floor and she jumped to her feet, her eyes fixed on Emily. 'I'm off to the priest's house – would you be able to phone Matron and let her know? If the poor child isn't to last the night, then he can leave this world in the light and go straight to Jesus. He could be Irish for all we know.'

Seconds later, Noleen was flying down the path towards St Chad's. The nurses might have a life to save, but she would see to it that his soul was given the same consideration. Emily raced off to the nearest phone box to call Matron, the baby clothes tucked tightly under her arm.

Chapter 10

The girls were silent as they left the ward to walk back to Lovely Lane, both pondering on the busiest and strangest day they had ever worked. Pammy, as always, was the first to speak. 'Did you see his eyes?' she asked. 'I've never seen such sunken eyes on a child or such a desolate look in them.' There was a catch in her throat and Beth saw the tears in her eyes. She hooked her arm through her friend's. 'But he's safe,' Pammy continued, 'and, frankly, it might be good that he's unconscious. At least he doesn't know anything.'

'He didn't move when Sister passed the nasogastric tube,' said Beth. 'I've always thought that's the worst thing for a child to have to endure and I expected him to thrash about, but he was just out of it. He's barely been conscious or cried all day, not a peep.'

'Sister said he probably won't cry even if he does come round,' replied Pammy. 'That he's probably learnt that crying doesn't achieve anything. She said that most babies cry because they've come to understand that if they do, someone will come running. And there's something inside a mother that makes it impossible to ignore her baby's cry. Whatever kind of life little Louis has had, it hasn't been the sort where someone comes running whenever he cries.'

Beth pulled her cape close around her body as if to fend off the feelings of upset and uselessness that had swamped them both.

Pammy carried on talking. 'I think Sister Paige was expecting some improvement by tonight. She seemed really frustrated that there's been none. Can you imagine the patience she has? Putting that feed down him, almost a teaspoon at a time at first, straight into the tube.'

'That's why he hasn't vomited,' said Beth. 'It was just a drop he could absorb without demanding too much effort from his body.'

Pammy nodded and also pulled her cape tighter. 'Did you see Matron going into the office to talk to the policemen today? She looked awful and so disappointed.' She sighed and shivered in the late-evening chill. 'God, I'm whacked – it's been such a long day. I don't know about you, but to me it doesn't feel like Christmas is coming, with this going on.'

'I know what you mean,' said Beth, 'but in the next day or two everything might change. He will improve, or, sadly, he may not. And it's probably good that we've got the Christmas decorations competition to distract us. It's a shame we couldn't get to the meeting at your mam's – she would have cheered us up, wouldn't she?' She flashed a smile at Pammy. 'I bet she and the other ladies have hatched us some good plans.'

Pammy nodded back, glad of the change of subject. 'You're right. And we need to try and look more positive now – Matron will have our guts for garters if we say a thing to anyone at Lovely Lane about what's gone on today.'

*

Exhausted at the end of a very long day, Aileen wandered out of the ward and came face to face with Freddie, who was bounding up the stairs with a packet of sandwiches for Norman, to see him through the night shift.

'Oh, hello,' Freddie said, trying desperately to stop his usually pale complexion from turning puce. He could feel it happening and he felt like he wanted to die of the embarrassment.

Aileen just stood there, smiling at him. 'Hello,' she said. 'You didn't have to go home for those – Branna said she'd make you some in the ward kitchen.'

'Oh, no, we couldn't,' stammered Freddie. 'You haven't seen how much Norman can put away. I'm not kidding you – he would eat every sandwich on that trolley and come back for more.'

Aileen laughed. 'Where is he now?' she asked.

'He's gone to the... er...'

Aileen got the message and blushed herself. 'Oh, right, and he's going to be here all night?'

'He is that. How is the little fella?' he asked, his voice soft, his expression anxious.

Aileen felt her stomach flutter. 'He's still here.' Her smile had disappeared and her tone was serious. 'We've inserted a nasogastric tube and are trying feeding – you know the situation.'

Freddie nodded. 'Is there a chance then?' he asked.

'I hope so, I really do. We all do. We are fighting hard for him in there.' She looked back to the ward doors. 'Dr Mackintosh is coming back at ten to check on him. The night will be a long one, I imagine, and all we can do now is pray.'

Freddie cleared his throat, and then a thought struck him. 'One of the nurses mentioned that you're in a choir. I don't suppose you're doing the St George's concert are you?'

'I am,' said Aileen. 'I'm in the choir here, at St Angelus, although there aren't that many of us. There's a big joint rehearsal tomorrow.'

'I know,' said Freddie. 'It's in the Anglican cathedral.'

Aileen smiled enthusiastically. 'Aren't the acoustics in there just amazing! It makes our small choir sound huge and as if we can properly sing.'

She pulled her cloak around her and Freddie thought that, shrouded in the cloak and with her frilly white hat, she looked more like an angel than anyone he had ever seen in his whole life.

'Will you be there too?' she asked nervously. Was she being too bold even asking, she wondered. It sounded as if she hoped his answer would be yes – which, she realized, was exactly what she was hoping for. For the first time in years, she could hear David's voice in her head. It had come back to her, as clear as if he was standing next to her, as if he was encouraging her, pushing her on. She was holding her breath, waiting for Freddie's reply, and she swallowed hard before she looked back up from the floor.

'I will!' Freddie sounded positively excited. 'Would you fancy a drink and a bite to eat afterwards? There's a few nice places now in town where you can get food, you know.'

Aileen laughed and before she knew what she was doing or saying, she replied, 'Yes, that would be really nice.' But no sooner had the words left her mouth than her thoughts turned to her mother and she pulled herself up short. How could she? The smile crashed from her face and Freddie noticed.

'Is that all right?' he said. 'Don't worry, I'll see you safely home on the bus afterwards.'

Panic settled in the pit of Aileen's stomach. If he did that, her mother might see him. She frowned.

Freddie felt the moment slipping away and, confused, had no idea what to say next. So he repeated himself. 'Is that all right?'

Despairing thoughts flashed through Aileen's mind. Was it all right? No, it was not. It could never happen. She could not tempt fate and certainly not with someone who made her feel as Freddie did. Back when she'd dated David, Josie had been too young to have a boyfriend, but her father had been happy for her and had stuck up for her. Now both her father and David were dead. Things had just not gone her way – she had drawn the short straw. Josie was the one who had a life and Aileen's lot was to look after their mother. It was far from all right.

'I'm sorry,' she said. 'I don't think it is. I don't think I can. I have no idea why I said it would be nice.' She laughed. It sounded shrill to her own ears, as well as his. 'I can't. I'm so sorry.' And to Freddie's complete surprise, she ran past him and down the stairs.

Freddie stood on the spot and listened to her footsteps clopping along the main corridor. Lifting his helmet, he scratched his head as Norman lumbered around the corner from the visitors' toilets, breathing in hard and fastening the last button on his trousers.

'Aha, you got my sarnies. Good boy.'

Freddie held out the packet wrapped in greaseproof paper and didn't say a word.

'What's up with you?' Norman said. 'I didn't ask you to bring them, you offered. I was quite happy with the little pile Branna left me sat under that damp tea towel on the trolley in the kitchen. Me eyes aren't bigger than me belly you know.'

Freddie slumped on to the wooden bench he'd been sitting on for most of the afternoon. 'The strangest thing has just happened.'

Norman sat down next to him, causing the back of the bench to hit the wall with a thud. 'What? Stranger than finding that half-starved little lad in a garage? There's not much that's stranger than that. I'll remember that night for a long time, and the look on your face when you ran out with him in your arms. Was Trevor from the CID here today?'

'He was here all day,' said Freddie.

'Jumped-up little toad. Thinks he's the bloody chief, he does. I've been after getting into CID for the past six years, been waiting for the nod. Next minute, Trevor Jones, the moaning Minnie from Wales, is in the job.' Norman shook his head in disgust. 'Did Sister Paige burst out laughing when she heard his voice? Do you reckon he's been castrated? It's not natural for a man to talk like that.' Resentment had festered in Norman's gut ever since the day he'd walked into the refreshments room at the station to be told that Trevor Jones, who was younger than him and had fewer years' experience in the force, had been promoted to CID. His anger was never far from the surface and always quick to erupt.

'Pack it in, Norman, you'll get indigestion,' said Freddie, looking forlorn. He leant forward and placed his chin in his hands.

'What's the story then?' said Norman grudgingly, curiosity

supressing his resentment. 'Who do they reckon did it? Are they looking for the mam and dad?'

Freddie sat upright again and folded his arms. 'According to Trevor on CID, the parents were German and had a maid. No one knew them or spoke to them, apparently. CID are tracking them down now.'

'German, eh? They must have been brave, living in Liverpool after the war.'

'Well, it seems no one ever talked to them and I'm guessing it was a one-way thing,' said Freddie.

'Were they Jewish?'

'Apparently not. If they had been, we would have more information because then people would have spoken to them.'

'That'll pass one day,' said Norman. 'You wait and see. As the generations age, people will feel less resentful. And anyway, it wasn't the German people's fault, was it?'

Freddie found that hard to imagine. Liverpool had been hurt particularly badly in the war and there'd been many civilian deaths. Liverpool people never forgot. They could be your best friend and the most warm and generous, funny and friendly people ever, but cross them and you would be crossed for life. They also stuck together: Scousers against the world. If you were an outsider and you kicked one of them, everyone in Liverpool would shout ouch. He crossed and uncrossed his arms several times, then sighed.

'What's up with you?' asked Norman. 'You can't sit still.'

'It's Sister Paige,' said Freddie, now staring glumly at the corridor floor. 'I asked her if I could take her for a drink after the choir rehearsal and she said yes, and then quick as a flash she said no and ran down the stairs. I mean, I know it's a woman's prerogative and all that to change her mind, but the words had barely left her mouth before she came out with the exact opposite.'

Norman peeled back the greaseproof paper on the packet Freddie had given him and peered inside. 'There's nothing odd about that, lad,' he said. 'Women change their mind all the time. They are the most contrary things to deal with, you know. Have to be handled with kid gloves. That's why I've never married. Is this Shippam's paste? Branna's made me egg and cress.'

'You're as good as married,' said Freddie.

Norman bit into his sandwich. 'No, I am not. I go back to my own house every night. I'm not always in my own bed mind, but it is an arrangement that suits me very well. I've never understood women, me. Never.' He was more interested in the provenance of the sandwiches than Freddie's love life. 'Did your landlady make these?'

Freddie nodded again. He had never felt so miserable. 'What do I do, then? Just leave it? Pretend she never said yes the first time?'

Norman laughed out loud. 'No, lad. Jeez, you really don't get it, do you? The reason she said yes and then no was so that you would ask her again, another time, like. They like to keep you guessing and wondering. They don't give much away, women don't, and they make you work for everything. She's just starting as she means to go on. She is a bit special, though, lad – top drawer, that one. Are you sure she hasn't already got a fella of her own?'

Freddie frowned. He was confused but now a bit more hopeful. 'No. I mean yes. If she did have, she wouldn't have said yes in the first place, would she?'

'There you go again, asking me a question about a woman

and expecting a simple answer. Freddie, mate, there is no simple answer. You will just have to try again.'

'So I should ask her then? Shall I ask her at the rehearsal?'

Norman was about to place an entire half a sandwich into his mouth. 'I would say so, because if you don't, there is only one thing going to happen and that is sweet Fanny Adams and you will be left swinging your truncheon all on your own.' He began to laugh, a long, dirty laugh, and his shoulders heaved up and down as he did so.

Freddie looked at him in disgust.

As Norman stopped laughing, he wiped his mouth with the back of his hand. His face was flushed red and his eyes were bright. 'Oh, where's your sense of humour, Freddie? My, you have it bad, don't you? Look, if you don't ask again, you have no chance, me old son. Do it. Find her at your rehearsal thing and ask her straight up. Say, "This is me last offer, Sister Paige. I won't be asking again."'

Freddie grinned, visibly cheered by Norman's endorsement of his own instincts. 'Right, I don't understand any of this, but that is what I will do. I know she likes me, Norm, I can see it in her – like it's in me, you know. It's there, the spark everyone talks about. I've never had it before, but you know, when we talk, it's as if we talk to each other every day. It's like she's not Sister Paige but someone I've known for ages.'

'Oh dear,' said Norman between bites. 'Just be prepared for a broken heart, my lad. I told you, she's top drawer, that one. So are you, mind, but she is a bit special, everyone says so. Oi, any ciggies in your pocket? My advice doesn't come for free, you know. And go and fetch me a cuppa, there's a good lad.'

★

Gina had only been home from the Paiges' for an hour or so when her mam came clattering through the back door, humming to herself and in good spirits after her meeting with the other St Angelus domestics round at Maisie Tanner's.

Sister Paige had got back from the hospital later than usual, but Gina didn't mind. Her mam had told her that Aileen had one of the most important jobs at St Angelus and that Gina was to do her best to help her in whatever way she could. 'She can't be saving babies' lives as well as scrubbing her own floors – that's your job and what she pays you for,' Branna had told her.

Gina would have loved to be the one saving babies' lives and not the floor scrubber. She loved babies. When the day was done and she pulled the bed covers over her shoulders, she closed her eyes and saw the face of her future child. She dreamt about the clothes it would wear and the pram she would buy. She longed for the day when she would become a mother and, as a natural consequence of that, an independent woman of substance, with her own home and her own life, doing things her way.

There were so many new things coming into the shops, she could barely wait. Gina was the opposite of her mother – she drooled over ornaments, frivolous cushions and lamp-shades with fringes. Every week, something she could never have imagined appeared in Blacklers' windows. But wait she had to. She had promised her mam that she wouldn't court anyone until she was past her seventeenth birthday. There were enough lads locally to choose from and that was something else she thought about as she drifted off to sleep. Which one would it be? In the meantime, she scrubbed floors.

Branna set her empty basket on the kitchen table and shot

a concerned glance at her daughter. 'Hello, love, you all right? You look done in. Has that Mrs Paige been giving you the runaround again?'

Gina nodded and rolled her eyes. 'God, Mam, she's a right old witch. An evil woman, she is. You should see and hear the way she talks to Sister Paige and carries on about being "a poorly woman". I swear to God, there is nothing wrong with her.'

Branna had lost no time in getting on with her chores and was already wiping down the kitchen table. She walked over to the sink to shake out the crumbs from the dishcloth. 'Don't be ridiculous, love – she is a poorly woman, there's no doubt about that. No one is right again after a stroke, Gina. A stroke is a stroke and most people die from them.'

'Oh, I know that, Mam. What I mean is, she's not a well woman, but, well...' Gina hesitated. She had thought it would be a good idea to tell Branna, but now she just felt mean. It was one thing to know what Mrs Paige did and keep it in her own head, another altogether to say it out loud.

'It's just that she's not as poorly as she makes out. I swear it – I've watched her. She pretends she can't move in the chair, but then as soon as Sister Paige leaves for work, she's up and out of that chair as fast as you like.'

Branna placed her hands on her hips. 'No! You are kidding me, Gina, aren't you? That can't be right. It's common knowledge she's lost the proper use of one of her legs and one of her arms, so unless she's hopping across the floor – and I'm guessing she isn't – then she can't be. And, besides, what about when you are on your day off, when Sister Paige is there on her own, she must see her do that too. It can't just be you she's hopping around for.'

'She's not hopping, Mam, you eejit.' Gina was giggling now at the thought of the grumpy Mrs Paige hopping across her bedroom floor. 'She is walking, Mam, I tell you. Oh, not perfect, mind, and she does use the stick, but she can put some weight on that bad leg, and she does walk. And she's quick too. I wondered about when I'm not there too, but I don't think she does it then.'

Branna was perplexed. She had no idea what to make of her daughter's revelation and a series of thoughts were flashing through her mind, the first of which was: if Mrs Paige could walk, why was Aileen having to pay for someone to sit with her?

'How do you know this, Gina, because surely if she's keeping it secret from Sister Paige, she'll be keeping it secret from you too?'

'Mam, I know because the keyhole in her bedroom door is a great big thing and when I polished it the other day, I took the key out and put it on the table next to the door on the landing.'

'Pass me those dishes while you talk,' said Branna. 'I want to get to bed soon, my feet are killing me.' She shuffled over to the sink and filled the enamel bowl as Gina carried the dishes over.

They both worked at cleaning jobs all day, but when they were at home, they shared everything. As Branna often said, cleaning their own home was as nothing compared to St Angelus. 'We don't have much, which means there's not a lot to polish,' was her common refrain, and she wasn't lying. Branna wasn't interested in material possessions and the house was almost bare of ornamentation or frills. There was nothing tolerated in her house that didn't have a useful purpose, just a selection of ornaments depicting the Stations of the Cross on the mantelpiece, a clock and a mirror over the fire in the parlour, the minimum of furniture, and a mere two rugs that needed beating.

Gina let the dishes slide from her hands into the bowl and turned away to collect the teacups. 'Anyway, sometime later she rang the bell and I was on the landing, standing on the chair, cleaning the big window. She must have thought I was downstairs in the scullery and would have to run back up. I heard her clomping about and I don't know what came over me, but I could see the key was still on the table, so I got off the chair, bent down and had a look through the keyhole. And, Mam, it's the size of my hand, so I know what I saw, and there she was, hobbling back from the window to the chair, as fast as you like.'

'Get the tea towel,' said Branna, up to her elbows in soapy water. 'You can dry and talk at the same time.' Looking sideways at Gina, she asked, 'Did she know you'd seen her?'

'No!' Gina shot back, shocked. 'If she had, I think she'd have got Sister Paige to sack me. She's not a bit like Sister Paige – really mean she is. Never says thank you or please and I've never heard anyone moan so much. I'm glad in a way that she's stuck to her room, otherwise I would have to be creeping around her all day long.'

Branna passed the last plate to Gina. 'Does that other daughter of hers ever come to visit? The one who lives in the Old Roan. Does she know she walks about?'

'That's their Josie. She comes and has lunch with Mrs Paige once a week and do you know, she's as bad as the mother. I feel so sorry for Sister Paige, you should hear how they talk about her. So mean, they are. The sister has married well and, my God, can't you tell. That's all the mother cares about – a right money-grabber she is.'

'Most people are, Gina. You will learn that in life. For almost everyone, money is more important than family or faith. Although it beats me why she should be so concerned. They live in a nice house and seem to be very comfortable.'

'Oh no, I don't think they are.' Gina stacked the dried plates on to the shelf on the press. 'That's something else I overheard. Mrs Paige was telling Josie that they needed all of Sister Paige's wages to pay the bills, and she said, "There's very little left, Josie. If Aileen had ever got married and moved away, I would have had to sell this place. I wouldn't want any strange man to have lived here. Married to Aileen or not."'

'Well, well, well, just shows you, you never know, do you,' said Branna, a thoughtful look on her face.

'Mam, do you think I should tell Sister Paige that I saw her mother moving around like a good'un?' Gina folded the wet tea towel and laid it across the bar of the range. Then she crossed her arms and leant against the blackened metal door and warmed her backside.

'Cup of tea before bed?' Branna held the kettle up.

'Please. What do you think? Should I?'

Branna filled the kettle, placed it on the range, folded her own arms and leant against the bar right next to her daughter, their arms touching. Mother and daughter: workers, survivors, confidantes. 'Hmm. Let me think a second.'

Gina watched her mam. She could almost hear the cogs in her brain turning.

'The thing is, Gina, you have to weigh up all of the options. If you tell Sister Paige and she believes you and is happy to know, then nothing really alters for you. But if she isn't happy and doesn't believe you, you could be out of a job. My advice is to keep your own counsel. But I tell you what, I'll ask the mafia. We're having a night of making stars and moons around at Maisie's house in a day or two – to help decorate the children's ward for Christmas. Matron wants us to enter a competition and she's asked everyone to help. Would you believe it, so close to Christmas! We decided on it tonight – we're going to do the Christmas Eve sky with the Star of Bethlehem for the shepherds to follow. Dessie and Jake are going to pin them all up on to the ceiling for us.'

'Oh, that sounds lovely,' said Gina. 'Mam, are we going to be all right for Christmas – for money?' she added nervously. 'With Da having being off sick from the docks for so long.'

Branna put her arm around her daughter's shoulders. 'Well, I'm not going to lie to you, if we didn't have your money coming in, it would be hard. But no, I've been paying into the clubs religiously, every week. Never missed one, so we're going to have a whopper of a turkey and all the trimmings, and you would not believe the amount of fancy things coming into the shop and I've got almost five pounds in me club book.'

Gina grinned from ear to ear. 'Does me da know?' She raised her eyes to the ceiling and the room above, where her father had taken himself to bed as soon as he'd finished eating, having exhausted himself coughing.

'Behave! Tell him? He'd go down there, carrying on and demanding they give it back to him. He'd be shouting and saying by rights it was his – you know what he's like – and then he'd spend it in the pub and on fags in one night, what I took a year to save. Not bleedin' likely.' Branna gave her daughter a squeeze. 'Why don't you come to the shop with me after work tomorrow and choose the Christmas treats? I'm going to be calling in there every day now on my way home from work to make sure I've got everything in. I can only carry so much at a time and I'm not telling your father. I'm hiding it all in the copper boiler in the scullery. We'll get all the fresh stuff on Christmas Eve and pick up the meat then too – that way he can say what the hell he likes 'cause I'll have spent the bleedin' lot.'

Gina grinned. Her and her mam outwitted her da every single day. They were a team and Gina loved it.

'I can't, Mam. Sister Paige is singing in the Christmas choir and they're all getting together for a big rehearsal,' she said. 'I'm going to be late tomorrow because she's asked me to cover for her while she's gone.'

'Well at least that's something nice poor Sister Paige can look forward to,' said Branna. 'Anyway, it's better to keep yourself to yourself, queen. Only tell your mam, no one else. I'll consult the mafia girls and see what they think, eh? They might think of a way we can let her know, like. Stop her being so worried.'

The kettle began to whistle behind them and they both lunged forward together, away from the range, united as always, mother and daughter acting as one.

Chapter 11

Matron could hear the telephone ringing as she mounted the stairs from the main reception area of St Angelus to her accommodation on the first floor. Blackie trotted obediently at her heels, grumpier than usual, having spent his day in the care of Elsie, Matron's housekeeper. Having known him since he was a puppy, Elsie took none of Blackie's nonsense and Blackie was never happy about that.

'Come along, slow coach.' Matron tugged at his lead and chivvied him up the last few steps as she removed her keys from her coat pocket with her free hand. Once through the door, she dropped the lead to the floor and hurried to the black Bakelite phone that stood on the hall table. It was almost dancing with irritation as it rang out.

'Hello? Matron's rooms.' She pressed the phone to her ear and held her breath in her throat as she waited for a reply. It was 8.30 p.m. No one ever rang her at that time unless there was a problem.

'Oh, Sister Haycock, it's you!' she exclaimed, audibly relieved. 'I thought it was Night Sister.' She would not admit it even to herself as she began to breathe normally again, but her heart had been thumping with the dread of it being Night

Sister on the phone, about to tell her that baby Louis had passed away.

During her time as matron hundreds of children had died at St Angelus. Her wards had seen countless cases of whooping cough, pneumonia, rheumatic fever and polio, not to mention the litany of infectious diseases that had a disproportionate impact on the poor, already weakened as they were by bad diets, and cold, damp, rat-infested slum housing. But anti-biotics were now becoming freely available and things were changing. Premature death was not the routine outcome it had once been and she wondered whether the greater number of more hopeful prognoses had eroded her natural defences, leaving her more vulnerable and emotional.

Over the years, she had learnt to deal with the inevitable sadness that came with the death of a child and to move on to care for the living. She had become inured to the acute pain and grief in a parent's eyes – she had had to. She had seen nurses brought to the point of sobbing, and sometimes she had to send them back to Lovely Lane, to the care of Mrs Duffy. Left on the children's ward, they were no use to anyone and certainly not to the surviving children who were poorly and afraid. Those nurses always returned the following morning, remorseful and slightly ashamed. Some she would find outside her door, wanting to apologize for having become so distraught, and although she put on her most professional face, she understood. Some of the children had been with them for months and the nurses couldn't help but form a bond – it was only natural, but she couldn't say that. She always accepted the apologies, assured them it would not be held against them on their performance record and wrote a thank you note to Mrs Duffy. There would never be another Sister Tapps. She would guard against that at all costs.

But Louis... He had touched a cord in her and it was a shock to realize that she dreaded hearing the all but inevitable news that he had passed.

Emily began to speak. 'Matron, I've just been round at the Tanners' house, and it seems that the domestics all know about baby Louis. Biddy has asked me to find out whether or not Father Brennan has been sent for. You know what they're like...' Her voice tailed off. It was her own secret that she was a non-believer herself; life had been too cruel for her to have taken a different course.

'I had thought about sending for the priest, you know. I always do. It was just so busy on children's today, and, you know, at times we thought he was about to rally, but then...' Matron's own voice faltered. 'I think, maybe, sadly, I am just in denial with this little one. I keep on expecting him to pull through.'

Emily could sense the sadness in Matron's voice. This was a new experience – she'd never heard it there before. 'Would you like me to come to the ward, Matron?' Emily didn't like to mention that Noleen Delaney, the most devout woman who worked at the hospital, had already hot-footed it to tell the priest that he was needed. 'I can see to Father Brennan, and besides, I have two bags of baby clothes Mrs Tanner has sent that would fit him, if he makes it.'

Matron was about to ask how Mrs Tanner knew. She trusted Nurse Tanner, she knew she wouldn't have told her mother, and besides, she'd been on the ward for a straight twelve hours before heading back to Lovely Lane with Nurse Harper – she would have had no time to tell anyone anything.

Matron opened her mouth and closed it again. There was no use her asking for the unexplainable to be explained. The goings-on in St Angelus were sometimes beyond her. She had to accept that she wasn't the only one with the interests of the hospital at heart, and sometimes she was very definitely kept in the dark. 'Well... are you sure you wouldn't mind doing that, Sister Haycock?' she asked.

'Of course I don't mind. Look, I'll be there in fifteen minutes. I'll tell Night Sister I'll stay until the morning. It's my day off tomorrow, as it happens, so that makes it even easier.'

Matron could barely hide her relief. 'Thank you. It won't be long before the plight of this poor child gets out, one way or the other, but thank you. I will away to bed now.'

'You do that, Matron, because you need your rest. Goodnight.'

Emily stepped out of the phone box and hurried straight to Dessie's house. She stopped there just long enough to place the brown paper bags of baby clothes in a wicker basket and to lay the table for Dessie's breakfast. She pulled her hood up over her hair, scooped up the basket, scribbled a note for Dessie and propped it up against the jar of homemade marmalade which she set next to his plate and knife. He would find it when he got back from the pub.

Just as she was about to leave, she remembered that she had one more call to make, to the priest's house. She would call herself, just to make sure he knew the urgency of the situation. In a trice she was out of the back door and stepping into the dark, damp entry. She nipped back into the phone box on her way to St Angelus and had a brief conversation with Father Brennan's housekeeper, who informed her that he was not at home. She impressed upon her that it was a matter of life and death and then she hurried on along the cobbles and up to the hospital.

The ward was in darkness when she arrived. The red night lights cast an eerie glow and as she walked up the stairs she noticed that PC Norman Bartlett's black uniform both absorbed and reflected the light as he sat at the entrance to the ward.

He jumped to his feet when he heard her footsteps. 'Who might you be?' he asked, one hand flying to his leather truncheon-holster as he spoke.

'I'm Sister Emily Haycock,' she replied as she moved the basket handle from one hand to two and held it out in front.

Basket met truncheon. Basket won and Norman's hand flew to his helmet as he raised it in acknowledgement.

'Matron has asked me to call over and check on baby Louis. We've sent for the priest, Father Brennan. Has he arrived yet?'

'Oh, sorry, Sister.' Norman replaced his helmet. 'No, no priest. But that doesn't sound good, does it?'

Emily looked down. She would never discuss the condition of a patient with anyone, not even a police officer, not without good reason. 'Well, we will see,' she said. 'If Father Brennan does arrive, just send him into the cubicle, would you please.'

Norman almost laughed out loud. 'Father Brennan? You'll be lucky. He's usually asleep in his cups by now. Speak to him yourself, did you? Loves a bit of the Irish, does the father.'

Emily turned towards the door. 'He will be here,' she said, with more confidence than she felt.

As she opened the ward doors she was greeted by the familiar sight of the night nurses gathered around the large wooden table in the bay at the bottom of the ward. This was where they always sat at this time of night, when the children had been settled, the medicine round finished and the sluice and clean utility tidied. The dirty laundry would have been packed into the wicker basket on wheels at the end of the ward, ready for collection by the porter's lad, who would replace it with a basket full of clean linen. Breakfast trays had been laid up by the auxiliary in the kitchen ready for the morning. In the pristine milk kitchen, bottles of feed stood lined up on the marble shelf for use during the night. Each had a chart next to it, ready to be completed and placed back on the end of the cot by the nurse who gave the feed.

The fire in the grate cast a halo around the bay and Emily could make out the white caps bobbing around. She looked up at the clock. They would be finishing their reports now and enjoying a cup of tea. The ward was still and quiet. Emily had always loved nights on children's ward. The large ward windows that looked out on to nothing but the black night outside; the stillness and the calm; the hushed footsteps and the sound of snuffled snores drifting on the air. Maybe it was because she thought she would never have children of her own; or perhaps it was that in the sleeping faces of the little boys she would see those of her late brothers, Richard and Harry.

Emily thought children's ward was special, but she'd loved working nights on adult wards too. She was especially attentive if she found a patient who was unable to sleep, perhaps worrying about work, home, their family or their children. She would make them a cup of tea and, breaking all the rules, would sit on the bed and chat through their concerns in the small hours, the time when demons plagued patients the most. It worked every time – on her next round the patient would always be fast asleep, totally oblivious to her creeping up with the torch and collecting the empty cup and saucer.

Emily smiled at the sound of the night nurses' hushed chatter and the sight of the auxiliary nurse in her daffodil-yellow uniform lifting her knitting out of a bag and settling herself into one of the large leather visitors' chairs. She knew that baby Louis would be in cubicle one and so, not wanting to disturb the others or force them to do anything different because she was on the ward, she slipped into the cubicle with her basket.

'Oh, hello, Sister Haycock.' Newly qualified Night Staff Nurse McGee jumped to her feet. She was clearly taken aback by Emily's sudden arrival.

'Hello,' Emily replied. 'Matron knows I am here, and the priest has been called.'

Staff Nurse McGee blessed herself. 'Oh, thank goodness. I was going to call Night Sister and make just that suggestion.'

'No improvement then?'

'None. Sister Paige fed him half-strength milk down the nasogastric tube every ten minutes this afternoon. He even had a drip up, but it was useless. It's as if he doesn't want to wake up. He's also burning up, all over. His pulse and respirations are fast. The poor thing has nothing to fight with. He's very, very poorly.'

Emily placed her basket on the floor. 'Baby clothes,' she said by way of explanation.

The night staff nurse smiled. 'I know it sounds daft, but I was just thinking of giving him a bit of a wash. Night Sister told me not to take his clothes off though, and to keep him warm, but he's boiling up as it is. He still smells a bit and I thought that maybe it would cool him down, and the stimulation might do something. Get the blood flowing, you know? But I don't know, maybe I'm just being fanciful.'

Emily was bent over the cot, looking at baby Louis. Turning to the staff nurse, she smiled and began to undo the knot of the headscarf tied under her chin. 'Not at all. That sounds like a jolly good idea to me.' And then she dropped her voice to the lowest whisper. 'Night Sister can be a bit old-fashioned about these things. What harm can it do? My own theory, and I teach this in the school now, is that if we can bring the temperature down using damp sponges, then the aspirin has a fighting chance at keeping it down. We are asking a lot otherwise, and nothing else appears to be working. It's too late to worry about him getting sick. Why hasn't he got a steam tent?'

Staff Nurse looked embarrassed and shrugged her shoulders. 'Maybe because he's a "no further treatment" baby? Although Dr Mackintosh said his breathing isn't too bad yet, and he's right, he does seem to be managing, it's just the awful high temperature.'

Emily breathed in sharply. She had nursed premature babies in her day and been instructed to hang a sign on the cot they were laid in, LTP – Leave To Perish, and that had tested her resolve to the extreme. Seeing a breathing baby on maternity, wheeled into the sluice room without the warmth of its mother's arms around it, the mother already having been told her baby had died, had been very hard to deal with. But she was as shocked as anyone that the decision had been taken and applied to a six-month-old. 'Look, have you had your break yet?'

Staff Nurse stuttered her reply. 'Oh... no... but I'm not bothered really.'

'Well, tell you what, you fetch me a bowl of nice warm water and a bath trolley and then you go and tell the others that I am in here for the night now and then you can all have your breaks.'

Staff Nurse knew better than to argue with Sister Haycock, and without another word she slipped out of the cubicle and into the sluice room to do exactly as she had been ordered.

Emily picked up the charts at the end of the cot and saw that Louis had been given the feed of watered-down milk just five minutes earlier. Removing the cloth draped over the jug, she sniffed the solution and noted the syringe ready to be attached to the thin orange rubber tube snaking out of baby Louis's nostril and pinned to the nightgown he was wearing. She slipped her hands under his burning back and head and lifted him as gently as it was possible to do. His bony form felt like a small bag of kindling; the only part of his body to weigh anything at all was his skull.

Sitting down carefully, she began cradling Louis in her arms, just as Staff Nurse pushed the trolley through the door. 'Thank you,' she whispered. 'Off you go and have your break now and then take charge back from the student nurse. Tell her she is relieved. I will stay in here for the night. Matron will have informed Night Sister I'm here, so she may just pop in to say hello later.'

Emily was letting her know in the nicest way possible that just because she would be trapped in the cubicle, the night nurses would still be monitored on the ward.

As Staff Nurse left the cubicle, Emily felt the heat from baby Louis seeping into her side through her dress. Her nostrils filled with the stale odour of vomited milk and sleeping child. One thing was sure, baby Louis would spend the entire night in her arms, not in the cot. She was the sister in charge of Louis for the following ten hours and she would look after him her way. If they were making it up as they went along, why shouldn't she? Hadn't the child spent enough time without knowing the warmth of a mother or even another human being next to him? Judging by the state of his skin and hair and the bed sores on his back and ankles, it had been far too long.

She half stood, crouching over the baby with her body as if to protect him, and picked up a towel from the bath trolley. Laying it across her knee like she would a napkin in a restaurant, with great tenderness she set Louis down on her lap and removed the hospital gown. Despite herself, she gasped at the sight of his skeletal form and distended belly. His nappy, as dry as a bone, had been folded into four in order to fit him, but it still hung halfway down his legs. Emily undid the large blue-topped safety pin. The thick nappy raised the bottom half of Louis's body and legs almost clear of Emily's lap, allowing the heat to escape.

She stood up and as she carried him to the trolley she had a brainwave. He was so tiny that instead of just washing him she could actually bathe him in the enamel bowl. She dipped her elbow into the water – the temperature was perfect. Checking that the baby soap and towel were within easy reach, she slipped Louis into the water, supporting him with one arm while using the other to wash him down with the translucent brown Pears baby soap that Sister Paige had chosen to use on this ward.

She massaged his warm soapy limbs and scooped the water over what hair he had. She could see it was working as the water, even in the night light, was turning murky, and, more importantly, as it trickled down his limbs, his body began to cool down as the water in the bowl warmed.

For the briefest second, she froze as she thought she saw the stiffening of his little legs and sensed the slightest tension in his tiny shoulders as they pushed against her hand. But then his cooled and flaccid form flopped from side to side in the crook of her arm. Her mind was playing tricks, imagining things – it was what she had wanted to happen, she had almost willed it.

But Emily could definitely feel the life flowing through his veins; she could feel him struggling to survive. He was not closing down, had not died yet. She refused to believe he would not last the night if he was cradled and given the love he had been missing so far. She would will all the love she held for him to flow straight from her heart to Louis's and pray that somehow this poorly child would understand that he was wanted. That they – Matron and the staff of St Angelus – were on his side, fighting desperately, each and every one involved in the plan to defy the doctor's orders, for his survival. She quickly sat down with him in her arms and patted his skin with the towel. Rubbing with long strokes across his limbs, bringing his blood to the surface to cool. She reached over and took the thermometer that staff nurse had placed on the bath trolley in a kidney dish of diluted Dettol and shook the mercury down with two swift flicks of the wrist. Lifting his legs by the ankles, she gently inserted it into his anus. She had no fob watch to count down the minute and so with her free hand, she stroked his arm and guessed the time instead. His temperature had plummeted and was now within normal limits. Emily smiled, happy knowing that the aspirin could now do its work and the chances of him keeping down and absorbing his feed were greatly enhanced. She drew up the milky solution into the syringe and, removing the rubber bung on the end of the nasogastric tube, made to insert the feed.

'We are flying by the seat of our pants here, Louis, but this is hardly brain surgery,' she whispered. She decided to increase his dose to eight fluid ounces. 'You've been tolerating four for three hours now.'

Emily was sure that if Sister Paige were there, she would agree. They were doing what nurses sometimes had to do, often on instinct alone, when they felt that someone was worth fighting for even though the doctors had long since given up. But defying orders was a serious risk – they could lose their jobs. In such cases, it was absolutely essential that they made the right call and won.

She slowly injected the syringe into the nasogastric tube. It was as if Louis was sleeping deeply and contentedly as he neither stirred nor made a sound. Emily fixed her eyes on his chest and tried to count his respirations as it moved up and down. They were slower now than they had been before his bath. She placed her fingers on his wrist and although his pulse was too fast to count without the aid of her fob watch, it felt less thready. Did she dare think that it felt stronger?

She had noted that the streptomycin had been given throughout the day and would be due again at midnight, ground up in a solution and passed into the tube at the same time as a dose of dispersible aspirin. That's one stat dose of streptomycin when he was brought in and four on the ward over the day, she mused. If it's going to have any impact at all, we should begin to see something soon. She looked hopefully down at the form in her arms, but there was nothing, no sign of waking or moving. Wherever Louis was, it was far away.

Wasting no time, Emily lifted a clean nappy from the trolley, then leant down to reach into the basket at the side of her. From the clothes Maisie had supplied, she extracted a lemon matinee coat but then put it back down again. She would leave him loosely covered in the towel and his limbs exposed in order that the heat could evaporate. If Night Sister called in, she would be horrified, but Emily was driven by her instinct that the old way of keeping babies and children with a temperature wrapped up, was a dangerously wrong thing to do. Instead, she lifted out of the basket a crocheted baby blanket to lay him on, which Emily guessed had probably once been wrapped around Nurse Pammy Tanner.

Within minutes she was sitting with him huddled into her chest, her arms firmly circled around him, and his back, arms and legs exposed to the air and still cool to the touch.

Staff Nurse popped her head around the door with a cup of tea in her hand and two biscuits perched on the plate. 'How's it going?' she asked. 'Oh, goodness me, would you look at him! He looks better already. He has a bit of colour.'

'Do you think so?' said Emily, feeling secretly pleased with herself. Being director of the school of nursing meant that she missed the day-to-day contact with patients, and that had always been the part of the job that she had loved the most. 'It's so hard to tell in here. I think it's just because he's clean. You can see the colour of his skin now. Would you take the bath trolley out for me, please? I didn't want to leave him.' She was embarrassed, apologetic. One of the rules of the school of nursing was that you always cleared up your own mess and never expected someone else to clean your trolley away, no matter how senior you might be.

'Sure, of course I will.' Staff Nurse kicked off the brake,

grabbed the trolley with both hands and began to wheel it towards the door. 'I'll leave you to explain to Night Sister why he isn't covered up if she calls in.' She winked as she spoke, something she would never have done had they been on day duty. The night brought with it an air of informality. Status was forgotten until the dawn came. 'Are you not going to put him back in the cot?'

'No, I'm not. I'm going to keep him in my arms, something I'm guessing he's not used to. No sign of Father Brennan then?'

Staff Nurse opened the cubicle door to remove the trolley. 'None at all, I'm afraid.'

'Well, let's hope we don't need him. I'm going to settle myself in the comfy nursing chair with this little one after his next tube feed. I've upped the dose.'

'Good on you, I was thinking that too. He's not passed urine, which is not a good sign, is it...'

Emily smiled and held up the damp towel. 'He has now,' she said as she revealed a small dark-brown stain. 'Pass me a nappy from that trolley before you take it, please.' She felt a surge of excitement run through her, and yet she had only been with this child for half an hour. His kidneys were working and that was a new vital sign of life they could pin their hopes on, a justification of their defiance.

Staff Nurse grinned and handed one over. 'Don't you move. I'll pass you a soapy cloth and the zinc and castor oil cream. That looks quite concentrated, it will burn his skin.'

Five minutes later, Emily was settled back in the nursing chair. The lights were off and apart from the faint chatter and the clatter of metal knitting needles, the ward was almost silent. She strained to hear the sound of Louis's breathing and gently brushed her fingers across the delicate papery skin on his shoulders and along the back of his neck.

The clock on St Chad's struck ten and Emily bent her head and kissed the top of Louis's head. 'Do you hear that, little one?' she whispered. 'That's the church bell and you are going to hear it chime on the hour all night and safely into tomorrow morning. Do you hear me?'

She kissed his downy hair again and her eyes filled with tears as she hugged the baby closer to her.

Through the night, Emily sat with Louis in her arms, his head tucked under her chin, his weak body pressed against the towel, flat against her, his back and limbs kept cool and exposed, his ear up close to her ribs, breathing in time to her own heartbeat. She administered the feed every fifteen minutes without fail, and the medicine at midnight and 4 a.m.

'I can't possibly sleep,' she whispered at one point to Staff Nurse, who came in every quarter of an hour and was now crouched down at the side of her chair.

'I don't see how not,' said Staff. 'Have a rest with him. We've been in bed all day, but you've been up and done a day's work already. Besides, what does it matter? What else can you do?' Using the lever on the side of the feeding chair, she tilted it back so that Emily and Louis could at least try and doze together.

Emily couldn't answer her and knew she was right. So, safely tipped back in the chair, she allowed herself to drift off between the feeds on the provision that Staff Nurse popped back in every fifteen minutes to ensure that she didn't miss one.

The moment Louis turned the corner came just before six.

As Emily's eyelids fluttered open, she could sense the dawn pushing through the blackness of the winter's night. She looked up through the window and saw the ominous clouds parting to reveal a strip of inky blue dawn sky. She heard a tug blow its horn as it made its way across the Mersey and out to the bar to meet a ship that had docked overnight, waiting to be guided into berth. The bore must be early today, she thought. Having grown up so close to the dockside, she was as aware as anyone of its rhythms. The klaxon wouldn't sound for two hours yet, but when it did, the men would file down the steps and find at least one ship ready and waiting to be unloaded.

Her thumb unconsciously caressed the back of Louis's head. He was still lying flat on her chest, the side of his face now pressed to the side of her breast, close to her heart. She looked down and a profound thrill shot through her as two huge, dark, unblinking eyes stared back up at her. Louis was awake!

Her breath caught in her throat. 'Oh, my goodness! Hello, little one,' she whispered. And then the second shock hit her as she saw that grasped in Louis's hand was the complete nasogastric tube. 'Oh my Lord, how did you do that?' She gasped and sat forward just as Staff Nurse came into the room.

'Well, would you look at that,' Staff Nurse said. 'Wide awake or what?'

Emily grinned. 'I know, and he's pulled out the flaming tube. I knew I should have kept my eye on him.'

'Well, that's not a problem. If he's got the strength to pull, he should have the strength now to suck. Why don't we try him with a bottle? It's worth a go.'

Ten minutes later, Emily could not keep the smile from

her face as Louis guzzled away at the eight ounces of fluid – half formula, half water – that Staff Nurse had made up and brought in. Louis neither smiled nor cried as he sucked, his entire focus being concentrated on extracting the contents of the bottle, but all the while his eyes never left Emily's and, in turn, Emily's never left his.

'Well I never,' said Staff Nurse, 'he's so much better. I think we should try him with another couple of ounces in thirty minutes. We could try not watering it down this time?'

While Emily had been feeding Louis, Staff Nurse had slipped a thermometer into his bottom. Now she removed it. 'His pyrexia has gone,' she said, shaking the thermometer as she spoke. 'It's ninety-nine. Under control. You did that, with a little help from the streptomycin.' She smiled. 'It always amazes me how rapidly babies and children recover. Literally dying one minute, right as rain the next.' She placed the thermometer into the kidney dish of diluted Dettol she had brought with her into the cubicle and, turning to Emily, noted that neither Emily nor Louis appeared to be aware that she was there. It was as if they were in their own exclusive world.

The bottle was finished. Emily grinned from ear to ear and, lifting Louis on to her chest to wind him, she looked up at Staff Nurse. 'Isn't he marvellous,' she said. 'If he keeps this down, we'll have cause to be optimistic, I'd say.'

Staff Nurse made no comment. It was as plain as the morning that was rolling in that something had happened. Sister Haycock had broken the golden rule. She hadn't nursed Louis like a nurse would but more like a mother and Staff Nurse could see it in her eyes as clear as day. Sister Haycock had fallen in love and there could be only one outcome – her heart would be broken. It was the unspoken code: never become involved because the heartbreak could be lasting and painful and in some cases, as with Sister Tapps, debilitating. 'You need to be careful there, with that little fella,' she said.

'Oh, don't worry,' said Emily, immediately understanding the nurse's meaning but still not taking her eyes from those that were staring back up at her. 'I'm not Sister Tapps.'

'That's a relief then, because you know the older staff on here, they still talk about her. About how she persuaded the doctors to keep that little girl in here for far longer than she should, and how after the girl was finally discharged, Matron had to send Tappsy on holiday to recover because she was so broken.'

'Yes, I know,' said Emily. 'Tappsy's breakdown is the worst-kept secret on children's. But I promise you, that's not happening to me. I love this little fella already, but I know the rules all right. I have to, I teach them.'

'Good, because it sounds awful. Did you know that the little girl threw her teddy at Tappsy when her parents dragged her away and now it sits on the windowsill in her office and woe betide anyone who touches it.'

Emily hadn't heard that bit of the story before and her heart crumpled with sympathy for poor Sister Tapps. But she was well aware of the outcome, and of the fact that from then on Matron had insisted that all nurses in the school be taught about detachment and professional care.

Staff Nurse had been taught this by Sister Haycock herself, and yet here Sister Haycock was, seemingly unaware that she had broken her own rules, disregarded her own teaching. As she lifted Louis's face up to her own and smiled a smile of such kindness and love, Staff Nurse almost groaned out loud. Sister Haycock was in for a fall. But as her actions had obviously had a huge part to play in the revival of baby Louis, it would seem that nothing could be done about it.

'Isn't he beautiful,' said Emily as she held Louis into her. 'The streptomycin has done its work. Sister Paige will be so pleased and if it wasn't so early, I would ring Matron myself.'

'There's still a long way to go, Sister.' Staff Nurse sounded her note of caution. 'I should think he'll be here for a long time before he can go anywhere, given the state of him.' She crouched down on to her knees and laid her finger into the palm of Louis's own. 'Hey, little one,' she cooed. And Louis, although now exhausted from the effort of feeding and unable to move his head to see where the voice had come from, responded by lightly grasping her finger. Staff Nurse smiled fondly and said, 'Well, would you look at that.'

Emily felt a stab of unreasonable jealousy shoot right through her heart. A frown crossed her brow and, imperceptibly, she moved Louis closer to her. 'Wonderful, such an improvement,' she said, but her words were tightly spoken and Staff Nurse could tell. 'Could you get me some more dispersible aspirin, please.'

The informality of her manner through the night had disappeared as quickly as the black sky and Staff Nurse had received the message. Sister Haycock was now pulling rank, and, worse than that, she had found an excuse to remove her from Louis's presence. As she left to fetch the keys for the medicine trolley, she felt a sense of foreboding. Louis had pulled through, but at what cost to Sister Haycock.

As her footsteps receded, Emily's eyes never left Louis's. 'Don't worry, little one, I will take care of you and we will get you better,' she whispered. She scanned Louis's face for a sign of recognition. How much did he understand, she wondered. How impaired was his development? Had anyone ever spoken to him, or loved him, even?

'I will put Auntie Maisie's nice clothes on you and you will be looked after so well on ward three – everyone will love you.'

Again, that stab of jealousy at the thought that Sister Paige would be with Louis and in charge of him all day. She had no power to make good on her promise to look after him. Louis was not her responsibility. When she left the ward that morning, she would have no excuse to return, other than to assess her nurses.

Get a grip, Emily, she admonished herself as, in a flash, she realized what she was doing. Breaking her own rules, defying her own teaching.

She smiled down at him, beaming with joy. But before she could pull back her heart and temper her feelings, Louis sealed the deal. It was as if he sensed what Emily was thinking, so he threw out his only weapon and Emily was snared for ever. The corners of Louis's mouth lifted. A twitch at first, which halted Emily in her thoughts. But he persevered, demonstrating the determination that had seen him survive for longer than he should have. His facial muscles were weak, it wasn't easy, but he tried again and this time the twitch at the side of his lips spread into a crease and then he beamed his final salvo up at Emily.

Tears sprang into Emily's eyes at the same time as they sprang into Louis's. She laughed, wishing Dessie were next to her to share the moment. Being very careful not to hurt him, she held Louis into her chest. Her tears dropped on to the top of his now cool and almost bald head and she felt something burn in her heart: a need that was like nothing she had ever felt before; a longing, a desire, and at the same time a fulfilment. For all she knew, this could have been the first time baby Louis had ever smiled, and his smile had been directed at her, Emily.

'That makes us special,' she whispered into the room. 'Very special.'

Chapter 12

Gina had been working flat out at the Paiges' since first thing and it was now well past five o'clock. She'd just finished scrubbing the grate when she heard the latch rise on the back door. She picked up the cloth from the floor, wrung it out and let it plop on to the metal grille in the bucket. Pushing back an errant curl that had escaped from the headscarf she wore tied with a knot at the nape of her neck, she pulled her forearm across her face. She was hot from the exertion of scrubbing, and her pale, freckly face was flushed. She leant back on her heels as a weary Aileen Paige walked towards her.

'Are you still all right for tonight?' Aileen asked.

'Of course I am. I said I would be, didn't I?' said Gina kindly. Since finding out about the wicked game that Mrs Paige was up to, she'd felt a protective fondness towards the hard-working Sister Paige. Even more so since she'd discussed it with her mam. 'I've kept the fire stoked and made sure the water is hot so that you can have a nice bath.'

'Oh, you angel,' said Aileen as she flung her headscarf on to the hall stand.

'No,' said Gina, 'that is definitely you, not me.'

Aileen laughed. It wasn't often that Gina heard that sound. 'And how is Mother?'

A note of caution crept into Gina's voice. 'Oh, you know, just the same as always.'

'Did she eat her lunch?'

Gina thought how Sister Paige must never stop worrying about people – at the hospital all day, and now here she was straight into enquiring about her mother as soon as she got home.

'Yes, she ate all of it.' She swallowed hard. That wasn't quite the whole story.

Gina had gone into the room after lunch to collect the tray and it was empty, but Mrs Paige denied having eaten her meal. She'd held the plate up to Gina and snarled, 'I couldn't eat that disgusting food. You gave me mouldy bread. I threw it into the fire.'

Gina's eyes had shot to the fireplace. Nothing was burning, nothing smelt and she very definitely had not made the sandwiches out of mouldy bread. 'Oh, I'm sorry, Mrs Paige, shall I make some more or would you like me to take you to the bathroom now?'

Mrs Paige hadn't bothered to answer. She just pretended to struggle up from the chair, putting on her usual elaborate act as, awkwardly and with no consideration for Gina, she leant her full weight against her. Whereas previously Gina had been happy to help her, now, knowing what she did, she felt resentful. Not least because her back often hurt for hours after she got home.

Gina glanced up at Sister Paige. If she rumbled her, she'd say she'd forgotten what Mrs Paige had told her about the sandwiches.

'Oh, well,' Aileen replied, oblivious, 'that's something at least. I'll go up and see her before I get ready to go out.'

'Are you enjoying the choir, Sister Paige?' asked Gina. She almost bit her lip. Her mother had told her to speak only when she was spoken to, but she couldn't help it because Sister Paige was so friendly. She wanted to talk to her. The days were long and lonely with just Mrs Paige for company and she always looked forward to getting home to her mam and the chance to have a good natter.

'Oh, I am. I really am. The singing, it just lifts your heart, and... you know... you forget everything else.' Aileen blushed. 'I'm not actually a very good singer, but it doesn't seem to matter. No one cares, and the thing is, when we all sing together, it sounds wonderful.' Her face lit up.

Gina grinned. 'Lovely. That sounds really nice. I feel like that sometimes at Mass, when we're singing. Can I come and hear you on Christmas Eve?' Now she really did flush. She wanted to take her words right back. She was overstepping the line.

'Oh yes. Anyone can.' Aileen seemed unperturbed that Gina was talking to her as though she had known her for ever. 'We'll be on the steps of St George's Hall, and then those of us who are from St Angelus will go back there and sing some more carols – first on the hospital steps and then inside, stopping at the entrance to every ward.'

'Will your mam be all right on her own?' asked Gina. 'With it being Christmas Eve?'

'Oh yes.' The smile vanished from Aileen's face. 'Josie and her family always spend Christmas with her. I always work Christmas Day, so they have no option. Either they come here or Mother goes to them. It's the one time of year I put my foot down. My sister and her husband and children will probably take Mother to the Grand for her Christmas lunch and I will have mine on the ward.' Her Christmas would be like every other: fun on the ward, in the company of patients and colleagues, then back to a dull evening at home. She quickly changed the subject. 'If that's Mother's supper on the range, I'll take it up to her, but I won't be long. She doesn't really mind me being in the choir – I just think she worries about me doing too much.' Aileen was lying and they both knew it.

Gina had the sensitivity to look away and, lifting herself off her knees, carried the bucket to the door of the scullery.

'I'll have a quick bath and change and then we can have our supper together.'

Gina almost stopped in her tracks. She was both touched and surprised. She had expected to eat her supper alone, at the big kitchen table. Not only was Sister Paige going to eat with her, it sounded as though she really wanted to. It struck her that Sister Paige must be lonely too. She wanted the company of someone younger and Gina's heart went out to her.

Aileen was slightly late and the choir had already begun to rehearse as she slipped in through the back doors of the cathedral. The sopranos were furthest from the door and she tried to edge her way inconspicuously around the sides and up to her section. As she turned into the first row, the first pair of eyes she was aware of were Freddie's. He was standing with the tenors, awaiting instruction from the choirmaster. For a moment he stopped concentrating and she stopped trying to find her place and it was as if no one was singing, as if just for that split second the world had ceased to turn.

She felt herself sinking into the large brown eyes with the curly lashes. Neither of them blinked or swallowed – their moment was frozen and they both felt the significance. This meant something. By the time they heard the choirmaster shouting out 'Stop, everyone! Stop! What is going on with the tenors? Freddie, are you singing with us tonight, or not?', their fate was sealed.

The cathedral was freezing and the rehearsal was to last for two and a half hours. Everyone kept their coats on as they sang and most people were still wearing their woollen gloves. In the break halfway through the session they gathered round the glasses of hot squash and biscuits that had been laid out on a trestle table covered in a long white cloth. Buoyed by his earlier conversation with Norman, Freddie came straight over and spoke to Aileen.

'You made it then. I thought that after such a busy couple of days with the little one and the ward you might have changed your mind.'

Aileen smiled; she couldn't help herself. Being in his presence made her feel as though a flame had been lit in her heart. 'Oh no. I didn't want to miss this. Besides, it's a good distraction. We don't often get a case like little Louis's, thank goodness,' she said. She picked up a glass of warm squash and handed it to Freddie. 'Do you want one of these?'

He smiled down at her. It was a dangerous smile and it did something to her. Her tummy flipped and her mouth dried.

'Thanks, I do. I won't be able to sing much longer if I don't have something to drink. I thought I'd be too tired for tonight, but I don't feel tired at all now.' He was feeling confident: she had smiled back at him and he knew he hadn't got this wrong. Her eyes were looking straight into his and they were smiling, dark and beckoning. 'I know you said no yesterday, but that was after you said yes – can I have a choice which answer it is I accept?'

Aileen laughed and almost choked on her squash.

He took advantage of the moment as he lifted the glass out of her hand and left her free to root around in her handbag for a handkerchief. 'Well, that definitely sounded like a yes to me, so, here, I have an idea – let's go to a pub, a nice pub – I know one, I checked it out before I came in here tonight. We can just have the one drink. I'm not being pushy, honest. I can either see you on to the bus afterwards, or if you will let me, I can see you to your door, it's up to you. I'm not a monster, you know – we can even have a nice conversation about something other than work.'

He was now holding out the squash for Aileen as she went to put the handkerchief away. She would have to tell him no. Her mother would never allow things between them to go any further. She'd make life very difficult for both of them, so what was the point? Aileen almost remonstrated with herself as she played for time and pretended to be searching for the right pocket in her handbag to put the handkerchief in. She was Aileen the carer, not Aileen the girlfriend or lover or wife. Aileen the servant of her very sick mother was who she was. She clicked the clasp shut and as she turned her head towards him a voice rang out.

'Back to your positions, everyone. We only have one more rehearsal before Christmas Eve.'

Freddie was speaking. 'Quick, drink up. You'll need it to keep you warm.' He smiled and as he did so, his hands went to the scarf that had slipped off her shoulder and was hanging down the back of her coat. He reached over her, picked it up and wrapped it around her neck. 'You need to keep your throat warm too. You don't look after yourself, you don't.'

Her heart melted. It was so rare to have someone expressing concern about whether she was warm or cold. She didn't think about her words before she spoke them. Quite the opposite, in fact – if she'd verbalized what was running through her mind, she would have refused his invitation. She simply heard herself replying, 'Why not! That would be nice.'

They both stood there grinning until their moment of warmth was interrupted. 'Freddie, Sister Paige, do you think we have all night to wait for you?' And as they turned around, it felt as though every member of the choir was looking and smiling at the two of them.

Mrs Paige had become more and more irritated with Gina as the evening had worn on. She'd rung the bell almost incessantly.

'The fire is low, why have you allowed it to burn down so much?'

Gina ran off to fill up the bucket and soon had the fire blazing up the chimney. 'Is that all right for you, Mrs Paige?' she said. Receiving only a grunt in response, she made her way back down to the kitchen, where she had decided to take the opportunity to clean the silver she'd found in a wooden canteen. Even if Sister Paige was at the hospital on Christmas Day, it would be nice to do the silver for her, just in case. She laid newspaper on the kitchen table and lined everything up. She was just opening the baking soda paste she'd found in a jar under the sink when the bell rang again.

'Blimey, what now?' She threw the cloth down and hurried back up the stairs. She didn't want Aileen to come back and find her halfway through her job. 'Yes, Mrs Paige?' she said breezily as she entered the room, no hint of irritation in her voice.

'Fetch me my whisky and water, would you. It's in the cupboard over there.' Mrs Paige pointed to a polished mahogany cabinet fixed to the wall.

Gina had wondered what went into the glass she removed from the bedside table every morning. It always smelt stale to her and left a translucent brown stain in the bottom.

'I have it for medicinal proposes.'

Gina made her way to the cabinet. She always made sure there was a clean glass back on the bedside table every day, but she would have to go all the way back down to the kitchen for the water. She supressed a sigh, lifted the bottle out and, placing it on the table beside Mrs Paige, said, 'I will fetch some water then, but you will have to show me how much to pour in.'

'I will indeed. I wouldn't expect you to know how much is the right amount.'

Ten minutes later, Gina had taken Mrs Paige to the toilet, fixed her cushions and poured her whisky, but instead of going all the way down the stairs to the scullery, she sat on the chair on the landing for a minute, just in case she was called again.

She heard the glass being placed on the table a number of times in quick succession and then she heard the chair squeak. She's getting up, Gina thought, and she quietly shifted herself off her seat, placed her eye at the keyhole and watched as Mrs Paige walked over to the window.

She was not as fast as she was in the mornings, Gina would give her that, but there was no drag on what was supposed to be her bad leg, like there was when Gina was in the room. She definitely lifted the leg and placed it back down again.

Mrs Paige switched off the lamp that stood on the table at the window and stood next to the navy velvet drapes. Gina wondered whether she'd turned the light off deliberately, so that she couldn't be seen from the street. Then Gina heard the squeal of the brakes on the bus as the clock struck ten. Aileen had told her that she might be on the ten o'clock bus. Flip, she thought, I wanted to finish that silver before Sister Paige got home. It didn't even occur to her to worry that she'd been working non-stop for fifteen hours or that it would be later still by the time she got home herself. She rose slowly, ready to sneak down the stairs, aware for the first time that her limbs felt heavy.

Just as she went to put her foot on the top stair, she heard a loud gasp from Mrs Paige and then her stick banged on the floor, twice. This was her way of demanding attention, as Gina was well aware. It was either that or shouting.

Gina moved to the window on the landing and parted the curtains to see what it was that had made Mrs Paige gasp. A smile spread across her face. Under the lamp-post at the bottom of the street, a man was kissing a woman. He had his arms around her waist and the woman he was embracing was definitely Sister Paige.

Gina almost clapped her hands together with excitement. Poor lonely Sister Paige, at the grand old spinsterish age of thirty, was being kissed. The kiss was brief and although she felt that watching was wrong, she couldn't bring herself to turn away. Under the lamp-post in the deserted street they drew apart and talked briefly and then he turned on his heel and headed back down Green Lane, towards the bus stop.

Gina looked away as Sister Paige thrust her hands in her pockets and walked towards the house. Just at that moment she heard Mrs Paige start hobbling back to her chair.

Sister Paige! Who would have imagined it! Gina grinned to herself as she raced back down to the kitchen and the unfinished silver. And why not? Why shouldn't she? Gina was pleased for Sister Paige. She couldn't wait to tell her mam.

On the other side of the bedroom door, Mrs Paige slumped into her armchair, her mind racing at what she'd just seen. What if Aileen had finally found herself a young man and was planning to leave home? She knocked back the remains of the whisky in her glass and glared at the window. Even more pressing was the problem of Christmas Day, now that Josie had decided to leave her in the lurch. She knew it would take something big to tear Aileen away from her ward duties that day, but she was determined to find a way. Gina had left the whisky bottle and the jug of water on the table. She lifted the bottle with ease and poured herself a large measure. If Aileen dared to comment that it was disappearing faster than usual, she would blame Gina without any hesitation at all.

By the time Aileen arrived in her room to put her to bed, she had hatched a plan. She would make her daughter suffer for her selfishness.

Chapter 13

The morning was sharp and it felt like Christmas for the very first time. The front steps of St Angelus were covered in a silvery frost that sparkled underfoot as Emily made her way into the school of nursing. She was desperate to pop into ward three and see how baby Louis was doing – she'd not heard any news of him in the twenty-four hours since she'd left him – but first she needed to see Biddy.

'Morning, Biddy, did Sister Ryan leave any paperwork for me?' she asked.

'Morning to you, Sister Haycock. You're in early. Yes, she did. There's a little pile waiting for you over there on your desk. Did you have a nice day off? Sounds like you needed it, from what I heard, after your night with that poor wee baby. Jesus, Mary and Joseph, what a sad case. And I understand Father Brennan didn't turn up?'

'No, he didn't,' said Emily. 'And I have to say – although you know we aren't supposed to talk about it, so hush – it was no bad thing he didn't come. I kept baby Louis in my arms all night and I know it sounds daft, especially coming from me who teaches that everything has to be done by the book, but I think it made a difference. Oh, Biddy, he's adorable.

Six months old, the notes say, but so small and fragile and helpless.'

Biddy had returned to pushing the Ewbank carpet sweeper over the rug in front of the fire, but now she stopped abruptly. It was as though someone had trickled icy water down her back. 'Well, don't go getting all attached – he's not your worry. Sister Paige is in charge of ward three now, your work is done there. You won't be needing to go back. We'll be seeing you at one for lunch as usual, will we?'

The way Biddy had dismissed her and her news about baby Louis made Emily feel uncomfortable and upset. She had wanted to tell Biddy much more about her night. About how little Louis had smiled up at her and snuggled his head almost under her arm until she had to lift him on to her shoulder. She frowned. She wanted to answer Biddy back, to find something to say to set her straight and let her know that of course she would be seeing baby Louis again. She had to, didn't she? Sister Paige needed help. But even as she thought that, she knew it wasn't true. Instead, she replied, 'I suppose you're right. There's no one better than Sister Paige.'

No sooner had the words come out than she was overcome with jealousy. She was shocked – she'd never felt like that towards anyone she worked with. She had voluntarily and happily chosen a non-clinical route as the director of nursing; it was what she had always wanted to do and she enjoyed it. But now, as she watched Biddy straighten the rug the Ewbank had ruffled up, for the first time she missed her uniform and ward work. How she longed to be ward sister on children's. Aileen Paige would spend her entire day with Louis. What pride she must feel at the end of each shift, Emily thought. How lucky she is to be able to count her achievements every day.

Biddy stood upright and smiled at Emily. She felt her pain. Poor Sister Haycock, childless as well as motherless. 'I'll have a nice hot lunch ready for you,' she said kindly. 'You get off and see to your paperwork now. But don't slip, it's as icy as hell out there.'

'Oh, drat,' said Emily, startled, almost irritated.

'What now?' said Biddy from halfway inside the tall broom cupboard, into which she was shoving the Ewbank with a clatter.

'I was, er, going to pop over to the porter's lodge to have a few minutes with Dessie before settling down to work, but I've left something in my rooms. Oh, gosh, I totally forgot. I have to fly – see you at one.'

Before Biddy could answer, she was away down the corridor. Biddy was left standing with her hands on her hips, staring after her as the door banged shut.

'Having a few minutes with Dessie, is she, the lucky madam,' said Madge, who had appeared from behind the coat stand around the corner. 'I thought she might have smelt me ciggie smoke and known I was here. I almost burnt a hole in my skirt trying to keep it away from your coat.'

Both women began to giggle. 'Holy Mary and Joseph! I shoved mine in the ashtray quick,' said Biddy. 'She would never have known.'

'I don't know why I had to hide in the first place,' said Madge, sounding mildly offended.

'Because we keep secrets, Madge, don't we, and we don't ever want any lines drawn straight back to you. One day someone will cotton on to the fact that half of our information comes from you working the switchboard, and when that happens, you might lose your job and we will lose all our power. Even someone as madly smitten as that one…' Biddy jabbed the cigarette now wedged between her fingers towards the door. '… would be suspicious about me and you gabbing in her room this early in the morning. This is her office and sitting room, not the kitchen.'

'Well, she would have a right to be suspicious, I suppose,' said Madge. 'Listen, you finish the cleaning and I'll see you in the greasy spoon at ten. I've got a bit of news meself this morning.' She winked as she made for the door.

'I'll see you there,' said Biddy. 'I'll have to collect soft girl Elsie on the way. She's becoming so puddled, she forgets when it's break time.'

'Forgets?' said Madge. 'She does not. She sits in Matron's kitchen all day long. Our Elsie's problem is that she can't be bothered walking all the way over there.'

Biddy laughed. 'You're probably right, but don't knock it because after you she's our second most valuable source of information. Remember, it was Elsie who told us about Sister Paige's promotion and how she beat Sister Antrobus to the job on children's.'

'Well, I don't call that useful, nowhere near as good as the information I find out,' said Madge.

Biddy shuffled towards Emily's desk with a duster in her hand. 'What I say, Madge, is everything counts and you never know what little bit of information we pick up might come in useful. Now, off away with you or I'll be late myself for the coffee.'

Aileen's mother was sitting waiting in her chair as usual when Aileen came in with the tray, but today she was smiling.

She seemed grateful for her breakfast, which was out of the ordinary to say the least, and there was something markedly different about her manner – the way she set her jaw, the way she watched Aileen walk across the room. It made Aileen uncomfortable; it was as if her mother was harbouring a secret she had chosen not to share.

'Are you feeling well, Mother?' Aileen asked as she unscrewed the top on the brown glass bottle to begin dispensing her assortment of morning pills. 'Here is your water tablet and your vitamin K. We mustn't forget those.'

'No, dear,' said her mother, 'I never do. You, however, did forget to leave the bottle for me yesterday morning.'

Aileen's head shot up. 'Did I?' she asked, startled.

'Yes, you did. Have you got something on your mind? Something that's distracting you? I had to ask the girl to fetch me the bottle from the cabinet and despite my telling her which one it was, she brought the wrong one three times. Stupid girl.'

Aileen blushed. 'Her name is Gina, Mother, and you know that.'

She had never been able to lie to her mother, but now she would have to, no matter how awful it made her feel. If she didn't, there'd be no more spending time with Freddie. She had to resist giving in to her guilt and letting her mother abuse the power she had over her. If she didn't resist, there would be no Freddie and no choir. All that would be gone. Over.

She took a deep breath as she handed over the pills. 'Nothing is distracting me, Mother.'

It was a lie. She hadn't been able to get Freddie out of her mind. She had relived yesterday evening over and over, and every time she did so, a thrill shot through her very core.

She would close her eyes, replay the kiss and feel herself becoming light-headed with the memory and the knowledge that it would happen again if she wanted it to.

She felt her mother's eyes scrutinizing her every move. 'Shall I butter your toast for you?'

'Yes, please, dear, because as you know, I cannot do it myself. It isn't soft, is it? You know I cannot abide soft toast. I may as well eat bread and be done with it.'

'No, Mother, it isn't soft. When did I ever bring you soft toast?'

'You may not do, but that useless girl, Gina, she does. She slopped the tea yesterday and the toast was wet on the corner and she didn't even offer to fetch me a fresh piece. What would have been the point anyway? The tea would have been cold by the time she got back. Is there really no one better? I tell you she will have to go.'

Aileen was holding out the plate with the buttered toast for her mother to take. Regardless of her guilt, if it hadn't been for Gina, Aileen would never have been able to join the choir, would never have been able to see Freddie, would never have been kissed. A surge of determination coursed through her veins.

'Well, she can't go, Mother, because there's no one else. We've been through everyone else hereabouts and you apparently cannot abide anyone. You have developed something of a reputation locally, it seems, and I was quite unable to get any-one to work here before I found Gina. If Gina leaves, I shall have to give up being a ward sister.'

Her mother reached out her good hand, but instead of taking her toast from Aileen straight away, she sat still for a moment, waiting until Aileen had finished speaking and she had her full attention. Aileen's unusually forthright manner did not perturb her, in fact she was amused by it.

'Well, do you know, I think that's not a bad idea.'

Aileen looked up from stirring the sugar into her own teacup. The colour drained from her face and was replaced by two bright red spots on her cheeks.

Mrs Paige's tone became cajoling, a note that Aileen knew only too well from when her father was alive. Her mother had always got her own way with him and now she used the same tactics on Aileen. 'It is so unfair, you having to leave here early every morning, and you work such long hours. All that responsibility cannot be good for you or the patients.'

Aileen felt a deep resentment bordering on anger that she had never experienced before. She took a breath, scrabbled for words that would not sound aggressive and then swallowed before she spoke. She returned her mother's fixed gaze and noted that somewhere behind her eyes lay something deep. Her mother had a plan and Aileen was suddenly aware that she was not the one in charge. Her mother was plotting something, manipulating her, just as she had her father.

'The patients? What do you mean, the patients?' She had tried to sound normal and had begun to butter her toast, but her hand was shaking so she abandoned the task. The butter knife was suspended mid air, between the plate and the toast, as Aileen stared back at her mother, waiting for a reply.

'Well, you know, you are still very young. It cannot go unnoticed by those in authority that you are far too inexperienced to carry all that responsibility on your shoulders. I mean, surely I am not the first person to wonder what Matron was thinking of when she promoted you to such an important position?'

Aileen did not dare allow herself to speak, and even if she had wanted to, the words were stuck in her throat. To give her time to compose her thoughts, she laid down the knife, picked up her teacup and sipped at the scalding liquid. Her mother's eyes never left her face.

'I have spoken to Josie about it many times and she agrees with me that it would be best if you left St Angelus altogether. We could sell this house and buy something much smaller, nearer to Josie, and then we could use the money left over to live on. I think we could be quite comfortable.'

This was too much and Aileen almost spluttered her tea on to the saucer. 'You might be quite comfortable with that, Mother, but I am only thirty. The money might last you out, but what will I do when I get old? The money would be long gone by then. And besides, I love my job.'

Tears had begun to sting Aileen's eyes, much to her annoyance. She could not believe that her mother had discussed this with Josie. Neither of them had congratulated her on her promotion – instead, they'd hatched a scheme that benefited the two of them and took no account of her life or her happiness. She swiftly took the decision to say no more. She simply did not trust herself. Her anger was burning like bile in the back of her throat. The heat from the fire felt oppressive. They were trying to drown her, own her. Why?

'Oh goodness, is that the time?' She looked up at the clock on the mantelshelf. Her eye caught that of her father in the photograph and it was pleading with her: *Run, Aileen! Run!* 'I must dash. I shall miss my bus.' They both knew that was a lie.

She jumped up from the chair. 'I have choir tomorrow night, Mother. Gina will be here until I return, and that will probably be quite late as we're all meeting in the cathedral hall afterwards for a Christmas celebration and I would like to join in.'

Her head was spinning. She would have to think about her mother's words later. For now she had to get out of the room as fast as she could. Her emotions were in turmoil – how could Josie not have told her what their mother was planning?

She turned from the door. For once, her mother had not tried to prevent her from leaving. There was no objection, no complaint. Instead, to Aileen's confusion, she was smiling again. 'That's nice. You'll enjoy that, Aileen, dear,' she said.

Aileen closed the door without replying. What is going on, Mother, she wondered as she made her way downstairs. What are you up to?

Sister Tapps perched on the edge of the bed. Her battered old trunk sat on the floor next to her. The lid was open, hinged backwards like a gaping mouth and reinforced by brown leather straps, and she stared into the cavernous expanse inside. In the bottom lay a tartan rug, the rug her parents had bought for her when she was sent off to boarding school. Apart from its occasional use during her schooldays, it had spent its entire time lining the base of the trunk and was now musty-smelling and riddled with moth holes. She remembered that she had always kept a photograph of her sister Edith tucked inside it, along with the original receipt. She blinked and almost shook her head. When did that rug get so old? It didn't seem so long ago that it was brand-new and wrapped in brown paper. But the rug was far from new any more and she sighed at the faded and tattered thing it had become.

She stood up from the bed and lifted the rug. There on

the leather-lined base of the trunk lay the yellowing paper receipt. She held it to her face and breathed deeply, and memories came flooding back. Memories of herself as a girl, holding her mother's gloved hand. She could even remember the shop assistant who'd served them in her smart overall and bobbed hair, and how her mother had embarrassed her by asking in exasperation, 'How much?', and then turning to her and saying, 'Look after that rug now, won't you. It's made of good wool and it's cost a pretty penny.'

The assistant had wrapped it up and given the young Olive Tapps a pitiful and knowing smile.

'I don't know why you have to go away to school,' her mother had said. 'Your grandmother and her money... But it seems I have no say in the matter. I'm just your mother, after all.' That was in 1904. Within the next ten years, now institutionalized into the boarding-school way of life, she lost her father to a bullet in the First World War, her domineering paternal grandmother to TB and her mother to madness.

She moved from boarding school to a nurses' home to the sisters' accommodation. She knew nothing else. Family life was something she learnt about via occasional conversations with the parents of her patients, but even though she and Edith had spent very little time together, she had loved her sister very much. She was uncomfortable in company and found it hard to converse in a jolly way with the other sisters. She'd given her entire life to her job and her patients, whom she had cared for with all she had to give. But only they knew that.

Tappsy was jolted out of her melancholy by the sound of doors banging in the room next to hers. It was Sister Haycock's room and she now heard the crashing of drawers opening and closing, then the wardrobe door being slammed shut.

It occurred to her that Sister Haycock's room had been very quiet of late. She used to hear her washing in the bathroom and there'd often be the hum of the radio playing softly in the background. But Tappsy didn't put two and two together nor let herself contemplate the possibility of illicit liaisons and her fellow nurses falling in love. Such thoughts had been far from her own experience for such a long time, they didn't even come into her head any more.

Time to get back to the ward, she thought. She had been about to try and begin to pack up. Abandoned by Matron, thrown out into the world she was so unfamiliar with, she had found that she couldn't. The physical act of opening her neatly lined and carefully organized dressing-table drawers had been impossible, and besides, where would she go?

She thought of her sister Edith and the guilt almost swamped her. 'Oh God,' she murmured as the image of her loving sister filled her head – the sister who'd been too young to attend boarding school, then too sick with rheumatic fever, which had trapped her in a wheelchair; the sister who'd been the only one to care for their mother. And she'd cared for Tappsy too, but Tappsy hadn't even attended her funeral.

'Edith,' she gasped, her eyes full of tears. It had been impossible for her to leave the hospital for the funeral, absolutely impossible. It just couldn't happen. But it seemed that her niece and nephew had not forgiven her, for her letters to them had gone unanswered. And her brother-in-law, the man who had loved Edith above all else, he would have taken her absence as a slight on Edith and would likely never forgive her. He must have turned Edith's children against her – her only blood relatives – and there was nothing she could do. The clock could not be turned back. So now she had nowhere to go and no one to spend Christmas with, and there was no incentive to pack.

She dropped the receipt into the trunk, watched it flutter back to its dark resting place of many years and closed the lid with a clunk. She walked over to the mirror next to the door and fastened her belt. She had doubled up on the Petersham and the buckle would allow it to tighten no further. Her eyes squinted in confusion. She would have to go to the seamstress and ask her to make it smaller. She felt no pleasure at the sight of her own reflection. She had eaten nothing but hospital food for the last forty years, and it showed. Her skin was sallow and grey, her frame almost skeletal. She sighed. 'You are old,' she said to herself.

Her hand reached out to the mirror and touched it lightly, as if to wipe away the image before her. She leant her head against the cool glass. 'I don't want to go away,' she whispered. Her sick children needed her, and she needed them. She lived in fear of losing what kept her stable and happy. That was the reason she never took a holiday or had a day off.

She closed her bedroom door behind her as quietly as possible, not wanting to attract attention, but she was too late: Emily Haycock was already out in the corridor, lugging a big case.

'Oh, hello, Sister Tapps, how are you? Have you heard about the new baby in ward three? What a stoke of luck we've had. It looks as though he's going to pull through.'

Sister Tapps blinked. She had no idea what Emily was talking about. Emily Haycock didn't even work on the children's ward. No one had told her about a baby on ward three, but then no one told her anything any more – it was as if she was invisible.

Emily's gaze wandered over Sister Tapps and although she was far too polite to say it out loud, she immediately registered that Tappsy had lost weight. It's because she works too hard, she thought.

'No, I haven't heard. We have been er... a little busy on ward four,' said Sister Tapps.

Emily's eyes widened. 'Oh yes, you're going to have your first Christmas off in ages, aren't you.' She suddenly felt relieved. Tappsy really needs that holiday, she thought. 'When are the children moving to three?'

Sister Tapps stiffened and glued the smile to her face. 'Tomorrow, I believe. Or so Matron informs me. They are making decorations for ward three and the trees have arrived – apparently they are going to look lovely.' A lump formed in her throat and she immediately changed the subject. 'Are you going away yourself?'

Emily looked down at her suitcase and her cheeks coloured. 'Oh, er, yes, I suppose I am really. Well, yes, I mean I definitely am, but I'm just staying with a friend – locally, that is.'

She prayed that Tappsy wouldn't ask who the friend was. She was quite sure that she would have no idea about her and Dessie. She wasn't the kind of ward sister the others gossiped to or included in their coffee breaks or soirees in their sitting rooms. It had been like that ever since the incident with little Laura, when they had almost all judged her. They'd seen her lack of professionalism as a slur against themselves and St Angelus, but most of all they hated the fact that she worked every day and never took a holiday.

'It has to stop,' Sister Antrobus had told Matron many times. 'We can't have her showing the rest of us up. Some of us have friends and relatives we like to visit and I for one look forward to my coach trip around the North Wales coast during the summer months. Her insistence on working every singe day makes me very uncomfortable.'

The most recent complaint had come only that week and Matron had almost rubbed her hands in glee at finally having the chance to bring Sister Antrobus up short. 'Well, as a matter of fact, she is having a holiday.' She paused for effect and had to stop herself from smiling as Sister Antrobus's eyes popped and her jaw fell open. 'She is away for the whole of Christmas and we are transferring many of her patients home.'

Sister Antrobus had recovered quickly, folding her arms and harrumphing with indignation. 'About time, Matron. She hasn't left St Angelus in nigh on seven years now.'

'Thank you, Sister Antrobus.' Matron raised her voice and there was no mistaking the meaning in her tone. 'I think I shall be the one to decide who does and doesn't have leave, if you'd be so kind – unless the board has failed to inform me that you have been promoted to Matron and I am no longer required? And may I say, as we are talking about incidents, it's not that long since you had one of your own.'

Matron finished her reprimand with a flourish and Sister Antrobus blushed to the roots of her hair. The memory of her having been caught red-handed in the arms of Mr Scriven, the disgraced consultant, was still fresh in everyone's minds and Matron would not let her forget it. Information was power and Matron used it well.

Sister Tapps sensed Emily's eyes on her as they stood facing each other at the top of the stairs. She wasn't very fond of small talk and much preferred reading a book to having a chat. She was suddenly afraid that Emily might be about to ask her where she would be spending Christmas. Everyone was talking about Christmas – the trees arriving, the preparations for the carol concert, the presents for the children. What could she say now? Her readymade answers about Christmas morning on the ward were useless this year. She acted quickly. 'I'm so sorry, I do beg your pardon, I've left something in my room. You have a lovely Christmas if I don't see you again, won't you.' And without waiting for a reply, she turned her back on Emily and nipped back into her room.

Pressing her back against her bedroom door, Tappsy waited until she could no longer hear Emily's footsteps racing down the stairs. Despite the weight of her suitcase, Sister Haycock sounded nimble and young. She popped her head out to check that none of the other sisters were around, then stepped out into the corridor again and closed her door.

As she passed Emily's door, a thought struck her. While they'd been talking, she'd noticed that Emily had failed to lock her room. That was quite normal – very few of them ever locked their rooms, especially not day to day. She turned the handle and stuck her head inside. It was tidy and clean and you would struggle to believe that anyone used it. It seemed so unlived in. She let her gaze rest on the bare dressing table, the open wardrobe door and the top of the fireplace. There was nothing there. She moved to close the wardrobe door and saw that it was empty. Sister Haycock is not coming back, she thought. There is nothing here to come back for. She's left. How odd – why didn't she say? Why be so secretive?

As Tappsy made her way over to the ward, a plan began to crystallize in her head, and for the first time since Matron had given her her Christmas marching orders, she smiled. Well, why not, she thought.

There was an *On off duty/holiday* sign to hang on each doorknob and Emily had turned hers over as she left. No one would clean her room or even enter it now, and besides, the accommodation domestics took holiday themselves over the Christmas break. She could hide out in Sister Haycock's room! No one would even know she was there. She could sneak out at night and if ward four was to be closed, she could stash anything she might need in there and use the fire escape to the kitchen if she wanted to cook anything. She could smuggle things out over the next day or two and hide them in her trunk. That way, she wouldn't need to go anywhere. She could spend her Christmas in St Angelus, just as she always had. She wouldn't have a great deal of warm food or her beloved children around her, and she wouldn't dare even put the radio on in case anyone heard, but it would only be for a short while.

She chuckled as she made her way down the steps, feeling lighter of heart than she had since she and Matron had had their little talk. But then without any warning she came to a sudden standstill. The pain had returned and it was intense, as if someone had crept up behind her and stabbed her in the side. She emitted the first note of a scream but quickly clamped her hand over her mouth and, grabbing the banister, took long deep breaths until the waves of sickening pain ebbed away.

'Deep breaths, deep breaths,' she whispered to herself as she sank down and sat on the stair. She had given that advice so often and to so many of her poorly children.

Once she knew she was safe, she removed her hand from her mouth, gripped the banister with both hands and dragged herself back up to standing. She felt weak and drained. That was maybe the fourth or fifth time it had happened that month. She'd had no other symptoms though, and she was sure she'd be able to identify any that might be cause for alarm.

As her heartbeat steadied, she took her handkerchief from her pocket and wiped the beads of perspiration from her brow and top lip. I need some magnesium, she thought. I have a bit of an ulcer and a bit of regular magnesium will fix it. Moments later, she strode down the corridor towards the laundry to find the seamstress and ask her to adjust her belt.

Chapter 14

Branna was the first to arrive at the greasy spoon and, as was the custom, that meant she had to fetch the hot milky drinks ready for everyone else. The urns sat on a long table at the front of the café and the coffee was scalding hot. She took a wooden tray from the table next to the urn, laid out the pale green national issue cups and saucers and was just holding the first one under the tap when she was joined by Biddy.

'Oh, you're a good'un,' said Biddy as she leant over and inhaled appreciatively. 'You get the coffees, I'll fetch the toast.'

'Don't forget to get a second ashtray, Biddy,' said Branna over her shoulder, keeping an eye on the steady stream of coffee, being careful not to miss and burn herself. 'I don't like putting the ash in me saucer. I missed yesterday and it fell into the coffee.'

Ten minutes later, surrounded by a haze of blue smoke, Biddy, Elsie, Madge, Branna and Betty had finished their coffee and toast and were all about to light up their second cigarette.

'What have you left your toast for, Elsie?' said Biddy as she pointed the lit end of her cigarette towards Elsie's plate.

Elsie looked miserable. 'I left me teeth out this morning and

I can eat nothing but a bit of porridge and suck on a sponge cake,' she replied with a frown and a shrug.

'Why, have you broken them?' Biddy furrowed her brow. 'You had them in yesterday. You haven't been inviting the coalman in again, have you, for an Elsie special?'

The table erupted into raucous laughter. Biddy made the most of the moment and played to the gallery. 'I thought he was a long time in yours. Hadn't wanted a cuppa from me, he hadn't, girls, and when I heard him grunting, I thought, oh, it's one of Elsie's buns he's chewing on. I was right, eh, Elsie?'

Tears fell down Madge's face as she dropped her cigarette into the ashtray and removed her handkerchief from her handbag to wipe her eyes. 'Oh my God,' she gasped as she blew her nose. 'Biddy, what are you like!'

Biddy stopped laughing and, noticing Elsie's forlorn expression, replied, 'Oh come on, Elsie, what's wrong with you? Have you left your sense of humour at home along with yer teeth?'

Elsie grinned. The arrival of the coalman was the highlight of her week – not that he would ever have known it. She blushed and said, 'No, the most the coalman has ever given me is an extra few lumps in me hundredweight. I haven't lost my teeth, or broken them either. God in heaven, the ulcers… would you look at them.' She leant forward and opened her mouth to Biddy, who flinched and looked away.

'Bloody Nora, you need a bit of something on that,' she said, wrinkling her nose. 'Go and see Sister Antrobus. Doreen on reception will sort you out. They're a bit quieter at the moment. Everyone's too busy getting ready for Christmas to be sick.'

'I work for Matron, Biddy, I think I might know that,' said Elsie, always quick to assert her position at the top of the food chain.

'Oh, excuse me, madam, I thought you made the tea, not sorted the rota.'

Elsie winced. 'I need something,' she said. 'Miserable it is. I can't go through Christmas like this or it'll be turkey soup for me.'

'Who has news?' asked Biddy, keen to change the subject. She blew out the match she'd been holding for Madge to light her cigarette with.

'I do,' said Branna. 'And you'll never guess, but Sister Paige has got a fella.'

'Go away, she has not! She never has and she never will,' said Betty Hutch. 'She's wedded to her job, that one, just like Sister Tapps.'

'Our Gina has seen him,' said Branna, looking smug and making the most of her moment of glory. 'Having a good old necking session, they were, under the lamp-post at the bottom of the street. And what's more, her mother isn't as poorly as she makes out and apparently she's putting it all on. And Mrs Paige saw Sister Paige and the fella too and our Gina says she sounded none too happy.'

'Ooh!' They gasped in unison and, open-mouthed, turned to each other.

'Bless her,' said Elsie, 'she deserves a bit of fun. Blimey, they are all at it – her and Sister Haycock. Think I'll have to do a bit better than a quick fuck once a week with the coalman and find meself a proper fella.' She looked serious as she drew on her cigarette and her toothless cheeks caved inwards.

The table was stunned into silence and they all stared at Elsie. But as she blew out her smoke and grinned, they exploded into laughter.

'That's how Bessie Green has always paid for her coal,' said

Branna. 'She makes no secret of it. He takes three minutes,' she said, 'and she's had it all taken away, so she's not bothered about getting caught and her money stays put in her purse.'

'Did,' said Elsie. 'Their Kev caught her out a few weeks ago.'

'Oh my giddy aunt, is that really true? How?' asked Madge.

Elsie took a sip of her coffee and made them wait. 'Their Kev's not the brightest spark, but they were stood in the yard at the time and he was brushing the coal dust back down the coal hole after the delivery. He wanted to know why there were two big black handprints on her fat arse. She was caught red-handed.'

'Black-handed, more like,' said Biddy, and the table hooted with laughter once more.

'And Sally on the Dock Road,' said Madge. 'With her it's the milkman and he's a cheeky bastard as he only lives in the dairy around the corner. Trouble is though, she complains 'cause sometimes he wants it every day. Mind you, I suppose she wants her daily pinta. Anyway, you get your ulcers sorted first, before you go looking for a new fella, eh, Elsie? Give yourself a fighting chance.'

Elsie grinned her toothless grin.

'Well,' said Betty, 'one more evening of making stars and we should be finished. Everyone OK for tonight? Pammy Tanner says they'll probably decorate the wards tomorrow. I think we've done really well, you know. I reckon we could even win that competition. Maisie has gone all out. One more push, ladies, and we're done.'

'Thank God for that,' said Biddy. 'If I have to make another golden star with that fiddly paper, me fingers will drop off. I can still feel it in me joints after the last session.' She wriggled her left hand to make the point.

'Well, I think it's magical,' said Branna, 'all that crepe and tinsel. And do you know what's the most magical bit? That little lad, Louis, he's doing so well, he'll be able to see it all. If anything made me want to decorate that ward, it's that. I can't wait to see his face.'

'Just think, if we'd been decorating two wards, it would have taken twice as long. Sister Tapps, I don't reckon she wanted to take Christmas off, you know,' said Biddy.

'She needs to,' said Betty. 'Something's not right there and I don't know if she asked or Matron made her, but she needs a bit of a rest, I'd say.'

'Oh, Matron definitely made her, I heard all of that,' whistled Elsie through her gums. 'No, she wasn't at all happy about it. And do you know what else – her sister has died and she didn't even go to the funeral. I heard her telling Matron. Too busy on the ward, she said.'

One by one they stubbed out their cigarettes in the ashtray.

'Come on,' said Biddy, 'let's get back.'

As they scraped back their chairs, Betty looked thoughtful. 'That's not right, that isn't,' she said.

'What isn't, Betty?' asked Madge as she shoved her cigarettes back into her bag.

'Not attending her own sister's funeral. I have a sister, and I would never do that. Don't you think it's just not right? Like there must be something wrong. It's not normal.'

'Oh, don't be daft, Betty. She's Sister Tapps by name and Sister Tapped by nature. She's always been a bit funny, and anyway, what do we know? They might not even have got on. Could have been sworn enemies for all we know. My mam, she never saw her sister at all between the two wars. Even now they only write a letter every now and then, and that's only because

I got them back together. But the jealousy! Jesus, I sometimes wish I hadn't. I swear to God, the only reason my mam keeps going is because she is determined to outlive her sister, and she will do that by making sure that every day she outdoes her in some way or another. She booked a photographer last week, to take a photo of herself stood next to the new electric mangle so she can post it to her, that's how bad it is.'

'She's losing too much weight if you ask me, Sister Tapps,' said Biddy as she loaded the empty cups on to the tray. 'I think it's a good idea if Matron is making her take Christmas off. Everyone needs a rest. What she needs is to put her feet up and have a few roast dinners.'

They all left the greasy spoon quieter than usual, lost in their thoughts, but not one of them wondered where Sister Tapps would go, where she would find her rest and those roast dinners. For the women of the dockside streets had no idea what solitude was like. They were never short of friends or company and spent their days at home with neighbours and children freely wandering in and out. It never occurred to them that for Sister Tapps there was no one and nothing other than St Angelus, her ward and the sick children of Liverpool's dockside.

Over in the Lovely Lane home, Mrs Duffy was arranging for Jake to give her a lift in his van to collect the decorations from Maisie and take them both up to the hospital. 'It's to be tomorrow, Jake, when everything's ready. You'll wait for me after your morning delivery so I can see my nurses off first.' She wiped her hands on her apron and fixed him with a smile. 'There'll be a cooked breakfast in it for you, lad.'

241

'I'd like to, Mrs Duffy, but Dessie won't let me if I'm not back by nine for the deliveries.'

Mrs Duffy was unimpressed. 'You tell Dessie, he may be the head porter and all, but we have to get cracking, on Matron's orders, and I don't have a magic carpet at my disposal.'

Jake shook his head. 'Mrs Duffy, you have me stuck between a rock and a hard place. What will I do?'

'I'll tell you what you will do, you will inform Dessie that there will be no decorations on the children's ward if we don't get on to it tomorrow. Is that what he wants now?'

Jake fled the nurses' home and drove straight back to the porter's lodge to plead with Dessie. 'If I don't do what Mrs Duffy asks, I reckon she'll be coming up here to deal with you directly. She's a woman who won't be taking no for an answer.'

Much to Jake's surprise, Dessie grinned. 'You do whatever Mrs Duffy asks of you,' he said. 'I'll put Bryan on the deliveries.'

Jake was standing in the doorway to the porter's hut and Dessie was sitting behind the desk, filling in the work chart for the day. 'Right you are,' said Jake. 'I'll be off then.' And to Jake's additional surprise, Dessie didn't invite him to take a cup of tea from the pot and nor did he even look up and crack a joke – he was fully focused on filling out his chart.

Seconds after Jake had run back down the steps, Dessie said, 'You can come out now,' and leant back in his chair, grinning.

'You are a cheeky monkey, Dessie Horton,' said Emily. 'I only came in here to drop off my case, I didn't expect to be trapped. You know better than I do that this hut is in full view of Matron's window.'

'Aye, I do.' Dessie stood up. 'Is that the last of your things?'

'It is. There's nothing left in my room now, it's all either already at your house or in this case. Will it be all right here?' She looked him full in the eye, more serious now. 'You know I'm not going to tell Matron yet, Dessie? Not till the new year at least. I'm keeping my room on and I've put a sign up for the domestics so they won't come in and clean over the holidays. You do understand, don't you?'

'I do. Don't you worry. I have no problem with that, and your suitcase will be fine. I'll bring it home in the van tonight.' His calm tone belied his inner turmoil; he couldn't help worrying that she might not stay, that one day she would pack her bags and walk right back out of his life. 'And don't worry about Matron seeing you. I happen to know she is helping decorate the tree in the main entrance. She took two of the lads and a set of ladders with her not half an hour ago. So we are safe.'

He moved towards Emily. There was no mistaking the look in his eye.

'Oh no you don't,' Emily said, a look of horror on her face. 'I will remind you that I am the director of the school of nursing. I lead by example.'

'Just one,' whispered Dessie with a grin. 'No one will know.'

'No! Certainly not!' Emily squealed. 'You cannot kiss me here, Dessie Horton. Can you imagine? The next thing you know, we'll have nurses breaking the rules all over St Angelus. They'll be kissing on the wards before we know it. You keep your hands to yourself.' And then she grinned as she backed towards the door. 'Until tonight then.'

Dessie stood and watched as Emily flew down the steps and across the cobbled yard to the school of nursing. He smiled as she pulled her cape around her, protecting herself from the biting wind that was whistling up from the Mersey. In the distance he heard the familiar horns of the tugs sounding their farewells and sail safes to the ships they had just led out to the deeper waters beyond the bar. Over to the far side of the yard he could hear the clatter of the oxygen bottles as they were wheeled away to whichever wards had requested them. All around him life went on as usual. Everything was as it always had been – everything except the contents of his heart.

He marvelled at the ways in which Emily had turned his life upside down. He had always been very busy, his days fully occupied with looking after the needs of others, but he'd also been lonely. There had always been that point at the end of the day when he could no longer escape the inevitable. When he had to leave work, the pool hall, the pub or the kitchen of whoever had invited him in for a bite and a cuppa. He knew that he was just a small part of the lives of most of the families he helped, the lads he employed, and that he likely got just a passing mention in their conversations – 'Oh by the way, I saw Dessie today' – before they turned out the light. But for him, those families amounted to the whole of his life, and when he closed his door at night he could run from his loneliness no more. He'd been aware that the way to end his misery was to find a wife, but he hadn't known how. And now here she was, his Emily. His house was full of her. Her clothes and bags and possessions. She had transformed his life and he was loving it. A lifetime of orderliness turned into chaos, and he didn't mind one little bit. He revelled in his new-found joy.

Every time he opened his back door of an evening and her voice shouted out 'Hello!' to welcome him home, his heart smiled. He wanted her there with him for ever, to hear that hello singing out to him every night for the rest of his days.

He would have liked to shout his happiness from the rooftops; he wanted to share it with everyone, wanted to brag about having Emily Haycock safely tucked into his terrace house. But Emily wanted to keep their living arrangements discreet until they had officially tied the knot, and he respected that. Matron, Mrs Duffy, Hattie Lloyd – they would all have something to say if they knew. So he would bide his time, let Emily do things her way.

Across the yard, Emily had reached the door to the school of nursing. As if she sensed him watching her, she turned and beamed, flashing him that mischievous smile that sent his pulse racing. She waved before she disappeared inside the building and, lifting his hand from the pocket of his brown porter's coat, he waved back.

Maura's feet were chilled to the bone. She'd spent all afternoon doing the laundry in the freezing back kitchen and now the warmth of the fire was making her toes tingle. Tommy had just got back from the docks and they were sitting in front of the fire together, enjoying a rare half hour of peace while the twins were napping. Maura was knitting a jumper for Kitty, having discovered that the only way she could stop fretting was to keep her hands and mind busy. Tommy was studying the form of the horses that had run that day and struggling to read all of the words in the *Racing Post*.

'Why are you even bothering with that when you lost?' asked Maura. 'You lost nearly a shilling and we can ill afford to do that just before Christmas, Tommy.'

Tommy felt chastened. He was studying the form because he wanted to know where he'd gone wrong. He'd been brought up around horses in Ireland and they had been his passion ever since. Everyone in the four streets knew Tommy to be the horse man and they looked to him for the tips. He hated to lose and was still smarting. 'It's the worrying about our Angela, it put me off.'

'Don't be blaming our Angela,' said Maura. 'Don't you even think about it. That poor kid is lying in a hospital bed and we're none the wiser. You bet on the wrong horse and you lost.'

Before Tommy could reply, their next-door neighbour, Peggy, came bustling in through the back door.

Tommy wrinkled his nose. He always said he could smell Peggy before he saw her. 'And what can we be getting for ye, Peggy?' he asked, before Peggy had even opened her mouth.

'Who says I'm wanting anything?' said Peggy.

Tommy looked over the rim of his glasses. 'Well, Peggy, I don't know of a day when you've walked out of me house empty-handed. Is that the sugar bowl in yer hand?'

Peggy looked down at her hand as though seeing the sugar bowl for the first time. 'Oh aye, it is, I nearly forgot.' Turning from Tommy, Peggy said to Maura, 'I've run out until payday, can I borrow a bowl of sugar?'

Maura raised her eyebrows and looked at Tommy. What she wanted to say was, 'Peggy, how is it I never run out of sugar and yet the same wage comes into my house as yours?' But she didn't. She rose and took the bowl out of Peggy's hand and went to the press to fill it. 'I can't give you a full bowl, Peggy, I need a bit extra to make a cake this weekend.'

'Oh, don't be worrying – anything ye can spare.' Peggy followed her to the press and peered inside without even attempting to conceal her nosiness. 'You have Camp Coffee?' she said as she put her hand in and pulled the bottle out.

Maura refilled the sugar bowl and, barely managing to conceal her irritation, snatched the Camp Coffee out of Peggy's hand, placed it firmly back where it had come from and almost slammed the press door shut. 'I do. I have it because I pay into the Christmas club every week without fail. Do you?'

Peggy didn't have to reply to the question. They both knew the answer. If Peggy needed extra fags, she didn't think twice about buying some. If she wanted a Saturday night in the clubhouse, she would get her hair set even if it meant there wouldn't be enough money for food to see them through the week. 'She pushes us all too far,' Maura often complained to Tommy. 'What if we had nothing, eh? What if Kathleen kicked off and didn't let her have whatever she borrows. I swear to God, they survive in that house on every bugger else's leftovers. It's poor little Paddy I feel sorry for. His legs are as bandy as hell. I'm going to tell the welfare.'

'No you're not, Maura,' Tommy would say, and he'd pat his knee invitingly, so that she'd come over and sit in his lap. 'You won't be telling no one now.' And she'd walk over and flop on to his knee. Even with her slim frame, the chair always groaned at having to support the weight of them both. The springs, half of them missing, would stretch and give so that Tommy's backside was almost touching the floor. 'That's not how we do things round here. We look after each other, even the neighbours you want to knock into the middle of next week. And little Paddy, don't be worrying about him now. He has his tea in here with our lot most nights, and the welfare would look at your cooking and think he was a lucky little lad. I know me and our Kitty do. Jesus, all the kids do.'

The conversation always went the same way whenever

Peggy tested Maura's patience to breaking point. And it always ended with Maura throwing her arms around Tommy's neck and him clasping her around her waist and holding her tight. 'There now, you know I'm making sense, don't you, Maura. We all have to look after each other. Look at the way we was brought up in Ireland. We never had so much as a pair of shoes. Our kids do and they get to school every day and they have never gone a day without a warm meal in their bellies. I've always had work, so what have we to complain about? If it's nothing more than having Peggy and big Paddy in our lives, we can manage that, can't we?'

Maura would silently nod into his neck. Tommy would stroke her back. Maura would kiss him. Tommy would search for the bottom of her skirt and with skilful ease slide his hand up her legs. Maura would lift his cap from his head, slap it back down and, pushing his hand away, say, 'Get off, Tommy Doherty, I've 'tatoes to peel and scones in the range.'

Tommy would chuckle as she leapt off his knee, then bend down to rescue his paper from beside the chair. 'Well you can't blame a man for trying, can you, and I'm dying of the thirst here.'

Peggy would never have guessed that it was Tommy and his unquenchable lust that stood between her and the welfare man knocking on her door.

Now in possession of a full sugar bowl, if not quite as full as she would have liked, Peggy shuffled across to the chair opposite Tommy and without being asked collapsed into it. 'Is the kettle on, Maura?' she said as she took the tobacco tin from her apron pocket.

'Is it ever not?' replied Maura tartly and she pushed the kettle back along the range and on to the hot plate.

Peggy, thick-skinned and not the brightest button in the box, failed to notice the dig.

Maura had been busy. She was a woman of routine and if there was one thing she could not bear, it was her routine being disturbed. Managing a family on a docker's wage took time and skill and Maura knew that Peggy, having no routine of her own, would quite often just copy her. If she saw Maura take her nets down, Peggy would do the same. If Maura's sheets were on the line, Peggy's would follow an hour later. It was one way Maura could sometimes get Peggy out of her house, and she wanted her out right now. It was worth a try at least. 'I'm going to start on my ironing in a minute, Peggy,' she said, shooting her a meaningful look. 'You done yours yet?'

But Peggy ignored the question. 'What's the news of Angela?' she asked. 'Big Paddy said he saw you both coming out of the pub and you weren't in long enough to have had a drink, Tommy.'

'We used the phone,' said Tommy, quite used to his neighbours discussing his every movement. 'They said she's doing well. Responding to the medication and we will see a great improvement when we visit.' He spoke with authority, as though he himself were the doctor imparting the news.

Maura grinned. Peggy was irritating, for sure, but hearing once more how well Angela was doing was music to her ears. They knew of too many children who'd died on the dockside streets. The war might be long over and Hitler himself defeated, but the new housing that was supposed to be coming had yet to arrive. There were no complaints – their homes had survived where many others hadn't. The Dohertys along with lots of others were still grateful for the grace of God.

Peggy rolled a cigarette. 'Did ye have a winner today, Tommy?' she asked.

Tommy pushed the pencil behind his ear and folded the paper on to his lap. 'I did not. I'm mighty disappointed about that, Peggy. Did Paddy have a flutter?'

Peggy snorted. 'He did not. We haven't two ha'pennies left until payday. I don't know what we're to do for dinner tomorrow.'

Maura bit her tongue. She felt like she was about to explode. This news equated to fair warning that Peggy's kids would be round for their tea when they found none on their own table, but Peggy, she would still have tobacco in her tin.

Peggy failed to notice the set of Maura's jaw and prattled on. 'I hear Helen's daughter is to be up at St Angelus to have her baby. They're saying when the mother is under eighteen they want their babies born in a hospital now, 'cause of the NHS. They have to be fecking joking. That'd be about half of them around here. You wouldn't catch me doing that.'

'Me neither,' said Maura as she handed Peggy her tea. 'But 'tis a long time since either of us were eighteen, Peggy. They tell me Helen's daughter's having twins.' Maura blessed herself. 'I know what that's like and I'd be wanting them at home meself. Just to be safe.'

She briefly recalled the image of her trying to cope with her twin baby boys as well as running the house, dealing with Angela, who was a crier and still a baby at the time, and looking after their Kitty, too young yet to help, made her blood run cold just with the memory of it.

'Imagine that,' said Peggy, omitting to say thanks as she took the cup of tea. 'Another set of twins on the streets. They're not like you in that house though, Maura. Filthy, it is. Helen hung her stockings on the line the other day to air the smell out and they were so dirty, they took themselves down and walked off with the shame. Anyway, I hope her girl copes with the twins better than you did. Yours were a right handful.'

Maura was carrying Tommy's tea over and almost tripped up in surprise. 'A right handful? Was that what you said, Peggy? Well, I'm not sure what you mean by that?' Her eyes blazed as she handed Tommy his cuppa.

'Did you see Sister Tapps when you was up the hospital?' Peggy asked. 'She looked after our little Paddy when he had his appendix out. He still talks about her. It was weeks before he stopped saying Sister Tapps lets me have this and that. Jesus, I nearly took him back. Drove me mad, he did. I think he preferred it in hospital to home.'

'Who wouldn't, Peggy?' said Maura. 'He would have got his food regular and not had to come asking for it some nights in the kitchens of others.'

Peggy inhaled the last of her cigarette and threw the stub into the fire. 'Aye, you're probably right,' she said, clearly having taken no offence at Maura's gibe. 'Kitty was under Sister Tapps too, wasn't she?' She squinted through the cigarette smoke that still hovered around her face and stung her eyes.

'Funnily enough,' said Maura, who was back by the range and pouring her own tea, 'she was. She has never forgotten Sister Tapps either. Often mentions her. She wanted to go and see her when we were waiting to go in with our Angela, and then, blow me down, wasn't the woman only coming along the path when we went back outside. Couldn't stop Kitty, ran straight for her, she did, and Sister Tapps remembered her! You know, Peggy, the only reason I can make you this tea right now without me hands shaking is because I know our

Angela is being looked after by Sister Tapps, and Kitty tells me that the woman is an angel wearing a blue dress.'

'Well, I never. You saw her!' Peggy smiled.

'We all did and she had a lovely chat with Kitty. Until some fearsome ward sister called Sister Antrobus stopped her. She was your one from outpatients.'

Peggy had finished her tea and was now standing up, ready to leave. She picked up her sugar bowl from the floor.

'She scared the shite out of me, that one,' said Tommy. 'I told Maura, if she has to go back to the outpatients when our Angela comes home, she can take you with her, Peggy. I'm not squaring up to that one again. She was bigger than our outside lavvy and twice as hard. Shaking half to death we was. She scared our Kitty too.'

'Really?' said Peggy, her hand on the back-door latch. 'Well, there's a surprise she scared you, and you being married to your Maura for all of this time. She must have been a right scold, that sister. Not sure I'll be going. Wouldn't want to meet her meself if she's worse than Maura.' And before either Tommy or Maura could reply, the back door had clicked shut.

'You're welcome, Peggy. Any time you need a cup of sugar from me rations, come right on in,' said Maura and both she and Tommy dissolved into giggles.

Emily had laid the table with a tablecloth and a candle in the middle. She had made a shepherd's pie, Dessie's favourite, and before he came home she ran into the bedroom to apply her make-up.

'What's all this in aid of?' he asked as he walked through

the door, puffing slightly from the weight of her suitcase he'd brought back from the hospital.

Emily barely let him finish his sentence before she threw her arms around his neck. 'Dessie, I want to talk.'

'Do we have to?' he asked as he nuzzled at her neck.

'We do,' she said. 'It's about baby Louis.'

Dessie's head shot up, his expression grave. 'What about him? He's OK, isn't he? I thought he was doing well, or so Jake told me.'

'Yes, yes, of course.' Emily was pulling the sleeves of Dessie's donkey jacket down over his arms to remove it. She hung it on the back of the kitchen door.

'Is that shepherd's pie I can smell?' Dessie put his nose in the air.

'Yes, and look, I went to the pub all by myself and got your tankard full of beer to have with the food.'

'Oh, Emily, it doesn't taste the same at home, but thank you anyway. Now...' He pulled his sweater up and over his head, making his hair stand on end. 'What's all this about? I'm not complaining, mind, but I know you, Emily, you are up to something.'

Just for good measure, Emily pulled him to her and kissed him in a way that promised much more to come. But first there was a serious conversation they needed to have.

Chapter 15

The sky above the Lovely Lane nurses' home was heavy with black clouds and daylight had yet to break through. The morning promised to be bleak and cold, but that didn't bother Jake, who was sitting at the kitchen table enjoying bacon, sausages and blackened eggs with a side of fried bread. Scamp's head rested on the toe of his boot as the nurses piled in for their own breakfasts.

'As soon as I've cleared up, we will be off to the Tanners' house to collect the decorations. And from there you'll be taking Maisie, the decorations, and me of course, up to the children's ward.'

'Right you are, Mrs Duffy,' said Jake and he took a huge bite of the crispy fried bread, made with the leftover fat from the sausages and bacon.

Mrs Duffy threw a tea towel across the table towards him. 'Jake, you're dribbling. Wipe your chin.' Without waiting for a reply, she continued, 'And at the ward we will meet Nurse Tanner and Nurse Harper, along with the other nurses, to begin the decorating. There's a competition to be won, so we can't be messing about. If we don't get a move on, it will be

Twelfth Night before we know it and it'll be time to take them all back down again.'

'I'm ready for anything after this, Mrs Duffy,' said Jake, spearing the last sausage with his fork.

Beth had been standing in the kitchen drinking her tea and waiting for Pammy, as usual. Any minute now she'd run down the stairs, exclaim that she didn't know where the time had gone, grab a piece of toast, drink a whole mug of tea in about thirty seconds flat, put her cap on in the mirror over the fireplace, and fly out of the door.

Sure enough, before Beth could reply to Mrs Duffy about the decorations, Pammy hurtled into the room.

'I think it's going to snow, you know,' she said, without so much as a good morning to either of them. 'Have you seen the frost out there? Freezing, it is, and it's so dark, it could still be night. I could scrape my name into the ice on the window.'

'Oh, I really hope it doesn't snow,' said Mrs Duffy. 'I know everyone thinks it would be nice for Christmas, but you know what happens, the buses stop running and then none of the patients can have any visitors. Terrible way to be, that is. Imagine being sick in hospital at Christmas and having no one from home to come in and spend some of it with you.'

Pammy looked guilty. 'OK, I'm sorry. I really hope it doesn't snow then. I'm so excited that you are coming to the ward today, Mrs D. Wait until you see baby Louis! Oh, he will steal your heart, he will. Has me wrapped right around his little finger.'

Beth straightened up from leaning against the worktop and walked over to the sink to rinse her mug. 'So much so, Mrs Duffy, that during morning report, when Sister Paige asks for a volunteer to special him, she's the first nurse to put her hand up and say, "I will." Aren't you, Nurse Tanner?'

'Well, I don't mind,' said Pammy turning to Beth, a bunch of kirby grips clasped between her fingers. 'Anthony says I should think myself very lucky to be nursing a little boy as unique as Louis. You don't get the likes of him in through the casualty doors very often. Do you know he's gaining weight every single day. I can't wait to weigh him each morning, and he's learning to smile. God, you would not believe how he stares at your mouth when you talk to him and he looks straight into your eyes. Studies you, he does. Anyway, are we off to the rehearsal tonight, Beth?'

'We are indeed,' said Beth. 'And don't cook anything for us, Mrs Duffy. There's a bit of a party with food in the hall afterwards. It's one of the last rehearsals before the concert and so it's a sort of celebration.'

'Well, lucky you,' said Mrs Duffy. 'Would you like me to make something for you to take with you?'

Both girls turned to look at her. 'Would you mind?' said Beth. 'They did ask. I was going to call into the bakery so as not to bother you, what with you having so much on.' She didn't add, 'And you've been so quiet over the last few days, we weren't sure if we'd done something wrong.'

'Of course I don't mind. I'll rustle up something just as soon as I get back. It'll have to be something easy, mind. How about a sausage plait?'

Beth kissed Mrs Duffy on the cheek. 'You are a love – but you know that.'

'Come on, Beth, I don't want to be late,' said Pammy, already reaching for her cape.

Beth laughed. 'Yes, and we know why, don't we.'

★

Beth and Pammy were almost through the gates of St Angelus when they saw Dr Walker drive past. They looked at each other in alarm.

'Oh, my giddy aunt,' said Pammy. 'He's back. Do you think he'll go straight to the ward?'

'I doubt it,' said Beth. 'He'll probably go and see Matron first, to let her know he's here. Anyway, what can he say? The little boy he thought should be left to die is fighting fit.'

'Quite. I'd love to see his face when he finds that one out.' Pammy's eyes were bright with mischief. 'Tell you what, though, we had better let Sister Paige know so she can swap the cover on the notes back over to his original ones.'

And with that, as though the devil was at their heels, they dashed in to ward three to warn her.

Mrs Duffy alighted from Jake's van just as Maisie opened her front door.

'There you are, Jake,' Maisie said. 'The decorations are all stacked up in tea chests in the parlour. I didn't think I was going to get them all in. Can't believe how many we made. You couldn't stop Betty Hutch once she got going. Look at me, covered all over in shreds of crepe paper and glitter, I am. It's all over the house too.' She stopped talking and looked over her shoulder towards the van. 'I thought our Pammy was off today?'

'You must be joking,' said Mrs Duffy. 'She couldn't get to St Angelus fast enough. She has persuaded Sister Paige to let her be the special nurse for Louis. She's turning into Sister

Tapps – won't take a day off. But she'll be helping with the decorating, and her Anthony. He's on call, apparently, and will be coming up too.'

'Smashing. What about Emily Haycock, is she coming?'

Mrs Duffy seemed not to hear Maisie as she looked straight past her and asked, 'Do you need a hand, Jake?'

Maisie caught the cold tone in her voice and frowned. 'Mrs Duffy, is Emily Haycock coming?'

Mrs Duffy looked at Maisie and paused for a moment before she answered, just as she did with her nurses when she was displeased. 'I have no idea, Mrs Tanner. I am just the chief cook and bottle washer at the Lovely Lane home, there to tend to the needs of others. I am under no illusion that Emily Haycock, despite the fact that I mothered her for all the years she lived at the home, has any obligation to tell me what her movements are any longer – nor anything of any consequence, it would appear.'

Maisie breathed in the icy air, but it was warm compared to the words of Mrs Duffy. She decided to let the moment pass, fearing that if she probed any further, it could derail the morning's plans. 'Right we are, Mrs Duffy. Jake, hold that tea chest at the bottom, it's got a crack in it and we don't want the pavement littered with glitter.'

The last of the children and babies had just been transferred over from ward four. Aileen was inspecting the milk kitchen, checking that the probationers had prepared the feeds correctly and labelled them with the right names and feed times.

With all the extra babies, it was a hive of activity and the fridge was full. The bottles were lined up in the order they were to be used. Aileen had never really understood why the feed rotas were organized to such an inflexible timetable – at 6 a.m., 10 a.m., 2 p.m., 6 p.m., 10 p.m., 2 a.m., and then 6 a.m. again – other than that it kept things orderly. It broke her heart to see the babies grizzling with hunger between the four-hourly feeds so she often fed them herself in-between times, with some watered-down dextrose solution, to keep them going. She'd been caught red-handed doing that by Dr Walker once, when she was a staff nurse on the ward.

'What is it that you have in the bottle?' he'd asked her.

'Dextrose, Dr Walker. I'm sorry, but this little one is so big and hungry, he's been screaming the place down.' The red-faced baby in her arms had duly bawled and pulled away from the teat, furious that the bottle didn't contain milk. 'Can we not be more flexible with each baby and the feeds? Some can't wait for the full four hours.' She was embarrassed at having been caught out for using her own initiative, but it was worth a try. 'Is there really any reason why the babies who are hungry can't be fed at the times they need it?'

'Absolutely out of the question,' Dr Walker had said. 'I think you'll agree that as the clinician responsible for children's services, I know what I am talking about. The stomach of a baby is no different to that of an adult. Four hours is an acceptable gap and the routine of this ward has worked very well on that basis.'

Aileen had gritted her teeth and left the screaming baby in his cot while she disposed of the dextrose solution in the milk kitchen. On that occasion she had no choice but to carry out his orders to the letter, but when Dr Walker wasn't on the ward she made her own decisions whenever a baby's cries became too pitiful to ignore. She didn't care if she got into trouble, she had to do something.

She had confided in Matron a few days after her reprimand. 'Look at this little fella...' She pointed towards a baby in the arms of a first-year nurse who was walking him up and down the cubicle as he guzzled yet another supplementary two-ounce feed of dextrose. The nurse had sneaked it in to try and satisfy him while Aileen kept an eye on the ward door. 'They sent him up from maternity. He's less than twenty-four hours old and ten pounds in weight and he's been yelling the place down.'

Matron had been sympathetic. 'I quite agree. A roast dinner wouldn't satisfy that one. It seems unnecessarily cruel to make a baby wait for a feed and I don't agree about the timings, I never have. But paediatrics is the ward where I have the least say, as you know.' She sighed. 'What Liverpool children's services says goes, I'm afraid, and it's the same in every children's ward in the city, unfortunately.'

Matron watched the first-year nurse desperately trying to placate the child and frowned. 'The poor thing. They are so full of wind from crying, by the time the four hours comes around it's even harder to keep the feed down, and then it starts all over again, a vicious circle. But I'm not the doctor and I'm afraid that there are only so many rules I can break at any one time.' She raised her eyebrows despairingly.

If Matron could have had her way, doctors would only be allowed on to the wards for one ward round and emergency calls. And children's services would have no say in anything beyond outpatients. But that was never going to happen. In fact Dr Walker was never away from the place, except when he was on one course or another. Aileen loved it when he wasn't around.

Closing the kitchen fridge, Aileen scanned the work surfaces and opened the door of the steamer to check that all the glass bottles had been stood upside down, the rubber teats turned inside out and the milk cleaned out properly. Satisfied, she turned around and nearly jumped out of her skin to find Sister Tapps right behind her.

'Oh, hello! You surprised me there. How are you? Are you looking forward to your Christmas break? I have to say, I envy you. I've never had a Christmas off.'

Sister Tapps looked confused. She was gripping a bedraggled teddy bear in her hand. Aileen quickly recognized it as 'that' teddy. The one that sat in her office and which no one was allowed to move. She thought it rather endearing that Tappsy was so attached to it and even felt the need to take it with her when she went away.

'Are you spending Christmas with your family?'

But Tappsy continued to look muddled, and Aileen felt both embarrassed and guilty at having put her on the spot. She heard footsteps on the stairs and looked towards the door. Freddie had promised to pop in sometime today, and they needed to talk about meeting at the rehearsal later and the party afterwards.

Sister Tapps interrupted her train of thought. 'Yes, I'm off to my brother-in-law's. I'm having Christmas with him and my niece and nephew. I'm leaving now in fact. You have the last of my babies on your ward and so there is no need for me to stay any longer.'

Aileen felt her heart contract. The look on Sister Tapps's face near killed her, and the way she was gripping on to the teddy. Impulsively, she threw her arm around Tappsy's shoulders and hugged her, trying not to recoil at the unexpected sharpness of her bones. 'Don't give this place another thought. I will look after your children. I have your nurses, and I will look after them too. What we want is for you to have a lovely Christmas and a good rest. You will do that, won't you?'

Sister Tapps nodded. 'I will miss the carol singing on Christmas Eve – the children always love that, with the nurses coming round and stopping for a singsong at every ward. When we hear the nurses downstairs on ward one, I know they'll be coming to us next. It's when Christmas really starts, and we switch on the Christmas lights.'

Tappsy's eyes were bright, almost tearful. Aileen had never heard her talk so much.

'I know,' she said. 'I trained on your ward, remember. You taught me everything I know, and that's why you can trust me. I know it's my first Christmas on here as ward sister, but I will follow your routine, do everything the way you do it. It will be just like you're still here.'

She heard Freddie moving around outside and she was torn. He was impatiently shuffling from foot to foot and she heard the wood of the visitors' bench complain as it creaked under his weight.

She smiled down at Sister Tapps and this time there was no mistaking the tears that rushed into Tappsy's eyes. 'Sshh, don't you get upset,' she said. 'Goodness me, what would your nephew and niece think if they saw you. Come on, it's time for you to begin your much needed rest from this place. Time for you to have a Christmas where it's all about you and not twenty demanding little people. If you ask me, you deserve a medal, not just a break.'

She walked down the corridor with her arm still around Sister Tapps. As they reached the top of the stairs she exclaimed, 'Oh my! You can't go yet! What was I thinking of? Wait here.'

She spun round and winked at Freddie, who was looking at her with amusement and anticipation. He didn't mind waiting – just watching her was a treat.

Two minutes later she came flying back out of her office, carrying a Christmas present and a card.

'This is for you,' she said. 'I guessed you would be travelling somewhere and so I didn't want to make it anything cumbersome to carry. It's just my way of saying thank you. I am so happy to be up here with you on paediatrics and, well, anyway, merry Christmas.'

Sister Tapps's face flushed and for a moment she stared at the gift Aileen had thrust into her hand as though it might explode. Recovering, she stammered, 'Oh, thank you. Thank you so much. With having to move all the children and nurses, and with all that needed to be done for the ward handover and everything, I haven't—'

'Don't be silly,' said Aileen. 'I especially wanted you to have this, because I want to make sure you don't forget us on Christmas morning. I know you'll be busy with your family, but when you open this, I expect you to feel thoroughly guilty and miss us, just for the briefest moment, and really, more importantly, I want you to know that however much you're missing us, we'll be missing you ten times more. And I'll tell you this, I bet there won't be ten minutes while you're away when someone doesn't say, "What would Sister Tapps do?"'

Aileen laughed – she had to, because Sister Tapps looked like she was about to burst into tears. Freddie coughed and both women glanced towards the policeman sitting on the visitors' bench with a sheepish grin on his face.

'You have a lovely Christmas too,' said Sister Tapps, 'and I shall certainly be thinking about you.'

Just at that moment, Pammy Tanner raced out on to the landing between the two wards.

'You weren't running just then, were you, Nurse Tanner?' Aileen asked with far more authority in her voice than she realized she possessed.

'Er, no, Sister Paige. Louis is asleep and so I thought I'd just nip down to the laundry to fetch his clean clothes. The housekeeper said she would be washing them by hand because they're made of wool. I'll be five minutes.'

Aileen smiled. At the mention of Louis's name, everyone smiled. Restoring his life and health had been a joint effort and they all took pride in his progress.

'I will be thinking about you all more than you know,' Tappsy said as she watched Pammy disappear from view. 'If you don't mind, I'll just go and wish my nurses a merry Christmas and say a final goodbye, before I... er... leave.'

Without waiting for a response, she turned towards the doors of ward three. It was not her ward and they were not her doors. Half of the children in there were not hers, but as soon as she stepped inside and could see her own charges, positioned in a semicircle in the bay at the bottom in front of the roaring fire, she beamed a happy smile. The pain in her side faded and the sadness slipped away.

Freddie wasted no time. As the ward doors swung shut, he sprang to his feet. 'About time,' he said, taking a quick glance down the stairs to check the coast was still clear. 'Have you a minute for a word?'

He grinned and Aileen felt that thing that kept happening every time he smiled at her. Her stomach flipped somersaults and her mouth went dry. Right now she didn't feel like the confident and organized Sister Paige she normally was, the Sister Paige who was to be responsible for the lives and wellbeing of twenty poorly children and babies over Christmas. Right now she felt as though she were seventeen again, and her heart fluttered just like it had back then.

'Let's step into the milk kitchen,' she said, worried that one of her nurses would come looking for her. 'There are an awful lot of staff on the ward today. I have almost one nurse to four patients, and Sister Tapps is down there just now too. And it seems Dr Walker is back as well – two of my nurses saw him driving in earlier. Goodness knows how he'll react to seeing the baby he wanted to be left to die now looking so healthy, but let's cross that bridge when we—'

Freddie wasn't listening, and before she could finish her sentence he had pulled her into his arms and was kissing her. That was by far the most important thing he had to do that morning – to get over any awkwardness and take them back to their goodbye kiss at the bus stop. To the night of their first date. The hours since had been agony and he could not bear the small talk. He had made his mind up and there was nothing that would change it. Aileen was the woman he had been waiting for. He wanted to marry her and he didn't care how long it took, he was determined to make it happen.

Aileen broke away quickly and looked out of the door towards the ward. 'Freddie, I'm on duty – don't! I have to get back. I'm taking over looking after Louis shortly, when Nurse Tanner has her break.'

Freddie's voice was husky with emotion. 'God, I've been

looking forward to that!' he said. 'I know it was wrong and I'm sorry, but I wanted you to know that I'm not playing games here. This is real for me.' He tried to kiss her again.

'Stop,' she said, pushing him away. 'You can't do that. We're both on duty – are you mad or what?' Even as she protested, she had to fight to keep the smile from her face. 'It's a good job everyone's busy and there's still plenty of time until the feeds. But I have to get back to the ward.' Both hands flew to her frilled sister's cap to check it was still in place. 'It will be fine once we've got to know all the new children, but it's a little bit on the hectic side right now, and with baby Louis and all.'

'How is he today?' asked Freddie. He couldn't tear his eyes away from the buttons at the top of her dress and the only thought in his mind was how, when and where he would get to undo them. He had rehearsed the moment so many times in his mind that he felt almost guilty.

'And here, put that back on.' She picked up his helmet from the table where he'd put it down when he walked in. 'Honestly! Now, please, this a hospital ward.'

He noted she was smiling. He was back on safer ground. He grinned as he fastened the buckle on his chinstrap. 'Have you got cover for your mother for tonight?' he asked, looking her in the eye. For the first time in his life he was in love with a woman he had met only a handful of times.

'I have. I told her about it yesterday morning, said I'd be later than usual tonight. Gina's sitting in for me.'

Freddie grinned from ear to ear, but Aileen felt uneasy. Lying to her mother had been difficult – she had been difficult. And yet something deep inside Aileen had made her hold her ground. She would have to think longer about her mother's comments about selling the house and Aileen giving up her job. She had already decided she would go and see Josie and ask her what she was playing at, but that would have to wait because right now she had a ward to run.

Mrs Duffy huffed and puffed her way up to the children's ward. 'Oh, those stairs,' she said, just as Freddie turned the corner and began to take the steps two at a time down towards her.

'Here, let me take that,' he said as he lifted the box from her arms.

'Oh, you are a good boy. Freddie, is it? You're the new policeman on the docklands roads, aren't you? Nurse Tanner told me about you being on the ward.'

Freddie didn't have time to reply as Biddy and Branna appeared at the bottom of the stairs.

'Mrs Duffy, what a sight for sore eyes you are,' said Biddy. 'I thought they kept you locked in that home and never let you out.'

Mrs Duffy pointedly ignored Biddy and turning to Branna said, 'Morning, Branna, what a treat to see you. Are you helping us with the decorations?'

'I am that,' Branna replied. 'Apparently I'm a dab hand at the decorating, even though I've never put one up in me life.'

Emily arrived at the bottom of the stairs behind them, with Dr Mackintosh at her side, just as Pammy joined them from the opposite direction with her arms full of freshly laundered baby clothes. She looked at the gathering and said, 'Oh, Mam, it's you lot making all that noise!' And then in her most officious manner, she added, 'Excuse me, can I get past, please. Some of us have work to do.'

The air filled with the familiar clatter of a hospital trolley being pulled along. Jake had commandeered one for the decorations and was dragging it along with the handle behind his back just as he did with the trolleyloads of linen that he transported up and down the corridors day after day.

'Oi! No hello for your mam then, high-and-mighty Nurse Tanner?' said Maisie as Pammy grabbed the banister ready to mount the stairs.

Maisie had been joking, but Pammy was totally serious. 'No, Mam,' she said firmly. 'I have a patient waiting for me.' And then in a softer tone, and casting a glance towards Sister Haycock, who was talking to Biddy, she added, 'I'll see you on the ward. The children are all very excited about the decorations. Beside themselves, some of them are.'

They all stood aside to let Pammy pass. Emily smiled at Mrs Duffy and was somewhat surprised not to have her smile returned. Instead, a distinctly cold shoulder was presented her way. She was about to complain and ask Mrs Duffy what on earth was wrong when Aileen Paige ran out on to the landing screaming.

'It's Louis! He's gone! Where is he? Has someone taken him?'

Chapter 16

Freddie ran to the office, picked up the telephone and asked Madge to put him through to the Whitechapel police station as fast as possible. A child had disappeared on his watch! He paced the stairs and the corridor for what seemed like hours as he waited for CID, periodically peering down the ward through the circular windows in the doors to see if by happy chance someone had found baby Louis.

Aileen was crying and was nothing short of distraught. Staff Nurse was frantically looking in the cupboards of the sluice room, and no one knew why. Nurses were searching under beds and almost shouting to each other. 'Have you found him?' Emily was comforting Aileen and trying her best to take control. The children were sitting in their beds, watching and frightened.

The only people not in a panic were the worldly-wise domestics, who had all survived the May Blitz and knew the difference between a life-and-death drama and a missing baby. Maisie and Biddy found themselves stepping quite naturally into nursing roles as they set about calming what had rapidly become a tense atmosphere on the ward.

'But no one came past us in the corridor,' said Biddy. 'How can that have happened? Surely to God one of the nurses would have seen the ward doors open? And anyone not in a uniform would have stuck out like a sore thumb. No one comes on to these wards if they aren't in some sort of uniform.'

Mrs Duffy was shaking her head in bewilderment. 'I didn't see a single person the entire length of the corridor with a baby in their arms,' she said.

'Right, I'm going to make tea for all of us and set up a drinks trolley with a few treats on it for those littl'uns,' said Branna. 'We need to do something here to help out, and fast.'

'I'll help you, Branna,' said Mrs Duffy, who always made tea in moments of crisis.

'Smashing, ladies,' said Maisie. 'I'll move Sister Haycock and Sister Paige into the office and close the door. They can talk in there. And we'll go and cheer the kids up, won't we, Biddy? Our Pammy and these poor nurses are going to have their hands full today.'

'We will,' said Biddy, 'but first I'm ringing for Dessie to come up with some ladders. The best way we can distract those kids is to get on with putting up the decorations. I'll use the phone in the ward four office. Where's Madge? She was supposed to be here.'

They all turned towards the office to see that Madge had arrived, and was already on the phone, calling Matron.

'I think you need to get to ward three quickly, Matron,' Madge was saying. 'It's baby Louis, he's gone.'

Matron sank down on to the chair in her office. 'Oh no,' she said. 'And we all thought he was doing so well. Sister Paige was looking forward to him enjoying his first Christmas Day.'

'The policeman who was here, he's just told me that the CID are on their way, Matron.'

'How is everyone on the ward? And, Madge, why is it you

telling me this and not Sister or one of the nurses? It should be Sister Paige telephoning me, not you.'

'I'm not on switch today – Bryan is covering for me while I help with the decorations for the competition. Sister Haycock is just calming Sister Paige down. She was a bit shocked like, said she had never lost a baby before.'

Matron's brow furrowed. 'Never lost a baby before? Sadly, she has lost plenty. Especially during that bout of whooping cough last winter.'

Now it was Madge's turn to be confused.

'And what of the nurses, why are they too busy to call?'

'Because, Matron, they are looking for the baby. They've looked everywhere. Nurse Tanner is checking the beds of the children in the bay to see if one of them has slipped him in there and Nurse Harper is looking in the cupboards in the milk kitchen, and Staff Nurse, she has all the sheets out from the linen cupboard all over the floor, looking for him in there. Matron, I don't think anyone knows what to do, they are all a bit frantic on here, they need you.'

'What on earth…?' Matron's heart was pounding. She was struggling to make sense of what Madge was saying to her. 'They should be preparing the child for the morgue, not going through the cupboards.'

'But, Matron, there has been no death. Louis's gone missing – he's disappeared.'

'Missing?' Matron almost shouted the word down the phone. 'Missing? How can that be?'

'I wish I knew, Matron. You are needed on three, and jolly quickly, I would say.'

★

Maisie had tipped up and emptied out the large wicker trolley of decorations and now it stood upside down, ready to be used as a platform for them to stand on. Dessie and Jake pushed open the ward doors, each with a set of ladders over one shoulder. 'Here you are, ladies,' said Dessie, casting a nervous glance towards the window of the office to see his Emily sitting on the arm of a chair with her arms around the shoulders of Sister Paige, and Matron opposite her. 'Is it true?' he whispered. 'Has he just disappeared?'

'He has that,' said Biddy. 'Into thin air, it would seem. He is nowhere to be found and what's more, Sister Paige is adamant that no one came up the stairs when she was in the milk kitchen and that policeman, Freddie, was fixing the light.'

Lights needing to be fixed were Dessie's responsibility and his alone, and his ears instantly pricked up. 'What light?' he asked. 'No one has reported the light to me. What was up with it? I was only up here yesterday and in fact Sister Paige called down and reported that the fridge in the milk kitchen was noisy. She would have mentioned the light to me.'

'Oh Jesus, Dessie, I don't know,' said Biddy, looking weary. 'Honest to God, we just came up here to decorate this ward and try and win the competition to please Matron. They have the judging lady and a photographer from the *Nursing Times* coming tomorrow and we just wanted to get it done and out of the way, but now all this has kicked off.'

'It's obvious, if you ask me,' said Maisie as she laid the decorations out on the large polished wood table in the middle of the ward. She was surrounded by gold-paper stars in five different sizes, a crescent moon two feet across, a huge Star of Bethlehem on a gold ribbon, a flock of cotton-wool sheep and their shepherds, and a glittery tangle of tinsel and paper chains. Stanley had made a manger and had been given straw from the dairy and in it, lay one of Pammy's old dolls as the baby Jesus. 'His mother must have taken him. How do we know what the circumstances were, eh? No one knows who she was, so, frankly, if she has found a way to look after him and loves him so much she is prepared to sneak into the hospital to get him back, then good luck to her, I say.'

'We don't know that, Maisie,' said Biddy. 'And in my book, no mother who lets a child get that sick deserves to be a mother.' Before they got the chance to bicker, she nodded towards the tinsel and paper chains on the table. 'Has that lot to be strung around the windows?' she asked.

'It has, and the moon and all the golden stars to be hung in the middle. It'll be all the easier now that Dessie has the ladder, won't it, Andrew?' Maisie turned to the little boy lying in the bed nearest to them, his leg encased in plaster of Paris and suspended from a pulley at the foot of his bed. He was one of several children on the ward who had limbs in traction to keep the broken bones in place as they mended. She looped a string of paper chains around the pulley weights hanging off the end of the bed.

He smiled back at her. 'Can I help?' he asked.

'I wish you could, love,' said Maisie. 'Tell you what, how about blowing up some balloons. Your leg might be out of action, but I bet there's nothing wrong with your lungs, eh?'

'All this faff and palaver,' said Biddy as she took some balloons out of a brown paper bag and handed them to the eager young Andrew. 'In two weeks we'll be up here to take it all back down again.'

Dessie propped up one of the ladders and then whacked

it open and checked that the rope in the middle was in good enough condition to hold his weight.

'You get the tree set up in the corner, Jake,' said Biddy as Jake whacked open the second set of ladders and set it up below one of the glass orb lights that hung from the ceiling on an iron pole. 'You help him, Dessie. It's too big and awkward for us to manage. If you can get it straight, I can put Branna and Mrs Duffy on to that. We'll start on the windows.'

Several of the children were now sitting up in their beds, transfixed by all the activity. 'Are the decorations really going up today?' came a timid voice from halfway down the ward.

'They are, queen, and we are going to hang the nicest over your bed. What's your name?'

'Angela,' came the reply.

Biddy noted the steam tent suspended over her bed, folded back like the hood of a pram, ready to be deployed when it was needed, and the drip in her arm. It was obvious that little Angela had been one very sick little girl. 'How are you doin', queen?' she asked, concerned at her pale complexion and wide dark eyes.

'I'm nearly better now,' Angela replied. 'I want to go home to Mammy and Daddy and our Kitty, even the twins.' Her bottom lip began to tremble just as Pammy Tanner came over.

Pammy had been nursing Angela and she knew it took only one word of kindness or two seconds of conversation to start her crying. 'Hey, hey now,' she said as she approached the bed. 'What did Dr Mackintosh tell you? Didn't he say that every tear you cry is an extra hour in hospital and every smile you smile is a day sooner home?' She placed her arm around Angela's shoulders and gave her a quick hug.

Angela looked up at Pammy and to cancel out the tears

that had escaped down her cheeks she gave her the biggest smile.

Biddy thought she recognized Angela. 'Where do you live, queen?' she asked.

'On the four streets.'

'I thought so. Are you one of the Doherty girls?'

Angela sat up in her bed but began to cough with the effort. 'I am,' she said.

'Well, listen, tell you what,' said Biddy, 'I'm going to the bingo with my mate Kathleen tonight and she is your neighbour. If you like, I'll knock at your Mammy's and tell her how brave you are and what a good girl you've been. Would you like that?'

Angela nodded and the tears filling her eyes threatened to spill.

As Biddy turned to Maisie, she whispered, 'It's bloody cruel if you ask me, only letting the parents visit on Sunday afternoons.'

'I can't argue with you, Biddy,' said Maisie as she unfurled a roll of tinsel. 'They were waiting by the tea post on the day she came in. I could see she wasn't well. Tommy, her da is.'

'That's right,' said Biddy. 'Tommy and Maura. They're neighbours to Kathleen. Kathleen's come over from Mayo on a visit to her son – staying for Christmas, she is. I bet you Maura is right out of her mind with the worry.'

She took a strand of the tinsel and flicked it to Pammy. 'Here you are, put this round the littl'un's neck. You can be our own Christmas angel, Angela – the Christmas angel of St Angelus, how about that?'

This time there were no tears, just a beaming smile that took her closer to home.

★

In the ward three office, the head of CID was talking to Aileen, Matron and Freddie about what he thought had happened. 'Seems to me,' he said, 'that the little boy's mother has been watching the ward, slipped in and taken him. Though seeing as she's neglected him once, it's a mystery to me why she would want him back again. We've sent a message out to all police officers.'

'Please, sit down,' said Matron, nodding at the CID officer as she lowered herself into a chair. 'Do we even know who this child is yet?'

The CID officer took out his notebook. 'I'm afraid to say, Matron, that our enquiries have led us absolutely nowhere. What we do know is that the little fella wasn't born in Liverpool, or wasn't registered here anyway. Over the last few days we've been through the registry records, identified every male child born around here in the past twelve months and traced his whereabouts. He's not from here. There is no report of any child missing in Liverpool or unaccounted for. We've been on to London and there is no child of this age reported missing nationwide. It would seem that every mother in the UK knows exactly where her baby is, except for this little fella's. He must have been abandoned. Except now it appears his mam has had a change of heart and regretted her actions or maybe had a change of circumstances.'

He lifted the bridge of his glasses and scrunched his eyes together, as though to clear his vision. Matron could see that he was a busy man, probably overworked, and a case like this was possibly one he could do without.

Letting his spectacles drop back, he placed both hands on

his open notebook. 'As you know, we have identified his blood group, but that doesn't really help us. I've never known anything like it. London has suggested that he might be the child of a foreign alien. Some of them who were known to be here before the war went missing around '42 and have lived off the radar since. We just don't know. Has anyone seen anything suspicious here on the ward before today?' He turned to Freddie. 'Where were you, constable, when the child went missing?'

Freddie looked down at his feet. When Louis had disappeared he'd been in the milk kitchen with Aileen. If he admitted that, they would probably both lose their jobs.

Before he could make any comment, Matron spoke. 'I don't understand why he was left alone?'

Aileen spoke up. 'Nurse Tanner had gone to the laundry to collect his clothes. As you know, he has been coming on in leaps and bounds and there was no real medical reason to special him. But as we had Sister Tapps's nurses join us from this morning, we thought it would be good for him to have some human contact and interaction. He has obviously been badly deprived in the past.'

'And where were you?' asked Matron.

Aileen's mouth dried in an instant. How could she say that she'd been in the milk kitchen being kissed by Freddie? However briefly, that was what had happened. The most vulnerable child in the ward had gone missing on her watch, while she was in charge. Aileen's palms went sweaty and she began to feel light-headed. She would have to own up. Her career would be over and her mistake would haunt her for the rest of her life. Her mother would have her wish. She was not fit to be a ward sister at St Angelus. Her life was over before it had begun.

But before she could say anything, Freddie interjected. 'There was a problem with the light in the kitchen, Matron. It was flickering on and off and I offered to take a look for Sister.'

Aileen felt no relief at what Freddie had just said. She could tell by the set of Matron's jaw and the way she bristled in her chair that she did not believe him.

'Oh, really, and how long did that take?'

'No more than three minutes, Matron,' said Aileen.

That was the truth. Aileen felt sick inside and decided that she would have to confess. Whatever the cost to her and Freddie, she could never live with herself if she didn't own up to the fact that it was all her fault. If she had not stepped back into the kitchen with Freddie, had not lost her mind for those thirty seconds... But her mind was whirling. If anyone had passed by, she would have heard them. Heard the ward doors open and close. But she had heard nothing.

She looked across the office to Freddie. He had remained standing in the company of his superior. His eyes met hers and his instructions were clear. There was an all but imperceptible shake of his head. He was telling her no, don't say anything, and she decided in that instant that he was right, because none of it was making sense. There was something very wrong about this. She would swear by all that was holy, if the ward doors had opened, even if Freddie had been kissing her at the time, she would have heard it and jumped out of her skin. But Louis wasn't on the ward any more; he wasn't anywhere.

'I have to say, this is all very odd,' said the CID officer. 'For someone to know when to steal a baby, to know exactly when a nurse would decide to go to the laundry to fetch the ironing and the precise moment a light fixture would break in the kitchen. Not your usual pattern for a kidnapping, I would say

– not that we have to deal with such things very often, but you get my drift?'

Everyone nodded in unison. They did get his drift and they were all thinking the same thing. How could a series of coincidences so bizarre have been used by an individual to such effect?

'Do you think it was his mother?' said Aileen.

The CID officer looked up from his notepad. 'I think it has to be,' he said as he scratched his scalp with his pencil. 'But the fact remains that I cannot for the life of me understand how she knew when to strike. Is it possible that his mother was on the ward?'

Matron tutted indignantly. 'Totally impossible,' she said. 'We have a very strict visiting policy, and besides, we know who is visiting who. It's not Lime Street in here. It is a hospital ward, a place of peace and quiet. Calmness aids recovery, that is the motto on this children's ward.'

No sooner had she finished speaking than there was a loud shriek from ward three. Heads shot up to see Maisie balanced on the top of a swaying ladder, with Biddy and Branna holding the bottom as it rocked to and fro.

'Oh my goodness me, what on earth is going on?' Matron jumped to her feet.

Aileen beat her to the door and as she opened it she was greeted by shrieks of laughter from the children in the bay. Jake was clowning around pretending to have been flattened to the ground by the weight of the Christmas tree and the kids were loving every moment.

'Well, peace and quiet for most of the time,' Matron said, raising an eyebrow at the CID officer. 'What on earth is going on, Sister Paige? Has mayhem broken out on this ward?'

Aileen was already half out the door. 'Sorry, Matron, it's the day for decorating the ward. Everyone is very keen to win the competition. I'll go and see what's going on.' Relief washed through her as she left the office. She had never felt so unworthy of her position, so dreadfully deceitful in all of her life.

'Where is Sister Tapps?' a little boy wearing hospital pyjamas and clutching a teddy bear asked Aileen as she hurried past. He was one of the children who'd been transferred from ward four earlier in the day.

Aileen had been on her way to see if the ladies with the decorations were safe, but she stopped in her tracks and with her usual kindness took hold of the little boy's hand and spoke to him. 'Well, she has gone to have Christmas this year with her own family,' she said. 'It was time for Sister Tapps to have a little holiday.'

The little boy's face fell. 'She promised me…' he said as his bottom lip began to tremble. 'She promised me she would be here and that we would have presents on Christmas morning.'

'Oh dear,' said Aileen. 'Listen, I'll be back in just a moment. You will have presents. Everyone's parents will bring presents with them, I'm sure. Look! What are these silly ladies doing up the ladder with ribbons and stars hanging around their necks? What's your name, little one?'

Aileen had yet to combine the two wards' Kardexes into one and she only knew half of the patients on Sister Tapps's ward. Her stomach was churning. A baby on her ward had disappeared into thin air and now there was mayhem everywhere she looked.

'Jonny,' squeaked the little boy through his tears.

Biddy was waddling up the ward towards her. 'Sister Paige,'

she said, 'now don't be worrying, it'll all be all right, I promise you that. Maisie knows what she's doing and with the gorgeous decorations she's made, I'll tell ye what, I think we might just win this thing, mightn't we kids?'

A cheer went up from the children in the bay. They had been delighted by the antics of Maisie Tanner. Her daughter Pammy, on the other hand, was holding her head in her hands.

Aileen could hardly believe what she was hearing. She glanced towards the office, her heart in her mouth. Those children who were able to do so had escaped their bedclothes and were practically bouncing up and down on the ends of their beds – being cheered on, she noted, by Maisie and Dessie. To Aileen's utter relief, she could see through the window of the office that Matron had a smile on her face as she turned to Emily.

'Sister Haycock,' Matron said, turning away from the office window and suppressing her smile, 'Sister Paige is in danger of losing control of this ward. The children are taking over. Go out and help her, would you. And tell Father Christmas down there to keep some of his playacting fresh for Christmas Day.'

Emily was also glad to escape the office. She hurried out before Matron could change her mind, and strode straight down the ward towards the grinning Dessie.

Matron continued with the CID officer. 'So what do we do now? There's no point in me keeping a nurse in the cubicle – no one is going to come back for a baby who isn't there.'

'No, Matron, I'm sure that's true. It's all down to us now. We've come to a standstill regarding the boy's identity and parentage and I can't see that's about to change now the child has gone missing. I'm not sure that reclaiming your own child is a crime. Especially as the baby is now so much better, as you say.'

Matron nearly exploded. 'I will have you know that it is only due to intensive nursing care that that baby is alive. As far as I am concerned, it is still attempted murder.'

The officer scratched the top of his head. He looked perplexed. He had nothing to say other than, 'Yes, Matron.' He would have liked to have said that they had a great deal on their books at present and that half of the staff were missing, thanks to the Christmas holidays. He wished he could prove that it was Louis's mother who had come back and claimed him. He could close the case then and be done with it. He would like nothing more than for her to have a nice excuse to hand as to what had happened and then all would be happy ever after. A seventeen-year-old boy had been found in the Mersey that morning with his throat cut. He hadn't wanted to shock Matron, but that was where his attention was needed.

As he stood and motioned for his officer to follow him, he left his final instructions. 'We will do our bit, Matron, but, please, keep a close eye on this ward for anything unusual. Police officers are the most observant of people – if our officer heard nothing while he was fixing the light, I would say there was nothing to hear, which is why this is all the more confusing.'

As Matron opened the office door, the telephone rang. 'Just a moment, please,' she said as she turned back to answer it.

'Did you look under the cot and in the cupboards?' said the CID officer, turning to Freddie, who was standing guard outside the office door.

'Yes, sir. We looked everywhere, but who would hide a baby and why?'

The CID officer lifted his hat and scratched his head again. 'There is no rhyme or reason to this,' he said. 'I'm not happy. I would swear on my old lady's grave that that baby is still here somewhere on this ward and hasn't been taken. Unless we have the first case of a child disappearing into thin air.'

'What? You think he's still on the ward? But that doesn't make sense.' But Freddie knew that it didn't make sense that Louis had been taken off the ward, either.

Emily caught up with Aileen as she continued comforting little Jonny and tried to stop him missing Sister Tapps.

'Are you feeling all right?' she asked as she placed her arm on Aileen's and smiled down apologetically at the little boy. 'It's a bit of a shock, isn't it, and I have to say, I think it's a first for St Angelus.'

Aileen looked up at Emily. She was trembling slightly and Emily could tell she was hiding something.

'Look, come here,' Emily said and she led Aileen away. 'We will be back in a moment, pet,' she said to Jonny. 'Could you keep an eye on those two clowns for me? I think they're going to break something soon. You tell me when I come back if they have both behaved.'

'Oi, I heard that,' said Dessie. 'You're on my side, aren't you, lad? We men stick together.'

Jonny didn't reply, but, shoving the arm of the teddy in his mouth, he grinned up at Dessie and with his other hand wiped at his wet eyes. Big boys didn't cry.

Emily and Aileen walked down the ward. 'Look, it wasn't

your fault. Louis was doing so well, he was improving by the hour.'

Aileen looked thoroughly dejected. 'But that's just it – I think it is my fault.'

'No,' said Emily, 'it isn't. He no longer needed to be specialled and he was thriving, and that was down to you. That's what you have to remember. And besides, I'm sure the police will find him very soon. If his mother has taken him, she's got him back a lot healthier than when he arrived here. It really isn't your fault that a mother, for reasons we don't yet know, wanted her son back.' What Emily didn't express was her own heartache at not even having had the chance to kiss Louis goodbye, let alone start putting into action what she'd discussed with Dessie the night before.

Aileen took a set of keys out of the side pocket of her navy-blue uniform. 'Would you help me do the drugs round?' She looked up imploringly. 'I know it's gone a bit mad on here today, but I would rather the nurses cracked on with the decorating. Maybe we can do something right and win the competition… And it's giving the children so much fun.'

She sorted through the bunch of keys for the one to the drugs trolley and Emily could see there were tears in her eyes.

'Are you going to tell me what else is bothering you?' she asked.

Aileen looked up sharply and met Emily's eye. She had never felt more in her life like she wanted to unburden herself. She glanced nervously towards the office. Through the window she could see Matron on the phone, and there in the doorway was Freddie, gazing at her while his superiors talked among themselves. His eyes were pleading with her, and the set of his jaw, the way he was wringing his hands, told her he was desperately sorry for the mess they were in. But it didn't matter how sorry he was – it was all her fault.

'I am to blame,' she whispered to Emily as she pulled the trolley away from the wall. 'I was in the milk kitchen with Freddie and he came in and we were... er... talking. I was distracted. Oh God, Sister Haycock, it was my fault.' She looked distraught.

'Why? How could it have been? Have you taken Louis?'

'Of course not,' said Aileen, 'but I was distracted and if I hadn't been, I would have heard someone coming through the ward doors and across the landing and down the stairs.'

'And did you?'

'No. There has been lots of coming and going today because of the transfer and the decorations and everything, and I'd just spoken to Nurse Tanner on her way to the laundry, and then to Sister Tapps on her way in to say goodbye to her nurses, and Freddie and I were in the kitchen and we were... we were...' She gulped and her face blushed a bright crimson and she almost screwed up her eyes as she lifted the lid of the medicine trolley and rested her head against the smooth wood.

Emily smiled. She was about to break a rule, but she didn't care. Times were changing. She would always be a stickler for standards, but she had the feeling that she and Aileen would become good friends. 'Let me tell you something,' she said. 'Do you see that gorgeous man down there?' She looked towards Dessie, who now had little Jonny on his shoulders. He was reaching up to the crown of the Christmas tree to place an angel on the top.

Both of them stopped for a moment and smiled. 'He's been with Sister Tapps for ten months, apparently, little Jonny,' said

Aileen. 'Dessie's just made his day. There are some benefits to being the longest-serving patient.'

'Well, that man,' said Emily, 'kissed me in the porter's hut yesterday.'

Aileen's eyes opened wide and she gasped. 'Sister Haycock!'

Emily grinned back. 'Don't you "Sister Haycock" me! And do you know something, when he did, the sky didn't fall in and I wasn't held responsible for every bad thing that occurred in those few minutes.' She shot Aileen a mischievous smile. 'And the same applies to you. Now, I think we both know that this sort of thing shouldn't happen, and I know that neither of us will ever let it happen again, but I also know this: you must not let your guilt or what's gone on stand in the way of finding your own little bit of happiness. That Freddie, he looks very nice. And by the way, he's gazing at you like someone who cares.'

For the first time in what seemed like hours, Aileen felt relief wash over her.

'Now, we know how these things work,' said Emily. 'A child or a patient we have nursed for a long time and really care for dies – or in this case disappears without warning. It feels like the ward will never be the same again, or even like you want to give up nursing altogether. But pretty quickly the ward does get back to feeling the same, and we don't give up nursing, not ever. So what I am saying is: keep going. Let's just carry on and get this ward back to normal – once we can get rid of this rabble! And by teatime all will be well.'

Aileen nodded. 'I know you're right,' she said.

'I am,' said Emily with confidence. 'And I will let you into another little secret. I nearly broke the golden rule with little Louis. I was besotted after I spent that night nursing him and I was thinking of ways I could get back here on to ward three to spend more time with him. But we all break rules occasionally and I'm not beating myself up over it. Now, when are you seeing Freddie again?'

'Tonight,' said Aileen. 'We're both in the choir. There's a big rehearsal and then a bit of a party afterwards. I'm really looking forward to it.' Her face lit up and she looked down towards the end of the ward to see if he was still there. He was. Matron was still on the phone and as their eyes met, she smiled at him to let him know that everything was all right. I'm fine. We are fine. He looked as though he wanted to run down the ward and kiss her there and then.

She opened the medicine Kardex. 'Right, no one in cubicle one, sadly. Cubicle two…'

But they had barely pushed the trolley to the door of cubicle two before Matron reached them. 'Sister Paige!' she said as she hurried over. 'Sister Paige, that was Sister Antrobus. It's your mother – I'm afraid she is in casualty. You had better get down there right away.'

Branna stood in front of the fridge in the ward four kitchen, its door in her hand, peering into its dark and empty interior. Mrs Duffy fussed about with the trolley and laid out the plastic squash beakers for the children and the cups and saucers for the adults. 'Now, where do you keep the plates?' she asked. Branna didn't answer. Mrs Duffy tried again. 'Branna, where do they keep the plates in this kitchen? And the biscuits for the children, where are they?'

Branna looked back and closed the fridge door. 'Mrs Duffy,' she said, 'I think there must be a ghost in this kitchen.'

Mrs Duffy laughed. 'A ghost? Why would that be?'

'Because since a couple of hours ago someone has been and stolen all the bleedin' milk, bread and butter and the other few bits that were left over in this kitchen after the transfer on to ward three.'

'What are we to do then?' asked Mrs Duffy, looking shocked.

'We push this trolley to the kitchen on ward three,' said Branna. 'I was going to use up the ward four supplies before I cleared the fridge out. But there's nothing to use now, is there! There's something in the air and I don't like it one little bit. I'm off to Mass tonight.' She cocked her head at Mrs Duffy. 'And are you going to tell me why you're being so funny with Emily Haycock? Isn't there enough going on today without you adding to it?'

Chapter 17

Sister Tapps couldn't bear to hear a child cry. She had never subscribed to the commonly held view that if a child wasn't in pain it should be left to cry out its tears. But Sister Paige's predecessor had been very much of that mindset. She had operated on the principle that leaving a child to cry helped with the healing and taught them a lesson; that it maintained peace and quiet on the ward if you quickly trained children to understand that crying was a fruitless exercise. There was no medical treatment available for a child who was simply missing its parents, and therefore, as most children were inpatients for several weeks at the very least, and sometimes for months or even years, the quicker they adjusted from their old life to the busy reality of a hospital ward, the better.

But Sister Tapps had no truck with any of that, and nor did she think that having their parents visit hindered a child's recovery. It was one of the reasons she and Sister Carter had never hit it off, despite having worked in adjacent wards for twenty-five years. There was also the fact that Sister Carter didn't like Sister Tapps working her days off and not taking any holidays; it was she who'd wanted to complain to Matron about that, but she'd asked Sister Antrobus to do her dirty work for her instead.

'I'm sure she's trying to show me up,' Tappsy had heard Sister Carter say one evening to Sister Antrobus on the landing that divided the wards.

Tappsy had stepped back into the shadows of ward four and listened.

'Can you have a word with Matron for me?' Sister Carter continued. 'She makes the rest of us look bad and you know I want to retire next year. Wouldn't we all go mad if we didn't have our breaks away? And you are so much closer to Matron than the rest of us.'

'Well, of course we would, my dear,' Sister Antrobus had said, 'but no one thinks Sister Tapps is sane, I can assure you. Not since that dreadful incident.'

There came the sound of approaching footsteps at the bottom of the stairs and the two women fell silent for a moment. Tappsy stayed put, sure that there was more to come.

'In my opinion,' Sister Antrobus went on, in a softer voice now, 'she has never recovered from that. But never fear, I shall have a word with Matron.'

'Excellent,' replied Sister Carter. 'Well, I shall put in a good word for you when Matron comes to talk to me about my replacement. You should get ward three all to yourself when I go, if I have anything to do with it. I cannot think of anyone better.'

'It would be such a privilege to take over from you,' Sister Antrobus replied. 'Such an orderly ward. Not like ward four – I swear I often see children running around in there. I have complained to Matron so many times, but when it comes to

Sister Tapps she makes special allowances. However, I shall try my very best.'

Sister Tapps had allowed the door to close softly behind her. She had heard enough, and she knew she had nothing to fear. All the ward sisters were unmarried and childless – that had been the rule at St Antrobus until recently – and they fell into two groups when it came to children on the wards. There were those who were full of resentment at being single and childless and took this out on the children, regarding them with poorly concealed resentment. And there were those who took the opposite view and lavished all the loving care they possessed on their young patients. Both she and Matron fell into the latter group, but only Sister Tapps was aware of Matron's soft spot. She hid it well.

For all those reasons, Tappsy had been relieved when Sister Carter had finally retired. She smiled to herself as she made her way upstairs to the sisters' accommodation, thinking about how different Sister Paige was to her predecessor and how fortunate it was that Matron had decided not to put Sister Antrobus on ward three. She stopped to catch her breath at the top, then continued down the corridor to Emily Haycock's room. She closed the door behind her and lay Louis down on the bed.

Sister Haycock's secret vacating of her room had been a real stroke of luck for Tappsy. It hadn't taken her long to realize that this could be the solution to her enforced Christmas break. She wouldn't need to go far after all – just next door, in fact. It had taken her less than fifteen minutes to pile into her trunk the things she thought she might need and to drag it from her own room to Emily's. She'd had to stop once to allow her heart rate to slow, but it hadn't been too difficult. This way, if the maids ignored the sign on her door or if anyone did pop into her room, they would think she had gone away as she was supposed to have done. She left her wardrobe door open so that anyone would see straight away that her outdoor coat and hat had gone, and she stripped off the sheets, stuffed them into a pillow case and left them for collection outside of her door, just as she always did.

No sooner had she closed her door, left her laundry out and retreated into Emily's room to get organized than she heard the sound of footsteps and voices on the stairs. She immediately recognized them as belonging to the accommodation maids, Enid and Dora.

'Nothing like the old days, this isn't, not at all,' said Enid.

'Not from what I've heard,' replied Dora. 'Who would have thought – two weeks' holiday at Christmas. What a thing, eh?'

'It is, but if it carries on like this, they'll be using the sisters' block for something else and we'll be out of a job. It's only a matter of time before Sister Haycock declares her hand, and we've only four of them living in now as it is. And to think, before the war there were more than twenty.'

'Gosh, that must have been hard work,' said Dora.

'It was that, but it could be a laugh too. They used to make their own fun – it was bingo for money one night, and the priest invited to supper in the sitting room the next. He used to give them all a ticking-off about the gambling, but it didn't stop 'em. I saw any number of bottles of sherry carted up those stairs behind Matron's back.'

'No! Never!'

'Oh yes I did. I'm not making it up. They were all right old scolds during the day, gave the nurses hell, they did, but by night in their own sitting room, two glasses in, they soon loosened up. They had a big radio on in the corner and they had their little rituals, all to the clock. Pored over the war news, they did – nothing else in their lives to talk about or look forward to. I swear to God, when the war ended they all looked lost. I mean, don't get me wrong, there was more drunk that night than any other, but they had nothing else to hold them together, no more running back to find out what had happened to the regiments their relatives were serving in.'

'Imagine not being able to get married,' said Dora.

'No, not a man between them, and not allowed one anyway. Every one of them a virgin. In those days, if they met a fella and wanted to marry, they was out on their ear. It's not like that now though, and not before time. Anyway, our days are numbered, my girl. Sister Tapps won't be here for much longer, she'll retire or be found dead in her bed, and they'll move Antrobus out into digs somewhere and we all know what's happening to Emily Haycock. Trying to kid us she's sleeping in the bed every night! I haven't changed those sheets for a month. I'm not daft, I know she hasn't slept in them. Buggered if I'm wasting me time.'

Sister Tapps heard the polished oak locker doors crash shut at the end of the corridor. In her mind's eye she could visualize the two domestics putting their coats on and fastening the buttons as they chattered. 'Anyway, are you coming to the concert on Christmas Eve night?'

'I am,' said Dora. 'It'll be lovely, that will.'

'Right, well, I'll see you there. Come on, time to get shot of this place for a couple of weeks. We have earned a break and if we don't get a move on, we'll miss our bus.'

Sister Tapps leant against the wall. There would be no one

anywhere near the rooms for the next two weeks. It is meant to be, she thought to herself.

It had been surprisingly easy. She almost marvelled at her own audacity and how the idea had just come from nowhere. She'd been down on the wards, talking to Sister Paige in the milk kitchen, and then she'd gone into ward three to say goodbye to her newly transferred children. The nurses were all gathered in the bay, filling in the morning charts that were piled up on the central table, and the office was empty. She'd stopped at little Andrew's bed to check that his leg was comfortable and to reassure him that she wouldn't be far away, when she heard a cry from cubicle one. It was little Louis, the best-kept secret in the hospital, the one Sister Haycock had told her about. The Christmas miracle.

Curiosity won out and she made her way towards his cubicle door. He had heaved himself up in his cot and tears were running down his face. He stretched both of his arms out towards her as she approached.

'Oh, you poor little thing, come here,' she said as she walked over and picked him up. It was the way he nuzzled his wet face into her cheek and placed his spindly arms around her neck and clung to her that did it. She was defenceless. He smelt just like Laura had. Of Pears soap and Johnson's baby powder. She hadn't used either on her ward since Laura had gone. She had bathed Laura every single morning herself and she had loved the smell of the Johnson's baby powder.

'Laura,' she whispered into the nape of his soft neck. 'You smell just like Laura.'

With Louis's sleepy head laid on her shoulder, she walked

out on to the ward and without even thinking what she was doing stepped on to the landing. She made straight for the milk kitchen – true, she was tiptoeing, and if she was honest, perhaps she was hoping not to be noticed, to have an excuse to spend a bit more time with the baby in her arms, but it had been so easy. When she got to the milk kitchen she glanced in for the briefest second and saw that Sister Paige was wrapped in the arms of the young policeman. Without a moment's hesitation, she and Louis slipped on down the corridor across the landing and into ward four.

Tappsy had spent her life tiptoeing around her ward, between the cots and beds of sleeping children, intent on ensuring that they didn't wake. Now that she weighed less than ever, being light of foot was even easier. She found a string bag hanging on the back of the kitchen door in ward four and, opening the fridge, took just a few minutes to fill it with food. Hastily, she tiptoed down the now eerily empty ward four to the locked single oak door at the end, the door she used most nights to return to the sisters' accommodation. She had the key on her ring. Placing the food down on the floor, she put the key in the lock and, checking that the coast was clear, slipped through, straight on to the accommodation landing and into Emily's room. It had all taken less than five minutes.

She was the only person to ever use that door. No one would think to ask her permission to walk down ward four and take a shortcut. Sister Carter had moved out to live with her widowed sister only two years after the war had begun and she had been the only other person to use the door. Even then, the etiquette was that she had to ask Sister Tapps's permission first. More often than not she preferred to walk down the steps, along the main corridor, all the way to the main entrance and then back up the administration offices steps and past Matron's rooms. It was a long walk after a hard day, but pride had often come before a weary hike for Sister Carter.

Louis gurgled and smiled up at her and as he did so her heart fluttered. He had been in St Angelus for only a few days but already she could see soft chestnut hair peeping through. Within a month his scalp would be full of tufts of long-overdue baby hair. She packed the pillows around him, placed him between the bed bolster and the wall and checked he was safe.

'Shhh, little boy,' she said. 'I will be back soon. I'm just popping out for more supplies – a bottle for you, for a start.'

As she tried to lay him down, he fought against her, struggling to raise his head above the eyeline of the bolster and to take in more of the room, but his full belly from the feed Nurse Tanner had given him just before she'd left to collect the laundry, and tiredness from his brief spell of crying, had worn him down. He was improving, but he was nowhere near good health yet. Tappsy hadn't needed to ask him to shush. His eyelids were already closing and he was fast asleep before she left the room.

'There, you can spend Christmas with me,' she whispered. 'We can enjoy it together, in here.' Her heart lifted – she would be spending this Christmas just as she had every Christmas she could remember, looking after a poorly child.

But as she bent to pull the cover up and over his tiny form, she had no time to think what her next step was going to be. A wave of pain engulfed her and she staggered back, grabbed the side of the chest of drawers with her hand and slid down the wall and on to her bottom. She clamped her other hand over her mouth, desperate not to scream out loud.

This pain was worse than any she'd had before. It had come on without warning and surged from her side and her back across her entire body. Beads of perspiration stood out on her top lip. Her face flushed from hot to cold and then went clammy.

When the pain had passed, she looked at the back of her hand and saw that her skin was sallow. Brown stains she was sure had not been there before glared up at her. As the pain ebbed away, she took her handkerchief from her pocket, wiped the tears from her eyes and steadied her shaking hands. She would take some diamorphine from the medicine chest when she went back through ward four to her own milk kitchen to fetch the formula and dried food for Louis. She thought he was ready for some now and she would be the first to try him.

She decided to wait for her pulse to return to normal before she stood up. This was the perfect time, she thought. Ward four would be completely empty. The nurses had stripped the beds, and the dirty linen had been collected. But she knew how diligent Branna and her team were, so she would avoid returning there tomorrow morning. She'd already heard Branna discussing how the holiday period would be a good time to get the porters to clean the top of the high window frames and the glass light shades.

Satisfied that the pain had now disappeared and Louis was asleep, she rose with care, not wanting the pain to return, and stood straight, holding on to her side. It had gone. She was becoming used to the pattern and, reassured, she crept back out on to the corridor and through the door at the end on to ward four.

She headed for the medicine chest first and slipped some diamorphine tablets into her pocket. They were a low dose, but she would double up. Checking through the window that there was no one about, she popped into the milk kitchen and, grabbing a cardboard delivery box from the side, filled it with formula, dried egg, and bottles and teats. She looked longingly at the tap, desperate to quench her sudden and burning thirst, and did something she had never done before – she turned on the cold tap, allowed it to puddle in her cupped hands and sipped the water. After a couple of sips, she pulled away sharply and looked down at the water in her hand with a puzzled frown. She checked the tap, placed her other hand underneath and felt the end. Her mouth tasted of metal. There was something in the water. She allowed more to puddle in her hand and, putting her face close, examined the water. It was clear and yet it tasted very strongly of something metallic. Lead. The pipes are lead, she thought. Is there lead in the water? She spat it out into the sink.

Gathering her cache in the box, she made her way to the laundry room for nappies, zinc and castor oil cream, and clothes. In no time at all she was safely back through the door and ensconced in Emily's room once more.

Louis was where she had left him, his arms stretched out above his head, his legs akimbo. She was exhausted from her efforts and, even though she refused to admit it to herself, from the pain as well, which had turned into a dull but persistent ache in her side. She took one of the diamorphine tablets. 'It's enough,' she said as she swallowed it with water from the sink, noting again that the water tasted metallic.

She wanted to lie down. Needed to lie down. She sat on the bed next to Louis and slowly lowered herself until she was stretched out alongside his thin but perfect form. Moving her face close to his, she breathed in his heavenly baby smell and her senses heightened, conjuring memories of the child she had loved as her own. She inhaled again, filling her nostrils, and that was all it took for her to remember Laura and all the days they had spent together, all seven hundred and eighty-two of them. As the tears escaped and rolled down the bones of her jutting cheeks, she sobbed her name. 'Laura. Laura.' Not a day had passed since Laura was removed from her care that she hadn't thought of her and worried about her. She longed to see her grown and to know that she was being loved and cared for. Laura had been neglected, she knew that. Louis had also been neglected. 'I'm here now,' she whispered. 'I'm here.'

Moments later, exhaustion swept through her and sleep came quickly, relieving her of her pain and her loneliness.

'I will come to casualty with you,' Matron had said to Aileen. What she didn't say was that she was about to put Sister Antrobus in charge of Aileen's mother. Dr Mackintosh had told her on the phone that he could find nothing wrong.

'If I had to guess,' he had almost whispered down the phone, 'I would say that there is nothing wrong with her, but she's Sister Paige's mother, so I can't really do that. And besides, given her history, I daren't discharge her. She's already made Doreen on reception cry, she was so rude to her.'

Matron remembered exactly what Mrs Paige was like and there was only one woman she knew who was bigger, scarier and more used to getting her own way. She was definitely handing this case over to Sister Antrobus. She could come in very useful sometimes.

'Can you take over ward three for the time being?' Matron had asked Emily. 'Sister Paige's mother has been admitted downstairs and we don't know what it is yet.' She raised her eyebrows and they both looked towards Aileen, who was grabbing her cloak from the staff room. She appeared shaken.

'I'm ready, Matron,' she said and she almost flew out of the door.

'I'm happy to hold the fort, Matron. Let me know what's happening and if I can do anything other than cover the ward,' said Emily as she escorted them to the bottom of the stairs. She reached out and squeezed Aileen's hand.

'Can you tell Freddie?' Aileen said. 'He thinks we're meeting at the rehearsal tonight, but I doubt I'll be able to make it now.'

'Of course I will,' said Emily. 'Leave it to me. I'm sure your mother will be fine, so don't worry. And don't worry about the ward either. I have no nurses in the school from now until we return in January, so you aren't inconveniencing me.'

The backs of Matron's and Aileen's cloaks swung from side to side as they hurried down the main corridor towards the front door and casualty. Emily marvelled at Matron's ability to take everything in her stride and the way she always had an answer ready. Her confidence never wavered. Her assured walk down the corridor of the hospital she was responsible for belied her age and gave the impression that she was a much younger woman.

Emily folded her arms and looked back up the stairs towards the landing. Matron had given her a meaningful stare when Aileen had asked her to tell Freddie what had happened. She wondered whether she'd be in Matron's bad books now for not telling her what was going on right under her nose. Matron liked to know absolutely everything that went on in St Angelus.

She turned and looked back down the corridor. Freddie was nowhere to be seen. The CID officers had left and it appeared they may have taken Freddie with them. Emily had the distinct impression that they weren't as concerned about Louis now as they had been when he was first admitted. That was a big mistake, in her view. She took the stairs back up to the ward with her usual quick, delicate steps and was met by Maisie Tanner on the landing as the ward doors shuddered closed behind her. Through the circular glass porthole windows, Emily could detect activity on the ward.

'Oh, there you are. Are you in charge now? Branna said Sister Paige's mam has been admitted.'

'She has, so it looks as though I'm the replacement sister until we know what's going on.'

'Well, you'll never guess what,' Maisie said, 'we're almost done with decorating the ward! Come and have a look. The kids are dying to show it off to someone. It's a crying shame these poor kids are only allowed to see their mams and das once a week. It's shocking, that, Emily – who makes up these rules?'

Emily shook her head. 'Do you know what, I never questioned it during the war, and it's just hung on, but now it really feels like a bonkers rule. I think Matron would have dropped it earlier, but Sister Carter was vehemently against her doing that. She used to say that visitors would bring bacteria into her ward, cause infections and disrupt the routine. She said the children wouldn't get enough rest and how was she supposed to nurse poorly and dying children with the noise of visitors traipsing in and out. I think Matron found it hard to argue against that.'

'Emily, I'm a mam and I know that if me and my kids were

separated, they would be so upset and that surely would mean they'd take longer to get better.'

'Well, everyone's talking about it in London apparently, and with the new NHS things are changing so fast. I wouldn't be surprised if new rules were announced soon. I even read that they're thinking of scrapping the Nightingale wards and dividing them into smaller sections, to give patients more privacy and make it easier to have visitors coming in and out.'

Before she pushed open the doors, Maisie owned up to the fact that the children in the bay had become more than a little involved in the decorating. 'We couldn't stop them, Emily. The kids were all helping and I thought Matron wouldn't mind. To be honest, they were no trouble – all the bedlam seemed to be coming from elsewhere, what with everything that's been going on.'

'I can't argue with that,' said Emily. 'And to top it all, Dessie acting like he's just flown in from Lapland.' She shook her head as Maisie began to giggle. 'Do you think we have a winner? Has all this effort been worth it?'

'Well, come and see for yourself, love. We've got everything you can think of and the ladies have been at it for nights. I don't know about green fingers, mine are golden glitter fingers now. Our Stanley will be spitting it out of his Christmas dinner at this rate.' Maisie placed the flat of her hand on the ward door. 'Any news about little Louis?'

Emily shook her head. 'No, nothing. Talk about a mysterious disappearance or what?'

'It's no mystery, Emily. No one walks away with a sick baby in their arms, not unless they really love him and think they can do better than is being done here to make him healthy again. The only reason any woman would do that would be because she can't bear to be apart from him. It's his mam, make no mistake. Only a mother's love would drive a woman to take that risk.'

'I'd like to think that,' said Emily, 'but it is one heck of a coincidence if she just happened to turn up at the hospital at the very moment there was no one to stop her. I mean, I'm not saying it didn't happen, but what are the chances?'

Emily thrust her hands into her pockets, something Matron had been telling her off about for years, but to no avail. A troubled look sat on her face. She wasn't convinced by Maisie's theory, but she had no alternative argument to put forward.

As Maisie opened the doors, Emily gasped in surprise. The ward had been transformed into a Christmas grotto and twenty pairs of earnest eyes were fixed on her as she looked around and walked towards them. Lights glittered everywhere, and on the table there was mistletoe and holly set into a block of oasis. She looked up above her to the huge star suspended from the ceiling. 'That's the star of Bethlehem that is,' said Maisie, who had crossed her arms and was studying Emily's face intently, looking for early signs of approval.

'Look at the manger,' said Emily, 'and the shepherds?'

'They aren't shepherds, them's dockers,' Maisie began to laugh.

Emily couldn't laugh, she was transfixed by the ceiling of glittery stars, the lights and candles and the sheer transformation of the ward. The flames from the ward fire reflected in the baubles on the Christmas tree. 'Oh my goodness, haven't you all done well,' Emily said as she looked around at the children and included them in her praise. 'It looks just magical.' The children grinned from ear to ear and Maisie sighed. Her work was done.

Outside the window the light was already beginning to fade and Emily could see the first flutter of snowflakes driving past on a squall thrown up from the Mersey.

'Do you like it, Sister?' little Jonny asked, clutching his teddy and holding Dessie's hand.

'I do!' Angela piped up and grinned.

'Oh, would you listen to you,' said Emily, 'you are looking better even in just a few hours.' She looked around her and grinned as she continued marvelling at the decorations around her.

'There's just one more little job Jonny here has to do, isn't there, lad?' Dessie looked down at him and winked.

Jonny seemed to rise to his full height as he said to Emily, 'Close your eyes, Sister Haycock.'

Emily looked at Biddy, who grinned and winked at her. 'Go on,' she said. 'Do as you're told for once. It's the little patients doing the ordering about now, not you.'

The ward, a place of sickness and healing, was full of smiles. The children who were to remain there over Christmas were either chronically ill, too poorly to be discharged or had home circumstances that were not conducive to recovery. Poor nutrition resulted in badly healed bones and the orthopaedic surgeon would not allow a fracture patient to return home to a diet of potatoes and bread until he was sure the bones had mended. For many of these children, this Christmas would be their first away from poverty and squalor.

A little girl's voice rang out. 'Sister, Dessie says we are in charge now because everyone's lost their heads and he doesn't know where they are.'

Everyone burst into laughter.

'Shush, you, you will get me into trouble,' said Dessie.

'Yes, come on, Sister, do as you are told,' said little Jonny.

Emily thought they were all enjoying this just a little bit too much.

'Eyes closed, everyone!' Dessie shouted.

'Honestly!' said Emily as she crossed her arms. 'I hope Sister Paige hurries back. I can't imagine what it's like for her being bossed around on here all the time by you lot.'

'Oh, Sister Paige is fine. I think they've saved this especially for you,' said Beth Harper as she elbowed Pammy in the ribs.

Despite the fact that Louis had gone missing, there was an air of excitement on the ward. 'It really feels like Christmas now, doesn't it?' said Pammy. 'And I tell you what, I'm going to go over to ward four and see if I can find out where Sister Tapps keeps her stash of sweets because I think you all deserve a reward for helping to decorate and clean up.' She suddenly looked sheepish. 'Is that all right with you, Sister?'

'Oh, don't worry about me, Nurse Tanner,' said Emily. 'No one else seems to be.'

There was more laughter at Emily's mock indignation.

'OK, Mr Horton, I think we are all ready. Shall we get this over and done with? How about a countdown, everyone?' said Maisie.

The children nodded enthusiastically.

'Right, everyone with me. I'll count backwards from number five – can you do that?'

Twenty little heads bobbed up and down, some more con-fidently than others.

'Let's start then. Close your eyes, Sister Haycock. Five, four, three, two, one! Eyes open, Sister.'

Jonny flicked the switch and the Christmas tree lights illuminated the bay. It stood ten feet tall and shimmered as the golden tinsel reflected the lights. The fire in the hearth in the middle of the ward was roaring, thanks to Branna and Biddy, and tears sprang to Emily's eyes. Feelings of happiness, sadness and delight mingled within her. This was the first Christmas in her life that she had someone to call her own and he was standing next to the Christmas tree, smiling at her. His eyes said: this is the first and the forever. And she knew that, after years of lonely Christmases when she had jumped at the chance to work and cover a ward, any ward, this one would be different.

Chapter 18

Dr Mackintosh was waiting for Aileen at the desk in casualty. Aileen could hear her mother before she saw her and the shame froze her to the spot.

'Take it away, you stupid woman. No, I do not want another of your cups of thick, bitter, Catholic tea. Has anyone called for my daughter? She can take me home now.'

'Now then, Mrs Paige...' The soothing voice of Doreen O'Prey, the casualty clerk, drifted out from behind a screen. 'Sister Paige knows. I have already telephoned ward three and I am sure that as soon as Sister Paige is free, she will be straight down here.'

'As soon as she is free?' Mrs Paige's voice rose in temper. 'Her own mother has been brought into hospital in an ambulance and she keeps her waiting until she is free?' She reached a climax on the word 'free', which came out almost as a screech.

All Aileen could do was stand and stare at Dr Mackintosh in horror.

'Come here,' he mouthed and motioned for her to step into the doctors' office.

Doreen continued to try and pacify Mrs Paige. 'It might be

some time before Sister Paige can get away. There has been an emergency on ward three and she has patients to look after. She will be needed up there for a while.'

'*This* is an emergency,' she heard her mother almost shout. 'Me being stuck here in this place – that's the only emergency my daughter should be concerning herself with.'

Dr Mackintosh placed his fingers on his lips, urging Aileen to be quiet as she tiptoed across the space that separated them.

'Is she all right?' asked Aileen as she untied her cape, the office door now closed. 'What happened? What's wrong? How did she get here?'

'The young girl who works for you, she called an ambulance. Apparently your mother told her she was having another stroke.'

Aileen hung her cape up on the coat stand. 'I take it from the sound of her that she wasn't?'

'Well, the signs and symptoms she described to me certainly sounded as though she might be. The first thing I did was a neurological examination, which was just fine. In fact, considering her previous stroke, I was very impressed by some of her reflexes. Tell me, how has she been managing at home?'

'Well, she doesn't really,' said Aileen, looking and sounding thoughtful. 'She can't really do very much for herself, which is why we have Gina, the girl who called the ambulance. She's Branna's daughter, from up on ward four. It was becoming difficult for me to get to work on some days and I desperately wanted to be made a ward sister...' Her voice trailed off. She thought she must sound very selfish, putting her career before her own mother.

'Well, let me tell you, her heart is as strong as an ox's, and beating twice as well. The grip in her affected hand is amazingly good, and you may be surprised to hear this, but it is much better than you have probably been led to believe. I say this because I had a slight suspicion and then I caught her out.'

Aileen's eyes opened wide.

'Please don't be cross with me,' said Dr Mackintosh, 'but I sensed she might have been playing for sympathy rather too much. When the ambulance men brought her in, she nearly hit one of them with her handbag, and when they transferred her to the bed, I saw through the curtains that she got herself off the gurney without assistance. I thought nothing of it, but when I examined her, she said she couldn't put the foot down at all on her bad side and yet I had seen her get down and take three steps towards the bed only moments before.'

The colour drained from Aileen's face. 'How did you catch her out?' she asked, too shocked to say anything more.

'Well, I pretended to be moving her stick out of the way. She took a few steps towards it and she grabbed it tight. Your mother, Sister Paige, is not as infirm as she makes out.'

Aileen lowered herself on to the chair. Anger began to bubble up from somewhere deep inside. The effort she put into nursing her mother at home, the effort Gina put in… The worry she had caused over the years, to the point where she'd nearly jeopardized Aileen's promotion. She didn't trust herself to speak, so all she said was, 'Thank you, Dr Mackintosh.'

'Gina's out there in the waiting room,' he said gently, all too aware of the hurt in her eyes.

Aileen looked up. 'Do you mind if I speak to her myself, in here? Can I see her now, before I see my mother?'

'Of course, Sister. As I've said, from my perspective I can't see any reason to admit your mother to the ward. However, we have plenty of beds – would it help you if I did admit her?'

'But it's Christmas in a few days.'

'Yes, and Matron tells me that you're working. Tell you what, I'll leave you with your Gina while I attend to the little boy with the profuse nosebleed in the next bay – which I think has something to do with the twig sticking out of his right nostril – and I'll come back in about ten minutes. You have a think and I'll send Gina in now.'

He didn't hear Aileen's thank you as he rushed out. Her mind was whirling as the realization dawned that there was nothing she would love more than for her mother to be in hospital for Christmas. Almost immediately she was filled with shame. How can you think that, she berated herself, then looked up to see Gina walking towards the office.

'I'm sorry, Sister Paige,' said Gina. 'She made me call the ambulance. She said she was having another stroke. I don't know what one of them looks like, but she had just eaten all her lunch and seemed as fit as a fiddle to me.'

Aileen shook her head in bemusement and could only ask, 'Why?'

'I don't know Sister, but she's been acting all funny since just before you came home the other night after choir.' Gina didn't want to say, 'Since she saw you kissing the handsome man on the corner of Green Lane.'

'Did she faint? Did she lose consciousness at all?'

'No, Sister. She waited for me to come back to her room after I took the lunch tray back downstairs. Told me to come straight back up, she did, when I was on my way down to the kitchen, and when I did get back up the stairs, she was flopped back in the chair with her hand to her brow and she was making this kind of gasping noise. She was complaining that she felt just like she did when she had her stroke a few years ago, and she told me not to waste time and to go straight down to the phone box to call the ambulance. So I did.' Gina looked fearful, as though she might be told off.

Aileen was quick to reassure her. 'You did absolutely the right thing, Gina. I will go in and see her now.' She furrowed her brow. 'Did she turn pale? Did her mouth look funny to you, or did her eye droop? Was she mumbling, unable to speak?'

'Oh no, Sister Paige. Doctor asked me all of those questions too. She had just had a big bowl of oxtail soup and the bread I made this morning with lots of butter and salt on it. She was a good old colour. She was out of sorts, that's why I did what she said, but she was none of those things.'

Aileen nodded, perplexed. 'You go to the WVS post and get yourself a cup of tea, Gina. I will join you there.'

As Gina left the unit, she passed Dr Mackintosh coming out of one of the cubicles. He had blood splattered down his long white coat and what looked like a bloody stick in his hand.

'He'll live,' he said as a look of horror crossed Gina's face. 'He didn't quite get it up far enough to pierce his brain.'

Gina grimaced and pulled a face, and then she leant in and whispered, 'Sister Paige doesn't know what I told you, does she doctor?'

He looked behind him to see the retreating back of Aileen as she passed through the curtains and into her mother's cubicle. 'Not a thing, and she never will,' he said and he tapped the side of his nose, leaving a smear of blood on it. 'You did the right thing to tell me, Gina. That young woman deserves a bit of a life of her own and you were absolutely spot on. I took a peep behind the curtain when Mrs Paige didn't know I was looking and I saw her with my own eyes, so don't worry. I told Sister Paige what I saw, not what you told me, and you did the right thing because if you hadn't, I wouldn't have known what to look for.'

Gina was the one who now felt faint. Relief flooded her face and she almost laughed out loud. 'Oh, thank goodness, I was worried there. I like working for Sister Paige, I didn't want her to think I was being a sneak. But like you say, her mother gives her the runaround something rotten. I feel sorry for her, I do.'

'Indeed.' Dr Mackintosh looked down into the blood-stained enamel kidney dish he was carrying. 'The mystery though is why? Why has she done this and brought herself here? For what purpose? But don't you worry, it's our little secret,' he repeated, and he turned into the office.

'Oh, darling, at last.' Mrs Paige switched from abusive to smarmy with zero effort. 'I thought you were never coming – I kept asking them where you were. I'm so sorry to be such a nuisance and to worry you.'

'You aren't a nuisance, Mother,' came Aileen's automatic reply. 'I was worried when I heard you had been admitted. I thought it might have been—'

'I know, darling. Another stroke. Me too.' Aileen's mother pulled a disconsolate face and for the first time that day Aileen doubted her mother's sincerity. That expression of hers, when she dragged her mouth down at the sides and looked forlorn, always made Aileen feel guilty. 'Anyway, if you can tell that nice lady who sits behind the hatch and makes the tea to let the ambulance know we are ready to go home now.'

'Doreen?' Aileen almost spluttered. 'Mother, I am going to have to see Doreen and apologize for the way I just heard you talking to her – for the way everyone heard you talking to her, in fact.'

Mrs Paige sat up sharply. 'Oh no, dear, not me. Either you are mistaken or she is telling tales. I have offended no one and I would never do such a thing. I just heard the doctor telling her to be the one to organize the transport – I've not said anything out of turn. It's her job, what she is paid to do.'

It had not been lost on Mrs Paige that Aileen appeared remarkably unruffled by her dramatic admission to St Angelus, but she put it down to her daughter's professionalism.

Aileen's eyes were fixed on her mother's face, as though watching her every move. 'Tell me, Mother, exactly what happened. How you felt when you became poorly and how you ended up here, at my place of work, because you are obviously fine now and the doctor can't find anything wrong.'

Mrs Paige glanced sideways at her daughter and began to wheedle. 'Well, darling, it may be your place of work, but it is a hospital and I was very sick. That doctor, have you seen how young he is – what can he possibly know? He's not the best, is he? Otherwise why would he be working here in this dockside hospital?'

Aileen felt a spike of fury course through her. It rendered her speechless. Dr Mackintosh was possibly the most popular doctor in the hospital, with patients and staff alike. He had introduced a new resuscitation method to St Angelus that was only being used in a few other hospitals across the country and it was saving lives already. He helped with things he had no responsibility for – teaching the nurses, standing in for the other doctors – which was quite some sacrifice, both for him and for his girlfriend, Nurse Tanner. For the first time in her life Aileen felt like she wanted to scream at her mother not because of anything she had done to Aileen but for what she had said about someone else.

Mrs Paige reached out her bad hand and grabbed hold of Aileen's – a significant and revealing mistake. Aileen looked down and saw the realization flash through her mother's eyes. She was in unfamiliar surroundings and Aileen was standing on the opposite side to where she would have been if they'd been at home.

Aileen gasped, but her mother acted with impressive speed. She let her arm drop to her side and banged it forcibly against the side of the trolley. 'Oh, my stupid arm,' she said as she heaved it up with her good hand, and, glancing quickly up at Aileen from under hooded lids, laid it on her lap.

It was a convincing performance and Aileen, her emotions all over the place, immediately reached out and gently rubbed the back of her mother's hand. 'Oh dear, that might bruise,' she said as she examined the delicate flesh on the hands that had never met a scrubbing brush to see if there were any broken veins or capillaries. 'Wait there. We have ice in casualty, I'll go and fetch some before it comes up in a nasty swelling.'

Her mother reached out again, this time with her good hand. 'No, Aileen, really, it will be fine. Please, just get that girl to order the ambulance.'

The overhead lights suddenly flicked on throughout the casualty unit, dispersing the gloom. Aileen hadn't realized how dark it had become and now she remembered that she hadn't eaten a thing all day. She felt more than a little light-headed herself. She checked the clock – there was no way on earth she would make the rehearsal and the party. She had so been looking forward to it, not just because she would be with Freddie but because it was a rare chance to do something for herself.

For a brief while her life had looked as though it might be on an upward trajectory, with a lovely man, new friends in the choir and somewhere to spend her evenings. For the first time in as long as she could remember she had felt Christmas coming and she'd been looking forward to it, for reasons she simply could not explain, not even to herself. She had put it down to a combination of having become a ward sister, being with the children, helping to organize the Christmas decorating competition and even to spending time with the exuberant Nurse Tanner, who never stopped talking about Christmas and all the goodies her mam was bringing home from the grocer's and the butcher's, using the Christmas club money.

But all that had now come crashing back down to earth with a bang. She had a sick mother and responsibilities that could not be escaped. Nothing had altered in Aileen's life. She had allowed herself to dream and now she would pay the penalty for that indulgence. She would not even be able to make the Christmas choir.

'Do you need to have a word with Matron?' said her mother. 'To tell her I shall be leaving the hospital and returning home with you.'

'Matron? Why?'

'Well, I would have thought it was quite obvious, Aileen. Wake up, child. And you call yourself a qualified nurse? It seems you really do know very little about things medical. "Why?" What a stupid question. To tell her your mother is ill, of course, and that you will need to take time off work from now on to look after me properly. This was a warning,

I believe. I may not be so lucky next time, and I'm afraid, darling, you won't be able to go out this evening to your rehearsal. I would be very nervous being left with that young girl, after all that has happened today.'

'All that has happened?' Aileen repeated her mother's words as though in a daze. Her mother didn't know the half of it. Here Aileen was, standing in casualty, a place to which life-or-death emergencies were brought, trying to work out why her seemingly healthy, rather rude and apparently duplicitous mother was there with her, wondering what she was going to say to Dr Walker when she saw him and exactly where Louis was. The fact that she had left her ward in disarray was the least of it right now – there was far more to worry about than the decorating competition and the antics of the porters, and anyway, she could rely on Sister Haycock to restore order. Much more pressing was the missing baby. Where was Louis?

'Did you hear me, darling?' Her mother was speaking to her again. 'Run along now and fetch that ambulance. They must listen to you. Go and take that one outside the door.'

Aileen turned her head and through the curtains saw an ambulance driver together with Doreen, the casualty clerk, wheeling an elderly man up the rear ramp and into a waiting ambulance. 'We can't have that one, Mother. They're busy taking someone back home.'

'Yes, yes, but can't you pull rank? Your father used to do that for me all the time.'

Aileen remembered how her mother used to bully her father. He always appeared to be doing something he didn't want to do, and his face would be red with embarrassment. 'I could ask if they are going our way – we could share,' she said.

'Share? I don't share. And another thing, you had better call Josie and tell her what's happened.'

'What has happened, Mother, if you are so eager go home? What has happened?'

Before Mrs Paige had time to answer, casualty filled with a voice Sister Paige instantly recognized. It was Sister Antrobus.

'Sister Paige, you are needed back on ward three as soon as possible, please.' She strode over towards the curtains and, grabbing them by the top, flung them back.

'I'm afraid I can't, Sister Antrobus,' said Aileen. 'This is my mother, she was brought in with a suspected stroke and I am going to have to get her back home.' The words were painful and for the first time Aileen knew how her father must have felt. The shame was inside of her; it shrank her from within, making her feel belittled and sick. She worried that her professionalism had been compromised and it hurt her deeply.

Sister Antrobus folded her arms across her wide expanse of navy-blue dress and supported her ample chest. 'Home? Suspected stroke? Suspected by whom?'

Aileen stopped speaking and looked down, expecting her forceful mother to reply for her. After all, it was what she had done for all of Aileen's life: spoken for her, made her decisions. But for the first time since she could remember, her mother was almost speechless and her expression resembled that of a fish.

'It was me,' Mrs Paige stuttered, far less confident now than she had been when shouting at Doreen or cajoling Aileen. 'I have had one before, I know exactly what it feels like.'

'Quite right,' said Sister Antrobus. 'You are the only one who does know what it feels like when you have a stroke, and as far as I'm concerned, if you were alarmed enough to call an ambulance, then I am quite sure you need to be admitted for observation. We can't be too careful about these things, can we?'

'Oh, no, that won't be necessary,' said Mrs Paige, finding her voice and her courage all at the same time. 'My daughter here will be looking after me, and after all she is a qualified nurse, and a ward sister, just like you.'

'Oh no, I'm afraid that won't be possible,' said Sister Antrobus. 'We have sent Sister Tapps home for Christmas and your daughter is the only paediatric ward sister in the hospital. We will have to admit you, Mrs Paige, otherwise you'll be sent home alone, for the whole of Christmas. You see, Mrs Paige, it's like this: Matron has sent me down here to tell Sister Paige that instead of going home for Christmas, could she stay in Sister Tapps's room in the sisters' accommodation, until she returns from her holiday. Starting the day after tomorrow. Absolutely no one in St Angelus says no to Matron, do they, Sister Paige? She really is the boss.'

Aileen nodded, slowly.

Sister Antrobus had looked straight into Mrs Paige's eyes as she'd said those last few words, daring her to raise an objection, half hoping she would. She was disappointed. The woman went down like a deflated balloon. Sister Antrobus could see her mind working through it all as the expression on her face moved from disbelief to a frown to the mildest semblance of resistance. She spluttered and attempted a few incoherent words, but to no avail. Sister Antrobus gave a good impression of not listening to a word of it and instead of responding turned to see which porter had just come through the casualty doors.

'Bryan,' she said as he walked in with Doreen, pushing a

wheelchair back into the long queue of chairs lined up just inside the doors, 'could you take Mrs Paige down to ward one, please. Sister Paige, you had better get back upstairs. I'm afraid you'll need to work late tonight, because of everything that's gone on. You can bring your mother's things in tomorrow – we can put her in a hospital gown for tonight.'

Mrs Paige made one last attempt to object. 'But I don't need to be in hospital if I have a daughter who is a ward sister, and the doctor said—'

'Oh yes you do, Mrs Paige. It's the doctor's orders. I have just overheard him talking to Matron on the telephone. They are both very much in agreement. We need to keep a very special eye on you. We don't like this sort of thing, not at all. You never know, it could have been a warning and that is the very reason we are keeping you in. We are going to give you very special treatment – so special that I am going to nurse you myself, right through Christmas.'

Chapter 19

Biddy knocked on the front door. She only walked round the back of a house if she was a regular visitor, and this was her first time at the Dohertys'. She'd been standing there for no more than twenty seconds before a small crowd of grubby faces gathered around her.

'Who d'ya want, missus?' asked a particularly dirty little boy. His shoes had no laces and there were holes in the toes and a grey sock poked through.

'Are you from the hospital?' asked the slightly older girl next to him with red ribbons in her hair. 'Is Angela dead?'

Biddy took a sixpence out of her pocket. 'Here you go. Get some sweets,' she said.

It was as though she had waved a wand. The children scattered, racing off towards the Dock Road and the sweet shop. They'd known by the look of Biddy that she was Irish and the chance of her purse being opened was high.

Biddy spotted a man walking on the opposite side of the road and recognized him immediately as the son of her friend Kathleen. 'Hello, Jerry!' she shouted over. 'Do you know if the Dohertys are in?'

'Oh aye. Hello, Biddy. Just knock harder,' Jerry shouted

back. 'It'll be the twins' bath-time – they make enough noise to raise the dead.'

Biddy raised her hand in thanks and knocked again. This time she heard a response from within.

'Is that someone at the door, Maura, is it?' It was a man's voice.

'How would I know, Tommy? Get off your big fat arse and go and look, would you.'

Biddy heard the shuffle of feet along the lino on the opposite side of the door. While she waited she studied the scrubbed step, the clean windowsill, the freshly washed front door and the polished brass knocker. Her gaze travelled to the parlour window and the net curtains, which were pristine and white. Biddy liked Maura before she'd even met her. She could tell she was a kindred spirit. They were both women with a sense of pride, members of a select club who maintained standards despite the daily battle against the grime from the docks. They made certain that every member of the family understood what was expected and, just as importantly, ensured that their homes would never be mistaken for the homes of slatterns or women of ill repute.

Maura's was clearly a God-fearing home, as the statue of Jesus on the cross in the windowsill testified. Biddy would bet Maura attended Mass twice a day, flying there in her curlers when she heard the call of the bells. She sensed that Tommy was also the sort who came straight home on a Friday night and put his wages on the table, waiting to have his spends returned before he dared disappear and join the other dockers down at the pub.

Suddenly the door was flung open. 'Oh, hello. How are ye?' Tommy, wearing his vest, trousers and a cap, looked puzzled to find a rotund lady, minus curlers and clutching a large handbag, on his doorstep.

Biddy noticed that the vest he wore was free from stains. 'I'm well, so I am. I've come to see Maura,' she said. 'I'm a friend of Kathleen's. You must be Tommy.'

At the mention of Kathleen's name, a grin spread across Tommy's face and the door was opened wider. 'Well come on away inside, would ye. Maura is just bathing the twins.'

The hallway was so narrow, it was almost impossible for Tommy to turn around and so he waddled into the kitchen ahead of Biddy, shouting, 'Evening, Peggy,' over his shoulder.

Biddy turned to close the front door and wondered why Tommy was calling her Peggy. But then she saw that the woman from the house next door – which, by contrast, could not have been described as clean – had come out on to her front step and was already trying to peer down the Dohertys' hallway after her. She was presumably the woman Tommy had been addressing. Peggy opened her mouth to speak, but Biddy pretended not to see her and closed the door in her face. She knew Peggy's type only too well. She would have been about to invent a spurious excuse to follow her inside, only to leave even before Biddy did and immediately report to the neighbours why she'd been there, along with any number of exaggerated details.

As Biddy entered the kitchen, Maura looked up from the tin bath in front of the fire in which she was bathing two young boys. One of them was full of energy, kicking about in protest as Maura attempted to douse his head with water; his twin, the exact same in looks and stature but seemingly the opposite in personality, sat still with his hands in his lap, looking forlorn and perhaps wishing that his brother would be still so that it could all be over. Through his dripping fringe he squinted up at Biddy. At the end of the bath, perched on a small wooden stool, was a little girl, whom Biddy presumed was Maura and Tommy's eldest, Kitty. She was holding out a grey towel, threadbare and holey in places but clean-looking nonetheless.

'Friend of Kathleen's here, Maura,' said Tommy by way of announcement. He made his way to the chair in front of the fire and, lifting the cushion, extracted his newspaper from beneath it.

Maura, drying her hands on her apron, pushed herself up from her knees and on to her feet. 'Oh hello,' she said. 'Is Kathleen all right?'

'Oh aye, she's fine. My name's Biddy and I'm after calling for her to go to the bingo. I work up at the hospital and I was on ward three today, with your little girl, Angela.'

Silence descended on the room; even the noisy twin ceased objecting to being lifted out of the tub and into the towel Kitty was holding. It felt as though the clock had stopped, along with time itself, as Tommy slowly laid his newspaper back on his knee with one hand and with the other held the stump of a cigarette he'd been trying to light midway to his mouth. Maura, who could say nothing in response, just stood with her mouth half open, her eyes frozen in fear, staring at Biddy. The statue of Our Lady looked down on her from the shelf over the range above her head and Kitty blinked as she thought she saw it smile.

'She's asked me to send a message,' said Biddy, 'to say that she's doing just grand and breathing much better and she can't wait to see ye all at visiting the day after tomorrow.'

A noise escaped from Maura that sounded like a gasp. Her hand flew to her mouth and tears filled her eyes. As much as she tried to remain composed in front of this stranger, this angel bearing good news, she failed. Seconds later, with Tommy at her side and his arm around her shoulders, all the tears, fears and pent-up emotion she had been forced to hide for the sake of her other children found release. Kitty, speechless, grinned from ear to ear as she towel-dried her concerned-looking brother's hair.

As Biddy left the Doherty house and made her way to Kathleen's, she felt both disturbed and elated. They'd all heard stories about parents who found it hard to leave the hospital even though they weren't allowed on the ward. In some cases, when a child was really very ill, the parents would spend half of their day at the WVS post, just in case. Maisie had plenty of tales to tell and had attended the funerals of more children whose parents she had befriended than Biddy thought could possibly be good for her.

Some mothers never left until the hospital lights were switched off and the army of night cleaners arrived, believing that their child would be able to sense that they were near. Biddy knew of one neighbour who'd lost weight and been physically ill during the week she'd had to leave her son at St Angelus. Relief only ever came once the parents finally got to meet Sister Tapps, on visiting day. She was such a reassuring presence that subsequent weeks tended to be not so agonizing.

'You are late, missus,' said Kathleen as Biddy walked through her back door.

'I am that,' said Biddy. 'I was just giving some good news to your woman, Maura, about Angela.'

'How is she?' asked Kathleen as she tied her headscarf

in the mirror over the fireplace. 'Maura has been out of her mind all week, it's been terrible. I've spent as much time over there as I have in me own house, trying to keep her going. I wouldn't mind, but Angela is such a crier, you'd think she'd be glad of the peace.'

'Aye, some of them are,' said Biddy. 'But I've heard there are women with a dozen kids who get that upset when they're apart. There are some that think the more kids you have, the less you feel for each one. I'm not kidding. At least we have Sister Paige on ward three now. The old sister, Sister Carter, she had terrible ways. When a child died she would make the nurses bathe them, lay them out and dress them in a shroud before the parents were allowed in. As though the parents cared how their children looked. By the time a mother got her little one back in her arms, the body was cold. Who knows how many little ones died alone, behind a screen, with no one holding their hand when the angel came. Terrible, it was. She was a right scold, that sister.'

Kathleen shook her head. 'God, isn't it awful, and if they were cold, the soul would have flown. Why have you tolerated it, Biddy? You're right, it has to change, but what power do you have anyway?'

Biddy shrugged. 'I have no clue. I'm just the housekeeper in the nursing school.'

'I'll tell you what I do know,' said Kathleen, 'if we don't get a move on, we'll be late for the bingo.'

And the trials and traumas of children separated from their parents were forgotten for now as Biddy and Kathleen ran for the bus.

★

Freddie stood outside on the red sandstone steps of the Angli-can cathedral waiting for Aileen to arrive. His eyes focused on every huddled and shadowy form that hurried up St James Mount towards the warm orange glow of the candlelight within. He even stared hopefully at the area to the side of the main doors, near where the workmen's wheelbarrows and tools were stacked, just in case she'd lost her way in the dark. He wondered briefly when the repairs to the bomb-damaged Lady Chapel would be completed; it had been more than a decade already, but it seemed nothing went quickly when it came to the building of the cathedral. There were still sections that hadn't even been finished in the first place, let alone the bits that got damaged in the war. Many thought it might never be done.

The sleet was becoming more forceful and as the wind blew, the icy blast stung his eyes, forcing him to blink as he squinted repeatedly into the distance, only to be disappointed as someone, anyone but Aileen, dashed past him and in through the door.

'Blimey, what a night,' said one lady as she almost knocked him over, her head bent in an attempt to keep her hair dry under her hood. The Mersey squalls were so ferocious, umbrellas were of no use.

'Flamin' buses. Thought I was late,' said a chap he recog-nized as being part of the firemen's choir.

When he saw the nurses from ward three tripping up the steps, wrapped in their capes, he almost dared himself to ask one of them where Aileen was, but he thought Aileen might not appreciate him doing that, revealing their private business to the nurses on her ward.

'God, what you doing out here, Freddie? It's freezing,' said Pammy as she shook the sleet from her cape.

'I'm just having a ciggie,' he replied. He wasn't surprised to see Dr Mackintosh running up behind Pammy and Beth. It was hardly a secret that he and Pammy were madly in love, a fact that even Matron seemed to tolerate.

Freddie took much ribbing from his fellow police officers as they arrived, and he pretended to be lighting up another cigarette to avoid having to follow them in. Every time he heard a set of running footsteps in the distance his heart leapt in anticipation then sank again when Aileen failed to materialize.

He almost visibly jumped at the sudden opening of the door behind him. 'Here you are, still here.' One of the tenors from the police choir had come to look for him. 'We were just about to begin and one of the nurses said you were out here. You know how mein Führer hates us to be late.'

Freddie half smiled at the reference to Hitler. There was barely a citizen of Liverpool who missed an opportunity to belittle or laugh at the man who had wreaked such havoc on their city and caused them all so much misery. The choirmaster was elderly, bald and not much over five foot tall; he wore half-moon spectacles and his love of God and his devotion to worship through music was obvious to all. He was as far from a representation of Hitler as it was possible to be. Churchill had been so right: their city may have been damaged, but the spirit of the people of Liverpool remained unconquered.

'I'm coming,' said Freddie reluctantly as he cast one last pleading glance backwards into the dark, towards the city. There were no more scurrying feet. The last latecomer had arrived and with a heavy heart he realized that what had happened today had almost certainly changed things between them. Aileen had obviously decided that it was their fault that Louis had gone missing. They were to blame, or rather, knowing Aileen – and he thought that even though he could count their conversations on two hands, he already knew her as well as he knew himself – she would be blaming herself. That was what he would do, and weren't they just the same, two halves of one whole? It was him, he was to blame as it was he who had kissed and distracted her. She must surely see that she was entirely innocent. Louis's disappearance was nothing to do with Aileen. She would obviously never forgive him, and he would never forgive himself.

He'd asked one of the police officers on the cathedral steps whether there'd been any news from the hospital. 'You mean about that baby you found? Not a whisper, mate. That little lad, he's back with his mam, he wasn't even reported missing in the first place.'

Freddie didn't bother to argue. It seemed that all his colleagues were of the same opinion and that the case was now closed. It dawned on him that as long as Louis was missing, Aileen would be lost to him. His future was over before it had begun and as he walked into the cathedral he found it difficult to blink back the tears that threatened to run down his cheeks.

'Nearly started without you there, Freddie,' said Pammy as he walked past her standing on the end of her row. She winked and grinned at him as he found his place and, taking the deepest breath, he forced back a smile of his own.

Candles burnt brightly all around them – on the window-sills, in the aisle and encircling the chancel. It was as freezing as always, but even though it was as cold inside as it was outdoors, the flickering flames gave the impression of warmth, taking the edge off and making it possible for him to open the carol sheet he'd been handed as he came in. The wood, the stained glass, the candles – everything shone expectantly. All that could be heard was the clearing of throats, the flicking over of the score and the shuffling of feet. And then there was nothing but silence as they waited.

Freddie kept his gaze to the front, focusing on the figure of Christ and his suffering, the windows, and the elaborate altar cloth. He was breathing in, holding it, and breathing out slowly. How has this terrible thing happened to me, to us, he wondered. How had something so wonderful come so close, only to be snatched away? He remembered the taste of Aileen's lips. The softness, the yielding. It was as though they had never been touched before. The image of her eyes, smiling at him, welcoming, floated in front of him.

There was the cough, the five-second warning, and then came the sweet voice of the soloist and the first strains of 'Once in Royal David's City'. The acoustics in the cathedral lifted the carol heavenwards and Freddie could hold it together no more. He did the thing he had been brought up to believe was wrong: his throat tightened, his eyes burnt and the tears cascaded down his cheeks. He missed the worried glances from Pammy and Anthony, who, if they could, would have walked over and stood next to him, one on each side.

Emily Haycock was kneeling on a kitchen chair mashing potatoes when Dessie arrived home from work. 'What a day, eh?' he said as his cap landed on the back of the kitchen door and he sat on the chair in front of the fire to take off his boots.

'I don't think I've ever known another like it,' said Emily.

'I thought the police would never go, the ward would never be decorated and the whole horrible nightmare of Louis going missing would end. And then Sister Paige's mother being admitted to top it all off.'

Dessie stood and, moving behind Emily, slipped his arms around her waist and kissed the back of her neck. He doubted he would ever get over the novelty of finding her in his kitchen when he got back from work. He couldn't take his eyes off her. Watching her mash a pan of potatoes was a delight to him and he wondered whether he was finally going mad.

'What's for tea?' he asked as he began to nibble her ear.

Emily squirmed. 'Dessie, stop! It's your favourite, mince and mash.'

He reached around her, freed her hands from the hot pan she'd been holding and turned her round to face him. It could have been ambrosia from the gods – it didn't matter how hungry he was, there was only one thing he needed at that moment.

Later, they were lying in bed, half awake, half asleep, both exhausted by the day and their lovemaking, when Emily sat up abruptly. 'Oh, God, no!' she almost shouted.

'What?' said Dessie, sitting bolt upright himself.

'I forgot to tell Freddie about Aileen – that her mother had been admitted and she wouldn't be at the choir rehearsal. I got the impression she might have been expecting him to call up to the house after. Oh bloody hell, Dessie.'

'Did you see him then?' Dessie asked as he reached for a cigarette.

'No, that's just it, I didn't. By the time I'd finished the observations and the medicine round, got the ward cleaned up and the children's tea sorted, the police had gone. I thought

Freddie might have come back, but it seems that now Louis has been taken back by his mother, no one is interested.'

'Don't worry, he'll catch up with Aileen tomorrow. Are you sure you don't want one of these?' He passed her a cigarette.

'No, I don't. Come on, let's go down and have that food. We aren't wasting it, and besides, I'm hungrier now than I was before.'

Aileen Paige had started packing her case and it sat open on her bed, already half full. Matron had brooked no argument. She was adamant that Aileen should move into Sister Tapps's room while she was away for Christmas. 'Besides, apart from the fact that there'll be no travelling for you, you can be closer to your mother and know she is being well cared for. I know it isn't ideal, but I think you need a break, young lady. It's true that working on the ward isn't exactly a break, but at least you won't be working when you get home as well, will you?'

Despite the awfulness of the day, there was one glimmer of light – Freddie. When Emily told him what had happened, he would surely make his way to Aileen's house to see her, knowing that her mother was in the hospital. Emily had said she would tell him that with everything going on and Aileen having to work late, it would be impossible to make the rehearsal but that she would be at home. Alone.

She sat in the window with the lights off. Every time she heard the squeal of the brakes on a bus she shrank back into the curtains, but there was no point. None of the nimble young men who alighted from the buses were him. He never came.

As she sat in the dark, replaying the events of the day in her mind, she began to shake. It had all been too much: Louis, her mother, her shame, and now this. Freddie just didn't care. She had got him all wrong. She'd been such an idiot. He was probably more concerned about his job than he was about her, and Louis going missing had scared him. It had scared her too, but she had gone over it so many times and the only explanation had to be that his mother had arrived at a time that happened to be fortuitous for her. She must have been scared at the prospect of having to speak to someone. It was not their fault. If they hadn't been in the kitchen, Louis's mother would probably have hidden and waited for the right moment. They were not to blame. Of that, Aileen was sure.

She waited until the last bus pulled away from the bottom of Green Lane and as she looked out into the dark night she felt sad at the turn her life had taken. No choir or party tonight, the first social gathering she would have been to in ages. No Freddie, no future to look forward to. As she stood to make her way to bed, it dawned on her that she was entirely alone and possibly always would be.

Chapter 20

Christmas was rapidly encroaching and Mrs Duffy still had a lot to do. She was removing the last tray of mince pies from the oven when Beth walked into the kitchen to help.

'Have they finished the tree?' Mrs Duffy enquired.

'They have, and they are all looking forward to the trolley full of treats coming in,' said Beth. 'You would think some of them had never tasted a glass of sherry before.'

'Well, maybe they haven't? But I think it's my mince pies that are getting everyone excited.'

Beth laughed and gave Mrs Duffy a gentle nudge in the ribs. 'Get you! If you weren't spot on, I might have the temerity to disagree with you, but honestly, if you said I could only have one or the other, the mince pie or the sherry, I'd choose the mince pie any day. You are the only person I have ever known who puts orange zest in the pastry – it's gorgeous.'

Mrs Duffy flushed with pride. These were the moments she lived for, the moments that made it all worthwhile. There was no one at home and there had never been a Mr Duffy. Like many women who had lived through both wars, she was certain that whoever it was that God had chosen for her had fallen in a muddy field long before she'd had the chance to meet him. All human contact in her life came in the form of hugs from grateful nurses, and their words of thanks or praise were the highlights of her life.

'I forgot to tell you, Sister Haycock is popping in too. She really wanted to help with the tree. She's not singing in the carol service on Christmas Eve, but she's coming to watch, with Dessie. I think he's taken the porter's lads out for a Christmas drink tonight.'

Mrs Duffy pressed the flat of her hand into the small of her back as she arched backwards, attempting to relieve her enduring stiffness, brought on by years of bending down to a low oven. 'Is she now? Well, wouldn't it have been nice to be asked first? I don't suppose my opinion counts for much though, does it?'

'Mrs Duffy,' Beth blurted out, 'what do you mean? No one takes you for granted.'

Instantly Mrs Duffy wished she could have bitten off her tongue. 'Oh, not you. Sure, no one helps me more than you do. I don't mean you, not at all. I swear to God, you spend as much time in this kitchen as you do on the wards. You're never out of here. I don't know what I would do without you some days.'

Beth had covered the distance of the kitchen between them and placed her arm around Mrs Duffy's shoulders. 'Well, that comment didn't come from nowhere. Tell me, why do you think that?'

Mrs Duffy would not be drawn. 'No, that's enough. No more talk – I won't discuss it. You know me, once I decide.'

Beth remained silent, but she was very much aware, as were they all, that if Mrs Duffy did have a fault, it was her stubbornness.

Mrs Duffy was already moving the conversation on. 'Anyway, isn't this just one of the best nights of the year, when we decorate the tree and have the mince pies and the sherry? We won't be spoiling it now, will we? Oh my giddy aunt, would you look at that!' She waved the tea towel in the air at Scamp, who was sloping away with a warm mince pie clamped gently between his teeth. 'How in God's name did that dog get in here?'

At the sound of Mrs Duffy's raised voice, Scamp quickened his step. With his ears flat against his head, he glanced backwards as she half-heartedly chased after him, flicking the tea towel back and forth in front of her. Scamp raced off, never loosening his grip on the mince pie, making a beeline for the sitting room. There would be safety in numbers and the nurses who'd gathered there would hide him under a chair.

Beth began to giggle, Mrs Duffy's surprisingly self-pitying comment forgotten. 'We won't miss one,' she said as Mrs Duffy gave up the chase and turned back into the kitchen. 'And don't tell me you didn't bake one for him anyway.'

'I did not. Are you mad? D'ye really think I spend my time baking cakes for the flamin' dog now when you are all at the hospital?' Her voice rose with her indignation, making Beth laugh all the more as she pushed the trolley and followed Scamp towards the sound of chatter and whoops of delight along with a chorus of 'Oh, Scamp, you naughty boy.'

As the trolley nudged open the sitting room door, both Beth and Mrs Duffy stopped for a moment to take in the sight before them. The large tree stood proudly in the bay window, decorated from top to bottom in the gaudiest decorations, some of which Mrs Duffy had brought back with her from their day on the ward. There was tinsel of every colour imaginable and lights within globes, painted and depicting nursery rhymes. Each nurse had brought something or had it sent from home to add to the festivities and each and every bauble clashed. But, it didn't matter, not to any of them. It was their tree and they loved it.

Pammy was hanging crepe bells and bows from the ceiling. She was standing on the top rung of a wooden ladder in one corner of the room while one of the probationers was balancing precariously on the sideboard at the other. 'My drawing pin has bent, flipping thing,' she said. 'Can someone reach me up another? The box is on the windowsill.'

One of the nurses quickly obliged and as Pammy pressed the pin into the ornate plaster coving, the tension in the paper garland gave and the crepe paper crackled and swayed in the thermals rising from the huge fire in the grate. The room was now crisscrossed with red and green streamers.

'There, that was the last, I think,' said Pammy as she carefully dismounted and snapped the ladder shut.

Mrs Duffy stood with her hands clasped together as if in prayer, her eyes bright with delight. 'Don't you just wish we had a camera?' she said to the girls who were picking up bits of tinsel from the chairs and the carpet. 'You know, like the one that photographer man had when he came to the children's ward. They should hold a competition for the best-decorated nurses' home next year – Lovely Lane would win hands down.'

'Shall we switch the lights on now?' said Pammy. 'Can I do it, Mrs Duffy?'

'You can that, Nurse Tanner. Wait a minute now while I turn the overhead lights off. Let me get back to the door, Nurse Harper.'

'Hang on,' said Beth, who had began laying out the glasses on the trolley, 'Sister Haycock is on her way, let's wait until she gets here, shall we?'

The nurses watched almost open-mouthed as Mrs Duffy's face set into a scowl. She took a breath and folded her arms and seemed to be on the point of saying something, but then they all heard the front door slam and the familiar tones of Emily Haycock as she sang out, 'Hello, everyone.'

The room fell silent. The only sounds were of the fire roaring up the chimney and the patter of the rain on the dark windows. The atmosphere had chilled and none of them could understand why. The only person who could make it right again was Mrs Duffy, but she had not responded to Emily's call and nor did she go hurrying down the corridor to take Emily's coat and tut over her having got wet as she normally would. Instead she crossed over to the fire that didn't need poking, poked it anyway, and firmly set her back to them all.

Emily burst in through the door. 'I am almost soaked to the skin! That rain is freezing cold. You haven't switched the lights on yet, have you?' She glanced towards the bay window and the tree. 'Oh, you haven't. Thank goodness. I'd hate to have missed that. Where's Mrs Duffy? She's not in the kitchen.'

Emily was not even aware of it herself, but this was the first time she had ever walked into the Lovely Lane nurses' home and not been greeted by the welcoming fussing of Mrs Duffy.

'Oh, there you are,' she said as she spotted Mrs Duffy's back. 'I've come for one of the best mince pies in Liverpool.'

There was a moment's silence, which hung as heavy as lead. Mrs Duffy threw the poker into the bucket with a clatter and said, 'Have you now? I'm surprised you bothered at all.' And with that she walked straight out of the room.

Not a single person spoke until they heard the kitchen door close behind her. Scamp had belly-crawled out from under one of the chairs and with a worried frown on his face glanced from one nurse to the other. Instead of greeting Emily, he sat with his head low and his tail tucked in. Even he knew that something was very wrong.

Pammy was the first to speak. 'What's wrong with her?' she asked. 'I've never seen her like that before. Has someone upset her?' She looked around the room at the assembled nurses.

There was a murmur of general confusion and a feeling of acute disappointment at the dramatic souring of what had been a joyous Christmas mood.

'Not at all.' One of the first years spoke up. 'She was as happy as Larry over supper and was excited about the tree being switched on.'

They all loved Mrs Duffy and no one wanted to think that she might be upset. Beth swallowed hard. She wanted to save the night but knew that what she was about to say might not be well received. 'I think it's you, Sister Haycock.'

'Me?' said Emily in surprise. 'But I've only just walked in, what can I have done?'

Beth was embarrassed and hoped this wouldn't backfire on her. 'I'm not sure, but I very definitely get the feeling it is you.'

All eyes were fixed on Beth now, and there was a collective intake of breath. The room was full of nurses who were in awe of Emily. She was the director of the school of nursing, a very important person, whereas Beth was just a nurse like the rest of them, and yet she was speaking to Sister Haycock as though they were equals. Not one of them would have dared say what Beth just had and they could see that Emily was wrestling with her response.

Emily looked around the room and was met with a lot of disappointed expressions. They were clearly waiting for her to make things right. 'Well then, you evidently all think it is me, so I suppose I had better go to the kitchen and see what I can do.' Her tone was almost sharp. She was very obviously offended, but the sight of the young nurses looking so downcast so close to Christmas was enough to make her bite the bullet. 'Don't worry, nurses, nothing is ever as bad as it seems, or so I am always being told. I have known Mrs Duffy for a very long time and I'm sure I can sort this out. Just give me ten minutes and don't you dare open the sherry until I return – or eat all of those mince pies,' she added over her shoulder as she left the room.

Emily popped her head around the kitchen door with much less confidence than she'd felt when addressing the anxious probationers. For the first time since she'd been a young nurse herself, living in the home, she felt that maybe she should wait to be invited in.

Mrs Duffy was standing at the sink, elbow deep in soapy water, vigorously scrubbing at the mince pie tray as though it had just sworn at her. Her back was to Emily, her shoulders tense, and a thought passed through Emily's mind as she watched her. How many hours of her life has that woman spent at that sink? They weren't an average family. The nurses' home housed twenty nurses and Mrs Duffy acted as a mother to all of them, albeit with help from the maids. She worked tirelessly in the kitchen, where she had no assistant, and until recently she'd had ration books to cope with as well.

'Mrs Duffy...' The words came out as a whisper. 'May I come in?'

There was no reply. Emily gulped. She stepped inside anyway and held the door as it clicked shut. She waited to see if Mrs Duffy would acknowledge that she was in the room. There was still no response other than the hot tap being opened with some ferocity to rinse the large baking bowl she had almost thrown into the sink after the tray.

Emily could see there were still some dirty dishes on the table waiting to be washed and so she collected them up and carried them over. As gently as she could, in contrast to the crashing and banging coming from the butler's sink, she said, 'You forgot these.'

Mrs Duffy didn't look up. 'I haven't forgotten anything,' she said. 'They will be done in good time.'

Emily's eyes widened in disbelief. If Mrs Duffy had turned around and slapped her, she could not have been more surprised. For a brief moment she felt as though she'd lost her breath. Gathering her thoughts and deciding that saying nothing was the best option, she laid the dishes down on the dirty side of the draining board and, pulling the tea towel from the hook, picked up the large bowl and began to dry it.

'I was leaving that to drain,' said Mrs Duffy, her voice now full of hurt, her anger seemingly spent.

Emily set the bowl down on the table with almost no noise at all and moving back to the sink said, 'Look, I know it's me. Will you tell me what I've done?'

'You haven't done anything.' Mrs Duffy stacked another plate on to the draining board. 'Nothing whatsoever.'

Emily sensed that there was a clue hidden in her cryptic response, but she couldn't fathom it out. 'Well, I obviously have done something, something that has upset you. I know you, I can tell.'

'Oh, know me, do you?'

It was obvious to Emily that Mrs Duffy's mood was volatile and that she would have to tread very carefully.

'I would say you don't know me at all well, actually. If you did know me half as well as you think, I wouldn't be the last person in the world to know what's going on in your life. Do you know, half the women at Mass know about you and Dessie Horton and do you think they don't tell me, that I don't know? Oh no, everyone tells me everything – except you.'

Emily's jaw almost dropped to the floor. She had never in her life seen Mrs Duffy as angry or upset as she was right now.

Mrs Duffy took her hands out of the sink, dried them on her apron and then, pulling her cardigan sleeve down, rooted inside for her handkerchief. Retrieving it, she noisily blew her nose. Emily had never seen her cry in all the time she'd known her and she was shocked to her core. She hadn't wanted to tell Mrs Duffy that she'd moved in with Dessie until the time was right. But as she stood there and witnessed the distress of the woman who, along with Biddy, had been the closest thing to a mother she'd known since her own had died, she had to be honest with herself. Mrs Duffy was of a certain type, a woman who did things by the book, and that was part of the reason she hadn't said anything. But more than anything it was because Mrs Duffy had always had high expectations of Emily, had supported her through her career, delighted in her progression. The main reason Emily hadn't told her was because she hadn't wanted to let her down, and now was the time to let her know that.

'Mrs Duffy, I am so, so sorry. I have been just the biggest idiot. I didn't want you to be disappointed in me. I didn't want to let you down, and now look, that is exactly what I have done.'

Mrs Duffy wiped her eyes. 'Is it true that you're staying at his house?'

Emily blushed bright red. Her embarrassment was excruciating, but she wasn't going to lie. 'Yes, I am. Are you mad with me?'

Mrs Duffy turned to her with an incredulous expression on her face. 'Mad at you? I'm mad that you didn't come to me for advice and tell me yourself. I'm mad that the woman who lives next door to Dessie, that nosey beak Hattie Lloyd, was the one to tell me. That's what I'm mad at.'

Emily sensed a softening in her anger and took that moment to reach out and take Mrs Duffy's hand. 'I'm so sorry,' she said again. 'You know I wouldn't hurt you for the world. We were going to tell you tomorrow, at the carol service, and that's the truth.'

She felt a further easing of the tension and, moving closer, gave Mrs Duffy a hug. 'Life's so short, you know, and it feels like we've got no more time to waste. I suppose I thought that after what we've both been through, you more than most would understand.'

Mrs Duffy heaved a deep sigh and smiled. Then she fastened her arms around Emily's waist and hugged her. 'I know, my dear. I do understand. You have my full approval because you couldn't have picked a nicer or better man.'

'Oh, thank goodness!' Emily began to laugh. 'What a relief it is now that you know. Am I forgiven?'

'Oh, away with you!' Mrs Duffy pushed her hankie back up her sleeve. 'Come on, let's have a sherry and switch on the lights.'

Five minutes later the two women walked into the sitting room, Emily with her arm around Mrs Duffy's shoulders, Mrs Duffy with her arm around Emily's waist. An audible sigh of relief swept across the room.

'Come along, everyone, a glass in your hand while we let bossy boots Nurse Tanner do the honours of switching on the lights.' Mrs Duffy began to pour.

Once the sherry had been transferred from the bottle to the glasses, Beth flicked off the light switch next to the door, plunging the room into darkness.

'One, two, three!' everyone shouted, and on three, Pammy dropped the switch for the tree. The lights flickered on and then off and then on again and the tree and the room were finally flooded with the twinkling bulbs of Christmas. There were oohs and aahs from the assembled nurses as they all commented on how wonderful the large tree looked.

'I'm surprised the lights worked,' said Emily. 'Remember the years they didn't?'

'I do,' said Mrs Duffy. 'I got Jake to come in today and test them. We have an extra set because the tree is so big this year.'

'It looks wonderful,' said Emily. 'You always manage to do this, Mrs Duffy – make Christmas special.'

And then came the warning. It was dropped in quietly amid the sips of sherry, the clink of glasses and plates, and the gasps of delight at the shortness of Mrs Duffy's pastry and the perfect consistency of her mincemeat. But it was clear that this was what was at the heart of Mrs Duffy's concern. 'Christmas is to celebrate the birth of a special child,' she said. 'You will be careful, won't you, Emily?'

Her meaning was clear. She would never refer directly to the fact that she knew that Emily and Dessie were sleeping together, but like all mothers, natural and adopted, it had been her main worry since the day she had overheard Emily talking to the girls. Mrs Duffy wasn't blind or daft. There was a mood in the air, a recklessness that had emerged during the war and only grown stronger since. No one knew what tomorrow would bring and the young in particular lived for the day.

She had whispered her words of warning so that the others wouldn't hear. Emily took her hand and gave it a squeeze. 'I will,' she said. 'Don't worry, I will.'

Chapter 21

Try as she might, Aileen had struggled to raise a smile all morning. If it hadn't been for the children, she might not have even bothered.

Pammy Tanner had been on a hunt and had discovered Sister Tapps's stash of Christmas presents on ward four. She'd brought them over to be wrapped. 'Why do you think she didn't tell us they were there?' she asked as she and Beth cut lengths of crepe paper.

Aileen had a wooden toy train balanced on her lap waiting for the wrapping. The wood had been polished and the funnel painted a shiny red. She pushed the wheels round and round with the tip of her index finger. Since the night before last, she'd been unable to think about anything but Freddie. He was always just under the surface of her thoughts and every single quiet moment she had, the enormity of her loss and what might have been washed through her. Her emotions zigzagged wildly, but she had convinced herself that she completely understood why he had chosen not to contact her. A child had gone missing and he must be blaming her. Perhaps he had got into trouble with his superiors.

Dragging her thoughts back into the room, she shook her

head and looked miserable and dazed. 'Sorry, what did you say, Nurse Tanner?'

'These – the presents.' Pammy lifted the tape up to her mouth, bit it and ripped a strip off.

'Gosh, I'm not sure. I expect Sister Tapps was so excited about heading off to see her family, she just forgot,' said Aileen. 'You have to admit, having the opportunity to spend Christmas with her own relatives for the first time in years must have been all she could think about, and she's a great present buyer. Every child who has a birthday while they're on ward four gets a present and a cake. I only just remembered to give her her present when she popped in the other morning to say goodbye to the children.'

'Really, she was here on the morning of the transfer? *That* morning? Blimey, I'm surprised you remembered at all, with the commotion that was going on. We need to be careful though. If word gets out that Sister Tapps buys them all presents, we'll have our own children from ward three transferring themselves en masse over there when she comes back. They'll be pushing their own beds and cots and dragging their pillows behind them. They must think they've drawn the shortest straw on here.'

'Well, that might have been true before,' said Beth as she wrestled with the wrapping for a spinning top, 'but not now.'

This finally brought a smile to Aileen's face. 'Thank you, Nurse Harper. I hope that's the case. I do try to be like Sister Tapps, she did train me, but I'm not sure it's possible for any human being to be as devoted and caring as she is.'

'She's a proper angel,' said Pammy. 'This is St Angelus hospital – we must have at least one.'

Beth handed Aileen a sheet of paper.

'We can't do all of this now,' Aileen said. 'Visiting is in an hour and I have to get my suitcase up to the accommodation corridor.'

'Can't you take it with you when night staff come on duty?' asked Pammy.

'No, I have to go and visit my mother on the ward and I'm not sure Sister Antrobus will like me heaving my case in as well. I might ask Dessie if he can get Bryan or one of the lads to take it up there for me. Right, the probationers will have cleared up lunch, let's get the obs done and the lockers tidied and then we can try and open the doors a little early for those who have caught the bus and are already waiting outside.'

'What if Matron comes up?' asked Pammy, sounding worried.

Aileen had stood up and was packing the toys back up into a cardboard box. 'Darn, I've just remembered, we need more diamorphine in the trolley and the pharmacist told me to take it out of ward four, with a witness. Could you come over with me, please. He said there were twenty-four tablets over there.'

'Rightyo,' said Pammy. 'Shall we do it now?'

Aileen unhooked the keys from the side of her belt and said the words Beth loved the most. 'Hold the fort, would you, please, Nurse Harper.'

The entire Doherty family were scrubbed clean to within an inch of their lives. Kitty and the twins sat on the settle, forbidden from setting a foot outside or even moving until their mam said they could.

'You aren't to go near the dirty entry, any of you,' said Maura. 'You will get your white socks filthy, Kitty.'

Kitty didn't scowl, although she wanted to. She just fixed her father with a glare in the only way she knew how. He responded with a helpless shrug and a pitying look, and mouthed the words, 'I can't, queen.'

They weren't due to leave for the hospital for nearly an hour. Even though they were to have a bath tomorrow night, before the Christmas Eve Mass, Maura had stood each one of them at the sink in the scullery and washed them down with just about enough warm water until their skin glowed a soft pink. Once they were dry they were dressed in clean, starched clothes that had dried in front of the fire overnight and been run over with the flat iron long before any of them had woken. 'What I can't get done whilst you lot are sleeping isn't worth doing,' Maura often said as they filed into the room for breakfast.

Kitty scratched her head. Her hair had been plaited and the ribbons tied so tight, her scalp was itching.

'There will be no children visiting that hospital today cleaner than mine,' Maura had announced. 'Or fathers,' she added as she finished ironing Tommy's shirt and held it out to him.

The back door opened as Jerry arrived in the kitchen, holding a present. 'Kathleen sent me over with this for Angela,' he said.

Maura stood stock still and even Tommy took notice. 'Well, Jerry, that's mighty kind,' he said. 'That should put a smile on her face.'

Jerry turned to Kitty and the boys. 'And don't you be worrying now, I think she has more for you, but not until Christmas morning. I think me mam must have won on the bingo,' he said. 'She's been treating us all.'

Both men looked over and saw that Maura had tears in her eyes. 'Eh, Maura, come on now,' said Tommy. 'We're off to see our Angela – what's up with you?'

'She won't be with us on Christmas morning, Tommy – the most important day in the year. She won't be coming into our bedroom and jumping on the bed waving her stocking. The poor child will be miserable and lonely and lost, and it breaks my heart.'

'I know, queen, but at least we will see her in the afternoon. We won't be all day without her.'

The kitchen door opened again and Peggy walked in, carrying her son, little Paddy, on one hip and with a small white paper bag in her hand, screwed up at the top. 'Take these for Angela,' she said as she placed them on the table, 'and when you get back come in and tell me how she is.'

Maura wasn't sure what she was the most surprised at, the fact that Peggy had brought something for Angela or that she hadn't asked to borrow something. 'Thank you, Peggy,' she said. 'Angela will be really pleased to know you are thinking of her.'

'We are missing her too, sure we are,' said Peggy. 'I never knew how much I didn't like the quiet – it's like something is wrong all the while. I'll never complain about her screeching again.'

Maura struggled to smile, but there was truth in Peggy's words. She had said a hundred times since Angela had been in hospital, 'I will never in me life tell our Angela off for crying again, so I won't.'

Tommy hadn't dared admit that even though he missed Angela and worried about her as much as everyone else, he loved the quiet. He hadn't realized how often Angela woke him up during the night with her yelling out, and to come down in the mornings with no one wailing at the table made a nice change. Whenever he found himself thinking that, he was consumed with guilt.

Jerry threw his arm around Maura's shoulders. 'Mammy says she will be in when you've gone, Maura. She'll peel your 'tatoes for you and turn the drying over.'

'You need to wrap up, Maura,' said Peggy. 'Jesus, 'tis brass monkeys weather out there. The wind cuts right through you.'

Maura took the knitted scarves and gloves that were warming in front of the fire and began to wrap them around the boys' necks and cross them over their chests. 'An extra layer to keep the cold out,' she said. Kitty grappled with her own scarf while Tommy picked up the brush to finish polishing the shoes.

Half an hour later and after two more visits from neighbours bearing gifts, the Doherty family were ready to leave. Peggy and little Paddy had hung on to the last, Peggy most interested to see what presents were being brought for Angela. Just as the back door was about to close on them, she said, 'I don't suppose there is a bit of steri milk left over from breakfast on your cold shelf, is there, Maura?'

Maura took a deep breath. There was – she'd saved it for the rice pudding she was going to make for that evening. But she knew that little Paddy probably hadn't even had any pobs that morning for his breakfast. She would rather Peggy hadn't been out and bought the sweets, although she really appreciated the thought. She would have preferred her to look after her own brood a little better. She sighed. 'Go on. There's nearly half a bottle. Take it, I will fetch another from the dairy on the way home. Water it down, it will go further.'

And with that, as Peggy clutched the milk, Maura and Tommy herded the Doherty brood out of the back gate, all of them impatient to set eyes on Angela.

Sister Tapps woke and for the first time she struggled to sit upright. Louis lay next to her, silent and staring as always, his eyes fixed on her face as though searching for her thoughts. Tappsy felt an itching on her abdomen, so intense she could barely stop scratching, and she hurried to open the buttons of her uniform, which she'd slept in, so that her nails could rake her skin directly. But no matter how much she scratched, she couldn't get relief. The metallic taste in her mouth was worse and she didn't feel like either eating or drinking. She turned her head to look at Louis, and the sight of him distracted her from what was now nagging, persistent pain as well as the new itchiness. She had barely slept with the discomfort and had taken all of the remaining diamorphine during the night.

'Now, we have to get you some food. Just give me a minute,' she said to Louis as she tried to heave herself up. It took her three attempts, but eventually she managed it. She'd got water from the washrooms the previous night and it stood in a jug next to the kettle. She'd scrubbed out the milk bottle for Louis and was sure that it was clean enough.

'I'll put the kettle on,' she said to him, 'and make you a bottle. And then we'll use what's left of the water to wash your bottom when I change your nappy.' She looked at the enamel bucket of nappies she'd stored under the sink; they were beginning to smell and she had already decided that while Sister Antrobus, whose room was round the corner at the other end of the corridor, was at work today, she would take them into the washroom. It would be a risk, but a very small one. There'd been not a murmur from the domestics since she'd heard them talking in the hallway the other day. She was certain she and Louis were the only ones in the corridor.

While she waited for the kettle to boil, she slipped out on to the landing to make her way to the bathroom. The coast was clear, but with each step she took, the pain dragged. The diamorphine had made her light-headed and she had to place the flat of her hand on the wall to navigate along it. She had woken a number of times during the night and thought she had seen her sister in the bedroom. Her dreams had been vivid, a girl shouting to her and it was Laura calling her name. Once in the bathroom she splashed water on her face and squinted at the mirror. She refused to acknowledge the gaunt, sallow woman staring back at her. Using the lavatory was difficult and painful and a glance at the dark tea-coloured urine shocked her so much she had to grab hold of the door handle. 'No,' she whispered. 'It can't be.'

Finding strength in her denial – something she'd become adept at over the last few weeks – she managed to wash her hands and make her way back to the room. Picking Louis up, she stood with him in her arms and rocked him. They moved over to the edge of the window, out of sight, as the clock on the church began to chime. It only chimed twice. Disbelievingly, she looked at the clock on the mantelpiece. The fire wasn't lit and she had run out of coal and emptied all the buckets in the adjoining rooms. The clock said 2 p.m.

Louis was beginning to grizzle. The baby who had forgotten how to cry because of the neglect he'd suffered was learning how to grizzle as a result of the care and love he'd been shown at St Angelus.

'You poor child,' she said. 'I don't know how that happened. I thought it was morning – I must have slept more than—' But she was confused. She hadn't slept, of that she was sure. The hallucinogenic effect of the diamorphine had dulled her brain and confused her further. The pain had been too great and now there was the itching. She screwed up her eyes in an attempt to ignore it, but it was almost too much to bear.

Louis became more uncomfortable and began to cry. She was awake and he was hungry, that was all he knew. But he had learnt that the sound of a boiling kettle meant milk was on its way, and as soon as he heard the familiar bubbling he became calmer.

Sister Tapps forgot herself for a moment – she wanted to check the clock on the church tower. Perhaps her own clock was wrong, or there'd been more than two chimes and she just hadn't heard them because they'd been carried down the Mersey on the wind. She moved to the window to crane her neck towards the church. It confirmed her worst fears: it really was two o'clock in the afternoon. She had lost seven hours and she didn't know where. She wondered why Louis hadn't woken her. She glanced at his face to check for any signs that he'd been distressed. There were none. He looked straight into her eyes and his baby thoughts seemed to shine through. 'Are you all right?' his quizzical expression appeared to say, and Tappsy's face immediately and automatically broke into the most loving smile. Her eyes filled with tears as she wondered how any Christmas could be better spent than in looking after a poorly child.

Louis became a blur to her, but through the pool of tears in her eyes she saw him smile at something beyond the window and then reach out with both his hands as if to grab at it. A seagull had flown past, screeching loudly as it did so. Tappsy caught her breath and held it as she moved. She had to – it had become too difficult to walk and breathe at the same time. She carried Louis a step closer to the window so that he could see the gulls flying inshore to escape the stormy river. And then, as she looked down to check that no one had seen them, she met the piercing and unwavering gaze of Kitty Doherty, staring straight back up at her.

Kitty gazed up at the window as she held on to her da's hand.

'Come on, queen,' he said as he gently tugged. 'We're going in for a nice warm orange squash and a biscuit for you and the lads.'

Kitty looked at her da and hesitated. She had definitely seen Sister Tapps, but something was wrong because Sister Tapps had neither smiled nor waved at her. Instead of following her da, Kitty dropped his hand and stepped back on to the gravel to take a better look up at the window.

'Kitty, what are you doing?' said Tommy as he also stepped back and took her hand again. 'Come on, love, your ma and the lads are waiting on the other side of the door.'

'Da, what's up there?' she asked, pointing.

Tommy looked up. 'I don't know, love. Offices, I think. Where they keep all the notes and things.'

Kitty didn't believe him. The towering walls were a blackened red brick and the red sandstone windowsill looked huge and solid. The dark, unyielding window reflected the slate-grey, snow-heavy sky. If it hadn't been for their yellow beaks, she would barely have noticed the seagulls against the snow clouds as they flew overhead. There was no longer any sign of life behind the window, but Kitty knew she had not imagined it. She had definitely seen Sister Tapps.

'Kitty, come on, we won't have time to get you a drink at this rate,' snapped Tommy, almost jerking her arm as he pulled her up the steps behind him.

'Well, would you look at you all. Ready for Christmas, are you?' Maisie called out to them as they made their way towards the counter. 'And don't you all look just smashing. I can see my face in those shoes, boys, which is just as it should be. Ah, look, they like the tree. Isn't it lovely.'

Maura and Tommy's twins were standing, mouths wide open, gawping at the wrapped presents under the Christmas tree and the dangling chocolate pennies.

'Mam, it's lovely,' said Kitty.

'It's Kitty, isn't it?' said Maisie to Maura and Tommy. 'Take one of the chocolates each, go on, love. Before everyone comes, go on.' Maisie pushed Kitty gently towards the tree, 'You too lads,' and moments later, they were each holding on to a golden penny, but no one spoke and Maura and Tommy knew immediately what was wrong. 'Can they take one for our Angela, Maisie, it's just that it's the way Maura had brought them up. One can't have without the other.'

'Of course,' said Maisie, who took one and handed to Kitty. 'There you go love, tell her it's from me.' Kitty and the boys now grinned. They were a team. If they hadn't managed to get one for Angela too, the chocolate pennies would have tasted like salt.

'Tea, love?' Maisie held the big brown pot up to Maura

with two hands, one on the main handle and the other on the small lifting handle on the brim of the lid. 'I doubt you get a cup of tea made for you very often, do you?'

Maura could see steam rising through the spout. After the cold walk there was nothing she would have liked more, but it being Christmas she was even worried about the ha'pennies and she had promised the children warm squash.

Maisie knew the look. 'There's no charge. It's nearly Christmas – look, we've even got mince pies too. I'm on me own today. No one else seemed to be organized enough to come in so close to Christmas. I swear to God, if I don't watch it, I'll be running this place single-handed soon. I'm not the usual type, me – I don't have the smart hats or paste brooches, and our Stanley, he wasn't an officer in the army. I think I only got finally accepted because our Pammy's a nurse here.'

Maura smiled as Maisie poured out the tea. Kitty and Tommy joined them from the side of the tree.

'And a nice glass of warm squash for you littl'uns, eh? Come here, Kitty, you can give me a hand pouring them out. I've just made a jug up.'

Kitty beamed at the copper jug on the trolley next to the urn. 'Should I come behind there with you, behind the counter?' she said, eyes wide.

'Well unless you have very long arms, love, and can reach all the way over to that shelf, yes.'

Maura and Tommy soon had two trays of drinks and mince pies ready to carry over to the wooden table, along with Tommy's ashtray.

'Now, you bring me back all the empties, Kitty, would you love,' Maisie instructed.

Kitty was all smiles, delighted to help, as always. Ten minutes later, she was standing by the hatch, setting down the dirty trays in front of a grateful Maisie.

'Thank you, love. Aren't you just the best. I bet your mam can't manage without you, can she?'

Kitty shook her head. 'She can't.'

Maisie laughed out loud. 'I guessed as much! Are you off to visit your sister now?'

Kitty, often shy, had warmed to Maisie on their first visit and felt even more comfortable with her today. 'I've got to take the boys to the toilet first and then we're going up to the ward. The doors won't open for another twenty minutes, mammy says. I wish our Angela was on Sister Tapps's ward.'

'Oh, love, Sister Paige is lovely and your Angela will be well looked after. Besides, my big girl Pammy is a nurse on that ward and even though I say it myself, I think she's marvellous. Tell you what, I'm so tired down here, I wish I could swap places with your Angela and jump into her bed. I'd say, "Oi, move over, Angela, let me in, me feet are killing me."'

Kitty began to giggle.

'And I'd wait there until our Pammy, that's Nurse Tanner to you, came along and tried to take my temperature, or gave me a bed bath or maybe brought the doctor to see me and said "Doctor, I don't think this patient looks very well," and they'd all be laughing, because she wouldn't know it was me.'

Kitty was now helpless. As the eldest in a large family, she had many responsibilities and laughing wasn't something she did very often.

'Besides, even if your sister had been on Sister Tapps's ward, Sister Tapps has gone home for Christmas and all her children have been transferred over to join your Angela on ward three, so she's not there anyway.'

Kitty looked at Maisie with a very confused expression on her face. 'Sister Tapps has gone home? Where?'

'Now that I don't know, love, but she left a couple of days ago. I know she's gone to stay with her family.'

'Do her family live here in the hospital?'

Now Maisie looked confused. 'No, love. I don't know where they live, but it's not around here. A train ride away, I believe.'

'No, she's not,' said Kitty.

'She's not what, love?' Maisie was slipping the squash glasses into a bowl of hot soapy water one by one and from the corner of her eye she saw Maura fastening the twins' coats and smiling over to her. Tommy was extinguishing his cigarette in the ashtray and chatting to the man on the table next to them. These were the busiest couple of hours of the day, as people arrived for visiting time.

'She's not gone home. I've just seen her upstairs at the window, with a baby in her arms.'

Chapter 22

Freddie took the steps up to the ward two at a time. He was at least five yards ahead of his super, who as far as he was concerned had driven the police car far too slowly from Whitechapel.

The familiar smell of the ward assailed his nostrils and he noted that it was visiting time, so the ward doors stood open, ready and welcoming. The warm glow of the Christmas tree in the bay almost took his breath away. The ward gleamed. The long polished table in the centre was mirror-like, the brass hand-bell for announcing the end of visiting time sparkled, and the brass knockers on the cupboards and the door to the sister's office shone.

It all felt very different to the last time he'd been there, the day Louis had gone missing. The ward was warm, the fire banked up for visiting and screened off with a metal guard, and the oxygen cubicles, well away from the fire and near to the office were almost unrecognizable beneath the paper-chains and pine branches that festooned the walls.

Freddie was nervous about seeing Aileen. She had as good as rejected him and he knew she was on the other side of the door, only feet away from him. His heart began to pound in his chest. As he waited for the super to catch him up, he glanced down the ward and observed the parents sitting by bedsides. Near him on the landing, children were waiting impatiently on the wooden benches, craning their necks to try and catch a glimpse of their siblings through the open doors. He provided a welcome distraction and a dozen pair of eyes considered him thoughtfully.

Branna came up to him as he stood there. 'Are you for Sister?' she asked. 'You had better go along in.'

Tommy headed towards the wide-open ward doors with Angela in his arms. 'Don't move, lads,' he said to the twins, who were waiting on the bench just outside. 'Angela can only have two at a time at her bedside, but I brought her to the door because she wants to see you.'

Angela buried her head in her father's neck.

'Come on, Ange, love, say hello.'

'Are you better, Angela?' asked Declan hopefully.

Angela shook her head.

Branna came out of the kitchen. 'Take her back to the bed,' she said to Tommy. 'Sister Paige will probably tell you off for standing there.'

'Are Maura and Kitty all right in there?' asked Tommy, peering through the window of the sister's office. The office was the last place Maura would want to be. It was Angela she wanted to be spending her time with.

'They're fine. Don't worry, Sister Paige isn't like some of the others, she'll let you stay longer if you've lost some of your visiting time. Come on, boys, give me your hands, let's go down to Angela's bed.'

The boys jumped up and grabbed hold of Branna's hands. 'But I thought it was only two at a time,' said Tommy.

'It is, strictly speaking,' said Branna. 'But as your wife and other daughter are in Sister's office, they don't count, do they? And these two, we can just stand them one on top of the other and they still don't make up the height of a grown-up, do you, lads?'

The boys laughed and skipped along beside Branna. Branna drew up next to Tommy as they walked down the ward. 'Where did you see her?' she whispered over the boys' heads, glancing backwards to check no one was listening.

'I didn't see anything,' said Tommy. 'I don't think our Kitty did either. I hope she's not going to get into trouble. It was Maisie who insisted that she come up here with us and have Kitty tell Sister Paige what she saw.'

'Where was Kitty when she thought she saw her then?'

'Jesus, I told Maisie, I don't know that either, but the only time Kitty looked at a window was when we were just about to come up the steps to the main entrance. She asked me what was up there and I told her it was probably offices.'

Branna stopped. 'Above the main steps as you come into the WVS?'

Tommy nodded as he laid Angela back down on her bed. 'Aye. But I'm not saying she was right – you know what kids are like. She's clever, our Kitty, though. Not one to be fanciful. I'm as surprised as anyone she said that.'

'There you go, boys. I'll get an extra chair,' said Branna. 'You can't sit on the bed or your legs will be chopped off.'

The twins looked suitably horrified.

Branna returned with a third wooden chair, then made her

way back down the ward. As she reached the kitchen entrance, Matron arrived at the top of the stairs.

'What's going on?' she asked.

'There's a child in the office with her mother, she thinks she saw Sister Tapps in a window above the main entrance – with a baby in her arms. That's what her father just told me,' said Branna. 'The police are in there too. The father told me the child is not the fanciful type. She's clever, like. Sister Paige didn't want to ask her any questions until the police got here.'

'The accommodation block...' Matron's voice was almost a whisper. 'With a baby?' She glanced into the office, saw Kitty on her mother's knee and the two police officers sitting in front of her. Sister Paige was standing against the window and, catching sight of Matron, she slipped out and closed the door behind her.

'Has the little girl said what she saw?' Matron asked.

'She has, yes, but her mother says it can't be true. She said they didn't see anyone.'

'The accommodation block – has anyone been up there?'

'No, not yet,' said Sister Paige. 'Why, do you think that's where she is? That the child is right?'

'I have no idea, but I intend to find out.' Matron opened the office door. 'Gentlemen, Sister Paige and I are going to make our way to the accommodation block to check the rooms. It seems to me that this is the quickest way to get to the bottom of this... er... situation, and then this poor mother can at last visit her sick child.'

Maura almost leapt out of the chair. 'Thank you,' she said, and pulling Kitty behind her, she hurried back into the ward.

Both Freddie and the super sat there with their mouths

open. Freddie's pen was poised over his notepad. 'But we haven't finished writing down what she said.'

Matron gave him a withering look and he promptly pushed both his notepad and pen back into his top pocket.

'Would anyone like to come with us?' she asked. She had no idea why it had already taken them so long to interview the poor child and she would have asked them to explain themselves, but she didn't want to waste any more precious time.

Freddie shook his head. It was obvious Aileen was upset with him – she hadn't met his gaze once – and he didn't want to have any awkward conversations in the presence of Matron or the super. 'I'll stay here and make sure nothing else untoward happens,' he said. Aileen, meanwhile, was already heading towards the stairs.

'We don't have to go that way,' said Matron. 'Come with us, Branna. There's a door at the end of ward four, behind the curtain.'

'Oh yes, of course,' said Aileen. 'Sister Tapps is the only one to use that shortcut. No one else would dare walk down her ward without permission.'

They trod softly down the ward, the highly polished floorboards creaking beneath every step. Matron led the way and the superintendent rather sheepishly followed behind. Matron thought how ghostlike ward four looked and wondered if she had done the wrong thing after all, closing it down and giving Sister Tapps a break. Her insides churned with fear at the possibility that her decision might have brought about something terrible. Maybe Sister Tapps had had another breakdown. 'Wait a moment,' she said. 'I just want to look in the office for something.'

She opened the door to Sister Tapps's office and her eyes went straight to the corner of her desk. It was gone – Laura's beloved teddy. The one Sister Tapps had bought her and Laura had thrown to her in the desperate hope that she would pick it up and run after her. But Matron had held on to Tappsy's arm, preventing her from following, and it had been Matron who had bent down, picked up the bear and whispered, 'There, you keep it. As a reminder.'

She now felt there was a possibility that Kitty Doherty might be right, that maybe she had seen Sister Tapps. But there couldn't have been a baby. Sister Tapps could not look after a baby in the accommodation block. It was the bear Kitty had seen, hugged close in Sister Tapps's arms, something Matron had herself seen many times.

Aileen reached the door to the accommodation landing to find that it was not locked and opened easily and quietly. Matron leant over and held the curtain open as Aileen slipped in behind her. She was followed by the policeman and Branna, who was not going to miss this for the world.

Letting the door slip back with the gentlest click, they all stood and waited for the silence to settle and their ears and eyes to adjust. There were no windows in the corridor other than a single skylight above them and it was dark and gloomy. No one spoke as their eyes took in the ghostly portraits lining the wall, showing the founders of the workhouse that had preceded St Angelus. A parade of dour-looking men in beards and hats sat in imposing armchairs and glared down at them with foreboding and hostile expressions.

Matron placed her fingers to her lips and they were all suddenly very aware of each other's breathing. At first there was nothing to be heard or seen and Matron almost let out a sigh of relief at the realization that this had been a false alarm. The child had been fantasizing after all. Maybe she had just wanted to see Sister Tapps so much that she had manifested an image of her in her mind. She turned to Aileen and was just about to suggest that they return to ward three when they heard the faintest sound.

'Was that a mouse?' whispered the superintendent.

'No,' said Matron, 'I don't think so. Shhh.'

Once again they all stood and waited. It came again and this time it was louder and unmistakably the sound of a child. Aileen's heart was racing and her mouth dried with anticipation and fear. She reached out and grabbed Matron's arm.

Matron raised her hand. 'Let me and Branna go,' she said. 'If it is Sister Tapps, she has known us both for many years. Branna, come.'

The police officer and Aileen stepped aside to let Branna past. Matron and Branna walked towards the room the noise had seemed to come from – Emily Haycock's room. They stopped again and listened and the noise came again, but this time it was much louder and then they heard a thump and a moan of pain.

Matron wasted no more time. She turned the handle and as she opened the door her hand flew to her mouth. It was not the fact that Louis, the missing baby that had caused so much trouble, was lying on the bed and kicking his legs, safe and sound and healthy. It was the sight of Sister Tapps, yellow, sallow and painfully thin, on her knees at the side of the bed, both of her hands clasped over her abnormally distended abdomen.

It took her only seconds to regain her composure and she took control immediately. 'Branna, take the baby over to ward three and hand him over to Nurse Tanner. Sister Paige, help me with Sister Tapps.'

She didn't have to ask. Aileen was already on her knees beside Sister Tapps, who appeared to be in too much pain to be aware of who was around her.

'Officer, please hurry down to the casualty unit and ask them to get a stretcher up to the accommodation landing, and to send Dr Mackintosh up here as quickly as possible. Tell him to bring some pain relief with him.'

The superintendent immediately raced along the landing at breakneck speed.

A minute later, Branna was walking at the pace of a trot with Louis in her arms. As she entered the ward and the nurses saw who she had with her, they were greeted by what was at first an outburst of disbelief, which morphed into delight and then concern.

'Where was he?' said Pammy.

'Matron said I was to hand him over to you,' Branna said, passing him over very gently.

Pammy felt a rush of pride followed by a warm glow. 'Matron said that?' she asked, her voice full of disbelief.

'Yes, that's what she said.' Branna had already decided that this would be the first thing she would tell Maisie when she saw her.

'Good job we left his cot made up. Who said they thought he was still here, eh?' Pammy never let an opportunity pass to score a point over Beth. 'I did, that's who. I knew he wasn't far.'

'I'll fetch him a bottle for you. He looks hungry,' said Beth, ignoring Pammy as she made her way to the milk kitchen.

'Sister Tapps is in a terrible state,' said Branna to Pammy. 'Matron has sent for your Anthony and a stretcher.'

'Oh God, no. Why?'

Branna looked as though she was in shock. 'I'm no doctor and I'm sure I haven't a clue, but I know this, it's not good.' She didn't want to say to Pammy that she'd seen enough people die at home who looked in a better state than Tappsy had just now. In the village she came from in Ireland it was the way. Hardly anyone went to a hospital: they got sick, were tended to by local women, given potions and medicines that bore no name, and then they died. Branna blessed herself, took her rosaries from her pocket and then, leaving the nurses, went to phone Biddy over in the school of nursing.

Matron sat and held Sister Tapps's hand as Dr Mackintosh examined her. The rash that covered her torso, her wasted frame and the symptoms she had managed to describe before the morphine injection had dulled both her pain and her senses were all too familiar to them both. The nurse on casualty had passed a catheter at Dr Mackintosh's request and the smallest offering of dark brown urine told the final story.

Matron could tell that the casualty nurse was nervous in her presence and so, not wanting to make anything worse for her beloved colleague and friend, she squeezed Sister Tapps's hand and decided to remove herself to the doctors' room. She paced the floor while she waited for Dr Mackintosh and it was not lost on her that she was behaving like so many of the visitors she had comforted over the years.

Doreen, the casualty clerk, arrived at the door with a cup and saucer in her hand. 'I've brought you some tea, Matron,' she said, placing it on the table then slipping away again.

Matron would have smiled if it all hadn't been so serious.

How many times a week did Doreen do exactly that for an anxious family member?

When Dr Mackintosh eventually returned, his expression was pained.

'It's all right,' Matron said as she leant against the desk, her hands folded in front of her. 'You don't have to spare me. It's CA isn't it? Advanced too.'

He moved to the sink to wash his hands. 'Sadly, you are absolutely right. I'm afraid it is cancer. That rash tells me it's in her liver and there is almost no kidney function. Her body is unable to drain away the toxins, so they're building up in her skin, hence that pinpoint rash that's so intolerably itchy. I have no cure for that, unfortunately. And the pain, well, you could see for yourself.' He ran the hot water and soaped his hands. 'I've palpated her abdomen and there are a number of masses. I can't even begin to guess where the primary is, but I'm afraid that's of no consequence now. There is no way she can be operated on. She had a quite noticeable abdominal ascites, so I drained off a fair amount of fluid, which might relieve some of the discomfort.'

Matron wanted to say so many things. About how Sister Tapps had dedicated her life to helping others and no one had done anything for her in return. She felt remorseful and terribly sad that this woman with whom she'd worked for so many years would never be given the acknowledgement and public thanks she deserved. There would be no retirement party, no cards, no thank you speeches – and no retirement.

'How long does she have?' she asked him as he pulled down the roller towel to dry his hands.

Thrusting his hands into his pockets, he let out a long, deep sigh. Sister Tapps was no ordinary patient; she was one of their own. An important person in the St Angelus family and one who got on with the job of caring and nursing. No one ever doubted that with Sister Tapps her patients came first – to the point that her dedication riled some of the other sisters.

'She's had a maximum dose of diamorphine and can have that again in four hours along with an oral diuretic and cortisone. My guess is that we can rally her, but it will just be for a few days.' His voice dropped as he looked up and saw the tears in Matron's eyes and the almost imperceptible tremble of her bottom lip. She may be experienced, know everything there is to know about running a hospital, but this was something she could never possibly have imagined, even in her worst dreams. 'A week at the most.'

He hesitated for the briefest moment. Was it appropriate to hug Matron, he wondered. He didn't care if it was or not. His instincts took over and he strode across the room, opened his arms and enveloped her. He felt her tears wet on the side of his face before she bent her head and they were absorbed by his starched white coat.

'This is hell,' he said. 'I don't know how you feel, but I'm asking myself why I never talked to her more. She was always asking about me and my family and I can't even think what I know about hers. She is the kindest sister in this hospital. She took the baby because she knew nothing else but how to care for others.'

Matron nodded and his starched coat crackled against her cheek. She pulled away, removed her handkerchief from her pocket to wipe her eyes and said, 'I've known her for nearly forty years. We arrived here at almost the same time and I have so taken her for granted. She was just always here doing the job, never asking for anything, not until she had a difficult patch a few years ago.'

'I heard,' said Dr Mackintosh.

'I shouldn't have sent her away for Christmas. I had no idea she'd lost touch with her niece and nephew. I sent her off because I could see she'd lost weight and I thought she was working too hard. She told me her sister had died, but I assumed she was going to find her relatives, to make it up to them somehow.' She let out another deep sigh and folded the handkerchief neatly back into her pocket. 'But look at me – so impatient to have things my own way, I didn't ask enough questions. And now I can't even throw a party for her on the ward she loves, something I've been thinking about doing for years. I'd already planned her retirement do, but now I've lost the chance to even tell her how much she is loved by the families around here. Look at the child who saw her at the window, she only saw and recognized her because she thought the world of her.'

Matron walked over to the window and looked out at the hospital complex. She had got many things right during her tenure at St Angelus, she was not so full of self-doubt that she did not know that, but perhaps she should have done things differently when it came Sister Tapps.

There was silence for a few moments as she let what was happening sink in. 'Let's have her transferred to the ward. I will nurse her myself. I will stay by her side until the end – it's the very least I can do to pay her back for the service she's given to this hospital.'

'She's been in a lot of pain and I intend to keep that under control – that's the best I can do for her.' Dr Mackintosh's words were loaded and his eyes met Matron's. She didn't question what he meant. They both knew. When the time came, he would not see her suffer.

Matron nodded. There was no need for words. It was what they did for every patient who required it when the end came.

'We'll give her another injection of diamorphine at about six o'clock and then again at ten and again at about two in the morning, unless you call me sooner. I'm going to put in another shot of the cortisone too. Just give me four hours – she won't be in pain and I think we'll see her come to. The itching has been driving her mad and we have to strike the balance with the cortisone and diamorphine to stop that.'

Again Matron simply nodded. There was a tap on the door and she shouted, 'Come in.'

The young nurse who had tended to Sister Tapps popped her head round. 'Sister is awake now, Matron. She says she's feeling much better and would like to go to the ward.'

Matron and Dr Mackintosh looked at each other and smiled.

'God, she's remarkable,' he said.

'Tell Sister I shall be there in just one minute,' said Matron.

When the door was closed, Dr Mackintosh ran his fingers through his hair and asked, 'Which ward do you want her to be nursed on?'

'Her ward. I shall be looking after her myself. I'll tell Dessie to put an adult bed up there and light the fire, and we're away.'

Dr Mackintosh didn't seem surprised by her response. 'Do we know who her family are?' he asked.

'I do,' said Matron. She lifted her head and looked straight at him. 'We are, and her ward is her home.'

★

Over on ward three, Baby Louis had settled straight back in.

Beth was trying to plug in a record player one of the parents had carried all the way up the stairs together with several records of Christmas carols.

'Right,' said Pammy, 'let's put this one on. Have you got the needle ready?'

'Yes. Give it to me.' Beth placed the record on the turntable and then, biting her lip in concentration, she moved the arm across and laid it gently on the record.

'It says here that's a diamond stylus,' said Pammy, who was reading the instructions the parent, Mr Thomas, had given her as he left.

'We always play these records at Christmas, Nurse,' he told her. 'I don't care if we don't have them at home, but I want our Richard to be able to listen to them if he can. If Sister doesn't mind.'

'I do not mind in the slightest,' Sister Paige had said. 'I just don't know how you managed that record player on the bus, Mr Carter.'

'I'd do anything for my boy, Sister. We only had two, me and the missus. The first one died in the war and then, lo and behold, this one arrived. The missus called him a change baby, because, you know, she was on the change and that's why he is like he is, a bit slow and different, like, but that doesn't mean we love him any the less.'

Richard was susceptible to chest infections and was a regular on ward three. But this was the first time he'd been a patient over Christmas. He usually made it through to the end of January before he was admitted.

The sound of a male choir singing 'Silent Night' filled the ward and Pammy turned off the main lights. She carried Louis on her hip and walked into the bay with him to join the other nurses and patients. Once the parents had left, they'd pushed the beds and cots into a semicircle around the Christmas tree. There was a strange quiet among the children. Some of them were reading and looked up from their books and smiled at Louis in her arms, some were sharing a jigsaw puzzle on a bedside table, and others who weren't so well were lying on their starched white pillows, staring into the fire.

Pammy went over to Sister Paige, who was sitting by the fire filling in a Kardex on her knee. 'Look at this little fella,' she said, nodding at Louis, who was almost asleep in her arms. 'You would think he had lived here all his life.'

Aileen looked up. 'That would be lovely for me if he did, but not for him, sadly.'

'You aren't going to be like Sister Tapps and the others,' said Pammy. 'You'll get married soon, you will. I think that policeman was sweet on you.'

'*Was* is the word,' said Aileen. 'He won't even look at me now.'

Pammy wanted to ask why, but thought better of it. Sister Paige had just returned from calling in to see her mother and she did not look best pleased. She walked over to the window with Louis to show him the river and saw a trolley being wheeled across the courtyard from casualty. It was taken through the side doors that led to the ramp to the lift. She could tell by the white hair splayed against the white pillow that it was Sister Tapps. Dessie was pushing the trolley and Dr Mackintosh was escorting it on one side, Matron on the other.

She turned to Sister Paige. 'Sister...'

She didn't have to say any more; the tone of her voice was enough to alert Aileen, who placed the Kardex on the chair next to her and joined her at the window. Dessie was just lining the trolley up to take it through the doors.

Pammy blessed herself then kissed Louis on the head, just as the choir on the record player faded and the needle began to scratch round and round.

Chapter 23

It was Christmas Eve and Aileen had been sitting at her mother's bedside for almost an hour, dutifully enduring her grumbles, as she always did, and never once challenging her over her behaviour or the fact that she had deceived Aileen for so long.

'The tea is cold... You aren't visiting me often enough... Josie hasn't been anywhere near... I can't bear the food... There's nothing wrong with me now...'

As the litany of complaints continued, Aileen felt her patience slipping away. She thought she might scream soon. But at least it was a distraction from thinking about Freddie. Having to see him yesterday in her office on the ward had been excruciating. They'd effectively ignored each other and it had broken her heart. When she'd bedded down in the sisters' accommodation last night she'd sobbed and sobbed, into the small hours.

She sighed, looked down the ward and was both surprised and relieved to see Sister Antrobus bearing down on them like a great white shark with prey in its sights.

'Oh God in heaven, here's that awful woman – thank goodness you're here, Aileen.' Mrs Paige reached out with her bad hand and grabbed Aileen's.

Aileen stared down, amazed at the force in her mother's grip. 'Don't leave me! She's a tyrant.'

Aileen was sure that this was exactly what the nursing staff thought of her mother. She was grateful to them for taking on the burden of caring for her over Christmas; it was a welcome reprieve from her routine responsibilities and she had already thanked Matron for making it happen. Despite all the sadness around losing Freddie, moving into the accommodation block had brought a feeling of lightness and unexpected relief. It felt almost like she was going on a vacation, and even if she was still working on the ward, which was certainly no holiday, she had been temporarily liberated from what was really her second job. She had forgotten what it felt like to wake up and only have herself to think about. It was bliss.

She had paid Gina two full weeks in advance and told her to take her own holiday. 'You enjoy a break too, Gina,' she'd said.

Gina wasn't so sure. She'd come to care so much for Aileen, she didn't want to leave her alone over Christmas. 'Are you sure you'll be all right on your own? You won't be lonely, will you? Mam and me, we have loads of food in, why don't you come to us after you've finished on Christmas night?'

Aileen's heart melted. 'I'd love to, but I still have to visit Mother every day and that will include Christmas evening. I promise you, though, I won't be lonely. It will be the busiest day of the year on children's ward.'

Sister Antrobus's voice boomed out as she approached. 'Now then, Mrs Paige, it's time for your enema. I'm sure Sister Paige has a lot to do up on the children's ward.' She reached up and with one deft tug pulled the curtains all the way down from the head to the foot of the bed, then strode round to finish the job on the opposite side.

'But I don't want an enema.' Mrs Paige had lost the stridency in her voice and sounded almost like a child. 'Tell her, Aileen! Tell her I don't want one and I don't need it either.'

Aileen opened her mouth to object on her mother's behalf, but she knew there was no point. Sister Antrobus was well known throughout the hospital for being obsessed with the bowel movements of her patients. A bowel chart was kept at the end of every bed and completed by the nurses during observations. One day missed and there was no argument brooked, an enema it was.

Aileen stood to leave and glanced down at her mother. 'I can't, I'm afraid, Mother. You aren't my patient.' Then she bent down and whispered, 'Just tell them in future that you've already been when they ask you in the morning.'

'"Been"?' her mother almost screeched. '"Been"? This woman, she demands evidence, she tells the nurses she wants to see when you've been. They have to write a description on the chart and whether it was a good movement. I ask you! She is a witch, Aileen. A witch, I say.' Mrs Paige had found her voice in the face of such indignity.

Aileen rolled her eyes. It hadn't taken long for the real Mother to shine through. She turned to Sister Antrobus. 'Maybe Mother could wait another day?' she said tremulously.

Sister Antrobus stood in her familiar pose, arms folded, and regarded her with a withering expression. 'Have you ever worked with me before?' she asked.

'I have, yes, Sister,' said Aileen with a sigh.

'In that case you will know how strict I am about regular bowel movements, and while I am responsible for your mother, we shall abide by my rules. Goodbye, Sister Paige.'

There was no ambiguity in Sister Antrobus's statement.

Ward sister or not, Aileen had been as good as ejected. As she made her way out, she enjoyed a brief moment of relief at having been released from her mother's company, but then she felt guilty. She almost allowed the guilt to swamp her, but something made her stop. She'd found a flicker of strength within, and that flicker had been growing throughout the day; she knew that if she didn't do something about her life herself, then others – her mother, Josie, the hospital – would make her choices for her.

A plan had taken root in her mind as she'd lain awake that morning with no need to jump out of bed and dash down to the icy-cold back kitchen. She'd only toyed with it at first, had been too shy and apprehensive to allow herself to linger over it, but it had grown in its insistence and had punched its way to the surface. Right now it was practically shouting to her: 'Never mind your mother, Aileen, tonight is about you and it's your only chance.'

She had one hour to return to the room and smarten up. She looked over her shoulder and saw an enema trolley being wheeled behind the curtains surrounding her mother's bed. She almost turned back to say to Sister Antrobus, who was pushing the trolley with her usual no-nonsense efficiency, 'Here, leave it to me, I will toilet her,' but from nowhere she felt as though a hand was tugging at her arm and propelling her away. She turned her head towards the door and almost came to a standstill as once again she heard her father's familiar voice whispering to her. *Run, Aileen! Run!*

The nurses from the choir had arranged to meet in the WVS post before they began their walk into town. There was a huge amount of pre-concert excitement as they giggled and chattered. Aileen felt proud to be wearing her ward sister's uniform as the nurses rushed over and deferred to her seniority as she walked in through the main doors. She was the only ward sister in the choir and as a newer and younger sister she was a favourite with those who'd worked with her.

'Here's your lantern, Sister,' one of her nurses shouted. She handed Aileen a wooden shepherd's crook with a glass jam jar suspended from it containing a candle, its flame fluttering.

'Isn't it thrilling,' said another. 'We're to be in the front row on the bottom steps because the choirmaster thinks our dresses and capes look pretty.'

The atmosphere was one of high excitement and Aileen grinned. She felt it too. It was a lovely way to spend Christmas Eve.

As they walked into town together, they passed the dockside houses, some with lights burning inside and many with a church candle, the light of Christ, flickering in the window. For many of the Irish Catholic homes this was the most joyous time in the religious calendar and a grand excuse for a celebration. The pubs were heaving, their doors open, men spilling out on to the streets, and through the windows of nearby homes Aileen caught glimpses of women cooking, bathing their children and wrapping presents. At one house, the windows were being cleaned. Everyone tried their utmost to make Christmas Day the one day when they wouldn't have any household chores to do other than the cooking and the dishes.

The sight of sixteen nurses walking down the street, lanterns lit, capes fastened and wrapped tight against the chill night air, caused a stir. Doors opened and neighbours called out.

'Merry Christmas, angels,' shouted several women as they

hurried to their front doors, their smallest children hanging on to their legs.

'Come in here for a singsong, angels,' shouted men outside the pubs.

The nurses smiled and waved as they wound their way down to St George's Hall.

Christmas Eve was officially Aileen's day off, but she'd chosen not to take all of the day for herself. She had very much wanted to spend it on her ward with the children and the nurses and even though the morning had been busy, she felt more elated than tired. More so when she thought of her plan. What if it works, she asked herself, and the prospect was so sweet, so delicious and exciting, that an intense thrill ran through her and she had to drag her thoughts back to the present, to the people she was with.

As the night darkened, the temperature dropped quite quickly and a sudden breeze blew in off the Mersey, threatening to extinguish the candles.

'Will anyone come in this cold?' a probationer asked Aileen.

'I hope so, after all the effort,' Aileen replied. 'As long as it doesn't snow.'

The bitter breeze put paid to their chatter. The nurses pulled their cloaks even more tightly across them and Aileen, with her head down, allowed her thoughts to drift to her sad conversation with Matron that morning.

'What are you doing here?' Matron had asked as she saw her across the landing between wards three and four. She wasted no time as she stormed over. 'Have you seen that poor woman in there? Have you? Just like you, she was, always in and out on her days off.'

Aileen looked sheepish, but she had her reply ready. 'No,

Matron, I haven't seen Sister Tapps yet. That's one of the reasons I've come in today, to visit Sister Tapps, and my mother too, and to meet up with the other staff for the carol concert. But I'm going to check that Louis is still doing well and help on the ward too. This is no ordinary day – it's Christmas Eve and my very first one as a ward sister.'

Matron's face softened. 'I'm sorry. You're quite right.'

'And,' said Aileen, 'we have Father Christmas visiting as soon as it gets dark – do you think I'm going to miss that? I mean, I've never seen him before, have I?'

Both women grinned.

'How is she?' asked Aileen, looking across to ward four.

'She's doing OK, but, you know, we only have a few days.' Matron paused. This fact was still hard to accept. 'I'm wondering if I've done the right thing putting her on her own ward with just me to look after her. Maybe she could do with seeing more of us?'

Aileen removed her cape and shook it out, away from them both, then folded it and hugged it into her body. 'Matron, I have an idea. Why don't we ask Sister Haycock to organize something, like a rota of people to sit with her, and then tomorrow we can wheel her bed into ward three to have Christmas lunch with the children and Dr Walker and his wife. If you think she's up to it, that is. And then if she's in the bed and she isn't so good, we can just wheel her back.'

'Oh, Sister Paige, I was hoping you'd say that. But it's just occurred to me – seeing you has reminded me – that there's a more pressing problem. She has a niece and nephew and I wonder, could you speak to the policeman who was on the ward and ask him if he could track them down for us?'

Aileen had been flustered by this. 'Oh, well, I can ask

someone else to do that, Matron,' she'd replied. 'Maybe Doreen in casualty? Someone who's behind a desk all day. I can't possibly do that today, I have so much to do.'

Matron was surprised. She was sure there was something going on between Sister Paige and the policeman, Freddie Watts. It wasn't often that she was wrong about such things. She had expected Aileen to jump at the chance. 'Quite right. I shall call Doreen immediately. Is everything quite all right, Sister Paige? Is your mother behaving herself?'

Aileen sighed. 'No, Matron, not really! But Sister Antrobus really does seem to have the measure of her and has things under control.'

'I'm delighted to hear it.' Matron smiled.

Aileen was about to head for the cloakroom door when Matron's words stopped her dead. 'Sister Paige, don't waste your life. Make the most of it. Nothing is ever as bad as it seems, you know, or so I am always being told, and there is an answer to most problems.'

Aileen looked down at her shoes. 'Oh, I'm not sure about that, Matron. Sometimes there are just too many problems to deal with at the same time and they all seem to merge into one.'

Matron sighed. She guessed something had gone horribly wrong with Sister Paige and that her mother was at the root of it. She was now convinced that her instinct to keep her mother in and to give Sister Paige a break had been right. But the young man... She'd been sure there was something. She put her hand on Aileen's arm. 'Sister Paige, I scrapped the marriage ban on nurses for a reason – because I never want to see another ward sister have to live the life of Sister Tapps and, yes, even Sister Antrobus, not to mention many others in this hospital.'

Aileen noted that she did not include herself.

'The ban was wrong and I realize that now. I don't know what has happened to take the smile from your face and the twinkle from your eye that I saw there so recently—'

Aileen looked up sharply, as though she were about to object. Matron raised her hand to ward off her words.

'Sister Paige, I am older than you by many years. I have worked with nurses all of my life, I have seen that look in your eye and I saw a matching one in his.'

Against her better judgement, Aileen let out a gasp.

'Oh yes I did, and don't try and tell me otherwise.'

And that was when the plan had begun to properly germinate.

'Sister Paige, sometimes, in order to achieve the things in life we want and, yes, deserve, we have to put aside our pride. We have to make the first move and perhaps even be the first to say sorry. I'm not suggesting you make a habit of it, mind – I certainly don't – however, if it helps to get you where you want to go... And remember, if something feels right, that's because it is right.'

Aileen didn't know how to respond so she just stood there in silence. Matron threw her a knowing smile and disappeared through the doors of ward four.

Josie was waiting outside the ward doors along with the rest of the visitors, but rather than sit on one of the wooden benches she remained standing, slightly aloof, away from the tapping feet and nervous, clenching hands. Not everyone enjoyed visiting, especially not those whose loved ones were failing to recover and might never return to their own home and bed. As she heard the brass hand-bell ring on the opposite side of the ward doors, she almost jumped.

The doors were flung open and Sister Antrobus boomed out, 'Visitors, please remember, visiting is for exactly one hour.' Turning her back, making it clear she wasn't the sort of ward sister who welcomed small talk, she strode away in her black brogues, taking one step for each of Josie's three in her beige suede kitten heels.

Scanning the ward for her mother, Josie eventually found her in the bed furthest from the door. She was sitting up against the starched white pillow, motionless, as though she too had been recently starched and ironed and placed there.

'For goodness' sake,' said Josie as she pulled out the chair, 'what on earth are you doing here? I said to get Aileen to stay at home from St Angelus for Christmas, not for you to book yourself in as a patient – it's not a hotel, Mother.'

Having spent the afternoon in the hands of Sister Antrobus, Mrs Paige was in no mood for Josie's intimidation tactics. 'I did my best,' she said. 'In order that you and your husband can hobnob on Christmas Day, I am being forced to spend my Christmas in here. I almost think Matron did it deliberately. You have no idea of the injustice and indignity I have had to face this afternoon, all for you and your husband. Come with you, has he?' She made much of leaning forward and peering down the ward at the last trail of visitors streaming in through the door. 'Concerned for the welfare of his mother-in-law, is he? Let me see now, when did I last see him? Oh, silly me, of course, it was Christmas Day last year, wasn't it? I thought he might want to at least come and witness the sacrifice I am making.'

'Oh, Mother, really.' Josie squirmed on her chair and looked around the ward to check that no one had been listening. 'You know he isn't here – he had to go all the way to London on the train today, even though it's Christmas Eve. He has a very responsible job, Mother.'

Her mother's next words took Josie completely by surprise. 'And so, my dear, does your sister. The one thing I would say about sitting here in this bed is that I have a lot of time to think. You don't know this, and, frankly, neither do I, not for definite, but I think Aileen may have a young man. And do you know, it has occurred to me that I wouldn't want to live with you, not in a month of Sundays, so you can stop fretting on that score.'

'A man? Who?' Josie shuffled her chair closer to the bed and Mrs Paige smirked. Now Josie was paying attention. Mrs Paige was no fool – Josie was always interested in the house and what would become of it. She was happy for Aileen to remain in it so long as she was single and paying for the upkeep, keeping her inheritance warm. But she wouldn't want the house sold and the money distributed; all or nothing was always Josie's way.

'Well we can worry about that when we know if it's true or not, can't we.' Mrs Paige laughed, which unnerved Josie. Her mother rarely laughed. 'Oh yes, my dear, we can worry about it then – or you can.'

Emily Haycock had been writing out the last of her notes and preparing for the January intake when Biddy came in with the tea tray. The room filled with the smell of hot buttered crumpets.

'Isn't it shocking?' said Biddy.

Emily put the cap back on her pen. She instantly knew what Biddy was talking about and sat back in her chair. 'Sit and have one with me, Biddy,' she said, having taken note of the second cup on the tray and the excessive number of crumpets. She had to think on her feet in order to keep one step ahead of Biddy. She was such a strong character and if Emily let her, she would completely take over the school of nursing, so a line had to be drawn. But Emily didn't mind – Biddy was like a mother to her.

Biddy sat down in the opposite chair. 'I can't get her out of my mind. Is there a kinder woman anywhere? Why would the good Lord choose her?' she said, visibly distressed. 'Everyone is talking about it, you know. We all feel so lost, we don't know what to do. Some of us have spoken to her pretty much every day for the last forty years.'

'Maybe he's chosen her because she's so good, he can't wait to take her to a better place?' Emily said, hoping to offer a shred of comfort. But in truth she felt so desperately sad herself, it didn't even feel like Christmas Eve.

Without asking, Biddy placed a crumpet on a plate and held it out to Emily. They both jumped as the phone on Emily's desk rang. Biddy poured the tea while Emily answered it.

'Well, Biddy is with me, Matron, I'm sure there's something we can do. … No, I think that's a very good idea, if Dr Mackintosh thinks she's up to it?'

The conversation continued and Biddy had polished off her first crumpet by the time Emily put the phone down. She waited – she knew Emily so well. She understood that Emily needed to process her thoughts and that if she sat and didn't speak and bided her time, Emily would tell her everything. Biddy had decorated the office and looked around with a degree of satisfaction at the holly branches on the windowsill. The fire needed more coal and she would attend to that before she left the room.

Emily gave a big sigh and transferred her gaze from the handset to Biddy. 'She only has days,' she said in a voice leaden with sadness.

Biddy dropped her second crumpet on to the plate and her hand flew to bless herself. 'Holy Mary, mother of God.'

'Matron is going to wheel her bed over to ward three tomorrow. She said she's bright and chatty, although a little bit away with the fairies because of the diamorphine, but she's confident that spending her day with the children will make her happier than being alone on ward four. She'll wheel her back before visiting. Matron wants to do something for her, but she doesn't know what. I hate to use the words "send off", but you know what I mean. Something to show her she was appreciated... loved, even.'

'Well, that's easy enough,' said Biddy. 'We can get on with that. We can give her the best Christmas Day ever.'

'But, Biddy, it's Christmas, everyone has their own families to see to and things to do.'

Biddy looked alarmed. 'What, you think people around here wouldn't want to do something for the woman who has done so much for so many? Are you kidding me?'

Emily smiled. She should have known.

'Christmas Day or not, what's a few hours?' Biddy was already on her feet and throwing coal on to the fire.

Emily stood at her desk. 'Right, well, I will speak to Dessie. We'll organize a group of staff to go to the ward at maybe twelve o'clock to see her. Everyone can bring a little something and we'll make it a thank you party for her. You know she loves teddies – I have one that I won at the fair, I'll take her that. Matron is asking Doreen to track down that little girl she looked after for over two years and loved so much – Laura Thomas, I think her name was – and the police are trying to trace a niece and nephew she lost touch with, her sister's children, though Matron tells me the sister died some years ago. I didn't even know she had any family.'

Biddy walked back over to Emily's desk and sat down. Her expression was grave. 'There's something you need to know,' she said, 'and something I want to do.'

Emily knew from both the tone and the look that this was serious. If experience had taught her anything, it was that she would end up doing whatever it was that Biddy had in mind, regardless of whether she approved or not.

As the nurses approached St George's Hall, all they could see was a mass of people and uniforms spreading right across St George's Place and William Brown Street and across to Lime Street Station. Politely pushing their way through the crowd, they heard a lot of whispered comments behind them:

'It's the angels from St Angelus.'

'As good as angels they are too. They looked after my father at the end…'

The comments brought smiles to the nurses' faces. Being appreciated was what kept them going through difficult days on the wards.

With a sigh of relief, Aileen spotted their choirmaster and shouted, 'This way, everyone.' Breathless from her last-minute dash to round them all up, she asked, 'Where do you want us to stand?'

'On the front steps.' The choirmaster beamed down at her. 'Everyone here is highly valued, but the audience hold you ladies close to their hearts.'

Aileen beamed. 'Come along, nurses, on this step, please,' she shouted. And then, as she turned to run up the steps herself, she saw Freddie. Her plan instantly flew out of her mind.

'Oh, hello,' he stuttered, his cheeks flushing. 'I... er... didn't think you would come. You weren't at the rehearsal or the party.' He coughed and fiddled with his scarf, then collected himself. 'I understand though. You must think very badly of me.'

Aileen made herself look him in the eye. She shook her head, searched for the right words. 'Me think badly of you?' Her heart was thumping now. 'No! That's not it at all!' The words came tumbling out in a rush, and she had to say them quick, before anything else interrupted them. 'I was waiting... hoping you would... The reason I couldn't come was because my mother was admitted to hospital. I sent a message with Emily Haycock, didn't you get it?'

'Shall we stand here, Sister?' a voice called out to Aileen.

'Yes, please, just there.'

'All line up, everyone, please. Am I talking to myself?' The choirmaster was trying his best to assemble people on the steps. 'This is like herding cats,' he shouted down to the firemen, who were flirting with the shop-girls pouring out of the stores on Church Street and down to the hall.

Aileen turned back to Freddie, who had a huge grin on his face. 'Emily didn't tell you?' she asked again.

At that moment they both heard a familiar voice calling out, 'Sister Paige! Aileen!' and as they turned around, Emily sprinted up the steps and was next to them. 'Oh God, please don't hate me – I am so sorry. Freddie, Aileen's mother was taken into hospital earlier this week and I was supposed to have told you and so much has happened I don't know where the hours went and I forgot. I just forgot!' She threw her arms in the air and almost screeched the last few words.

Both Aileen and Freddie began to laugh, as much with relief as anything else.

'That's all right,' said Aileen. She looked across at Freddie. 'It explains a lot, but I think we'll be OK now.'

'Phew, thank goodness for that. Thought I'd stopped fate in its tracks there.'

Aileen blushed, but Freddie didn't. He continued grinning; in fact he couldn't stop.

'Anyway, one more thing, when you leave here and return to the hospital for the night-time carols, make sure you go to ward four, won't you? We're arranging something for Tappsy tomorrow, but Matron doesn't want her to miss out on tonight. Everything is to be as normal as possible.'

'We'll do better than that,' said Aileen. 'What's the point of singing at the ward doors when she's the only patient? We'll go in and sing around her bed.'

Tears sprang into the eyes of both women and neither could say much more. Emily reached out and grabbed Aileen's hand. 'Bless you,' she said, her voice thick with tears.

They squeezed each other's hands tightly as their eyes met. This was for no one else to share. One of their own, a ward sister at their beloved St Angelus, was at the end of her life and they all knew what their responsibilities were, from Matron to the ward sisters to the domestics. Tappsy would die knowing she was cherished.

Emily hurried back down the steps to Dessie as the choir-master shouted out, 'Nurses on the first step, police officers on the second, tenors to the right, altos to the left, firemen on the top. Please take your places now.'

The air buzzed with excitement and chatter as the crowd waited. Knots of people gathered around the braziers in the concourse where vendors were roasting chestnuts.

Freddie, now standing behind Aileen, whispered in her ear. 'Shall I come to the hospital with you after this is over?'

Aileen turned around and the smile she gave him let him know his answer. She'd spent the whole day thinking about her plan, imagining it, refining it, and now here it was. Without her doing anything at all, it was all happening just as she'd hoped. An image of her fallen hero, David, flashed into her mind. He was smiling, egging her on and she didn't feel sad or even guilty. 'Yes, please,' she said. 'I have to sing on the wards first, though – it's traditional, what we always do.' She felt his hand squeeze her shoulder.

'I'll wait. I'm happy to wait for you for as long as it takes,' he whispered.

The crowd fell silent. The orchestra began tuning their instruments and then slowly the cacophony quieted as one by one the flutes, violins and then the harp stuttered to an expectant hush, awaiting the sign from their conductor. The choirmaster and the conductor looked towards each other and nodded.

Aileen noticed that it suddenly felt much warmer. She wondered was it the braziers that were lit all over William Brown Street and St George's Place. The night had been bitter, but that hadn't dampened their spirits – every one of them, amateur singers and professional musicians alike, had been looking forward to this evening for a long time. It was the perfect way to begin Liverpool's Christmas celebrations.

The violins began, alone. The haunting sound of the strings rose into the night sky and then came a piercingly beautiful voice singing the opening bars of 'In the Bleak Midwinter'. Aileen watched as the first snowflake floated down and landed on her dark cape and she thought to herself, this is the happiest moment of my life.

Chapter 24

It was eight o'clock when the nurses assembled outside ward one and began to sing. They had split into two groups, dividing the wards between them. The night nurse looked up from the desk where she had been writing her report and smiled as the sound of 'The Holly and the Ivy' floated down the ward. The traditional last carol was 'Silent Night' and she looked around to see which of her patients were still awake, waiting.

She and the two nurses she was on duty with walked to the end of the ward to greet the small choral group. They stepped in among them and, sharing the songsheets, sang with them. 'Wonderful,' said Sister as they finished. 'What a lovely way for our patients to fall asleep. Merry Christmas, everyone,' she said as the singers moved over to ward two.

As she made her way back down the ward to the desk and the lamp, Mrs Paige called out to her. 'Was my daughter with those nurses, Sister? Only I know she sings with the choir and she hasn't been in. I thought maybe that was her?'

'No, Mrs Paige, I think she's gone upstairs to her ward with the second group, to sing to the children. Listen – can you hear them?'

Mrs Paige stopped and turned her head to the side and they both heard the muffled sound of singing floating down from the ward above. 'Yes, I can,' she said. 'Fancy that! Yes. Will the night staff mind the children being awake?'

The night nurse smiled. 'Oh no. Many of them will be asleep already, but those that aren't will enjoy it, and besides, they have a special patient on ward four, an adult. Someone who isn't very well. They'll be putting on a special show for her.'

'That's nice,' said Mrs Paige.

Night Nurse noticed that Mrs Paige's attitude wasn't quite as abrasive as it had been on previous nights.

'Who is the patient?' she asked.

Night Nurse sat on the bed, but only after she'd looked around first to make sure no one was watching. 'She is a very special lady, a sister at this hospital. She's spent her whole life looking after others and she's known for always thinking of others first. There's no one quite like her and because of that, almost everyone who works at this hospital is pulling together to ensure she has a very special Christmas Day.'

Mrs Paige felt a pain in her heart. The night nurse was describing a woman who could not be more unlike herself, and her own daughter had chosen to go upstairs and sing to this apparently saintly being rather than come and sing in the ward where she was a patient.

'It's beginning to snow,' the nurse said. 'Getting really heavy. I hope the buses are running in the morning or it's a long walk for me. Shall I fetch you a cup of tea? I have a drop of medicinal brandy in the cupboard – how about I put a splash of that in to help you sleep.'

And for the first time in her life Mrs Paige answered, 'Only if it's not too much trouble, Nurse.'

★

Matron had made it clear that she wouldn't leave Sister Tapps until after the carol singers had come round, even though she'd placed a night nurse on specialling duty. She was sitting by the side of the bed, filling in a fluid intake and output chart, and watching with dismay as Sister Tapps's kidney function did exactly as Dr Mackintosh had predicted; it was diminishing as Tappsy dozed.

Matron's head shot up as she heard the ward doors open and the footsteps of the eight nurses, with Sister Paige at their head, tiptoeing down the dark ward.

'Do you still want us?' asked Sister Paige.

Matron glanced at her sleeping patient. She was about to answer 'No,' when Tappsy woke and asked, 'Is that Laura?'

Matron stood up and fixed her pillows and spoke to her with so much love and tenderness, as if Tappsy were her child. 'No, it's Sister Paige. She's brought the nurses to sing some carols to you. Would you like that, my dear?'

'Oh, yes, please.'

Sister Tapps tried to push herself up the bed and Aileen immediately dashed to the other side of her. Without any need for words, she and Matron linked their arms behind her back and weaved their fingers together under her knees. Making a cradle of human limbs and digits, they moved her up the bed, keeping her clear of the bedding so as not to drag her skin on the draw sheet below.

Both their faces were close to Tappsy's as they leant over her and she looked into them, one to the other. Aileen could see that her pupils were dilated and her eyes bright. The diamorphine was doing its work as she smiled at them both.

'What are you doing here now, 'tis the middle of the night,' she said as she laid the flat of her hand against Aileen's cheek. 'Oh, would you look at her,' she said to Matron. 'Who would have known she'd grow up to be such a fine colleen. The face on her, she'd take the eyes out of any man's head, she would. Blind them with her beauty.'

'Isn't that the truth,' said Matron as she rubbed Sister Tapps's back with a gentleness Aileen had never seen in her before. She smiled benevolently at Aileen. 'Sister Paige always was one of your favourites, wasn't she, Sister Tapps? Even when she was a patient here as a little girl, long before she became a nurse.'

Tappsy grinned. 'Aye, she was that. Are you here for the singing?' she asked Aileen.

Aileen found she could not control the tears that had rushed to her eyes or the tightening of her throat. Unable to answer without betraying her emotions and letting Matron down, she drew herself upright and turned away from Tappsy as she swiped at the tears with the back of her hand.

Matron threw her a look full of understanding and covered for her. 'She is – they all are. Let me pull up my chair before you start, nurses,' she said, putting on her brightest voice so that there was not even a hint that her heart was breaking. And then, looking over at the thin, frail form of Tappsy in the bed, she did something she had never done in her entire nursing career: she walked back to the bed and said, 'Move over, Sister Tapps.'

Tappsy grinned as she grabbed her hand. 'Oh, get away with you,' she said. 'You'll be getting me into trouble with Matron.'

Matron didn't know or care who Tappsy thought she was or who she was talking to. It didn't matter. It wasn't about her feelings. Tappsy was pain-free, comfortable, smiling and happy, and her job was to keep her like that for as long as she could, right to the end. That was her personal challenge.

She noticed that Tappsy's head was sinking deep into the feather pillow she'd brought in from her own rooms and that her eyes were growing heavy. 'Just the one,' she whispered to the nurses, holding up a single finger.

Aileen nodded. Her throat was tight, her eyes prickled and her shoulders were on the point of heaving with sobs, but she steeled herself and took a deep, shuddering breath. She felt seven pairs of tear-filled eyes being turned towards her, waiting for their cue. '"Silent Night",' she said.

They began in their softest voices, each nurse with her eyes fixed on Tappsy, wanting her to appreciate every note as she lay there smiling, seemingly listening while at the same time somewhere lost in her happy thoughts. Matron held her hand and gently caressed it. It wasn't until they reached the last line, 'Sleep in heavenly peace,' that their voices faltered and their tears threatened to break. But it was no matter: Tappsy was now asleep, the smile still on her face.

Biddy had taken two buses and she was cold. She held the piece of paper out in front of her, scanned the road and looked for the numbers on the doors.

The bus conductor had known exactly where the address was. 'I'll drop you before the stop,' he'd said. 'But you'll need to walk up to the Jolly Miller to get the bus back.'

Biddy thanked him profusely.

'It's Christmas, love,' he replied.

'Merry Christmas,' said Biddy as she dismounted, determined to achieve what she'd set out to do. Now that she was here in a part of Liverpool she had never set foot in before, her confidence was deserting her. 'Come on, you,' she said out loud. 'You've not come all the way here for nothing.'

Five minutes later she was lifting the latch on a gate she had never opened, walking down a path she had never trodden and knocking on a door she had never seen before.

A young woman aged about eighteen opened the door.

'Can I step inside, please?' asked Biddy, looking around nervously. 'I'm from St Angelus.'

Chapter 25

The feeling that comes just once a year and is special to Christmas morning was as strong on ward three as it was in every home in Liverpool. Even those children who were too ill to return home rallied when they opened their eyes and saw a stocking on the end of their bed.

'Will you all calm down!' said Night Staff Nurse as she stood in the middle of the bay, half leaning into the medicine trolley, trying to weigh out and dispense the morning medicines. As she walked into Louis's room, carrying his antibiotics, vitamin pills and iron tonic, she almost shrieked out in laughter. Louis was holding the bar on the side of his cot and had heaved himself up. He was bouncing on his stick-thin legs with all his might, his nappy hanging around his ankles and a full bowel movement trodden into the bottom sheet and smeared all over his body.

'Oh Holy Mary, mother of God,' she shrieked. 'Nurse!'

An exhausted nurse nearing the end of her twelve-hour shift dashed into the cubicle. 'Yes, Staff,' she said, before the smell hit her nostrils and her eyes processed what had happened. Her hand flew to her mouth in shock. 'Oh, would you look at the state of him. I bathed him and changed him not ten minutes since.'

Night Staff smiled. 'Well, Sister Paige will be here in fifteen minutes by my reckoning.' She craned her neck to take a better look at the ward clock above the door. 'You had better get a move on.'

'Yes, Staff,' said the nurse. She loosened the bottom sheet from the cot and wrapping it around Louis like a mummy scooped him up and carried him out of the room. 'Come on you, you little terror,' she said, laughing as Louis began to object. 'I'll take him to the sluice and I'll run the sink in there.'

'Yes, do. I can't think of any other way to manage him,' said Staff. 'I'll lock up my trolley, fetch the dirty linen basket and the Dettol and wash the bed down for you. Louis, you are a little pain in the rear end these days. Who would have thought that a week ago.'

Half an hour later, day and night nurses were in the office together, wishing each other a merry Christmas. Branna was setting up the long table in the bay as a dining table ready for when the guests arrived. It was a Christmas Day tradition that Matron, Sister Haycock, Dr and Mrs Walker, and the board members all gathered in the ward for a glass of sherry, and then, lo and behold, Father Christmas would arrive, to the great excitement of the children. The turkey would be sent up from the kitchens and Dr Walker would carve it for Matron before he and his wife returned home to their own children.

Those who had to work on Christmas Day liked to make the ward experience as close to a home Christmas as possible. Matron was the first to arrive, and then came Father Christmas, pushing Tappsy in her bed across the landing. Even Matron commented on how well she seemed.

'Well hello, all of you,' Tappsy called out. Her voice was thready, but her enthusiasm carried her words all the way into the office from the doorway. The nurses stopped mid conversation and their faces lifted in delight at the sight of Sister Tapps sitting up against her pillow, her hair pushed back and her eyes bright. Her face was painfully thin and drawn, but it didn't seem to matter, the energy within shone out and was like a magnet to the nurses. Forgetting sister–nurse protocol, they rushed to the side of her bed and took it in turns to plant kisses on her cheek and to call out, 'Merry Christmas, Sister Tapps.'

Aileen wanted to throw her arms around her and hug her, but she was too frail, so like everyone else she kissed her on her cheek and said, 'Look!' as she took a handkerchief out of her pocket. 'I opened your present before I came to work and it's lovely. And do you know, Father Christmas came here for you too – there's a stack of presents for you under the tree.'

Sister Tapps smiled like a child as she clasped her hands and said, 'No! Surely not for me?'

Aileen's heart constricted at the reminder that Tappsy was someone used to giving but not receiving. There were no relatives at her bedside – her St Angelus colleagues were the closest she had to family.

The morning passed in a haze of cheeriness and not a single person shed a tear or allowed a frown to cross their face. Matron didn't leave Tappsy's side and Emily Haycock arrived to help. Even the children commented on how much Father Christmas liked Sister Haycock.

They were all amazed at how much of her Christmas dinner Sister Tapps managed. 'I chopped up a roast potato and she even ate that,' said Matron to Emily. Straight after lunch, the ward began to fill with visitors and Sister Tapps found it within herself to refuse to return to ward four.

'Is Sister Tapps getting better now?' a young nurse infected with the informality of the day piped up as she came in to change the water jugs. The question played on everyone's mind. Even Matron, impressed and inspired by Tappsy's revival, wondered if that might be possible.

It became obvious halfway through visiting, however, as Tappsy began to close her eyes, that it was now time to take her back to ward four. 'She needs to sleep,' said Matron. 'I can't believe how she's kept going. I'm going to freshen her up and give her some painkillers.'

'Did you find the niece and nephew?'

'We didn't,' said Aileen. 'Doreen and the police did their best, but we didn't even have a surname.'

At that very moment the ward doors opened. Everyone stopped what they were doing at the sight of Biddy standing in the doorway with a young woman at her side. Matron had no idea who she was. No one did. But Tappsy put them right. She opened her eyes and her face shone with love as she called out the name. 'Laura! My Laura!'

Aileen had handed over ward three and all her charges and responsibilities to the night staff nurse and although the day had been filled with much laughter and jollity, she was delighted and relieved to hear the sound of the ward doors closing behind her. Now she was free.

Her heart skipped a beat and her face lit up at the sight of Freddie sitting on the wooden bench, no longer in his uniform but smart in a shirt and jacket.

'Are you sure you want to do this?' he asked as he sprang to his feet. After what had happened to Louis, he was far too nervous now to even touch her when she was in uniform.

'I am, but we just have to do something first, one last little job. Can you come with me?'

Five minutes later, Freddie was heading across to ward four carrying the heavy record player in his arms.

'She's asked to hear "Silent Night" sung again and we have it on the record, so I asked the parents today and they were more than happy for us to take it over to Tappsy. I can just pop across and say goodnight to Matron at the same time.' Aileen opened the doors to ward four and held them in place with her back to allow Freddie to pass though.

'Is Matron spending all night here?' he asked.

'Yes. She's made it all so cosy. Dessie and the porter's lads carried Matron's armchair and sofa down, along with the Christmas tree from her apartment, when we moved Sister Tapps on to ward four. The night nurse reported over there for duty, but Matron sent her away to ward three.'

'Shall I come with you?'

Aileen thought for a moment. 'Yes, why not. I think it might please Matron, and I need you to carry the record player down to the bay at the bottom anyway.'

She was surprised to see Matron in her armchair reading by the fire and not at Tappsy's side. The young woman, Laura Thomas, was on the bed next to Tappsy with her arm around her shoulders. She appeared to be talking to her.

Aileen gestured for Freddie to follow her and, smiling at Laura as she looked up, she tiptoed over to Matron. The ward was dark, but the lamp at Matron's side gave out a welcoming glow and the fire in the grate was crackling brightly, its flames reflected prettily in the lights on the Christmas tree.

'I've just popped over to say goodnight. Is there anything I can get or do for you?'

Matron almost ignored Aileen and looked straight at Freddie. 'Hello, young man,' she said. 'What a nice surprise. Merry Christmas to you.'

Freddie had removed his cap and holding it to his chest said, 'Merry Christmas, Matron.'

Turning to Aileen, Matron said, 'I'm fine here. I have everything I could possibly need. Have you seen that table? Between Branna, Biddy and Elsie, they've left me enough food to feed an army. Night Sister is popping in when she's finished her rounds to have supper with me, so I'll have company, don't worry about me. I'm not sure what time Laura over there will be leaving. They seem to have a lot to talk about. I'm utterly amazed at Sister Tapps – she hasn't stopped talking for hours, it seems, and it's as if they've never been apart – very odd.'

They all looked over to the bed. The overhead light threw an orange halo over Tappsy. Laura was mostly in the shade and Tappsy was nestled into the crook of her arm, staring into the fire as she spoke and holding a cup of tea in her hand. Aileen felt something wash through her, an emotion that moved her to tears. How she wished she'd known a mother's true love. She felt more like a servant than a daughter and it was only now, looking at Laura, that this came home to her.

'Do you know, Matron, I think she's had a lovely Christmas. I know that might be an odd thing to say, but look how happy she is.'

Matron gave a deep sigh. 'She really has and I think we can all be pleased with ourselves tonight for that and for the fact that all the patients on all the wards have had a lovely day. It has been a job well done. Oh! I forgot to tell you all yesterday, what with the excitement of Christmas Eve – I had a phone call from the *Nursing Times*, and guess what...?'

Aileen looked at her quizzically.

'We won the decorating competition! The lady who phoned said that it was quite clear from when she came round and judged it that the decorating had been done in the most collaborative way, and that's what swung it, apparently. She made special mention of how it was so heartwarming that the decorations had been made by "the community" – she meant the domestics, I think, and Mrs Tanner. All those golden stars they cut out and covered in glitter.' She beamed. 'Isn't that a lovely result, Sister Paige. And for your first Christmas as ward sister too. Do be sure to tell the others if you see them before I do.'

Aileen beamed back at her. Matron was right: winning the competition really was the icing on the cake. It felt like a good omen. Next year things were going to go right for her, she was sure.

'Are you off home?' Matron asked.

'Not yet, Matron. One more visit downstairs first. Let me show you how to work the record player.'

Ten minutes later, as the voices of the King's College Choir filled the ward, Matron looked at Aileen and Freddie and said, 'Whatever next! I mean, look at the size of it, only half the width of my desk. It's a strange world now with all these new-fangled gadgets.'

'We have to go down to Mother,' said Aileen.

Matron raised one eyebrow. 'Ah, well, good luck with that. See you in a couple of days. If Sister Tapps is in the same spirits tomorrow, I might even put her in a wheelchair and take her for a spin outside.'

Five minutes later, Aileen and Freddie walked into ward one. Aileen called in to the office first, where the night staff nurse was filling in the charts. 'How has she been?' she asked.

'Well, she could hear all the high jinks upstairs – we all could – and obviously she knew you were busy and couldn't come down, but I think you might find a change in your mother. I certainly have. I think Matron knew exactly what she was doing bringing her in for observation. You may find you're a little more appreciated when she returns home.'

Aileen didn't feel as confident as the night nurse sounded.

As they approached Mrs Paige's bed, they could see her lying there, awake, staring into the middle distance. Aileen's heart crunched. Her mother looked sad and childlike. As her gaze rested on Aileen, a smile slowly spread across her face and she sat upright in the bed.

'Aileen – at last. I thought you weren't coming.' She gave Freddie a glance and asked, 'Who is this?' But there was no malice in her voice and Aileen guessed she knew who he was.

'This is Freddie, Mother.'

Before she could say any more, Freddie picked up Aileen's hand and finished her sentence for her. 'And your daughter, Mrs Paige, is very important to me.'

They spent half an hour sitting by her mother's bedside, and the whole time they were there Aileen's heart soared. She barely spoke, just watched how Freddie used all the skills he possessed to start her mother eating out of his hand.

As they left the ward and ran down the main steps of

St Angelus, Freddie said, 'She's not a bad old stick. If I had to put money on it, I'd say she missed your father. She mentioned him a lot just then.' He took Aileen's arm and slipped it through his.

'You have no idea how much she gave my father the run-around,' said Aileen, almost snorting with disgust.

'And you probably have no idea how much he let her.'

Aileen came to a sudden standstill. 'I never thought of that,' she said, taking in his cheeky grin and feeling a sudden rush of happiness.

The snow had covered the black cinder surface of the car park with a dusting of white and the cloud was heavy and low, promising more snow. There was not a star to be seen in the sky. The buildings of St Angelus were the darkest red behind them and in the bay window of Aileen's ward the Christmas tree blazed. It occurred to Aileen that everywhere was silent. There was no traffic, no buses, no people scurrying past. It was Christmas night, a silent night.

'Why aren't you staying in the hospital tonight?' asked Freddie as he unlocked the car door with his key. Aileen noticed that his cap was now white and snowflakes rested on his eyelashes, dropping to his cheeks as he spoke.

'It's Christmas, I want to go home. Would you like to have supper with me? I told Branna I would be coming home and she said Gina would lay up a supper, even though she's meant to be off over the holidays. I'm sure we can make it stretch to two – she always leaves me a huge amount, and anyway, I have a feeling Gina will assume I won't be eating alone if I'm coming home. I'm not at work tomorrow, it's my day off.'

Freddie grinned. 'Same here.' He could resist no longer. She might be in uniform, but they were not on the ward, and besides, how could he let this moment pass. This magical moment on Christmas night, with snowflakes and Christmas lights and the sparkling brightness of Aileen's eyes burning brightly up at him. He placed his hand under her chin, but she needed no encouragement. Their lips were drawn to each other's and as they clung together, the warmth of their bodies kept the cold of the night at bay.

'Come on,' he said, his voice deep and thick. 'Home it is then.' He opened the passenger door for her.

Aileen slipped on to the leather seat and through the window saw out of the corner of her eye a young man in army uniform, at the base of the wall. He was no stranger to her. As Freddie walked around the car to the driver's door, she watched the young soldier slip away into the shadows. She had seen him before at the important moments in her life – when she was made a Sister, when she passed her finals – but she sensed that this time would be the last. Her heart ached as she wiped the tear from her eye and she almost jumped in fright as Freddie flopped into the driver's seat. He leant over and kissed her, his lips cool, his face wet with melted snowflakes.

'Are you ready?' he asked as he brushed the snow-dampened hair off her face.

'I am,' she said. 'I really am.' She looked into the eyes of Freddie, to the now, to her future, and without a backwards glance let David go.

Up on ward four, Night Sister had arrived. She was lifting the damp tea towels and examining the food that had been left for her and Matron to enjoy for supper. Matron walked back from the bay window. She'd seen Aileen and Freddie and had stepped away from the window, embarrassed but happy for Aileen.

'Is the weather any worse?' asked Sister.

Matron looked wistful. 'It is, but really it's not at all bad out there tonight.'

'Doesn't she look happy,' said Night Sister, nodding over at Tappsy as she bit on a sausage roll she'd taken from the table.

Matron also looked over and smiled. 'She does. You should have seen her opening her presents – like a child herself, she was. It was wonderful. At one point there was Father Christmas, also known as Dessie Horton, sat on the foot of her bed, and she had little Angela Doherty almost in bed with her all morning and then Kitty and the Doherty parents brought in a huge bag of presents for Tappsy from half the families in the dockside streets. Honestly, I didn't know when it was going to end. Fancy that, though. And look at the cards, many of them homemade by one child or another.' She pointed to a pile of cards alongside a half-wrapped tin of talcum powder, some gardenia soap, a pair of knitted gloves, a jigsaw and lots of sweets.

'Is the girl, Laura, staying with her? She's the one all the trouble was about, isn't she?' Night Sister had dropped her voice to a whisper so as not to be overheard.

'Yes, she is, but I'm glad of her now. Look at them. But, no, she's not staying overnight. Besides, Sister Tapps needs her sleep. I've rung Laura's father. He's coming to collect her and then he's bringing her back in the morning. Apparently the mother walked out years ago, and it seems the father's not as bad as we thought.'

They watched as Laura bent over to kiss Tappsy goodbye. The love that bound them together was apparent to all. She tiptoed over to Matron. 'I'll wait outside, Matron, for my father. I'll be back by eight in the morning. I don't want to keep her from her sleep.'

'We can't thank you enough for coming,' said Matron.

'Oh, not at all. When Biddy asked me, I didn't hesitate. Sister Tapps was my mother for more than two years when I was very sick. The worst two years of my life, but also the best in a way. She was the only woman ever to show me any affection. I thought about her all the time, but I never felt that I could turn up unannounced, I suppose. And besides, I wasn't even sure she would remember me. Honestly, I've thought about her every single day. You did *me* the favour, not the other way round.'

Matron looked at her as she spoke. She wanted to explain that there weren't many days left, but she decided that could wait for the morning. She didn't want to spoil such a magical night.

She saw Laura down the stairs and when she returned she said to Night Sister, 'Come on, let's do her back and bed and make her comfortable. I can give her her diamorphine and then we can have our supper and know she's comfortable.'

'I've already got the trolley ready,' said Night Sister. 'I'll be honest, I haven't spoken to her yet, but I saw the light fade when you and Laura left the ward.'

The two senior women, unused to carrying out basic nursing chores, laughed at the things they'd forgotten as they went to collect the trolley and a bedpan from the sluice.

'How are you, Sister Tapps?' said Night Sister in the most gentle of voices as they approached the bed and the pool of orange light.

Sister Tapps was quiet, looking down at her hands, but she

perked up as they approached. 'Oh, I'm doing just grand, and would you look at this, Matron herself and the most senior night sister looking after me! I'll be back on me feet in no time at all after all this fuss, and you know, I don't deserve it. I really don't. Now, I don't want to be any trouble to you, go and have your supper. Leave me be, there's nothing wrong with me, I'm fine.'

'You are no trouble at all,' Night Sister replied and she and Matron exchanged glances.

Much to Sister's surprise, Matron said, 'Oh, seriously, to hell with it,' and plonked herself down on the side of the bed. Night Sister gasped. Matron looked at her sternly and then at Tappsy. 'If either of you tell a single living nurse in this hospital that I sat on the bed, so help me God, I'll haunt the life out of the both of you when my time comes.'

They all three began to laugh and Matron turned and rested against Tappsy's pillow. The night light on the wall above illuminated her face as she took Tappsy's hand. She looked across at her with so much affection, Night Sister felt a lump form in her throat. Tappsy grinned and squeezed her hand back.

'Did you enjoy seeing Laura?'

Tappsy's eyes swam with tears. 'Oh, can you imagine how that happened? That she just turned up here out of the blue? She must have missed me as much as I did her, you know.'

Matron didn't answer but simply nodded and squeezed her hand again.

Tappsy frowned with concern. 'You've been working hard all day long – you're tired.'

'I have,' said Matron. 'And do you know what... How many years have I been nursing?'

Tappsy frowned. 'I can't remember.'

'Me neither. Anyway, the point is, this has been my best Christmas Day in this hospital ever – and I've spent it with you.'

The two women shared a long and knowing look.

'I'm not going to get better, am I?' said Tappsy.

Night Sister stepped back out of the pool of light and into the shadows, the clean draw sheet in her arms. It was obvious that time was running out. This time, these words, they were important. The draw sheet could wait.

'Of course you are. You have me looking after you night and day. Do you think I'm going to let anything else happen to you? I want you up soon and running about this ward, just as you have been for all these years. There's more for both of us to do, you know. This place would go to rack and ruin without us. Imagine!'

Tappsy's smile was feeble as she grasped Matron's hand. Her grip was weakening, but she held on. 'Thank you, Margaret. Thank you. It was my best Christmas Day ever, too. Since my sister died, I've had to live with the guilt. All these years, you know, I knew what I'd done.' Silent tears rolled down Tappsy's cheeks. 'Do you think she'll forgive me for being a terrible person, for not being there?'

'Oh, Tappsy…' For the first time ever, Matron used the nickname so familiar to everyone else. 'Of course she will. She has already. She knew you and what you were like. She knew you because she was your sister and she loved you without question. Of course she does. Would you have forgiven her if the boot was on the other foot?'

Tappsy nodded without any hesitation.

'Well, there you are then. You've answered your own question.' Matron suddenly felt a shiver run down her spine. A coolness had entered their space. They were speaking of an angel and she felt the flutter of her wings. 'Come on, you, we need to settle you down, and I'm not going to call Dessie, or rather Father Christmas – I've packed him off home. We will do this all ourselves. I want to bank that fire up before we have our supper.' Matron slipped off the bed and back on to her feet.

'Matron...' said Tappsy.

Matron smiled down at her. 'I think it's Margaret here, Olive. There's only us and Night Sister, who is helping herself to another sausage roll.'

'Margaret, can I have Blackie on my bed tonight? I don't want to be alone.'

'You can – that will be his canine dream come true. And you aren't alone, we are just over here, not even two yards away, sat by the fire watching you all night. We won't be taking our eyes off you, but I will be in that chair over there, because I don't want to keep you awake.'

Night Sister appeared in the light, no longer holding the draw sheet but with three glasses of sherry perched on a tray.

'What a flipping good idea,' said Matron.

'Ooh, lovely. Isn't this exciting,' said Tappsy. But the excitement was no longer in her voice and Matron picked up on it immediately. Even so, there was no stopping Tappsy as she picked up her glass. 'My first ever,' she said as she sniffed at it. 'Do you know what, I think I'm going to like this.'

'Hang on,' said Night Sister, 'I'm going to put the carols back on that record player. Give me a minute.'

Tappsy took her first sip of sherry and licked her lips, obviously pleased with the experience. The music crackled into life and the smooth tones of the King's College Choir filled the air.

'I can't believe this is your first sherry,' said Night Sister.

'Did you never just fancy a little try of it? Just look what you've been missing.'

And without them knowing where it went, time passed. The snow fell outside and the clock in the warm ward ticked on towards midnight. Matron repeatedly banked up the fire, and Tappsy looked radiant as she sipped her sherry and talked about Laura, and the children she'd cared for, and her sister Edith and their childhood singing of the very carols that were on the record player. 'That was my sister's favourite,' she said. 'She was the better singer of the two of us.' She recalled her memories one by one, and Matron and Night Sister refilled their glasses and listened to every word.

Dr Mackintosh stuck his head around the door just as they'd finished. 'How's my favourite patient?' he asked. 'I was just heading back to the doctors' residence and thought I'd pop in and see how you were doing before I turn in.'

'Well, you can see for yourself,' said Matron. 'She couldn't be better,' she lied.

'Can I have a little listen to your heart and see how things are going?' he asked, and Matron felt as though the magic of the day had vanished with his words.

She had nothing good to report. Tappsy's urine output had dropped to almost zero and her abdomen had slowly distended during the day. In the past half hour she'd noticed the scratching returning, and the breathlessness. Tappsy's spirit had won the day and yet Matron knew they were on borrowed hours.

Half an hour later, Tappsy had been examined, washed and tucked up in the cleanest sheets and the warmest blankets. She lay on her side, scratching and grimacing, with Blackie doing his duty, curled up next to her.

Matron stood in the clean utility with Dr Mackintosh as Night Sister tidied up. 'Give her this,' he said in the firmest voice as he handed Matron the syringe.

Matron's face was set. 'But she's doing so well and—'

'Matron...' Dr Mackintosh stopped her with nothing more than the gravity of his voice. 'Someone riddled with tumours the size of hers is not going to get better, I can assure you. I have palpated her abdomen and nothing has changed. Look at her, she's already relapsing from when I walked on to the ward just minutes ago.' He glanced up and looked Matron in the eyes. 'She's had a wonderful day and she has risen to the occasion. You know as well as I do that this can often happen just before the end.'

Matron looked over. Tappsy was scratching at her skin again, which was a sign that the diamorphine had worn off and the pain was returning. The dose that Dr Mackintosh was giving her to administer was larger than what Tappsy had been having so far. It was an act of kindness and it happened all the time with terminally ill patients – but this was a patient Matron knew and loved. She took the enamel kidney dish from his hand and he didn't miss the fact that hers was shaking. As she approached the bed and saw Tappsy tearing at her skin, her face contorted with the sudden searing pain, Matron knew he was right. They would give her enough diamorphine to keep her under. She would not rally again, she would not be able to. There would be no more conversations or smiles or happy memories to reveal. It was now just a question of time.

It was almost dawn when Maura Doherty woke with a start and lifted herself up on to her pillows.

'What's up love?' asked Tommy, rousing. Angela's breathing problems meant they were both light sleepers, always alert, even when asleep. Both had been delighted that day to see the progress Angela had made and even more delighted to be told she would be back home within the week when her course of antibiotics had finished and her breathing was fully back to normal. Both were more worried about Sister Tapps.

'That poor woman,' Maura whispered. 'She looked so awful, but wasn't it lovely, the way everyone was with her.' Tommy reached out an arm and took hold of Maura's hand.

'It was, but look where she is, in the best place to get better. Our Kitty is more bothered about her now than she is about our Angela.'

Maura shuffled back down the bed and lay her head on his shoulder, already feeling sleepy once more. She had chilled from being on the outside of the blankets and he pulled her into him and wrapped his arms around her as she turned her face towards him. 'Kitty made her a card, I'm going to drop it into Kathleen, and ask her to give it to her friend, Biddy, to pass on to Sister Tapps, just so she knows Kitty was thinking about her. We all are, I mean, surely the woman knows, she's a legend with every family on these streets.'

Dessie Horton was the only night porter on duty. He wouldn't let any of the lads miss their Christmas night, but he was at home, tucked up next to his warm Emily when he woke to the sound of the house phone ringing out. It was 4 a.m. His was the only house on the street to have a phone and that had been at Matron's insistence.

He crept back into the bedroom and tried not to wake

Emily, but it was no use. 'What's up?' she asked. 'Who was that? It's not Louis is it?'

They had talked again about Louis only a few hours previously. About the fact that he would be leaving the ward in a matter of weeks and would be transferred to the children's home. Emily had left Dessie in no doubt that she would like them both, as Mr and Mrs Horton, to be the couple to adopt him, if the police failed to find his mother.

Dessie planted a kiss on her forehead. She could feel the tremble in his lips, which transferred to his voice when he spoke. 'It's not about Louis. It was Matron on the phone – it's Tappsy, Emily. She's gone.'

Emily didn't speak; she couldn't. She swallowed hard and turned her head to the window and the snowfall, now silent and heavy. Death was no stranger to Emily.

'I'll be about an hour,' he said as he sat on the side of the bed to fasten his boots. 'I'll transfer her to the mortuary myself, with Matron. I want to.' Emily reached out and took his hand. 'Make sure Matron keeps her belt buckle safe, her angel wings. She can give it to Laura to remember her by.'

Dessie nodded. 'I will. I'll go now.' She lay perfectly still and heard the latch on the back gate drop. She wouldn't sleep until he returned.

Through the gloom of the struggling dawn, she watched as the snow gathered around the window's edge and her mind wandered back over the day and the hours they had spent with Tappsy, surrounded by children and in the company of her beloved Laura. She smiled as she replayed little Jonny's words in her head. Staring at the golden figurine on top of the ward three Christmas tree, he'd looked a bit puzzled, and then he'd said, 'But that's not a real angel, is it? She's not smiling and she hasn't got white hair and a blue dress. She's not like Sister Tapps. My mummy said Sister Tapps is a right proper angel.'

'She is now,' whispered Emily as the stars faded to allow the morning through. 'She is now.'

The Real Christmas Decorating Competition

In 1952 the *Nursing Times* held a nationwide Christmas competition in search of the best-decorated hospital ward. It was the early days of the NHS and the competition may have been conceived as a way of uniting the nation's hospitals that had been corralled together under one executive roof.

Many hospitals and wards responded to the initiative. One of the runners-up was the long gone Liverpool's Southern Hospital with an entry from the Robert Jones Ward, with a theme entitled 'Christmas in the Stratosphere'. The ward was named after the pioneering Liverpool-trained orthopaedic surgeon Sir Robert Jones. Any nurses reading this who had the privilege to work in either the Southern or the Northern, will recognize the descriptions of the wards with the bays, day rooms and central fireplaces.

The decorating competition is only a small part of the *Christmas Angels* story, but it is my way of capturing the atmosphere in hospitals such as my own fictional St Angelus and conveying some of the very real excitement, effort and love that the nurses and the children used to put into making the wards look so special at Christmas time.